THE
ANTIQUITIES
DEALER

A David Greenberg Mystery

ED PROTZEL

TouchPoint Press
Relax. Read. Repeat.

THE ANTIQUITIES DEALER
By Ed Protzel
Published by TouchPoint Press
Brookland, AR 72417
www.touchpointpress.com

ISBN-10: 1-946920-50-9
ISBN-13: 978-1-946920-50-8

Editor: Kimberly Coghlan
Cover Design: ColbieMyles, ColbieMyles.net

Visit the author's website at EdProtzel.com

First Edition

Printed in the United States of America.

To my old friends, both lost far too young: the real Solly, a brilliant scientist, and the real gambler, Daddy Markowitz. And to Janet, of course.

SECTION I. OPENING GAME

Believing as I do that man in the distant future will be a more perfect creature than he is now—

Charles Darwin

In three days you shall live, I, Gabriel, command you.

"Gabriel's Revelation" stone tablet, circa 1st Century BCE, anticipates a suffering Jewish Messiah who will be raised from the dead.

Ada Yardeni and Binyamin Elitzur
Cathedra Quarterly [Israel]

CHAPTER ONE
APHRODITE UNCLAIMED

Someone said Jesus Christ is alive.
Then I received a phone call that buckled my knees.

I closed my gallery, David Greenberg Antiquities, early that evening to play one of my rare but deadly chess matches against my diminutive gambler friend, Larry Finkel, a loser of epic proportions. In his daily desperation to support his local bookies, Finkel is a scavenger in the antiquities black market, preying upon unsuspecting collectors whom he can convince that vast windfalls await them at little risk. I only associate with him because, while Finkel may be a slimeball, his dragon variation of the Sicilian defense makes for breathtaking chess.

Outside in the falling dusk, the cold, hard rain dragged its feet, but I sensed a balmy April poised to elbow it aside. Umbrellas and raincoats rushed by my shop's window, doomed to be relegated to closets by morning. Life in the Midwest would soon emerge from its winter dormancy renewed, stretching its emerald luster toward blue skies and sunshine.

The little English shoppe bell above the door tinkled as the five-foot-five scam artist scurried into my gallery, his back-alley soiled shoes leaving *schmutz* on the Kashan Persian rug.

"Hey, Genius, ready for a knife fight?" Finkel flattered me with my old gambling crowd nickname, although his tone was more sarcasm than grudging compliment.

"Bring it on, Finkel!" I retorted.

I was surprised to see Finkel looking like a middle-aged accountant: black hair slicked back, wearing a tan sports coat over pressed khakis and a plaid shirt. The big annual Baptist convention was in town, and I had expected him to be sporting his black preacher suit with the phony white "Father Finkel" collar, like a predatory wolf in sheep's disguise. With a grimace on his skeletal face, he leaned away to block my view of his illuminated cell, hurriedly fingering the miniature screen. *Nothing.* He checked his watch with a bitter frown, then angrily shoved the cell into his pocket. Finkel is tightly wound.

It was an hour before post time at Fairmount Racetrack. I figured, if he wasn't at the track, he intended to snooker me. But how? I locked the door, then, returning to my desk, poured two cabernets and pulled my hand-carved ivory chess set from the drawer. The set is nothing special, 20th-Century Hong Kong, but I like the way the pieces make a solid *thunk* when brought down hard on the board. To make room, I cleared my desk, closed the safe, and—honored guest in mind—gave the tumbler an extra spin. I also shut down my computer so he couldn't thumb-drive my customer base when I left the room. There's no trusting Finkel.

During our second game, Finkel said pointedly, "Hey, there's a rumor going around that Jesus—*the* Jesus—is living somewhere in Israel. Now there's a chance for someone to make a buck."

I sneered, figuring either he was trying to break my concentration or he had a bizarre hustle lined up to snag me. Finkel knows I'm a relatively honest player in the antiquities game—despite my reputation in some circles—and it's difficult to cheat an even somewhat-honest man. Yet greed does spring eternal in the coldhearted, lowlife breast.

"Sure, Finkel," I laughed. "I'll leave the door unlocked for Him."

His eyes narrowing, he pulled out his cell phone and tapped the screen, listened for a single ring, then cut off the call. Turning to me, he sported a smug, superior grin. I didn't know what to make of his sudden change of demeanor.

I soon found out. Within moments, Finkel's cell rang out the Kentucky Derby "Call to the Gate." He noted the caller and handed it to me. "It's for you."

"David Greenberg," I growled.

"Hi David, it's Miriam," the familiar voice of a woman I hadn't heard in twenty years said cheerily. Instantly, I felt faint, unnerved—and at the same time, joyously aroused. It was, indeed, Miriam. My hand began to shake, and I went white blind, the ocean roaring in my ears. When I recovered from the shock, I stammered, "Miriam. Why...why are you calling me?"

"I can't tell you over the phone, David," she said urgently. "But we need to talk; it's important. How about lunch tomorrow? Blueberry Hill?" I quickly agreed, fool that I was.

Shaken, I returned to a won position in mid-game: a bishop ahead with the clear prospect of a passed pawn. But I couldn't concentrate. After I made a few desultory moves, Finkel locked a knight fork onto my rooks. Shortly thereafter, the black bishop had my queen skewered!

"Death to the bitch!" Finkel cried, undoubtedly alluding to his late-grandmother whose antiquities fortune he'd inherited and summarily blew at the track and in card games at the Eastside stockyards. But he was winners now. Faster than my king could fall on his sword, Finkel snapped up two crisp C-notes and shoved them into his coat. "Thanks, Greenberg. Got to get to the track. Lazy-Eye Lebowitz gave me a tip on the sixth race." Then he rushed so hurriedly out the door, the tiny shoppe bell rang like a violated canary.

Little did I suspect then, but Finkel and his card-shark buddy, Fat Daddy Markowitz, an old family friend of mine, would become adjunctive to my higher, or my *lower*, purposes.

At last, the stupid chess game was out of the way. *Screw the money.* Twenty years of yearning for Miriam, twenty years! I tried a sip of wine but had difficulty swallowing. Mortified, I turned out the lights and sat in the dark, a serrated longing plunging and ripping into my chest, remembering...

There, on her parents' darkened porch, our enduring first kiss, soft and long and tender, releasing luminous visions of a life together.

There, under the star-splashed sky by the park's Jewel Box fountain, we embraced, our bodies melting together, her breasts against me, our every sense bursting into life.

There, in my student apartment, I awoke on a sunny Sunday morning, Miriam's long black hair wild on my chest, her lips sensuously brushing my navel...

I drifted back to consciousness, numb and despondent, absently gazing at my gallery's locked display cases, their tarnished relics of epochs past now seemingly useless, meaningless, as I suddenly believed my life to have been. *Perhaps the gods cheat us at chess,* I mused.

Indeed, the mischievous Fates were playing a far deeper game than I could have imagined, about to spring a trap upon me they'd set twenty years before...or, perhaps, twenty *centuries* before.

***

The noon sun poured through the picture window of Blueberry Hill like aged scotch, spreading a warm, golden glow. I waited for Miriam in a scarred oak booth at the nostalgia bar named for the Fats Domino song. Then, as if she had planned it, Leonard Cohen's "Suzanne," a song about a woman you want to spend the night beside because she's "half-crazy"— so fitting the old Miriam—spoke to me from the luminescent Wurlitzer jukebox. Entranced, my thoughts drifted to the Miriam I had known so long ago, never imagining the singular historical destiny into which she had been cast.

Ironic to meet her at our favorite old haunt. Blueberry Hill touches the depths of its patrons' youthful memories, and I surmised that's probably why Miriam picked it. The long bar at the front of this museum of decades past is crowned by a semi-religious effigy of Elvis atop the cash register. Around me, the wall-to-wall icon collections—the Beatles and Chuck Berry displays, the Howdy Doody-themed phone booth and Whistle Orange Soda clock—all proclaimed that the thrill on Blueberry Hill augurs another time, another world, something primal that I had lost.

Then she was there, looking the same—yet so changed, emanating an inner glow I'd never seen. Ghostly white Jewish kewpie doll with long, black, exceedingly thick curls only slightly touched with gray. Compact, wispy, pale body, like a wood nymph, as if there wasn't material to waste when they put flesh on her bones.

Her dominant feature, large, expressive, black doe eyes, gave one the sense she was soulful. But now she was no longer the rebellious girl I'd known, wearing Salvation Army *schmattes*. Her dress, an off-the-rack Israeli brand I knew well, was simple, unadorned, of material too light for this latitude.

Thoughts of Israel always put a lump in my throat. Two decades before, Miriam had inexplicably emigrated there with my best friend, Solly— Professor Joseph Solomon—leaving no word of explanation. For two wonderful years prior to their disappearance, Miriam spent every weekend with me at the apartment Solly and I shared as I drifted through graduate school, more dabbling-in than dedicated-to history and archeology. Solly was merely our Mr. Spock fixture around the place—already obsessing on his second Ph.D. in the sciences, while engaging in his unsanctioned "personal" experiments. And then one day, Miriam was gone from my life…with Solly, dammit, a scientific whiz with a female-scoring quotient within degrees Celsius of absolute zero. And I never knew why.

To recover from my loss, I told myself Miriam never deserved my affections—that my youthful lustiness blew her better qualities out of proportion. But isn't there always one who continues to haunt you?

For the last decade, I've taken regular buying trips to Israel. Inevitably, though, whether drifting along a Tel Aviv beach awash in sun-drenched bikinis or strolling a sweltering Arab street market in Jerusalem, the first thing my eyes seek out is Miriam. Invariably in vain. Perhaps I could have found her and Solly, but I couldn't force myself to try.

"The years have filled you out nicely, David," she said with a sly smile, sliding across from me.

"How is Solly? Still testing the barriers of modern science?" I ventured.

"I hate to tell you, David…" She paused, thinking of how to frame the bad news. "Joseph died," she recited, revealing nothing.

I sighed deeply, shaken. My best friend from college…dead.

Solly could have won the Nobel Prize. He was that brilliant. At least, if his grad school experiments hadn't become drug-related, with himself as his own guinea pig. In his sophomore year in high school, before the drugs, he'd won a grant to explore original experiments at Pfizer. After school, he'd ride his bike to the corporation's laboratories to work on his concoctions, which he devised while daydreaming in right field during gym class—leaps of imagination that made the adult scientists' jaws drop. No telling how many discoveries Solly could have made.

"I'm sorry, Miriam. How did he…?"

"Suicide," she said, her voice flat as if she was ordering a Coke and wasn't thirsty.

"What happened? Was it drugs?"

"Joseph never touched drugs after we moved to Israel, David. Neither of us did. But the saving grace is that his work might live on long after we're all gone."

Bravado? Conviction? I'd have to find out for myself.

"Were you still married, when he…?"

"Yes. Although he'd been living in his lab for the last two years."

So Solly had reverted to his natural state, living in a laboratory without the real world to distract him from his research. Of course, if we're lucky, don't we all wind up where we belong? Was running a high-end gallery and chiseling the chiselers where I had intended to land? Lately, I hadn't been so sure. There was no special woman in my life, no future companion or wife on the horizon, and the proverbial missing leg stung.

"Was it recently when he…?"

She nodded 'yes,' with no intention of elaborating. I wanted to press her, but couldn't. I knew nothing of their last two decades, of their lives, their pursuits, if they had children. Let alone what took them to Israel. Most importantly, why Solly had slain himself.

"Why call me now?" I asked.

"I promised Joseph. He told me to visit you, on a mission of sorts," she answered.

Solly sent her! She had me by the tender warriors, and I couldn't resist. Had my friend wanted to atone for breaking us apart? Or was it because he knew I could be trusted?

"Where have you been living in Israel? I travel there frequently on business." There was a long silence.

"Outside of Netanya, near the Mediterranean coast," she whispered with some reluctance.

"I've been there. Why Netanya?"

"It's all connected to a Society we belong to." She was clearly unwilling to go further, and I let up on the interrogation. "So I understand you're in antiquities," she said.

"Right, I own a gallery on Euclid." *Which she already knew, so why ask?*

She flashed her warm, toothy smile. "You were always so smart," she said, her rare compliments, as always, melting my resistance.

"Why?" I countered, suspicious.

"Chick Markowitz tells me you also play the dark side of the antiquities market from time to time, sort of off the books. But he says you're honest. Are you?"

"If you're honest with me. Otherwise, all bets are off."

Chick is Daddy Markowitz's younger brother. Chick was a promising young artist Miriam and I had known who one day returned from a trip to San Francisco blathering about dead bodies and ghosts. His parents were forced to plant him in an institution. He was also, for a time, one-third of a spinning love triangle: I wanted to bed Miriam, she wanted to bed Chick, and he wanted to bed me. Frustrating to all concerned.

"So Chick is out of the mental ward?"

"He's living in Israel. That's all I know about him." She cut to the chase. "David, there's something Joseph instructed me to…to recover, and I need your help."

7

"All right." *Depending.* "Shoot."

She grew solemn. "Listen, this may seem a bit strange, but I'm perfectly serious. Now I'm not talking about a piece of the cross from a railroad tie, not even the shroud of Turin. David, there were only three nails on the cross."

"Nails? On *the* cross?"

"Yes, exactly. The only one that's still in existence is the one from the *feet.* You must have heard rumors."

"Well, Miriam, you hear stories all the time in my line of business, but the whole thing seems so farfetched. A nail from the crucifixion? It sounds like some Indiana Jones fantasy." My mood dropped; I wasn't going on any wild goose chase over an apocryphal legend. "I mean, assuming everything you'd need to—which is a stretch—after two thousand turbulent years, how do you document that a particular nail is the exact one? Carbon dating? Listen, the Romans crucified more Hebrews…"

Her cheeks flushed, and she blurted, "You don't think one of his followers or, heck, just some adoring fan wouldn't have held on to those nails as a keepsake? With the business you're in? David, come on."

"Okay," I said, exasperated. "Let's assume you're right. I mean, why would Solly, an atheist, even want such a thing? And no hocus-pocus or biblical exegesis clap-trap."

Seeing I was headed down the wrong trail, she laughed, shaking her head, her black crown of hair swirling. "I'm not authorized to discuss this yet, David, but it's nothing mystical, I assure you. You know Joseph and I never believed in that *bubbe-meise.* You'll know soon enough, I promise. The point is that the nail exists, and I need you to find it." Her eyes darted about, what poker players call a tell.

"Okay," I said. "You're holding something back. Out with it."

She merely stared at me with those dark eyes. I could see I was going to have to pry it from her.

I wondered what kind of Jews were so involved with historical Christianity that they'd invest their communal aspirations into the quest for a relic. Mainstream Jews wouldn't do that. This sounded more like a cult. Both Solly and Miriam were from typical middle-class Jewish families. But the young Miriam had been far too blatantly hedonistic to ever join a Jesus cult, and Solly's only religion, if any, was science.

From my own understanding, Jesus never claimed to be anything but a Jew. He preached in the countryside around Nazareth, avoiding the town, until his fatal trip to Jerusalem. At that time, like today, there were those Jews who kept the daily rituals, and those who didn't. Being a scholar, it is believed Jesus followed Jewish practices. Many believe the Last Supper was a Passover *seder*. Interesting speculation, but who knows for sure?

"So, what's involved?" I asked, my interest piqued. "An artifact like that, if such a thing exists, would cost millions."

"I can get you millions," she said matter-of-factly, meaning it.

"You? Millions?" I examined her department store clothing. "From whom, Miriam, this Society?"

At that moment, the tattooed waiter with a spiked Mohawk fluttered up to take our orders and refill our iced teas, then flitted away.

"Can you help us, David? It's for the ultimate cause, for humankind. I came to you because you have ethics…and because you loved Joseph."

Ethics aside, the twinkle in her eye indicated she much preferred that people on the seamy side of antiquities trusted me, which could be helpful to her. I nodded reluctantly.

***

Miriam reached into her worn shoulder bag and, without guile or fanfare, pulled out a large, thick envelop, Israeli-make. I could see my name written in the precise, left-leaning style of my late-friend. Then she reached casually for the sweetener, allowing me a glimpse of the pink sunrise on her left breast. Was this revelation on purpose? My thinking wasn't clear.

I absently turned my attention to the envelope. Inside, there was a letter written in Solly's hand—to me—and a thick stack of fresh American banknotes. Shocked at the sight of so much cash coming from Miriam's delicate hand, I quickly pulled the package under the table and extracted the letter.

I skipped to the end to see Solly's familiar, precise signature, matching that on the envelope. Considering the entire package was new, with crisp stationary and banknotes, Solly would most likely have written the letter shortly before he died. Recently. I wondered what had driven him to send this plea to me, then to do himself in. I was anxious to read the missive but preferred to savor it alone, so I folded it into my shirt pocket, where it burned my chest. Then, returning to Earth, I absently counted part way into the stack of greenbacks, but stopped abruptly, suddenly fearful.

Trying to act nonchalant, I scanned the room. Among the lunch crowd nursing their Becks and Heinekens, a ghostly pale-faced man at the bar, thin as death, ignored an untouched Coke. When he saw me examining him, he dropped a ten on the bar and slipped off. Suspicious, but I wasn't going to let myself get hung up in paranoia.

"There must be fifty thousand dollars in here," I whispered.

"I took a few cabs, meal expenses," she replied absently. *And she probably distributed a few tastes around town, seeking information or the cooperation of people like Finkel. Or worse.*

"I'm not taking this money from you," I said, tapping Miriam's knee with the envelope. She got the hint and dumped the money back into her purse.

"So tell me about this Society. What's its name?" I asked.

"Am Ha-b'rit," she whispered confidentially. "It means 'People of the Covenant.' You can't repeat that name to anyone. *Anyone.*"

"I won't. Is this Am Ha-b'rit like a *kibbutz?*"

"Kind of," she replied, clearly not meaning it. "They're all great people, David, doing important work. That's what attracted Joseph, why he gave up drugs for them." She paused to measure her words. "David, we're the original group that Jesus joined over two thousand years ago."

Not that "joined Jesus," but that "Jesus joined." Quite a claim.

"A group of Jews? You mean, a philosophical movement like…the *Essenes* or one of those offshoots?" I asked.

"Yes, sure. Kind of. But I'm not the best person to tell you," she said, avoiding the subject.

"Please try," I pressed.

She hesitated, then went on. "Am Ha-b'rit has always been an intellectual order: everyone seeking wisdom, during some eras—not so much today—living in common, working together, sharing material possessions. I mean, we live in modern communities now, with credit cards and single-family homes, but the basic idea still applies."

"Okay, I get the picture. And this group survived beyond the crucifixion?"

"Survived in varying degrees the Romans slaughtering the Jews, survived the Diaspora, the Inquisition, and the Holocaust as best we could. But with Israel reborn in 1948, we have taken root and prospered."

"Miriam, that's saying a lot," I said skeptically, but decided to drop it. She was right about one thing. They had certainly prospered if they were tossing around millions for a wild-goose-chase artifact. "But go on. How does your Society, this Am Ha-b'rit, support itself?"

"Well, Am Ha-b'rit's always been about philosophy, religion, sure, but the Society is also into the physical sciences. You know? Recruiting Joseph was part of that. We've made real advances, David, in biotechnology, medical science, and computer technologies."

"I see. There are a few bucks in those lines of work," I chuckled.

"We're cashing in, that's for sure. Not that anyone's trying to get rich," she cautioned, "but our successes enable us to do so much good. We all have different interests, but some members are pretty brilliant, like Joseph."

"I get it. And so...?"

"So the movement's thinking has evolved over the past two thousand years."

"Evolved?" I interjected. "That's a strange word for something that began as a religious order."

"Who doesn't believe in evolution in this day and age? I mean, not everyone in the Society is traditionally religious. And even if you do believe in God, evolution might be *His* method. Anyway, Am Ha-b'rit blends religion, philosophy, and science together, see? Science is on the ascendancy, but they're all just ways of understanding the world. Right?"

"I guess so," I agreed, still not fully grasping the idea.

Detecting the doubt on my face, she said, "You still don't believe me?"

"I want to, but, really, Miriam..."

"David, we have preserved writings spanning the last two thousand years—even books about Jesus, contemporaneous to His time, that weren't written by Paul or John, which contain *other* things He said. Not that the originals have survived, but they've been copied and translated over time. Maybe they're real, maybe not. But whether Jesus was divine or a historically significant genius, whether the writings are real or forgeries, what does it matter if the books themselves give us wisdom?"

"True, it doesn't matter." Fascinating. My bags were already half-packed for a Mediterranean climate. Maybe I'd find some unique acquisitions for my collection. If nothing else, I wanted to read the writings. "How long have you been in town?" I asked, changing the subject.

"Almost two weeks, visiting my family mostly."

Then I asked the big question and held my breath for the answer: "Are you going back?"

"I've got to, David," she said with startling urgency, the glint of a tear in her eye. A tear! From Miriam! Venus had me hooked through mouth and gills like a pool-hall patsy.

CHAPTER TWO
THOU SHALL MEET HIM

"Okay, so tell me about this nail," I said. "How do I fit in?"

We sat upon the alabaster stones beside the park's rushing waterfall, just Miriam and me, alone except for our turbulent images in the fall's roaring pool. We had walked from the restaurant to the secluded grotto to talk in private, the sunshine and blue skies no balm for the tension we felt. Miriam briefly related Am Ha-b'rit's quest for the cherished artifact, but she declined to reveal their motivation.

"…Anyway, when we located the nail, we gave Levi Asher a suitcase full of euros and sent him to buy it. That's the way the dealer wanted it done."

"Don't tell me," I interrupted. "The dealer who owned the supposed nail was Moise Shankman, and that's why you are here." I was knocked for a loop. Just two weeks earlier, my dear friend Moise Shankman, an eighty-year-old St. Louis antiquities restoration craftsman and trader, had been found lying in a pool of blood on the floor of his shop, his throat slashed from ear to ear. The police had no suspects for Moise's killer; nothing had been taken from his shelves, his cash drawer, or his wallet. Miriam nodded in affirmation, then grimaced and shrugged her shoulders, indicating they knew in Israel about poor Moise's demise.

"So you think the nail might still be here? Possibly, anyway? And with so much at stake, your group, this Am Ha-b'rit, is spreading a wide net."

"There's more at stake than you can imagine, David."

"All right, go on. Tell me about the Moise Shankman transaction."

"See, Levi is a biology student doing research in genetics, so he was the perfect one to send."

"They're into *genetics*, your Society?" I was aghast.

"Of course! What is cutting-edge medicine without genetics?"

She handed me a typical school photo of a young man who looked like a skinny nerd with acne and a bad haircut. Levi was smiling into the camera, as innocent-looking a kid as you'll ever see, eager to please and to be accepted. Not a line of guile in his earnest face. I slipped the picture into my pocket, sure she had more in her bag.

"How would your people know the nail was authentic, *if* such a thing could be determined? That's a lot of money to bet on the right needle in a gigantic haystack."

"The genetics are the key," she said haltingly. Then before my eyes, she was overcome by emotion, nearly to the point of tears. *What could have caused this upheaval in her heart?* I waited some minutes until she was able to compose herself.

"Okay, assuming…"

"Anyway," she said, wiping an eye and sniffling, "Levi must have thought he was being followed. A day after the purchase was supposed to take place, we received a hurried text message. That's the last we heard of him."

"A *day?* That means he had time to fly back to Israel."

"Possibly. His ticket was used, anyway."

"And the money?"

"Gone."

"And you want it back."

"The money means nothing. We want the nail."

"Do you think Levi absconded with the cash? Or could you have been betrayed by someone inside your Society?"

"Levi would never betray Am Ha-b'rit. He was among the most fervent believers in our special mission. He'd die first."

"Which you hope is not the case."

She nodded gravely. "But betrayal from someone or some faction within Am Ha-b'rit, a mole, is possible, very possible."

"Why would you suspect a traitor?"

"I can't tell you why just now, David, but some do suspect it may be one of our own. We just don't know who. Am Ha-b'rit has grown very large, with wide-ranging factions and viewpoints, some a bit radical. Like any academic organization, jealousies run thick as tar. Academics are always complaining about backstabbers among their colleagues, right?"

"A suitcase full of euros would turn many a professor's head. Moise Shankman's fate doesn't bode well for poor Levi."

"I'm afraid not," she replied, eyes downcast.

"So there are ruthless interests seeking the nail, bloodthirsty killers? I mean, I'm just a businessman. I'd be taking an enormous risk if I helped you."

"I promise, David, we have resources to protect you. It's important, the most important thing in my life—in the world's life."

I figured I'd be the judge of that. "So why didn't you provide Levi with help?"

"We were trying to keep his mission quiet. That's the way Mr. Shankman wanted it."

"And I would respect that confidence, Miriam." I paused to think. "Tell me what Levi's text message said. Tell me exactly, please."

"It read, in English..." and she wrote on a scrap of paper: 59CBZQ.

"That's obscure." I shook my head, unable to wrap my mind around the combination of digits and letters. "Do you have any idea what the fifty-nine means? Or the letters?"

We were silent for a few minutes while I puzzled out Levi's text. Then something clicked, and I tore the paper into pieces and shoved them into my pocket.

Miriam saw my eyes light. "You have an idea what this is about, don't you, David?"

I nodded with self-deprecating shrug. "Maybe."

Much relieved, Miriam took my hand. And I melted.

***

I thought over my conversation with Finkel and decided to shoot the works. What difference would it make? I was already on my way to losing whatever Miriam wanted to take—just another of her chumps.

"I hear rumors that Jesus Christ is alive and living in Israel," I ventured. "Is that crazy, or what?"

She stared at me hard. "Can we talk about that later?"

Oh, no! She does belong to some kind of a Jesus cult, or *she's setting me up. Perhaps she was the source of Finkel's claims, to lend credence to her pitch.*

"You know Larry Finkel, right?" I asked. "He's a friend of Chick's brother."

"I don't associate with any of Chick's brother's friends," she answered disdainfully, with finality. I'm sure Chick had complained to her about his brother's gambling crowd.

"Finkel's in antiquities. It was his cell you reached me on. I mean, come on, Miriam!" I was growing frustrated. She had come to St. Louis seeking antiquities traders, and Finkel had probably directed her to me for a price.

Suddenly, her eyes clouded, and she became so deadly serious, I was taken aback. "Can I trust you or not, David?" she pleaded.

I gave my most sincere nod. Her penetrating eyes searched my own. "If you come back with me, I'll see that you meet Him." Her eyes lowered; the air seemed to grow heavy with a pervasive sense of tragedy.

Was she expecting me to believe the second coming had arrived? If not, what was she implying? "You mean, I'll meet *Him?*" I gasped, my eyes growing large.

She nodded, trembling. Without warning, tears streamed down her tender, pale cheeks. Bewildered, I placed my hand on hers, already mentally scheduling my manager, Arnie, to run the shop for an extended period, maybe giving him a cut if I was absent for any length of time.

She couldn't fake what I saw: her shoulders shaking, face consumed with pain. I chastised myself for thinking ill of her. I was a rotten lowlife, cruel, black-hearted. I vowed to serve the purposes of my friends unreservedly. *A vow! Até, the goddess of mischief, had me pinned like a butterfly in a collection!*

I gave Miriam my handkerchief, and all my anger and frustration from bygone years evaporated. Love is scary, irrational, and memory plays tricks on you. *Were those years with Solly and Miriam as idyllic as I imagined? Was that young Miriam as glorious as I remembered her?* Regardless, the mature Miriam before me seemed to promise so much. *Am I, a divorced, childless man, falling for her again, or just delusional?*

I put my arm around her frail shoulders. Like a child, she buried her flushed, tear-dampened face into my chest. I knew she could hear my heart pounding, pounding.

In Gabriel Garcia Marquez's *Love in the Time of Cholera*, a couple waits over fifty-three years to be united, finding Heaven for the first time as love-smitten septuagenarians. In so doing, they discover what can only be revealed through love—that "It is life, more than death, that has no limits." In that context, I felt incredibly lucky. I had known Miriam barely twenty-three years!

Everything I owned, my very life, was at her disposal. Worldly David Greenberg had become one of those suckers P.T. Barnum declared was born every minute. Knew it and didn't care.

***

We strolled back to find a cab for Miriam, our steps in rhyme as if no time had intervened since we last trod these oak-lined pathways.

"What had Solly been up to? Until recently, of course."

"You see, Am Ha-b'rit supports a university for extremely gifted students, sort of like M.I.T. but with a different curriculum. Joseph was the top researcher over special biotech projects."

"Is the university exclusively for Jews?"

"Yes, for the most part, in a very liberal sense. We reject the traditional maternal lineage definition of who a Jew is, which we believe predates genetics. A group of us are trying to allow the university to take non-Jews—Arabs, Palestinians, Christians—but these things take time.

"Look, David, you're pretty smart. You should know as well as anyone, nature makes it hard for the truly gifted. They're detectibly different. Joseph believed society instinctively roots out, even destroys, people with exceptional minds. Our university supplies a nurturing environment where our students can follow their curiosity and fulfill their talents."

"What's this school's name?"

"Hadera University. It's a small, very private school. You can't repeat that."

A secret university! What crazy fantasy had I stumbled into? "Why so secretive about everything?"

"With business enterprises across the globe, we worry about paranoid anti-Semites who already believe the world is run by a Jewish oligarchy. Think of the suffering engendered by the phony *Protocols of the Elders of Zion*. As the American politicians say, 'Israel lives in a tough neighborhood.' Frankly, David, Jews all over the world live in a tough neighborhood. Always have."

I had more questions, but the moment we reached the street a cab braked at the curb, and Miriam climbed inside. I handed the cabbie a twenty and wistfully watched them pull away.

It was my move. Was fickle Fortuna, the Roman goddess, actually a diseased harlot whose come-hither wink entices men inexorably to madness? I was determined to find out.

CHAPTER THREE
HUBRIS NATION

After my heart-wrenching lunch with Miriam, I returned to my gallery, where time slipped away like a cash-laden con man.

My shop nestles on the sedate corner of Euclid and McPherson avenues in St. Louis' upscale Central West End, occupying a whitewashed-brick two-story. The neighborhood's cobblestone, maple tree-lined streets offer an enchanting collection of high-end art galleries, specialty boutiques, and the venerable Left Bank Books, interspersed with quaint cafes, fine restaurants, and theme bars. A bit of Heaven if you have taste and money—especially old money.

To steamroll Eros' hustle, or rather Miriam's—same thing—the afternoon proved spring-like with light breezes and cloudless skies. I floated through a gentle fog, tour guide to my private collection of busts and statues, enveloped by the giggle symphonies of effervescent coeds and clinging lovers grazing the shops and cafes. In harmony, a steady stream of flush collectors drifted weightlessly through my doors, eternity on their minds and accountant recommendations for tax-deductible museum bequests in their hearts. I even unloaded the Egyptian urn with its faded Amun-Ra image, which I had begun to believe would gather dust on my shelves for centuries, just as it had collected sand in a desert cave until 1907.

As daylight faded to purple, I glanced across the street. Then I froze. Leaning against the brick wall at Llewellyn's Pub, a crow-faced man in a solid black suit tugged his hat brim down like some forties movie dick—staring directly at me. I stared back hard, but he didn't budge. I remembered Moise Shankman, and an ice chill ran down my spine. I had an unsettling premonition that crazies were about to shatter the life I had worked so hard to achieve. *Had someone declared open season on antiquities dealers?* I reached for the phone to call the police, but when I glanced up, the man was gone.

Assuring myself I was imagining threats because of Moise's brutal murder, I shrugged off my apprehension and returned to the state of anticipation I'd felt since my lunch with Miriam. I had to kill time to allow Miriam to get her gear to my house using the diversionary methods we had planned. We wanted her to be free from any potential shadow, either hers or mine.

Following my daily routine, I turned out the lights and locked the door, before grabbing a bite at Dressel's Pub. Solly's note still burned my pocket, as yet unread. I was savoring the wait, holding off until my head cleared. I checked my watch to see if I'd given Miriam enough time to slip into my house. Then I went out into the fallen twilight. Welcome, oh Nyx, goddess of night.

Heading home, I passed celebrants from the suburbs ditching their BMWs and Jaguars in parking lots, forming a steady pilgrimage to worship at the temples of Bacchus. I passed a pair of younger women I vaguely recognized sitting outside a bar. "Buy you a drink, David?" one shouted. Without slowing, I merely smiled. *Sorry, can't stop.*

I live on one of the surrounding private streets a short walk from the gallery. These avenues sport well-kept, 19th-Century brick homes, considered mansions when first built. I turned onto my dimly lit street, with its rows of dusk-silhouetted Georgians, Tudors, and Victorians— blissfully unaware that a grizzly labyrinth of kidnapping, torture, and murder loomed just ahead.

Suddenly, a trio of huge men, big as NFL tackles, one black and two white, surrounded me from the shadows, and my heart squeezed for blood. When my eyes adjusted, I could see the three were nattily dressed in pinstriped suits like villainous muscle in some bad European action flick.

I proceeded, but the largest blocked my path. "Excuse me," I said, but the behemoth failed to yield. Bad sign. "You can have my money..." I ventured.

"We don't want your money, Mr. Greenberg," the large one replied in a surprisingly polite, high voice. "We have money for *you*, sir."

"I don't want it," I answered, attempting to circumvent the blockade. They closed in, shutting me off.

In the lamplight, I could see the glint of a golden cross on each of their lapels, where one might sport a boutonnière or American flag pin. Clearly, they didn't represent some chiseling *goniff*—too classy.

18

I glanced at my second story window fronting the street. In shadow, backlit by the hall light, I could see the outline of Miriam peering through the blinds. The arrival of whatever vehicle my guests were driving must have attracted her attention. She was secure, for now.

"Please come with us, sir," the soft-voiced tackle ordered.

I made a final attempt to walk around the leviathan, but agile as a cat, he sidestepped into my path like he was sealing off a swift defensive end on third-and-thirteen.

"What *is* this?"

"You're perfectly safe, Mr. Greenburg," the spokesman said as gently as a shrink to a hysterical child. "This will be quite worth your while."

"Will it now?" I asked sarcastically, to no reply. "Come see me Monday. I'm staying in tonight."

"We'll get you back early," the man reassured me. "You'll have plenty of time to relax."

"And if I won't go? I've got to tell you, having never been kidnapped, I'm predisposed to telling your boss to go to Hell." Seeing the three cringe at the H-word, I quickly added their master could go perform an act upon himself that nature designed for heterosexual couples, exasperating them to no end.

"Please, Mr. Greenburg, such language," the man said. Then I recognized him; any football fan would. Strong pockmarked face, red as windburn, framed by a swept-back, thick blonde mane. Six-feet-six of solid muscle.

"Aren't you Bear Brukowski? God's Left Tackle? Association of Faithful Athletes, right?" He nodded. "That block against the Eagles, where you took out the defensive end and the weak side linebacker, then chipped the safety going down, that was the best I ever saw. Touchdown!"

"Thank you," he replied modestly.

"And with whom am I to seek an audience, Bear?" I asked with exaggerated formality.

"The Reverend Nation, sir," Bear replied.

"Hubris Nation!" I laughed scornfully. Reverend Nation, the host of TV's own "Hallelujah Hour." Sermons available in print or on DVD for a modest Love Gift. "Jesus-Fucking-Christ! What does he want with me?"

"Please, Mr. Greenberg, the Lord's name!"

They were polite but giving me no choice. Scowling like a captured bandit, I let them guide me into the plush leather back seat of one of a pair of black Cadillac Escalades.

"And Jesus rode a fucking ass," I mumbled under my breath, running my hand over the sleek material.

***

Hubris Nation, the charismatic evangelist instantly recognizable to anyone with a television set, God's right-fisted warrior, famed for his crusades against the ever-encroaching manifestations of malevolent modernism. According to PR legend, the good reverend had risen from a humble sharecropper shack in the Missouri boot-heel town of Sikeston. In actuality, Nation's father was a respected judge in nearby Cape Girardeau, the county seat, and Hubris himself a private school dropout.

With only the strength of his Maker to guide him, and an infusion of capital from his father's fortune, Nation had turned himself into a one-man growth industry, wealthy beyond only God and His team of accountant angels knew—all gathered tax-exempt, which only encourages the practice.

Reverend Nation preaches, "God wants YOU to be RICH," one of theology's more lucrative incarnations. The Word of God is especially palatable when sweetened with a strong dose of material promise. Wouldn't John Calvin be shocked to see his justification for the avarice of a rather puritanical class of wealthy merchants usurped by struggling masses worshiping at TV's Cable Cathedral?

As for Reverend Nation's ethics, I'd read accounts in *Time* magazine of his ministry planes delivering food to starving Africa—with military weapons possibly hidden aboard—and returning with Blood Diamonds in exchange. I was skeptical about that, but couldn't help being curious. Sure, he's a showman, but in the few times I'd seen him on TV, he seemed genuine about his faith. More particularly, I wanted to know how he came by the name Hubris.

Since I wasn't blindfolded—somewhat reassuring—I paid attention to the direction my captors took, watching lighted highway signs pass in the night. We drove in silence forty-five minutes southwest on Highway 44, taking the second exit past the ghost of Fenton, Missouri's stark, shut-down Chrysler plant. From there, we followed a paved access road for five miles until a lit, twenty-foot-high gate appeared before us. Beyond the gate, a thick Missouri woods loomed. *Easy to lead the police back here,* I mused. *If I leave alive.*

As the Escalades skidded to a halt, we were blinded by a spotlight. From out of the glare, a sleepy security guard, unarmed, approached, casual and loose-jointed. After a glance through the window, the guard waved to what I took to be a camera perched high on a tree. Then he sauntered away, rubbing his eyes as the gate slid open, and we proceeded.

For ten minutes, we circled a darkened lake along a twisty gravel road, through solid black walls of woodlands, headlights our only guide. It was creepy, but the driver knew the way. At one point, a pair of deer leapt across the road, flashing arcs of delicate flight, and vanished into the pines and scrub.

Bad thoughts came fast, making my hands shake. No one knew I was out here, and I didn't have my cell phone. I could disappear, and that would be that. Considering the speculation I'd read about the good reverend's African operations, it was possible he'd hired armed killers to protect his interests.

Reaching a large clearing, we entered a paved circular drive leading to a magnificent three-story white colonial with eight massive columns illuminated by floodlights. Clearly God's summer residence. Reverend Nation may have given his cloak to the stranger, but he'd kept the dwelling for himself.

I got out of the Caddy, stretching, and noted the keys still in the ignition. Light security…good to know.

I was led to the massive brass front door, held open by a liveried butler who offered to take my jacket. I refused. "Not staying, thanks," I said. I'd already had my last supper.

The interior made Tammy Faye Baker's mansion look paltry by comparison. Enormous crystal chandeliers, richly carved cornices, valuable oils, and medieval tapestries hanging on red satin-covered walls. I was taken up the marble staircase to Nation's second-floor office overlooking the drive.

He sat behind a gilded French provincial desk, wearing an immaculate white Armani suit, a diamond-encrusted cross adorning his lapel, a glistening Rolex watch, and the Super Bowl-size ring that showed so well on television. *Nice loungewear for around the bungalow.*

Trim and tanned in his late-fifties, his powerful face had begun to sink inexorably toward folds in his chin. He wore his gray-streaked black hair slicked back into a pompadour with Elvis sideburns reaching to his jaw. I felt captured by the hungry and imposing will of his hazel eyes.

Seeing me, he rose to his full six-foot-four from what looked to be a Louis XIV throne, all white and gold leaf with red velvet cushions. He indicated a guest chair, and I sat, craning my neck like a Holy Land tourist. The office sported wall-to-ceiling bookshelves filled with orderly rows of leather-bound volumes and a conference table for sixteen, tastefully lit by brass lamps.

He waved Bear and the other two tackles away, and they closed the door behind themselves. Listening, I could distinguish three heavy gaits fade down the hall. We were alone.

"Thank you for coming, Mr. Greenberg," Nation said ever so cordially.

"It wasn't voluntary, Reverend Nation," I replied, still miffed.

"Please believe me," he said, displaying a wall of shining teeth, illuminated from within by tender mercy, "if it were not for my rugged schedule, the mountain would have come to Mohammed."

"I'd planned to spend a quiet night at home, Mr. Mountain," I said. We studied each other suspiciously.

"We tried to call but didn't have your cell number."

"I don't usually carry a cell phone; I don't want to be bothered."

Next, Nation suffocated me with charm. "You know, I own a few very high-quality ancient pieces myself, Mr. Greenberg, mostly early-Christian." He raised an eyebrow and flashed enough teeth to supplant Teddy Roosevelt.

"Look, Reverend, I do not want to see them, and I will not transact business under these conditions. Period."

"Then I'll come to the point so we can get you back home. As you know, there were three nails driven into His Beloved Flesh when our Lord and Savior was sacrificed on the cross to cleanse away our sins and save our souls…"

I thought of playing my cards close to the vest, but the desire to see Miriam overpowered me. "And you want the third one, for the feet," I conjectured.

"You people are smart; I'll give you that. You know, Greenberg, my accountant and lawyer are both Jews."

"So was your Master, the Prince of Peace," I added, teasing him.

"Why in Heaven's name God chose you people!" he blurted, flabbergasted. "Logically, God, not being human, cannot be a Jew;

therefore Jesus, being God, cannot be a Jew. The 'Hallelujah Hour' is struggling to expose that myth to an unsuspecting public."

"But Mary, his mother, was a Jew, which makes Jesus a Jew according to accepted Jewish norms," I stated firmly. "Mother a Jew, you're a Jew."

"Let us not get sidetracked by a finer theological point. '*Go, Daniel, for these words are concealed and sealed up until the end of time.*'"

"Splendid, I won't argue the point."

Nation rubbed his chin, ruminating on his next gambit. "Simply put, *I want that nail.*"

The very nail Miriam and my late-friend Solly also wanted. I wondered how Nation knew about the nail. And if Nation knew about it, who else was after it?

I met his eyes. "And if I demand millions?"

"Millions," he spat disdainfully. He spread both arms to draw my attention to our surroundings. "What are millions of dollars compared to *billions* of souls!"

"Mere fractions of a penny on the soul, by my calculation. What a deal!"

"Enough," he bellowed dramatically, rising to full height like a Kodiak bear, his golden voice echoing throughout the chamber like a prophet in the shower. He waved his hand, and magically, a panel slid open to expose a mountain of neatly bound bills. "What do you need?"

"Look, Nation, I suspect you must know you're not the only one seeking this relic. If you want my help, you're going to have to play straight with me. Now, what does everyone want with this nail?"

"I don't know," he said, sinking back onto his throne. "Truly."

"But you've heard the rumor Jesus has returned to Earth, right?" I dropped the other shoe.

"Yes, I've heard," he said wearily. "He is being sequestered by a Jewish cult, in Israel."

"Just like before," I jabbed, but my witticism fell on deaf ears.

"My sources tell me He's being held by the people hunting the nail. Why? Only God knows."

By Miriam's people? Curiosity, that insidious prestidigitator, had its hand in my pocket. "So why do you want the nail? Is it supposed to be magical or something?"

"Nobody believes in magic," he said disdainfully.

"Do you want to trade the spike for this Jesus? Do you think this group, this so-called cult, would make that trade?"

"Honestly, I don't want to possess Him, Mr. Greenberg," Hubris said, growing animated. "I merely want the chance to see His glowing face, to kiss the hem of His robe. I'd give every cent I own, my investment properties, my planes and yachts—everything—just to hear His loving voice. That's all I want." His tears looked real, just like on television; the guy really could tug at your heartstrings. He dabbed his eyes, catching a sneak glance at his watch, as I'd seen him pull off on TV.

"You'd still have your TV station and the Blood Diamond trade." Then it clicked. "Oh, I know, you want him on the 'Hallelujah Hour.' That would be the ratings coup of the millennia!"

"*Please!*" he pleaded so pitifully I drew in my horns—figuratively speaking, of course. He recovered instantly. "How much do you need in advance? A million in cash? Two? I'll fly you anywhere on the planet on one of my personal jets. And provide round-the-clock protection!"

"Protection?" I asked, my heart leaping into my throat.

"As you yourself said, I'm not the only one after the nail. Realize what's at stake and for whom. There are many views of God in countries where life is not held sacred or dear. When you add in millions of U.S. dollars, the acquisition, Mr. Greenberg, gets deadly serious. *Deadly.*" He smiled warmly. "I'll have Bear accompany you; he's a great guy."

"I…I don…don't know..." I stuttered.

"Now. Who killed Moise Shankman?" he asked ominously.

Was this a threat on my life? How did he know about Moise's murder? I could be lost at the bottom of the lake or filed neatly away in a hidden chamber out here in the sticks. An icy chill swept over me. "I'm willing to deal with you," I said, simple survival my sole interest.

"But I need your promise, your guarantee," he demanded.

"There are no guarantees on this Earth, not even those of eternal life written in the Bible—not with me."

***

Reverend Nation paced, staring out the window, then turned. "Look," he said, eyes ablaze, "this isn't about money. Read Irenaeus, the disciple of Polycarp, his treatise *Against Heresies*."

"2nd-Century CE." I had to show off just a little.

"Yes. Read Irenaeus' disciple, Hippolytus. They tell us, with the End of Days approaching, Satan will appear in the person of the Antichrist, the

Beast, seeking to reign over mankind…"

"*Oy*," I replied, thinking, *Here we go*. "And the Antichrist will be a Jew, you think? Like this rumored person in Israel?"

"Exactly. He will achieve power by convincing the world he is Christ, the messianic King of the Jews. Thereby, he will become the 'abomination of desolation,' as spoken of by the prophet Daniel. *'God will send upon them a deluding influence so that they might believe what is false,'* 2 Thessalonians."

"*Oy vey*," I said, my skepticism rising. "And this End of Days is coming soon?"

"Yes, within my lifetime."

"Reverend, which is it? First you want to see this guy because he is Jesus. Then you want him because he is the Antichrist about to take over the world."

"That's why I have to meet Him."

"But say you do meet Him; how will you know?"

"God has led me inerrantly—inerrantly!—to this moment in time, to prepare His children for the coming End of Days. I assure you, Mr. Greenberg, I will know the truth when I see Him."

It was getting late, and I wanted to be home rebuilding my relationship with Miriam. "What I said still applies, Reverend Nation: no guarantees. That's the best I can do."

Just then, his cell phone beeped, and he examined it. "You think about this, Mr. Greenberg. You think about it very hard. Because I am a gentleman, and I mean well. But there are many others who are not gentlemen, and they *do not* mean well. You are going to need my protection, and I would love to give it to you. So think about that. I'll be back shortly."

"I want to go home now," I demanded.

"You're not going anywhere until we have a deal." He dropped the cell into his pocket and left the room, slamming the door behind him.

I listened to his footsteps click-clacking down the long hallway, then cracked open the door quietly, peering out. One of the tackles waited at the opposite end of the hall.

Closing the door softly, I crossed to his desk, empty except for a white telephone beside an equally white, leather-bound Bible, which, with its gold lettering, appeared to have never been opened. I tried the phone. Dead, a showpiece like the Bible. Now I wished I'd brought my cell.

I went to a dormer window. Hip roof leading to a drainpipe, which dropped straight down to the front drive—to where the ministry Escalades sat, keys in the ignition.

On one hand, if I tried to climb down, the arc lights illuminating the mansion would make for easy discovery. On the other, with everything being well lit, I probably wouldn't break my neck. After all, this wasn't an old prison movie where a spotlight follows me and the guards shoot me down. If they see me, they'll capture me, and I'll be right back here. Why should I wait around to be outnumbered, which considering their size, would be in the company of any one of my abductors?

Taking a deep breath, out the window I went.

***

My driving was more Roman chariot race than Indy 500. The moment I put the Escalade into gear, a loud siren went off, and soon, the second Escalade was in pursuit. I sped off on the twisty gravel road through the black woods circling the darkened lake. Periodically I could see bright headlights at a distance in the rearview mirror. My pulse raced. Now I knew of Hubris Nation's interest in the current "Messiah" and in the nail, but little else, except for his willingness to kidnap me. And, of course, the article on Blood Diamonds wasn't reassuring. Considering Moise Shankman's fate, if they caught me, would they would kill me or hold me prisoner to get their way? I couldn't rule out either.

My "daring chase" is a tale of skid marks at blind turns, gravel flying, backing out of ditches, and near pitches into the cold waters. I almost made it to the fence, through which I was planning to smash like in a Steven Segal thriller, when a sharp turn landed my front tires in the muddy lake, bumper snagged on fallen timber. Spin my wheels as I might, I finally had to climb from the cabin, sinking to mid-ankle in the freezing water and clinging mud.

I headed for the road on foot, but within fifty yards, headlights blinded me, above which police lights flashed. I could have manned-up and slipped into the woods, but I saw the cop as a lifeline and waved my arms to flag him down. The cruiser braked, and a young deputy weighing about two-seventy came toward me.

"Raise them hands. I'll shoot," he called in trembling voice, aiming his revolver at me.

I raised my hands. "Officer, I was kidnapped."

He approached, sheer malevolence dominating his layers of face. "Ain't that the reverend's Caddy? Why, you got it stuck in the lake! Boy, you is in trouble..."

"Yes, but you see..."

"You better shut up, boy, or you gonna find this here gun upside your head."

"But officer..."

He raised the pistol again, and I clamped shut. "Spread 'em, boy, and make it quick."

I'd seen enough *Law and Order* to know the drill. I tried to speak, but that only made him search me more roughly. No profit in that. Meanwhile, two of the reverend's tackles, not Bear, pulled up.

"Is the reverend pressing charges?" the cop asked.

One of the tackles spoke into a cell, then confirmed that charges should be filed.

"Now you get in the cruiser, boy."

It was time for country justice. *Oy gevalt!*

CHAPTER FOUR
GREENBERG IN THE LION'S DEN

My evening had turned into a waking nightmare.

"You stole a church Caddy!" the sheriff growled, his righteous anger fueled by being awakened from the pleasant narcosis of a fried chicken supper. "That is a felony in these parts, Mistah Greenberg, a very serious crime."

Easily three-hundred pounds, he breathed laboriously every inch of the six-step journey to the coffee pot, brushing his sleep-tussled hair into a further tangle. The cramped room, lit by a single naked bulb, reeked of stale ashtrays, onions, and the sweat of week-old uniforms on rotund bodies. Yellowed, curling papers lay piled in earnest disorder upon the cigarette-scarred desk, interspersed with an unchained potpourri of half-filled coffee cups and Burger King wrappers.

The deputy shoved me hard into a chair, still handcuffed, then raised his meaty paw threateningly. I steeled myself for the blow.

"Now wait a minute, officer, I was kidnapped..."

"Shut up," the sheriff interrupted, waving the deputy away. "You expect me to believe a man like Reverend Nation would do that? You folks will tell any damn lie!"

"If I wasn't kidnapped, how did I get out here?" I parried, but the sheriff wasn't listening. He settled into his chair, which groaned and cracked in protest.

"Tell it to the judge at the bail hearing."

"Good. When can I see him?"

"He be in on Monday."

Monday. It's Saturday night! my head screamed.

God and Mammon being an irresistible combination, Hubris Nation and his largesse unquestionably had the whole threadbare county in his pocket. Neither the law nor my humanity had any weight on the blind woman's scales, which were heavily sunk in the reverend's favor. I could be charged with a felony, meaning, under federal law, it was possible I wouldn't be able to travel internationally. No helping Miriam, no buying trips abroad, at least until the lawyers cleared it up. Lawyers! Pain and expense, drawn out procedures, the appeals court, interminable injustice. Years!

"I get one call, right?"

"You can use your cell phone to call your Jew lawyer. County don't pay no station-to-station."

Tax attorney Burton Stephenson, a Jew? I wonder if his parish knows. "I don't have my cell phone, Sheriff. Look, if I can just speak to Reverend Nation..."

"The reverend is a busy man," he said like I'd asked to speak to the president.

"But Reverend Nation can explain this mix up. Please let me speak to him."

"Johnny, search Mistah Greenberg and put him in the cage."

So I was going to be stuck until Monday with nothing to occupy my time, a form of torture. Why didn't they just put me in solitary confinement! I was about to object, loudly, when the deputy dragged me to my feet, removed the cuffs, and began to search me in detail.

"He got sumpin' in his pocket, sheriff," the deputy noted, pulling Solly's letter from my shirt. Digging further down, he pulled out the Levi Asher photo.

"That's a letter from my friend. Who died. I haven't even read it yet. Have a little sensitivity." To avoid complications, I didn't mention Solly's suicide, fearing one of the intrepid lawmen—the earnest deputy was a prime candidate—might have notions of becoming Sherlock Holmes.

"Give them here, Johnny," the sheriff instructed. Ignoring my objections, he read until his eyes popped wide open. Then he reread several paragraphs, rubbing his chin. *He knew.* He also stared hard at Levi's photo, his face impassive.

"Make me copies for the record, Johnny, then give him back the originals." So the good reverend was going to end up with a copy of my letter through his intermediaries. Frustrating.

"That letter is extremely personal, Sheriff," I objected, hoping to keep it away from Nation.

"Just do what I say, Johnny. Lock him up."

***

I was trapped in a dank cell smelling of urine, sweat, and dust with nothing to read but Solly's letter.

I unfolded the note from the friend I hadn't seen since grad school, the friend who'd carried off the woman I'd loved, disappearing to a far-off land. Solly's writing style read more like a scientific footnote on the life cycle of the ordinary protozoa than a desperate man.

David, my oldest and dearest friend,

I have an interesting proposition for you, a request technically speaking. It may seem quite odd, inexplicable, but there is a logical reason for what I require, which soon will be revealed to you.

You know I am not frivolous to any degree but rely on facts alone. What you will learn, David, may sound like science fiction—or worse, a tale of horror. But I believe my work is almost a century ahead of the curve, and I have decades of well-documented, practical experiments and discoveries to prove its validity. Far more, your own eyes will allay any skepticism you may harbor. Your own eyes will see, accomplished in the real world, something seldom before imagined on this planet.

While still in graduate school, David, I was recruited by an organization to which you will be introduced when you arrive in Israel. These far-sighted people put me in charge of a project whose significance is no less than the scientific future of mankind and a transcendent basis for future human society. You know me; I do not exaggerate. I saw immediately that their project is clearly tangential to my own scientific aspirations, involving experiments I had been contemplating for years. I accepted their proposition.

Sorry, but Miriam, too, was adjunctive to my purposes, and I loved her at least as much as you did.

After years of planning, I have secured every resource needed to carry out my work. The advanced technology at my disposal is first-rate, world-class, my team of scientists and technicians dedicated and skilled.

David, once I am able to reveal my results, my work will change mankind's destiny. In the short run, it will certainly make me a household name and either earn me the Nobel Prize or land me in prison—with prison being the strongest probability. You know I do not say this lightly. It may sound like megalomania, but you will see for yourself when you arrive.

It is an unfortunate delay, but there remains an object I must have. Miriam will explain.

Please accompany her back to Israel, David. If you and I cannot meet again, there are many in my group to guide you through what has been accomplished here. You yourself will intuit where this is leading, I'm sure. David, help us complete this most critical work. Please retrieve the object we seek.

Your Friend still, I hope, Solly.

Not one hint of suicide.

More importantly, while his claims sounded preposterous, knowing Solly, I couldn't be sure they were. I always believed him capable of enormous discoveries. *But "the Nobel Prize or prison"? Had he become delusional? Or even dangerous?*

Miriam told me they'd given up drugs, but science can be a drug, too, especially with obsessives like Solly. I didn't know what to think. Sitting on an iron cot, my back supported by cinder block, I reread the note a number of times. No answers.

***

The sheriff spun the folder around for me, then shoved it across his desk, his faced pinched in a stern expression, like he'd bitten into a steak and found it tasted like dog food. The deputy sat immediately behind me, his holster unfastened, his hand resting on his pistol.

"These felonies are beginning to multiply," he said. "Big time."

I opened the folder, and a police photo shook me to the core. It was Moise Shankman's body curled up on the floor of his shop in a huge pool of his own blood, his throat slashed. It was a terrible thing to see, especially without any warning. I felt dizzy and a little nauseated.

The sheriff's eyes narrowed, silently accusing me. "Friend of yours, in the same business as you?"

"Reverend Nation seems to have tentacles everywhere," I groused, thinking that the fat body of the octopus is sitting right in the sheriff's chair.

"This is a big-time murder charge, Greenberg. First degree. It's a death penalty case. If nothing else, I should hold you as a material witness."

Clamming up, I took a few deep breaths to settle my nerves and my rebellious stomach. I was dying to insult him, to act tough, but the thought of being stuck in that stinking cell till Monday, with Miriam waiting for me at home, made me decide to play him, albeit reluctantly. It was my only chance.

"Moise was one of my dearest friends in the world, Sheriff. Look, I'd tell you anything I knew to help the police capture his killer. Whoever did this to him is worse than an animal."

"Your acquaintance didn't do him much good," the sheriff said. He pulled the photo back, then sat rubbing his chin for a long time, thinking.

"I had nothing to do with Moise's death. Look, I've got to get back to open my shop in the morning. Sunday is a big day for me."

"If you agree to turn over your passport, you can go home. The deputy can collect it when he drops you off."

"The reverend approved that, did he?" From the looks of things, the sheriff's office was a receiving station for Nation on a pretty broad scale. There was probably an office in the building with the latest computer equipment. Nevertheless, I wasn't going to let Nation control when I can leave the country. "Not a chance. You haven't even given me my phone call."

He nodded to the deputy. "Return him to his cell, would ya' Johnny?"

The deputy grabbed my arm roughly and yanked me to my feet. It hurt like hell; the big kid was strong. It was blackmail, but there was nothing I could do about it.

"Tell Reverend Nation I'm ready to deal," I said as I was being dragged from the room. "Tell him."

***

I had a hunch about the cryptic text message Levi had sent in his last moments of freedom, about the concluding letters *C B Z Q*. But guessing what the reference meant in relation to the nail's hiding place would pose another problem. Solving puzzles is not my forte.

Except, if unlocking the puzzle was so easy, the Israeli police or these Am Ha-b'rit geniuses would have figured it out. Or the killer, for that matter. *Did the Jerusalem police know about Levi's text message, and were they keeping it from the outside world? If so, why?*

After an hour, the young deputy came down the hall devouring a Double Whopper. "The reverend wants to speak to you," he said through full mouth. He handed me a cell phone before waddling back the way he'd come.

"Had time to think?" the velvet-toned voice said.

"Not to your advantage," I replied.

"Look, I am sorry, Mr. Greenberg, but you must understand, I have dedicated my whole sober life, my reborn life, solely to be touched by His Spirit. Millions believe I am the man closest to Him, that I hear His Word more clearly. To know He's returned and I can't meet Him, you can't imagine... Please believe me, David, I have no ulterior motive. None."

He sounded so sincere I nearly believed him. Well, if kidnapping and bearing false witness were okay, so was false swearing.

"Okay, Reverend, assuming the rumors are true, I swear to use my influence as best I can to get you an audience with him." Promise your beloved preacher anything, but get me out of jail. "As for the nail, if it exists, that's out of my league. Far too dangerous. I'll tip you off when, or if, I learn something, but I'm leaning toward not getting involved. That's all I can promise."

"I've already sent Bear to pick you up. You'll have round-the-clock protection."

"Don't want it."

"You don't realize, David, you may already be in grave danger. You must see that I'm only trying to protect my interest."

Bad transition. I'd gone from a dream date delayed two decades to mortal danger.

"It's a simple dilemma," the reverend continued. "Either I drop the charges against you or else a felony hangs over your head—no travel for business or for pleasure. Period."

We'll just see about that. I'll get home and work out the details later. "All right," I said, crossing my fingers. "You win."

"How much money do you need to start?" Nation asked.

"Keep your money. If this Messiah wants to meet you, it won't cost you a dime. That's what you say you want, just to meet him, right? We'll just take each other at our word."

"I think you people are more trustworthy when you get a retainer," he insisted.

"Nevertheless, Reverend, you don't want to be accused of committing counter-robbery," I barked threateningly.

"What the devil is *counter*-robbery?" he asked, puzzled.

"It's a Jew's worst nightmare: being forced by a good Christian clergyman to take money against our will." I chuckled, but the laugh on his end wasn't forthcoming.

"I will never understand you people," Reverend Nation growled disgustedly, then hung up the phone.

What a mishegas *I'd gotten into!*

CHAPTER FIVE
JERUSALEM BECKONS

Wearing only a light jacket, I walked out of the jailhouse into the shock of a late-season, icy-cold front. Refusing to retreat to the police station, I waited for Bear to arrive, shivering myself awake. The star-sprayed night felt like the atmosphere's shell had been punctured, allowing the weight of the infinite frozen nothingness to cascade down upon man's petty travails. Deserted by courage and reason, I sought the refuge of the ministry Escalade as eagerly as any broken-down sinner seeking church absolution against eternal oblivion.

As for the nail, I was leaning heavily toward just forgetting the whole thing, Miriam or no Miriam. Kidnapping and murder? I have my limits. If Reverend Nation wanted to fly me to Israel and supply me with a six-foot, six-inch bodyguard with a history of concussions and a balky knee to accompany my buying trip, that was his business. He can afford it. I was planning to leave shortly for Israel on a buying trip anyway.

Besides, Bear would make great company. Imagine traveling first-class, accompanied by God's Left Tackle, being regaled by his first-hand NFL tales. Hours and hours of inside-the-locker-room and on-the-field anecdotes straight from the Bear's mouth!

Plus, the guy knew his Christianity backwards and forwards. If I played my cards right, he could probably tip me off to which artifacts would be most in demand by his brethren. No reason I shouldn't take advantage of the arrangement.

In a way, I kind of liked the idea. Not that I had any intention of fulfilling my end of the bargain. I mean, what effect would it have on so powerful a religious force as Reverend Nation if he met, or believed he'd met, Jesus? The notion was too weird to contemplate.

For that matter, if I, myself, met the would-be Messiah, as hinted at by Miriam, what impact would that have on me, a modern secular Jew? Whose version of "Messiah" would he validate anyhow: Jewish, Christian, Muslim? I had to put the speculation aside, to deny the conflict even existed, because the concept was giving me a headache.

***

"I'm sorry, Bear," I said as I exited the Caddy, relieved to be home, "but this is as far as you go. If you want to protect me, you'll have to do it from the street."

"But the reverend said..."

"I don't care. The reverend's extortion stops at my front door. If you set one foot on my property, I'll call the cops. How will you protect me from your jail cell?"

Two could play this game. It was freezing, and Bear was a good guy, just following orders. But I'd made up my mind: chaperones from the almighty inside my house weren't part of our arrangement.

Besides, Miriam was waiting upstairs, and I didn't want Reverend Nation to know.

"I can't leave you alone," Bear said.

"Nobody's going to harm me before I have in hand what Reverend Nation wants."

Resigned, Bear handed me a cell phone. "Just press this button, and you'll get through to me instantly. I'll be in the car. If you can't talk, that's okay, I'll come running. Can I at least use your bathroom?"

"Sorry, again, Bear. There are restaurants and bars all up and down the street."

"My faith won't allow me to enter an establishment that sells alcohol," he said humbly.

"There's a 24-hour coffee shop with public restrooms right around the corner." I replied, unlocking my door.

His facial reaction touched me; he meant well and wasn't doing any of this for the money, which I assumed he didn't need. Before he became concussion-prone and hurt his knee, God's Left Tackle had cashed in with a long-term, guaranteed contract. The NFL can be lucrative for its star players, especially popular left tackles.

***

That day, I'd purposely left the security system off so Miriam would

35

have no problems getting into my house. Once inside, I touched the wall panel that controlled the lamp, shedding a warm glow over the spacious living room. People are surprised when they first see the contemporary style with which I decorated the house, free from adornment. But the restful simplicity and clean lines take my mind off work.

That's when the lamp revealed someone in the armchair, pointing a pistol at me.

"Hello, Greenberg," a familiar voice said. When my eyes adjusted, I could make out the stubby but powerful bulk of Finkel's pal, Joey "Daddy" Markowitz. Joey is called Daddy because of his rotund shape and assertive manner. From dissolute living, his weight long ago shifted to paunch. He sported a crew cut above his bright red cherub face, which was lined by a blunted will to riches and self-indulgence, all framed by the sadness of the gambler's serial impoverishment.

In their bio-niche, Daddy Markowitz preys upon Finkel and the stockyard munchkins until he can raise a stake large enough to re-enter the big games at a third-rate hotel. Then for a couple weeks, Daddy lives high on uncontrolled substances and gargantuan doses of saturated fat, devoting himself to his beloved cards until, naturally, his bankroll finds its way into the sieve-like pockets of a higher level of losers. As Tumor likes to say about the gambler scene, "The cream always settles to the top."

Like any gambler, Daddy is always shooting for the Big Score, compulsively drawing for the card so wild that he'll be flush with cash forever. But aren't we all seeking that jackpot in the lottery of life that will make us invulnerable to the vicissitudes of time? In fact, isn't the concept of Heaven, and thus most religion, irresistible because it soothes people into believing they can beat Death itself? Whatever. Hey, find balm in Gilead anywhere you can.

"Daddy!" I said, "How's it going? How's your mom?" Mrs. Markowitz, a fine lady, had always treated me well. Her sumptuous meals, with Daddy and Chick around the table, had made my student life and bachelorhood periods so much more, well, palatable. I felt at home there, in sharp contrast to my own parents' house.

"My mom's okay," he answered in his slight lisp.

"Last time I heard, you were flush," I lied, knowing that he'd be at the stockyards if he had money, not sitting in my living room brandishing a firearm.

"Tap City," he replied wearily.

"Too bad, Joey. My Hamburger Haven stock just took a nosedive." I plopped into a sofa where I could stare directly into his eyes and keep watch on the pistol.

"Fuckin'-A, Tweety," he replied. "I could go for a half dozen party dogs. I'll bet you I can eat two in two minutes."

"I've seen you win that one too many times. You want a drink? I've got some good Scotch."

"Thanks, I already found it." He took a major swig from a quarter-full fifth, sloppily splashing his chin, which he drew his sleeve across.

"You better get rid of that pistol before you harm yourself, Daddy. Since when did you start carrying a piece?"

"Since a friend of yours beat the shit out of me."

I looked closely, and through the shadows, I could see bruises and scars about his face. Threats were multiplying. "A friend of mine? Like who?"

"I don't know," he slurred, drunkenly. "Some foreign fucker."

"Where was he from, Daddy?"

"I don't know."

"Middle Eastern? East European? What?"

"Spoke broken English. He didn't take my money."

"What did he ask you?"

"Questions about you. That's all I know."

"How was he dressed? Any headgear?"

"He was dressed okay, nothing special. Just a guy, you know. Slightly dark-skinned with a black beard. Maybe it was fake; I couldn't tell."

"Anything else? Think, Daddy."

"No, nothing... Wait. He had a birthmark on his face, longish and pointy."

"Like a spike or a nail?"

Daddy nodded yes.

Was this a coincidence? Something otherworldly? The revelation nearly opened my bowels. *Could the reverend and the Bible be right about that Beast prophesy? Could this guy be Satan or one of his henchmen?* I was starting to lose it. *Or was the perpetrator one of the reverend's own associates?*

Just then, Daddy's cell went off, and he listened a moment. "The Blackhawks are a tough ticket—standing room only." He paused. "Maybe three, four hundred apiece...What time?...Okay, I'll be there." The phone disappeared. "Fuckin' eleven o'clock in the goddamn morning!" he grumbled.

"Prison taught you a trade," I acknowledged, impressed with his professionalism. "I need tickets from time to time—"

He flipped his business card on the table, bent and dirty with pocket lint. "Any time, Greenberg, you cheap shit.

"You just don't know, Genius," he continued, relieved he'd seized a friendly ear to unburden his existential angst. "You think about death all the time in the slammer. One time, I got into the dispensary; I had the pills in my hand!" he roared, thrusting his fist skyward as dramatically as any amateur Macbeth.

Ah, the fatal pills, a revered topic among the gambler tribe. Clearly, though his fortunes had more ups and downs than a commodity futures trader, he'd never built any tolerance for losing. The agony of defeat is only exacerbated by inglorious repetition.

"When did this man grab you, Daddy?"

"Yesterday."

Was Daddy's interrogator Moise Shankman's killer? If he was, why didn't he just dispose of Daddy, too? Perhaps the guy didn't want to attract unnecessary attention to himself; a possibility. The Evil One, whomever that might be—if there was only *one* in this game—was probably more clever than ruthless, and he was plenty ruthless.

On the other hand, if he was one of the reverend's people, and the birthmark was truly a coincidence, I was safe while I was in Nation's pocket.

It was possible, too, that Miriam had directed one of her greenback "help-me" packages into the wrong hands. She may have known of my connection to Markowitz through his younger brother, Chick, he of the spinning love triangle. Naiveté and desperation are a dangerous combination when money is involved.

I wanted to ask Markowitz more questions, but he was Scotch-submerged far below such detailed memories.

"You owe me money, Greenberg!" he barked, doing his best George C. Scott's *The Hustler* imitation.

"How, Daddy? How do I owe you money?" I recited in my best Jackie Gleason-Minnesota Fats voice, like a refrain to a priest's admonition, hoping to put us both in the same religion—gambling. It's never a bad idea to humor an aggrieved drunk holding a pistol, old friend or not.

"Proctor got busted. You turned him in."

"I had nothing to do with that. He was swindling people all over town."

"It had to be you. Seems like fuckin' thieves fencing goddamn ancient treasures always get busted right after they've been introduced to you."

"He was scamming museums, Daddy. He was a bad guy." Stan Proctor—DBA "Doctor" Proctor—preyed upon the willingness of museums and foundations to share with other institutions for educational purposes. Claiming he was putting together traveling displays, he "borrowed" Native American artifacts from their collections and sold many of them through shady dealers, of which, as people that know me well will attest, I am not one. I don't look for it, but if it finds me, it's *caveat venditor*—let the *seller* beware.

"He's talking like I turned him in," Markowitz decried, taking another swig directly from the bottle. "Maybe he has friends."

"Don't worry, Daddy; Proctor has no friends. In fact, you might get a piece of the insurance money. You can donate the proceeds to the 24-hour card game in the stockyards."

"Fuckin'-A, Tweety," he said, a drunken acknowledgement of the fate of all his liquid cash assets.

"Those pieces belonged to the public, Daddy, not to a bunch of scumbags."

"Proctor's a prick."

"He is. So what can I do for you?"

"I've been talking to Finkel..."

"Naturally. And you want a piece of the action. You'll wind up with Finkel's piece anyway."

"Fuckin'-A, Tweety." He took a gulp.

"I've never cheated you, right?" I paused for an objection, but it was a rolling stop. I changed the subject. "What do you know about Chick, Daddy?"

"Chick's living in Israel with this sculptor. Sometimes he helps fake antiquities for the guy's friend."

It felt good to know Chick was out of the mental hospital, which I had feared was a permanent thing.

"Good news, Daddy. Is Chick still painting?"

"Fuckin'-A, Tweety Bird, little brother's trying."

"So what's the deal, Daddy?"

39

"He wrote me a letter, said something about trying to find a nail...that he was going to get rich."

"You have Chick's contact info?"

He set the pistol on the table so he could fumble through his pockets. Finally, he found a torn wedge of brown paper bag with writing on it.

"I'll buy the gun, too, Daddy. Now that you've been questioned, you won't need it. How much did you pay for it?"

"Two C-notes," he lied.

"I'll give you one-fifty."

"Done," he said, nifty profit in hand.

"Let me call you a ride, Daddy." I pressed the button on the cell Bear had given me. "Bear, I've got a passenger for you. Meet me outside the house."

"I'm here now," Bear said through the cell.

As I helped Daddy from the chair, I thought about the birthmark clue. *Could this be the guy who killed Moise Shankman?*

I capped the Scotch bottle and slipped it into Daddy's pocket. I was now the proud owner of a loaded street-pistol, obviously well-equipped to face murderers and religious fanatics. Escaping this whole new dimension to my life seemed tempting for the moment. On the other hand, Vince Lombardi had it right: "Fatigue makes cowards of us all," and I was plenty tired. Furthermore, Miriam was waiting for me upstairs.

I needed some aspirin. It felt like a herd of obese angels were dancing on the pin of my head. *Gabriel, call them off!*

***

I watched Bear pull away in the Caddy with Daddy safely snoring in the back seat. Then I shouted the all clear to Miriam and went straight to the kitchen to take some aspirin and put on a large pot of coffee. I needed the caffeine. Once the dark stimulant was brewing, I headed upstairs to see Miriam and to analyze Levi Asher's clue.

Miriam met me at the top of the stairs wearing sweat clothes. She looked exhausted, her face drawn, her eyes red from crying. There would be no romantic reunion this evening, or probably any time soon. Even the dregs of optimism I clutched seemed at the mercy of some malicious deity with extra jokers up his, or her, sleeve.

"What happened to you?" she asked half-angrily, her voice strained. "You disappear for practically the entire night with three men from the planet Giganticus, into a pair of black battle tanks. Then I have to hide in a closet for hours while an armed drunk crashes around downstairs, shouting angry expletives at your ghost. I was afraid he'd come upstairs searching for you, but he was too polite, or too wasted, to climb the stairs."

"I'm sorry, Miriam. It's a long story. Do you want something to drink or to eat? Some coffee or soda?"

"I'll have a glass of wine, red if you have it. Let me get a cigarette," she said, disappearing into the first spare bedroom.

"Bring the whole pack," I said over my shoulder, heading downstairs. I'd quit smoking long ago, but needed one. "I'll uncork a really nice Cab I picked up in Napa." When playing the long game, some potential rewards, no matter how unlikely, are worth shooting the wad for.

In the living room, we both rested on leather, me in the chair Daddy Markowitz had abandoned, her stretched out on the matching lounge. As I worked to pop the cork on the Cabernet, she lit both cigarettes and stuck one in my mouth. I took a drag and laid it in the ashtray to continue my assault on the cork. Soon, with great relief, I was sipping coffee, and she was sipping red wine, and we were puffing some foreign brand with a white filter.

"So, your disappearance? I've never known you to be late for a date," she added sarcastically.

"Believe it or not, I wound up in a jail near Wentzville, but I think that's cleared up now." I also thought I had a possible clue to Moise's killer, the guy with the spike-shaped birthmark, but now was not the time for that conjecture; neither was this the moment to reveal my hunch as to the location of the nail.

"Jail?" She sat up straight.

"It's a long story."

I gave Miriam some private time, making busy getting a wine glass for myself. I poured a half-inch, then ran through the ritual, sniffing it, taking a sip, my eyes always downcast. That done, I crushed out the cigarette, which had burned down with no help from me.

"David, there's something you need to know," she said haltingly, handkerchief to her eyes.

"Okay," I said, bracing for the worst. "Give it to me."

"I have a son, Ari. He's fourteen and he's dying, David. Ari was fine when I left home, but the doctors had always said it could happen suddenly, and that time is here. I've got to get back. I've got to see him before..." She burst into tears.

A son? I'd always thought of Miriam as she once was, young and unattached. She hadn't asked me about offspring during lunch and, dumbfounded with seeing her and by her startling revelations, I never asked. Hell, kids are the first things a woman will tell you about, and she never breathed a word. This oversight, which couldn't have been accidental, had me wondering.

I crossed to the couch and put my arm on her shoulders until she indicated that she was in control of herself. Then I returned to my chair and put it to her straight. "Well, then, you have to go. If you want me along..."

"Of course I want you with me, David. I need you," she said with difficulty, voice emotionally charged. "Please."

"The good news is, we have a private jet at our disposal. Straight shot, no airport lines, no changing planes, nothing."

"Uh-huh." Her tone lifted. "Time-wise, that would be helpful."

"The problem is the plane belongs to a preacher named Hubris Nation. I can't leave the country unless I use his plane...and he comes along."

"Hubris Nation? Oh, God, David, not that nut-job. There's no other way?"

"I don't think so. It's possible they can tie up my passport. What if we *have to* do it this way? To fly in his plane? With him aboard?"

"I guess faster is better. I need you with me, David. I need you, either way." That's all I was waiting to hear. "Please hurry," she urged. "Ari's..." She fell silent.

"One last thing," I practically stuttered, not knowing how to say it. "This guy, Nation, he seems to think the Messiah is being held by some cult in Israel. Any idea why he'd think such a thing? Part of the deal is that he gets to meet this so-called savior."

"I'm not up to getting into that with you yet." She paused, thinking. "Yes, perhaps he could meet him. Maybe. I'll think about what I want to do."

"Whatever you decide, Miriam. Lying to him is okay. The guy *is* blackmailing me. So, does Am Ha-b'rit hold this 'Messiah'?"

"Please, David, I'll explain when I can," she pleaded, too overcome to go into detail. "Maybe on the plane or back home. Please, please, just call this Nation person. I can't let Ari die without being there!"

I'll just have to be patient, I thought as I pushed the button on the cell and told Bear we wanted to fly to Jerusalem in the morning. I said that I'd have a female companion along or I wasn't going. Then Miriam and I took time to settle down. I searched the fridge and heated up some ready-cooked basil chicken and pasta from Straub's. We ate together, with only Miriam breaking our relative silence as she poured out a dense, turgid stream-of-consciousness. She'd been hit hard—first Levi's disappearance and now her son—and all I could do was listen, nodding as she talked.

I contemplated Miriam's turmoil-consumed face, trying to understand what she was going through. I know this: some evil spirit was second-dealing from a marked deck. It just wasn't fair.

***

I went upstairs to my study. Frumpy and disorderly, the room is an anomaly to the house's otherwise neat and tidy space. On every surface, scraps of notes and books, pencils, and news clippings lie about in random piles, having landed wherever I last used them. These stacks will later be shoveled into large hunks to make way for my new project of the moment.

Miriam drifted into the room on bare feet, appearing beside me like vapor. I stared into her eyes, now wrenched by tears into a tableau of sorrow. But she had real starch in her will. "David, do you really have an insight into Levi's text?"

"59CBZQ? Maybe. Miriam, was Levi by any chance a chess player?"

"Yes, he was on the school's chess team," she replied, utterly shocked. "His lucky piece was a black knight, a horse's head with one ear broken off. He carried it around to rub for luck."

"And he studied Bobby Fischer?"

"Yes!" she exclaimed. "Bobby was Levi's hero. Levi was our resident expert on Bobby Fischer's games."

So Destiny had lined me up like a bank shot on the eight ball. Bobby Fischer was my boyhood idol, and Levi's, too. And playing the rare pickup game of chess against Finkel the evening before had put the late, great grandmaster in the forefront of my mind. Playing white, I always open with *faux*-Fischer pawn-to-king-four, the move Bobby called "the best by test." Otherwise, Levi's text might have been just a jumble.

"Okay, I may have a clue for you. This number fifty-nine, though, that'll be tough. Let me ask you, what were Levi's other interests?"

"Well, Torah studies, of course. Let's see…He was in a *Kabbalah* group; many of our students are."

I knew little of *Kabbalah*, a medieval rabbinical form of mysticism quite popular among Jews and even celebrities today. Madonna is one of its many learned Hollywood practitioners.

I wracked my brain, finding only one other thin straw to grasp. "Interesting. Was he also into *gematria?*" *Gematria*, used for many purposes by *Kabbalahists*, is an Assyro-Babylonian system of numerology adopted by the Jews centuries ago. In *gematria*, a word or phrase equates to a numerical value. This Jewish numerology tradition is, in fact, one of the thirty-two methods used to analyze the Torah and other Hebrew texts, using mathematics. I had read that the first known use of *gematria* was an inscription telling us the Assyrian ruler Sargon II, 700s BCE, built the wall of Khorsabad 16,283 cubits long to match the numerical value of his name. Even today, a monetary gift among Jews based on the number eighteen is considered lucky because the numbers for the two letters of the word *chai*, meaning "life," add up to eighteen.

"Yes," she replied, slightly taken aback that I'd struck a nerve a second time. "Levi was always playing with numbers, especially after his *Kabbalah* meetings. He was kind of obsessive about it." She could see where this was headed.

Unfortunately, I knew little about *gematria* either. Further, I'd read there are hundreds of *gematria* charts, any one of which Levi Asher could have been referring to with his number fifty-nine, if that was even his intention. In fact, according to Elazar Rokeach, there are 231 replacement ciphers alone related to the 231 mystical *Gates of the Sefer Yetzitah*—stuff way beyond me. Regardless, which of the thousands of charts would I use? And assuming I found the right chart, how would I connect the result to my Bobby Fischer theory in order to locate the nail? The task appeared daunting, far beyond my expertise.

"Do you think *gematria* might help us find the nail?" Miriam asked hopefully.

"Just a hunch," I replied, attempting to keep my grave doubts to myself. "Wish me luck—lots of it."

Seeking to flesh out my hunch, I went immediately to the general area of the disheveled bookshelves where I was most likely to find the tomes on chess. While Reverend Nation's books stand in line like soldiers in parade dress uniform, my hobo volumes of every size and description are in little discernable order, each despoiled by bookmarks, annotations, and mustard stains.

While Miriam watched, I found the hardcover containing some of Bobby Fischer's chess games: its back broken and partly missing, its pages dog-eared. I'd lifted the book from the high school library, a worn volume even then. The moves were still written in the old chess notation, P-KB4, pawn to king-bishop-four, instead of the new F4, pawn to F-file, fourth row. I had, undoubtedly, saved the book from eventual recycling or from the flames of modern pragmatism.

The volume contains The Game of the Century, bookmarked by a scrap of paper with a telephone number written on it in an unknown female hand. I had replayed this epic contest many times for my own pleasure, but I now had more urgent need for it.

The Game of the Century was won by Bobby Fischer, then a thirteen-year-old prodigy. Played in New York City on October 17, 1956, Bobby appeared to make the jaw-dropping "mistake" of allowing his opponent, Donald Byrne, an accomplished adult, to capture his queen, the most powerful piece on the board, with Byrne's bishop. Byrne, a future grandmaster, had already obtained first place in the 1953 U.S. Open Championship and would later represent the United States in three Chess Olympiads.

The loss of the queen would defeat any normal player in competition. More importantly, though, in chess, the player who sees more deeply into a position wins the game, and Bobby always saw the board more deeply than anyone. Thinking far ahead, Fischer had allowed his queen to be taken *on purpose!* In effect, he gave Byrne seemingly overwhelming material advantage to gain an extra move, to gain a tempo. Rather than resign, precise as a Swiss watch, Bobby forced capture after capture with lightning combinations of minor pieces, a series of unrelenting, unstoppable knight, rook, and bishop checks and captures called a "windmill effect," utterly destroying Byrne in the process and leading to checkmate. Who could have seen it coming...except Bobby?

What led me to intuit this untangling of Levi Asher's 59CBZQ? My attention had been drawn immediately to the B and the Q, in chess notation the letters for the bishop and the queen. I then guessed that, being in a frantic rush, young Levi had struck the Z in error, when he meant to strike an X, immediately beside it. That left me with BXQ, in chess notation, bishop takes queen.

From there, I had to account for the C. The letter C means a hundred or a century in Roman numerals, like a C-note being a hundred-dollar bill. So, I intuited, Game of the Century, bishop takes queen, the most significant move in the history of chess, in Levi's exact order. What else could it be? Was the puzzle on its way to being solved? I felt good about the quest. I was on the way.

I didn't realize the Fates had been setting me up. One, since I had just played an intense game with Finkel, a rare occurrence, chess vibes were near the front of my mind. Two, Bobby was my boyhood hero, just as he was Levi Asher's. Three, Miriam's presence, after a two-decade absence, was making me blind to the consequences of my actions. Frightening, no?

Just then, Miriam spoke in her soft voice, even in her great distress showing interest in me. "This is all impressive, David, the shop, the mansion..."

"It's not a mansion, Miriam. It's just a big house, which looks bigger because of a lone guy rattling around in it."

"I thought you were going to be a famous historian, a professor, or an archeologist. What happened to all those dreams? All your great plans?"

"Maybe when I lost my future, my hurt trumped the distant past," I lied, seemingly placing the blame for my escape from academia on losing her. I knew it rang false before it left my mouth.

She stared at me for many long seconds, seeing through my sham. "Ha, the books didn't interfere with your poker games. Sometimes it seemed you loved the games more than you so fervently claimed you loved me."

"The cards were my part-time job, Miriam. Seven-card, low-in-the-hole/roll-your-own was my scholarship supplement," I acknowledged, letting her know with my eyes that I was aware that she was right, that I had been rationalizing. "How do you think I bought that rattling old Sirocco we rode around in?"

"Yes? And becoming a gallery owner, was that done for chump change? You're a grown-up now."

She's holding my feet to the fire. "Path of least resistance." I shrugged, admitting my weakness, the unmistakable influence of the materialism I so angrily rejected in my youth. The death of Finkel's grandmother and his inheriting her antiquities business was the turning point in my career, my life. If Finkel was going to blow her assets at the track and table, no reason I shouldn't catch as many falling valuable relics as I could before they hit the skids. Didn't I save Finkel from the mob's juice men more than once? He could have been crippled or killed…or so I tell myself.

"With this money, David, you could run your own archeological expeditions like you talked about."

"Miriam, I'm past the age where I can spend years alone in the desert just to startle a few academics. I'm really not big on being alone."

"You don't ever have to be alone if you don't want to. You just choose to be. And you know it, David."

She kissed me long and hard, her lightness melting into my arms, and I returned the kiss. It so felt like she meant it, and I wanted her to have meant it. Then we were apart again.

"David, a woman, too, can have a compelling destiny that is greater than herself…and be true to it. When I can explain, maybe you'll understand." She turned to drag herself from the room.

"I left the wine on your nightstand," I called after her. "In case you have trouble sleeping. I'll be in here or in my bedroom if you need me. Good night."

Alone now, I called Arnie, my assistant, waking him, to cover for me being overseas; perhaps for some time.

That done, I took up my writing pad and sat at my chess table, replaying the moves of Fischer's Game of the Century, with its scintillating whirlwind of creativity.

I reached the game's ritornelle immediately before Byrne took Bobby's queen, trying to imagine the symphonic lines of attack Bobby must have already been hearing with full orchestration in his head. Then, Byrne says, "Bishop takes queen," and all hell broke loose: the brass section strokes and kettle drum-pounding pressures of Fischer's rook, the violin crescendo of the knight, the swirling trumpeting of the bishop.

The rest of the game was a soundless combination of metaphysical melodies of purely mental force. A heavenly rhapsody created under time pressure, fighting with lesser material as Donald Byrne's own brilliant mind worked fiercely to stop him at every move. A thing of timeless beauty.

But not yet the answer. I glanced at the clock: three a.m. Time for a shower and shave; no time for sleep. I took up my pocket chess set, the Fischer book, my laptop, and writing pad. I'd have to decode this mystery in Israel.

CHAPTER SIX
THE NAILS

I am among the least of these, of whom our Master often spoke in parable. I am not of sound mind because of the horrors I have witnessed in these last days of my life. And surely a man as sickly as I am, on his best day, navigating through life with three limbs defective by nature, cannot be called of sound body on his deathbed.

The least of these, yes. Women and children are more swift than I. And even my brother Jacob says everyone is smarter than I, which I cannot dispute. It is true; ideas do not stick easily in my head. I never learned the trick to reading and writing, so these words I speak to you will have to serve as my Last Bequest. Not that it matters, of course, for all our earthly possessions are held in common anyway.

What is indisputable, though, is no one loves our Master more.

He truly gave me my life: a helpless, crippled beggar on the street. Women and children spat upon me with impunity. And with a gentle smile, He told me I was not a beggar, not a cripple, but a carpenter like He was. And He taught me His craft. To honor Him, I have dedicated every day since to making the adze and saw and chisel sing with my good hand and my twisted one—to making cabinets that families entrust with their heirlooms and silver treasures, their menorahs and goblets for the wine blessing; to making tables upon which they light their holy candles and break bread to thank the Lord on the Sabbath. As the Master Carpenter poured life and beauty into dead wood, so did He make a man from this pitiful creature.

I have even so prospered that I own my own forge, in which I turn hot metal into hard objects of many uses. This I work with two men to assist me who once were lost, but now are devoted to our Master. One was a beggar, like I once was; one a thief.

Death will be a blessing for me, an end to suffering this madness. I averted my eyes because I could not bear to see the pain on His sweet face. But though I covered my ears, I could not shut out the pounding, pounding, pounding of the mallet driving the nails into his flesh, could not silence their foul Roman laughter from beating upon my ears.

Suddenly, I was enflamed by the need to scramble to His rescue on my shriveled legs, to combat them with my good arm. If the Lord gave strength to little David to defeat mighty Goliath, surely He would give me strength to slay these soldiers. I could envision us carrying our Master back to the bosom of those who adored Him, who would treat His wounds and dry His tears. And even if I failed, He would know I had given my life to save His.

How could I live another minute knowing no one at that cursed place dared risk his life for Him, least of all me, who loved Him more dearly than all the world? I shouted and started forward, intent on seizing one of their swords, determined to take as many as I could with me into the darkness. But Samuel, seeing my intent, held me firmly with his great arms, his hand over my mouth. Struggle and flail as I might—I'm sorry Samuel— I could not break free and grew quiet.

Then before our eyes, for sport—sport!—one of the Romans, sneering derisively at our Master, jammed a spear into His side, twisting and cutting. From this ragged wound, His life poured like a flood, down His bare stomach and legs unto His feet, to the rocks and soil below.

Our Master tried to teach us that we would gain the whole world by loving our enemies. And I do believe He saw far beyond others, far into the future. But with all the trouble and sorrow I have known and seen— and now this!—let me say, it is easier for a crippled hand to smooth the grain on a splinter than for a wounded heart to love a Roman soldier.

Why, I ask myself, through all of time, has the Lord allowed savages like these, with their shining armored shells and fearsome weapons, to hold sway over His own hardworking, modest worshipers? Why allow the brutal hordes to enter a peaceful village and put to the sword and to fire the innocent and loving? All slain and burned, fathers and mothers, babes and children, holy men and scholars! All faithful Jews, Samaritans, people of so many races whose sins cannot possibly warrant such an ignominious demise. Why does He permit cruelty to prosper, while the pious are crushed?

To a fool like me, such a ratiocination as "turn the other cheek" only proves that man will tell himself anything in order to deny the horror of an indifferent existence. But He saw so much further than I: perhaps believing the Romans could be taught to turn their cheek. I know He must be right, but to my last breath, I will so desire to strike a Roman cheek.

***

Joseph of Arimathea arrived at Golgotha bearing the scroll signed by Pilate allowing him to take possession of our Master's corpse. To his everlasting glory, Joseph had obtained the precious document at great personal peril, knowing that to do so would expose him to the Romans as a follower of our Master. He also carried the linen shroud he had purchased to wrap the precious body. Nicodemus had already brought the spices necessary for the burial. Then the signed scroll was given to Aharon, our go-between with the Romans, to intercede with the soldiers.

Alas, as Aharon soon discovered, the crucifixions completed, the Roman army's duplicarius had long since given his final orders and departed to Jerusalem, where it was rumored he had a woman whose name and dwelling were unknown to anyone but himself. Aharon presented the scroll to the leading gregaralis, but the man could not read and refused to allow anyone anywhere near the cross until the duplicarius returned, perhaps in the next day or two.

That would be far too late! As it was, the Sabbath was drawing near, and we knew we would have to hurry. Finally, we determined we would have to wait until God solved the insoluble for us—and He did...in a most earth-shattering way.

After the soldiers finished their grizzly duties, the most terrible tempest I have ever seen drove them into their tents, which being of the best military stock, withstood the gale. Huge limbs torn from trees flew through the blackened skies, and the very stones seemed alive. While the families of the thieves beside Him and the curious crowd ran down the hill in panic, calling out in fright, we hid together in a nearby copse, just as we had planned, watching and waiting.

So greatly did the heathen soldiers fear the storm that, through the crash of lightning and thunder, we could hear them crying out to their gods for mercy.

Finally, Yahweh's terrible anger broke, and we were left exposed to the cold, steady rain of His tears.

And our Master's tormentors? We could hear the soldiers, their duplicarius absent, rolling dice in their sturdy army tents, swearing and cursing and drinking and fighting among themselves. And all we could do was bide our time and have faith, shivering through the night, staring with envy at their glowing fires and listening to their blasphemous revels. My threadbare cloak and tunic were soaked through, like a washerwoman's rag, and I knew then I would be sick unto my death when our labors had ended.

Any one of us who was there can tell you, every moment waiting for the soldiers to tire of their games was torture. From our hiding place, we could see Him hanging there, so pitiful, so damaged. I cursed the moon that revealed him.

It was late by the time their drinking claimed the last pair, and they were all snoring under their blankets. Joseph gave the signal, and we crept from the brush in the darkness. My crutch sank into the muddy soil as I stumbled up the rock-strewn slope. In my hurry, I tripped over a fallen branch and, reaching to catch myself, slashed my good hand deeply on a sharp rock. It bled like a torrent.

Finally, I reached the structure where His mutilated body dangled in the chill. Even in the dark, I could smell and feel the cross was hewn from cedar, probably from Sidon. I rubbed my bloody hand along its length and was shocked to find a mass of splinters and irregular gouges. The Greek merchant who sells to the Romans—at top price, mind you—had been using unskilled slaves with crude tools to hack out the shaft. Oh, that the World's Carpenter should die on so primitive a piece of workmanship!

The able-bodied went about their tasks. Joseph climbed the sturdy ladder I had built, while those below supported our Master's body in place. With his great strength, he hammered the nail and plucked it from His right hand and tossed it aside. I heard it hit nearby, and, feeling my way, I crawled through the briars, which cut and scraped my knees and palms, until I found it.

I tested it with my teeth. A good army nail, forged strong and sharp, like they make in Ashkelon. The Greek merchant no doubt received a handsome sack of Roman coins bearing the Emperor's likeness for the lot. Oh, that a small bribe can perform such service for an unworthy sinner, and that the soldiers can turn such fine implements to such ignominious purposes. God may know everything, as my Master claimed, but I often wonder if there isn't much in human governance that is kept from Him.

51

By the time I transferred the nail from my bleeding hand to the claw, Joseph was tossing aside the nail from His right hand. I crawled after it as well, almost losing my crutch, before I was able to stuff it too into the claw.

When Joseph dropped the last bloody nail that held His feet, it hit the stones piled at the base of the cedar cross, making a sharp clanging that split the silence. As they lowered Him down, I crawled to the spot, but the commotion had awakened one of the soldiers, who shouted a drunken alarm.

We panicked, rushing to get away, with strong Yitzhak hoisting our Master upon his broad back. I did locate the third nail, but as you know, the crippled lamb is eaten by the lion. Hurrying to rise, while juggling my crutch and at the same time attempting to switch the nail into my claw, I dropped it.

Finally, I found it and picked it up. My fingers felt along its length until they came to the maker's mark. It was that of my own forge.

"It is my own mark! It is my own mark!" I shouted like a man gone mad, my tears pouring like a river from my breaking heart. "I made these nails that killed our Lord! I made the nails!"

All reason gone, I began to slash my wrist with the nail.

Joseph ordered that I be silenced, and two of ours brethren covered my mouth and dragged me away. I struggled and fought them. I wanted to go kill the Romans by myself, like little David, but our friends did not release me, cry as I might.

So, here, I bequeath to all of you beside my deathbed, which I made with my own hands, to you who believed in He who took me in from the streets and transformed me, these nails that tore His tender flesh. These good Roman army supplies sold at such a profit by the fat Greek. These nails that bear his precious blood—and my own—and how many others that were condemned to die so horribly on such poor workmanship. I leave them in trust to Deborah, who has washed my fevered face and given me sips of cool water...and who will wash and prepare my corpse. And who, I pray, will bestow upon a dying man one last taste of her delicious lentil soup. Unless, of course, there will not be enough for the mourners at my funeral, in which case, I will happily forego this last pleasure in gratitude to these beloved friends and to the Great Soul who saw to it that I would not die a solitary beggar.

CHAPTER SEVEN
MIRIAM'S TALE

Sometime during the night, the cold front had its chilling orgasm and cut out, leaving the pubescent spring violated, stunned. In the pleasant, cool sunrise, beneath the returning leaves budding on the maple and elm lining my street, the reverend's driver carried my bags to the limo. I paused on my front steps to take a deep breath of the brisk spring air. Clad in a light leather jacket to suit the coming desert nights and arid climate, I yawned and stretched, taking a minute to admire my placid block, its homes smug and secure. I wondered when, or if, I would luxuriate in that serenity again. Then I bent to pick up my morning *New York Times*, ready to head off, fool that I was.

Miriam appeared beside me, wearing denim jeans and jacket, and a print blouse. Our eyes met knowingly. Her features were lined with concern, but she managed a passing smile—more polite grimace than fond greeting. She whispered a heartfelt thanks. I could see she hadn't slept easily or long.

I locked my front door and rolled her suitcase to the curb for the driver to load, and then we climbed in the back of the limo.

The revolver Daddy Markowitz had sold me was concealed in my suitcase. Although we would be landing in Nation's private airstrip in Israel, the chance of discovery was still there, but I decided to chance it.

Miriam instructed the driver to stop at her parents' home in University City before we headed to the airport. After living away for two decades, except for occasional visits to her parents, she could hardly leave without saying goodbye.

In fifteen minutes, we braked at the modest, aging bungalow, and

Miriam disappeared inside. The small, wood-frame and brick structure was part of a neat, post-WWII development of nearly identical units that went on for blocks in every direction. Each street in this part of town was named after a major center of learning: Harvard, Yale, Stanford, Cornell. When it was first built, this middle-class suburb was heavily populated by second-generation Jews—hardworking, money-saving accountants, clerks, and shopkeepers, many of whose offspring did, indeed, attend the very schools to which their parents aspired to send them. Now it was a settled salt-and-pepper neighborhood, having been block busted by Italian real estate speculators decades before, opening the neighborhood to upwardly mobile blacks and Asian populations.

How many nights did I park my rattling old Sirocco in the spot where I now sat comfortably in the limo watching Miriam enter her parent's house? The parting was never easy.

Leaving the Dreyfus home, Miriam bent to embrace and kiss her mother farewell, lingering a long moment to brush away a tear. Then she turned and came toward me, while the aging woman anxiously watched her prodigal daughter disappear, once again, to that far-off, mythical land.

I stepped onto the street to help Miriam into the back seat, and as our hands touched, she glanced up at my face. A deep sigh passed her lips.

Twenty minutes of light highway traffic later, the limo pulled onto the tarmac, a few feet from the reverend's Cessna. The driver opened the car door on my side, then got busy stacking our luggage in the plane's bay. I offered Miriam a hand getting out, but her eyes were downcast. Not acknowledging my presence, she headed grimly for the steps to the plane.

We walked to the jet, no lines, no security check, no baggage in hand. Reverend Nation appeared at the door all smiles, with a pompously modest greeting. Nice way to travel, except for the company one must keep.

I didn't expect a magic carpet ride to the river Jordan, but neither could I have expected to be ferried by Charon down the river Lethe to Hades. But that's what I got.

***

Shortly after takeoff, Nation's valet served us a hot breakfast of rib-sticking country food from the jet's ovens, presented on bone China with Sterling silverware, our coffee in gold-rimmed Hallelujah Hour mugs. Miriam picked at her plate. Meanwhile, Nation, a man with appetites to fit his girth, devoured his first round of helpings, then went on to consume seconds. In my sleepy state, I became fascinated by the reverend's prominent teeth, like some gleaming machine tearing and chewing and grinding as he pitchforked in hearty blocks of carbs, sugar, nitrates, fat, and salt, drowning them with OJ and black caffeine. My new bodyguard/friend, Bear Brukowski, shoved down toast, fruit, rare steak, and pitchers of fruit juice.

My body clock was so off from lack of sleep that it took the pungent taste of the coffee, syrup-drenched pancakes, and hickory-smoked bacon to remind me how famished I truly was. I ate hungrily, then opened my paper.

An article in the *Times* caught my eye. "It seems they're trying to resurrect species that went extinct over the last sixty thousand years," I noted, amused. "For about ten million dollars, they could modify the DNA in an elephant's egg to produce a mammoth. Oh, ho!" I chortled. "And listen to this. Although there would be ethical issues, this article says they could possibly use a human egg to produce a Neanderthal."

I looked up to see the reverend in an apoplectic state, eyes bulging, face bright crimson, nearly choking on his grits.

"They can't do that!" Nation sputtered.

His discomfort with the story put a wide grin on my face. *Being still cross-eyed angry at the man, wouldn't it be fun to discuss a little evolution or stem cell technology with the good reverend?* "The article says there used to be technical barriers because ancient DNA always shreds into tiny pieces, but now they have these '454' DNA decoding machines that use tiny pieces as their starting point. Each '454' costs about a half million dollars." I scanned the column. "It names a genome technologist at Harvard, George Church, who developed a method that can modify 50,000 genomic sites at a time. Apparently, too, a Dr. Shinya Yamanaka has come up with a way to reprogram an elephant skin cell to an embryonic state. Voila! The cell, now a mammoth embryo, can be carried to term by the elephant. Wouldn't it be wild if the great mammoth could once again roam the Siberian steppes?" I glared at Nation, victorious, practically challenging him to a debate.

"Sixty thousand years is nonsense," the reverend huffed at me. "The whole world is only 6,000 years old!" Nation truly believed this "established fact," conceived when a 17th-Century theologian named Bishop Ussher determined the age of the universe as being six thousand years old, using the generations of the Bible for his calculations—a figure many religious minds still accept as gospel *and* proof that evolution is false.

"Ah, the six thousand-year-old flat Earth, right—give or take twenty to thirty years, depending on your interpretation of certain statistical variables in the Bible?" I said sarcastically.

"Bishop Ussher is all the evidence you need," Nation asserted. "The math is clear, black and white." A smug grin spread across his face. "I thought you atheists believed in mathematics, even if you fail to believe in the God that created it."

"Meaning dinosaurs, which Ussher never knew existed, are at most 6,000 years old?"

"Exactly," he said, "and there's nothing you *evil*-loutionists can do to change that. There's nothing relative about that fact."

Suddenly, Miriam dropped her fork with a clang onto her plate. Startled, I turned to see her face turning ashen, her eyes welling up. "Excuse me," she said and, laying her napkin down, left the table without further word. Stumbling onto the couch and facing away, she buried her head in her arms.

I excused myself and went to put my arm around her, my hand on her shoulder. She pulled away.

The reverend stood, wiping his mouth, wondering how he'd offended his female guest. Then he stretched. "You won't mind if we catch a little sleep. We were filming a sermon all night." I nodded, and he and Bear headed toward the back of the plane. "I'm going to get some shuteye," he told the valet. "Come on, Bear."

The two ducked into their separate sleeping quarters and closed the hatches, while the valet cleared the table and disappeared into the plane's galley.

"What's wrong, Miriam?" I whispered when they were gone.

She turned to me with bloodshot, tearing eyes. "I'm sorry, David, it's just the strain of everything. I've hardly slept for days. I'm afraid I won't get home in time."

"We'll make it in plenty of time," I replied calmly. "Why don't you get some sleep?"

I cradled her in my arms, breathing in her fragrant hair, until she stopped crying.

She wiped her tears and returned my handkerchief, then stared into my eyes. It was as if she saw me for the first time. Before we'd gotten together, I had been just another college guy in the background, someone she could

56

count on for a ride to a party—a chauffeur to meet up with her loser girlfriends and escort to a movie. At this moment, aboard this plane, for once, she knew I was someone who cared about her still.

"I've thought about you all these years, David. Perhaps more than you've thought about me."

"That's unlikely, Miriam."

Exhausted, she hugged me briefly. Then, yawning, she curled up, wrapping her arms around my leg, resting her face in my lap. I wanted to stroke her hair, but I held back.

Within seconds, her lips were puffing tiny regular breaths. I took a moment to admire her face, peacefully asleep, to feel her warm breathing through my lightweight pants. Then the fatigue set in, and I realized how tired and sore I was. I'd managed the shop on a busy day, following an oh-so-memorable lunch with a woman I hadn't seen in decades; been kidnapped, escaping down a drainpipe; chased in a stolen car; gone to jail; worked through the night on the chess puzzle, *and* not slept in 24 hours.

Weary, and with Miriam so close, long-repressed regrets rose to the surface, catching in my throat. All these years, I had convinced myself my life was purposeful; but in truth, I had let myself drift, immersed in fantasies of antiquity, seeking dusty objects to gather dollars. I'd squandered my love on novelty, on random women, and on the comforting caresses of illusory forgetfulness.

I closed my eyes. Turbulent dreams of a glowing Messiah, God of Brotherly Love and Redemption, and nightmares of a dark Beast, Angel of Evil, flooded my mind, just a moment—a moment—and that's all it took. Mercifully, Hypnos, the Greek god of sleep, flew me to an uncharted land.

***

When I woke up, the sky was dark. I had no idea how long I had slept. *Where are we? Over land, water? Over Europe, the Mediterranean?* I stretched, trying not to disturb Miriam, her long hair a sleepy pitch storm.

Soon she awoke, coming slowly into consciousness. Still in the embrace of slumber's tendrils, she retreated into restfulness, her cheek on my chest. Then she yawned and sat upright.

"Want some coffee?" I asked, rising.

While Miriam stretched, I filled two Hallelujah Hour mugs and rejoined her, sitting so close I could smell the sleep still upon her skin, her breath, feeling the intimacy of a companion's first few minutes of waking.

I gave the caffeine time to kick in, then prodded her, "So it's time you explained, don't you think?"

"Explain what?" she answered innocently.

"*Explain what?*" I replied, incredulously. "For starters, how about a mysterious cadre seeking a nail from the cross? How about Jesus Christ reborn? These types of things don't wander into my world every day. And what about Solly's suicide? I truly want to help you, Miriam, but if I'm risking my life, I'd like to know why."

"Where's Reverend Nation?" she asked, examining the empty cabin.

"He's still asleep." It struck me that the plane could be bugged, but I didn't care. I had to know the truth.

She sipped her coffee, then took a deep breath. "Okay," she said. "It's true. Some Am Ha-b'rit members believe Jesus Christ has returned. And I don't exaggerate."

Jesus Christ returned! My head was spinning. Here I was in a private jet, 40,000 feet above the planet, with an illuminated apparition disguised as the old Miriam of petty pursuits seated beside me like some spiritual Faerie Queen in a woodland bower. Everything I had assumed about reality was shattered. I felt as if I'd taken a flight to the moon, only to discover, upon arriving, it had disappeared from the heavens, leaving only black emptiness, with nothing in view but the unreachable sparkle of quasars, galaxies, and nebulae.

"You've got to explain," I said urgently, knowing she would be reluctant to say too much because Reverend Nation might overhear her. "I mean, Miriam, come on, you can't mean this."

"You see, David, like I said, our discoveries in science are really helping us now. But the majority of us are religious, too. After all, that's what we were originally. What do you expect?"

"Okay." I could see she was telling it as dispassionately as she could— clearly, as she'd practiced—but under the surface, her emotions were seething.

"Jesus was a Jew, sure, a rabbi, but God or not, some factions of Am Ha-b'rit once considered him their leader, right? Some in the Society still think it's possible he was the Messiah promised to the Jews. How many believe that, I can't be sure."

"And I'm sure there are some who are apoplectic at the whole notion."

"Are you kidding?" she chortled. "You can't imagine the half of it!"

"But those in your group who do believe this man is Jesus somehow..." My doubts must have shown.

"Don't pooh-pooh what I'm saying about Am Ha-b'rit, David. We have documented other sermons and teachings Jesus spoke in his day. Different from the Sermon on the Mount, but perhaps just as far-seeing. They don't contradict what's in the Hebrew or the Christian Bible, but add to it. Taken all together, it's amazing stuff. The scope of the man's mind, especially when you consider it was two thousand years ago! Of course, He was speaking in terms people back then understood. But even so, just reading His words takes your breath away."

This revelation of further sermons from Western Civilization's most-quoted rabbi, whether officially recognized as such by the authorities of his day or not, made me half-dizzy. Think of it: if the New Testament was composed of personal and fragmentary eyewitness accounts of Jesus' life, what might other fragments from other eyewitnesses, something like the Gnostic Gospels, tell us? After all, most of what we know about Aristotle's thinking comes from notes his students took, classroom-like scribble. How much more did Aristotle teach? Did he write a treatise on comedy as well as his iconic study of tragedy, as Humberto Eco invented—or posited—in *The Name of the Rose?*

"You've read them?" I asked, envious of anyone who had.

"Sure," she said nonchalantly. "All of us have. Wouldn't you? Not that everyone believes they're authentic or agrees with interpretations of them. I mean, we're Jews; we can't agree on anything," she chuckled.

"We *are* an independent-minded people for sure," I agreed. "So give me an example."

"There's so much, David." She sat up straight. "For instance, there are those who think Jesus believed in evolution, for civilizations anyway. Not necessarily Darwin, so to speak, but Jesus envisioned things improving over time."

"I guess he had to believe mankind could change, could improve, at least morally," I said, encouraging the conversation. "Isn't that what he was about?"

"Exactly," she said, relieved that I was catching on. She set down her cup and ran her fingers through her thick, dark hair, brushing it back. "Solly thinks of Jesus more as a super genius, an evolved human being, whose transcendent vision took the world to a less-primitive place. Not that he attaches anything mystical to him."

"Well, sure," I interjected, "I believe human evolution is still happening, ongoing. I mean, with billions of us on the planet, not to mention international air travel, we're evolving faster than ever. But enough speeches," I said, breaking the spell these ideas put into my head. I wasn't going to let her play on my curiosity to run out the clock until Reverend Nation appeared.

She got up and corralled the coffee pot, then refilled our cups like a delicate Japanese tea ceremony a la Jewish princess.

"All right, the nail, Miriam," I said impatiently. "The nail. Get to it before Nation wakes up."

"That's above my pay grade," she said.

"You must know why you were sent to recruit me to retrieve it."

"Someone in Am Ha-b'rit will have to explain it to you," she said haltingly. She paused, and I could see she was having difficulty controlling her emotions. Taking a deep breath, she blew on her coffee.

"You will forgive my saying this," I said. "I hope I'm not being callous or offensive, but I want to meet him. You promised I could meet your Jesus, right?"

"Yes, sure, I want you to," she answered without even having to think about it, and then she lowered her eyes. A long, pregnant silence hung between us.

Here I was, onboard the reverend's plane, headed blindly toward—what?—and I couldn't stop myself. In retrospect, perhaps I was being swindled by the ultimate grifter, God, a capricious, malevolent deity who toys with people's lives for amusement, and for perverse amusement at that.

Finally, I spoke. "And Solly, his death?" I asked cautiously, sympathetically.

"Who knows why a person does such a thing?" she replied, clearly perplexed and deeply worried about something. But what?

It was obvious her mind was not on anything but her son. I felt my inquiries were intrusive, insensitive.

"Let's forget all that now," I suggested. "Would you like to talk about Ari? You would, wouldn't you?"

"Ari was born with a genetic defect," she managed to say, her voice breaking. "All I ever wanted was for him to be happy, healthy, to be able to play with other children..." She covered her eyes and turned away.

From what she said, I assumed Ari's infirmities kept him from running outdoors in the sunshine—that she was now resigned to the fact that he would never jump toward the sky in a field of wildflowers, never climb a tree. It was gut-wrenching to watch her. I was unable to fathom what agonies she, as a mother, was undergoing. I couldn't imagine what suffering she had yet to endure.

Then, the kill shot. She took my hand and stared deeply into my eyes a long moment. "David, I do want another child who *is* healthy." She was instantly embarrassed. "I'm sorry. I should never have said that. I didn't mean...I never meant you...please forget it, and forgive a worried mother for talking so foolishly. I was terribly wrong to say such a thing."

Forget it? Right. I wanted her, and I knew she needed me. I also knew we were the potential prey of this killer, a beast, if not *the* Beast, with a possible payoff that would make the police cringe. My throat grew dry, and I had trouble swallowing.

All true. And yet, I was not seeing the chessboard through the pieces. I was a starry-eyed child living in a kaleidoscope of crystalline illusions. The gods were laughing so hard they made a lightning thunderstorm in the surrounding sky through which I was condemned to fly.

Just then, Reverend Nation emerged from his quarters, resplendent in a fine Armani suit, shoes shining, the picture of prosperous Christian hope. Yet his eyes were deeply suspicious, like overcast clouds and winds churning shallow waters. I suspected he had heard everything, knew everything. If so, what did he think about Miriam claiming her group had other sermons from his sworn Lord?

We were on the last leg of our journey to Jerusalem. Miriam went to the back of the plane to be alone, to sleep and to worry—to refresh herself, if that was possible.

I returned to the couch with my coffee to study Bobby Fischer's chess game. Book, laptop, and notepad in hand, I placed my magnetic chessboard on the table and set the pieces in the position leading up to Bobby's queen sacrifice, where my hunch told me the solution lay hidden.

But no pattern emerged.

I made a few of the moves, all of it a smokescreen for Reverend Nation. Then I began to enter the chess notation of the moves into an Excel spreadsheet in earnest, separating the letters from the numbers into different columns, making notes on my pad as thoughts came to me.

Next, I tried any number of permutations. I manipulated the spreadsheet on a number of tabs, sorting out just the letters, then just the numbers.

Nothing.

I transposed the numbers for letters in the alphabet several different ways.

Zilch, nada.

Then I sorted both players' moves together, vertically down the page, extrapolating every trick I could think of, jotting notes.

No luck.

This was going to be harder than I imagined.

I decided I'd go with *gematria* and, hopefully, work backwards toward the chess clue—*if* that's where Levi Asher had been directing us. Some may dismiss the mathematical meaning of the universe, but Einstein used math well to explain time, space, and gravity. Without math, modern science would still be alchemy. In my view, I'd much rather search for truth applying math to nature than use it to analyze ancient parchment texts. But, of course, that's just me.

While I puttered with numerology, the reverend worked at his desk planning his next telecast, going over his lines. Hearing his magnificent voice rumble, I forgot about him and immersed myself in my brain breaker, becoming so involved, I didn't notice when his righteous pronouncements ceased.

Oblivious of the reverend's scrutiny, I Googled *Kabbalah, gematria* charts, performing all manner of searches in myriad variations. Confusing stuff. I read that there are two types of *gematria*: the "revealed" form, which is prevalent in many methodologies to interpret scripture found throughout rabbinic literature, and the "mystical" form, a largely *Kabbalistic* practice. But I hoped it wouldn't be that complicated. During my initial search, dozens of sites appeared on my computer screen, displaying promising charts and formulae. Unfortunately, none of these remotely connected me to Levi's clue. About to give up, I tried one more chart that seemed simpler, more logical, using numbers increasing and decreasing like the yard markers on a football field. The old axiom about the simple solution often being the best came to mind, so I gave it a shot.

A	B	C	D	E	F	G	H	I	J	K	L	M
1	2	3	4	5	6	7	6	5	4	3	2	1

N	O	P	Q	R	S	T	U	V	W	X	Y	Z
1	2	3	4	5	6	7	6	5	4	3	2	1

What was I to take from that? I began to play with the chart, but nothing. Then, out of frustration, I wrote "Jesus Christ," not meaning it derogatorily. While my mind searched other avenues, I translated the letters into their equivalent numbers. On impulse, with no avenue forward, I absently added the resulting values together and—surprise!—they totaled 59, the number in Levi Asher's text.

J	E	S	U	S		C	H	R	I	S	T		Equals
4	5	6	6	6		3	6	5	5	6	7		**59**

When Levi sent the text, had he been in possession of the third nail used to crucify Jesus, as I hoped? Was my discovery a coincidence? Or was the chart I had uncovered the key to Levi Asher's clue, a product of the brilliant young *Kabbalist-gematria*-chess nerd fooling around and discovering some connection in the mathematical universe? It was certainly a better lead than any of the others I'd stumbled across. But how would this chart connect to the Bobby Fischer game? And even if I could discover how it did, how would that link direct me to the nail's location? I didn't even know whether the nail was in St. Louis or in Israel. I had no doubt Levi could concoct such a puzzle, even under pressure; perhaps much of the foundation for his clue was gathered during his spare time at Hadera University. But I had great doubts as to my abilities to solve it.

I quickly realized that Reverend Nation was standing behind me, staring over my shoulder at my computer screen. Startled, I did a quick save and slammed shut my laptop, notebook, and the Fischer book.

"I've been watching you study that chess book, Mr. Greenberg. You've made many, many notations on your pad. And played with spreadsheets. What is all this scribbling and calculating you're doing?"

He circled the couch and sat immediately across from me, deep shadows of suspicion darkening his eyes. I didn't like the looks of it.

"Do you play chess, Reverend?"

"No, I can't *say* I do."

"I've been analyzing a game to pass the time, my hobby. Long flight, you know."

"But you haven't moved a piece in quite a while," he said.

I pointed to my head. "I move the pieces up here."

"Can you show me what you've written?" he asked.

"I, um...I prefer not to," I replied, securing the book and pad under my arm.

"Those were spreadsheets on your laptop. What do spreadsheets have to do with playing chess?"

"I'm thinking about developing a chess app," I lied.

Disbelief covered the reverend's face as he leaned over the chessboard and moved a knight, checking the king. "I'm only a novice, but I do believe that move signals 'check,'" he said sarcastically. "Am I correct, sir?" Grinning broadly, he sat back.

"Yes, it is 'check,'" I replied, surprised. I cleared the board, putting the pieces away. When I turned to look at him, his eyes were ablaze.

"Jesus is Lord," he announced in his most prophet-like voice, the word *Lord* in three syllables: *Low-or*-and hard *d*. It was truly inspiring, impressive, moving.

"I can't argue with you," I replied. "The Council of Nicaea..."

"...called by Emperor Constantine in 325," he interjected.

"Yes. The Council of Nicaea voted overwhelmingly that Jesus was, indeed, 'God in the flesh.' You can read Eusebius of Caesarea if you want to get a sense of the majority's thinking." And that settled that. To my mind, you can always bet on a vote by religious scholars and hierarchies. Look at Copernicus. He bet against the church, and where did it land him?

"You *must* keep your promise to me, Mr. Greenberg," Reverend Nation said forcefully, with profound intensity. "I am determined to meet this...this natural, *or unnatural,* phenomenon." He wasn't joking.

"I keep my word, Reverend. You'll meet him, if I have my way."

SECTION II. MIDDLE GAME

The past is never dead. It's not even past…

William Faulkner, *Requiem for a Nun*

If there be nothing new, but that which is
Hath been before, how are our brains beguiled,
Which, lab'ring for invention, bear amiss
The second burthen of a former child!

William Shakespeare, "Sonnet 59"

CHAPTER EIGHT
THE NATURE OF THE BEAST

The mid-afternoon sun suffused the arid desert air as we touched down on the reverend's private landing strip just south of Jerusalem. Landing in Israel is always emotional for me. Standing atop the plane's rolled stairs, I could almost breathe in the centuries, as if the atmosphere was magically spiced, as if I'd stepped into a timeless era, into myriad parallel millennia. The sands stretching off to the rocky hills from Nation's air strip have known the feet of prophets and holy men, of power-mad princes and clever caliphs; have drunk the blood of Christians and Muslims and Jews—of the righteous and the vain, of the wise and the ignorant, the bloodthirsty and the peace-loving.

"For the people shall dwell in Zion at Jerusalem, when they come to the Rock of Israel." Isaiah 30," Reverend Nation intoned, his voice resonant, his demeanor grave.

I wondered, *Why a private airstrip? Was it because of his cargo, the rumored Blood Diamonds from Africa? If so, these could no doubt be polished and laundered through Jerusalem's extensive diamond industry. Was it because of the guns he would have to trade to acquire them? Or was the Blood Diamonds story just bad press some jealous scribe had foisted upon him? Were the special landing privileges merely grateful treatment for the extensive Hallelujah Hour tourism trade to the Holy Land? Or did the strip simply reflect pure megachurch vanity?*

Security was lackadaisical during slow season at the private strip, just one old geezer, and he didn't discover my pistol, which I was later able to pocket.

My arm around her waist, I guided Miriam to the waiting limo. Bear and the reverend's valet would follow in a white van. I looked toward

Reverend Nation as he entered the front seat, but his face was a mass of angst, his eyes consumed with suspicion like those of a paranoid schizophrenic that wouldn't meet mine.

"Smooth flight," I said to the glum reverend, attempting in vain to break his frosty silence.

No reply. He sat slumped, eyes downcast, in deep spiritual confusion for probably the first time since being "born again." He was searching his soul for guidance within a maelstrom of the incomprehensible, of the impossible, or, at least, of the improbable.

Bear came to the limo's window. "A severe storm off the Mediterranean hit Netanya last night. The government has blocked the coastal roads north of Kfar Saba until it's safe to travel."

"So I'm stuck here and can't get home?" Miriam protested.

"Soon, I'm sure, Miriam," I said hopefully.

"This would be a good time for Bear and me to visit a detective friend of mine with the Jerusalem police," I said to the reverend. "Well, maybe not 'friend.' It's kind of a love-hate thing, really, but he does owe me a favor."

"Take the van," the reverend said. "We'll meet you at the King David Hotel." I hopped into the van while the luggage was redirected to the limo. Miriam followed me to the van, but I quietly suggested she go with Nation, which she did.

"Toward the Old City," I told Bear as he climbed behind the wheel.

Windows down to feel the breeze, we were soon riding swift breezes toward the legendary "City of Gold," established high in the Judean Hills by King David 3000 years ago: Jerusalem, *Yerushalayim* in Hebrew, *Al-Quds* in Arabic. I couldn't help whistling the song "Yerushalayim Shel Zahav - Jerusalem of Gold." Written in 1967, a time when Jerusalem was torn apart by war, "Yerushalayim Shel Zahav" was already becoming an anthem when, three weeks later, the Six Day War broke out, and the song was sung at the Western Wall, a site which had been denied to Jews for nineteen years.

Along the route, I barely noticed modern West Jerusalem with its dynamic city centre and leafy suburbs, where I usually stay on my buying trips to Israel. I sank deeper into the seat to observe the city, to imagine the historic pageant of world spiritualism and folly glide past. Bear was a good guy, and we quickly began to warm to each other.

Along the way, we made one stop to lunch at a Syrian restaurant with

Dawud Nazari, a Palestinian trader who is considered the shrewdest and most honest antiquities expert in the Holy Land. Besides a pleasant repast with an old, dear friend, Dawud provided me with valuable intelligence about the current state of the antiquities market.

Since we had time, I wanted to experience with Bear the full effect of the Old City on foot. I hadn't exercised in two days, and this was as good a time as any to stretch my legs. We parked the van and entered Jerusalem through the Damascus Gate, heading south. Jammed together in a square kilometer, the Old City is a labyrinth of streets enclosed within 16th-Century walls of limestone from the reign of the Ottoman ruler Suleiman the Magnificent, who often defeated the Christians in battle. The air in the shop-lined streets was fragrant with the cooking of onions, the smell of spices, the frying of oils, vibrant with merchants hawking their goods and handicrafts. We passed an Armenian garden and beheld the splendor of a medieval citadel.

Soon, we crossed the *Via Dolorosa*, the "Way of Sorrow," where Jesus, condemned by Pontius Pilate, made his painful way to the place of execution, one of hundreds of Jewish victims of corrupt Roman justice. This was where he bore the cross through the streets. Where along the way he encountered his mother, was helped to carry his burden by Simon of Cyrene, was given a handkerchief by Veronica. Where, despite his agony, he comforted the women of Jerusalem. At the end of which, he was disrobed and crucified.

Left to my own thoughts, I felt the profound weight of the nearby holy places. Ahead was the Western Wall, a sacred site for Jews around the world. There, too, was the holy *Al-Aqsa* Mosque and the golden Dome of the Rock, from which Mohammed is said to have ascended to heaven.

On the other side stood the Church of the Holy Sepulcher, the place of the crucifixion and tomb of Jesus, the Christian messiah. Hadrian built a temple to Jupiter and Venus on the site to quell the early Christians. But knowing the site's history, in 331 CE, Helena, mother of Constantine, excavated the site to find the tomb of Joseph of Arimathea and three crosses, which she believed were those from the crucifixion. There she built a church, which was destroyed by the Persians in 614 and the Turks in 1009, and rebuilt each time. Tradition tells us the slab of rock at its entrance is the same rock upon which Jesus was anointed. If faith whets your happiness, the Old City is the place to drink in ecstatic fulfillment.

We stopped at the Church of the Holy Sepulcher so Bear could pay homage. It was obvious how much he was moved. He appeared to be a man of sincere heart, and I respected that.

When we finally moved on, his eyes were alight, and he regaled me with the story of his conversion by the reverend and how much Christ had done for his life. He'd been the toughest kid in a rough neighborhood, with numerous arrests for fighting, drinking, and drugs. Only football enabled him to escape. In college, he was suspended from the Gophers twice in his sophomore year for drugs and partying. Luckily, he became a workout warrior, which replaced the drugs and late nights. Bear straightened out enough to get drafted in the first round by the then St. Louis Rams.

Still, his life could have gone either way. His rookie season was beset by problems—DWIs and resisting arrest, and he nearly lost his starting job. Then a teammate turned him on to Reverend Nation, and he never looked back. All pro, a Super Bowl ring, a big contract, the works…until knee injuries and a series of concussions shut him down. The reverend had been good for him. Or, at least, his belief in Jesus had helped.

***

Bear and I were on the block where the police station sat, walking casually, chatting pleasantly, when we passed under a tin awning. Suddenly, a passing motorcyclist slammed on his brakes. The rider, his Arab *keffiyeh* wrapped around his face to conceal his identity, pulled an Uzi and began to spray the sidewalk with bullets, aiming for us.

In an instant, Bear wrapped one arm around me and pulled me down with him. Simultaneously, with the other hand, he pulled down the awning to cover us. Lying there beside Bear, I could hear bullets pinging off the awning immediately above. Then they stopped, and the motorcycle roared off.

Throwing off the awning, I scrambled to my feet, reaching for Markowitz's street-pistol in my jacket. Antiquities dealers can get mad, too. I hadn't fired a pistol since summer camp, but I did manage to get off a shot. As luck would have it, the motorcycle rider jerked as if he'd been winged, but that didn't slow him. In seconds, he was gone.

Shortly thereafter, the police arrived, running toward us from the station, alerted by the shots. While we were being questioned, the cops spread out, roping off the area and gathering bullet casings, just like on TV. But this time, I knew how it felt to almost be killed. Meanwhile, Bear paid off the awning's owner in Hallelujah Hour cash.

"Well," Bear said, "there goes your theory about nobody wanting to harm you until you get the nail."

I had to admit he was right.

"You haven't lost your hair trigger explosion off the snap of the ball," I said.

He merely shrugged with a modest grin, as if he'd pancaked a slow, undersized defensive end.

"Thanks, Bear. You saved my life, if not my soul."

In a half hour, we were seated in Detective Dov Landau's office, very shaken—me, nursing a cup of coffee, Bear, bottled water. The police station wasn't much, but it was a step up from Reverend Nation's cohorts near Wentzville. Dov, my detective friend, offered me a Noblesse cigarette from a pack, which I accepted, then took his own. I broke my abstinence, but as any soldier in combat will tell you, getting shot at will make you fatalistic about cancer and heart disease. Dov lit our cigarettes and passed me an ashtray. He examined Bear and me closely, tsk-tsking. My pistol, one shot fired, sat on his desk.

"Why would anyone try to kill you, David?" Dov asked in his precise Hebrew-accented English.

"I'm at a loss, Dov."

The detective turned questioningly to Bear.

"I'm only along for moral support," Bear said innocently.

"So, you're here to liven up my district? Why?" Dov probed.

"I may have a clue about the Levi Asher disappearance," I answered.

"Yes? Go on," he said, his curiosity piqued.

"I think the man who possibly abducted Levi may have a distinctive birthmark. I didn't see it personally, but I have a friend in St. Louis who did. The man gave my friend the third degree."

"In St. Louis, eh? And he was asking about you?"

I nodded yes.

"Why would this unknown person with the birthmark be seeking you in St. Louis?"

"I don't know."

"You don't know? And suddenly you are here, having walked into his lair?" Dov stood and began to pace, drawing heavily on his cigarette. "Is this birthmark shaped like a spike? Here?" Dov pointed to his right cheek.

"Yes!" I exclaimed. "How...?"

"Never mind. What interest do you have in this man, the one with the birthmark?" he asked harshly.

"I told you, Dov, I don't know."

"Let me put it this way; what interest would this man have in you? All the way in St. Louis, Missouri, U.S.A.?"

I merely shrugged my shoulders.

Dov rubbed his chin, thinking, growing angrier by the second. He took a drag from his Noblesse, then another. "I think I'll have to hold you here for your own protection. At least, until you are more forthcoming."

I could see my trip to Netanya, to the university, going right past me while I stared through the bars of a cell. Lately, I seemed destined for jail. "You can't hold me, detective. I haven't done anything wrong."

"You fired a shot outside the police station and participated in a dangerous disturbance. Do you have a permit for this pistol?"

A permit! Who knows where Daddy Markowitz got the pistol? "You can keep it," I said. "I'm just here on a buying trip."

Dov buzzed in a uniform. "Lock this man up before he gets himself killed," he said, indicating me. "Let the other one go."

"You can't do that. You owe me a favor for helping you break that art smuggling ring."

"You had to aid me or you'd be in prison along with the perpetrators."

"No, Dov, I volunteered my information *before* you had a clue that I was involved. I gave you the key to recovering the contraband, remember?"

Dov stared at me long and hard. Then he waved the uniform from the room, announcing that I would be free to go, too.

"I'll be safe," I claimed, not altogether convincingly. "Bear here was hired to protect me. And we're in Israel, right?"

"The person with the birthmark crosses borders with impunity. He's like a ghost, a very deadly ghost," Dov warned and returned to his seat. "Bring your chairs around." Dov turned his computer monitor toward us. He tapped a few keys, and two faces appeared in split screen. Except for their headwear and the cut of their beards, they looked very much alike. One wore the black hat of an ultra-Orthodox Jew, the other the Palestinian *keffiyeh*. Both had a nail-shaped birthmark on their right cheek.

"This is Jarad Weiner," he said pointing to the one on the left. "Weiner is a devout Jew, but he is a radical militant, too. We have many reasons to be suspicious of Weiner's activities. This one," he pointed to the other, "is Edan Shadid, a fanatical *jihadi*. In Arabic, *edan* means 'like a fire,' and his illegal activities certainly fit that description. Both are suspects in several cases, but they are slippery devils."

"It's uncanny," Bear noted. "They could be brothers."

"Except they are not," Dov replied. "We have documentation going back to their birth. One is a Jew, the other a Palestinian."

"Maybe, in some way, they're the same person," I guessed.

"No, that's impossible," Dov said. "We have video of them in different parts of Israel at similar times."

"You have records on them, why?"

"David, there have been many gruesome, unsolved murders—assassinations—some involving torture. In a peaceful place like Jerusalem, those types of events stand out like an explosion. But the pattern doesn't make sense. The victims have been Jews and Palestinians, allies of both Weiner and Shadid."

"Doesn't it seem that Shadid would be the perfect candidate for Levi's abduction?" I suggested.

Dov punched a few keys, and Shadid's grainy visage camped at a demonstration appeared on a video, with dates and times superimposed in the corners.

"I thought of that. Except we have footage of Shadid during the entire period when Levi went missing."

"Could the dates and times on the video be faked?" Bear asked.

"The people who made this video don't make mistakes," Dov replied, giving us a knowing lift of his eyebrow.

I had to guess Shin Bet, but said nothing.

Dov punched more keys, and a video showing Weiner speaking to a rally appeared, with times and dates. "Also, *jihadis* are murdered and we have coincident video on Weiner. I have investigated both for years now, and both have had alibis in situations that point directly to them. Even a ghost cannot be in two places at once."

"Could some of these anomalous crimes be due to internecine disputes with their own allies?" I suggested.

"I am operating on that assumption in those very cases," Dov replied.

"Maybe they're working together," Bear said.

"Impossible," Dov answered. "Either would kill the other at first glance. I know them too well. There is no limit to how much they hate each other."

"Are you sure?" I asked.

"As sure as the sun rises," Dov said. "Just the collateral damage from their plots to kill each other provides me with unending messes."

"Make me a print of both their faces," I said. This he did, and I pocketed them.

"Look, David," Dov said, "you don't know what you're involved with here. If you were wise, you'd head straight back to St. Louis and be grateful you are still alive. But I know you're not so wise, and so I expect to see you on a slab in the morgue soon enough. That's your business." He shrugged. "I'll let you keep your passport in the vain hope that you will have sense enough to go home. But I want you to keep the U.S. Embassy informed as to where you are at all times, so I can reach you if I need to. If I can't reach you, you'll be in my jail cell until we deport you for good."

I nodded. "What do you have on Levi Asher?" I asked. "Is he or, more likely, are his remains in St. Louis or somewhere in Israel?"

Dov studied me closely and then made a calculated decision. "All right, Mr. Greenberg. Apparently, Levi Asher left St. Louis on his scheduled return flight. Or, rather, his return ticket was used, but he never arrived in Israel. We've examined the airport tapes with his family and members of Netanya University's security team, and no Levi Asher stepped off that plane. How someone just vanishes, I cannot say."

"Was the plane's manifest short one passenger?" I asked.

"Good question. No, it was not."

"I think, Dov, you should reexamine those tapes. See if, perhaps, one of our birth-marked brothers disembarked from that flight. Either of them could fake a passport and assume Levi's identity, right?"

"Either would be quite adept at such a subterfuge, and have been." Dov thought this over. "I'll check those tapes again with that in mind, David, and let you know if I find anything."

"Also, Dov, I have a hunch that Levi's captor, perhaps his killer, will return to St. Louis. Can you track Weiner and Shadid to see if one of them leaves Israel—leaves Israel first, at least? That man would likely be the culprit."

"Why would you think that?"

"Because I believe Levi Asher never got on that plane. And the only person who would know that is his killer."

"How would you know such a thing? Why was Asher in St. Louis anyway, Mr. Businessman?"

"That I do not know, Dov," I replied keeping my best poker face. The detective's look told me he knew I was lying. "But whatever the reason was, it is likely his killer may not have gotten what he came for."

"All right, David," Detective Landau said. "I'll let you and the St. Louis police know immediately whenever we're sure one of these vultures has flown from Israel. That will be all." He waved Bear and me out of his office.

Torture, murder, assassination, perhaps even the Beast and all his evil minions, I was half ready to throw in my cards, Miriam or no, Messiah or no, ancient wisdom or no, except…except…

***

It was a pleasant, cool afternoon, and my conversation with Bear ran the gamut of friendly small talk: a little politics, some football, even some hockey, on which he was very knowledgeable, being close friends with Blues players during his years in St. Louis. Insightful stuff for a rabid sports fan, which I am. Bear parked the van a distance from the King David Hotel, and we walked, just to make certain we weren't being followed. The coastal road would be cleared at any time, and I was anxious to continue to Netanya. I wanted to see Miriam, too, like a drunk needs his next drink.

Three well-dressed men, appearing to be government agents, blocked our way.

"What is your purpose in Israel, Mr. Greenburg?" the leader of the group asked in his business-like, clipped Hebrew-accented English, with no smile or inflection.

"Who is asking?"

"We are with Shin Bet. I suggest you don't be coy." He showed me his documentation: Ephraim Ben-Hershel was his name.

"I'm in antiquities. I travel to Israel regularly." I held out my passport.

"Your visa application was for next week," he said, ignoring the passport.

I didn't say a word.

"And Mr. Brukowski?" he went on. "You two are quite an odd couple."

"Mr. Brukowski simply gave a friend a lift on the ministry plane," I said. "It was an emergency."

"Yes? What kind of emergency?"

"The doctors say my companion's son is dying, and we needed to get her home ASAP."

Ben-Hershel dismissed Bear, who went ahead to let Miriam and the reverend know I was delayed.

"You had difficulty in the Old City this morning, didn't you, Mr. Greenberg?"

"Yes, through no fault of my own. Probably a random attack by some *jihadi*, I don't know. I'm working with the police to help resolve it."

Ben-Hershel examined me skeptically from head to foot. "We can put you on a plane back to St. Louis by evening. Permanently. You need to be more helpful than you've been."

"My papers are in order," I objected, knowing my shop on Euclid Avenue closes without future trips to the Holy Land. "What are you getting at?"

"What is your ultimate destination?" the Shin Bet agent asked.

"Netanya. My companion's son is there."

The agent turned to his assistants. "Miriam Solomon, Hadera University. The Levi Asher abduction." He looked me straight in the eye. "What is your business with Hadera University?"

"Nothing. I've known Miriam for twenty years."

"Have you ever heard of an obscure organization named Am Ha-b'rit?"

"I have not."

"Am Ha-b'rit is the entity that funds and operates Hadera University. They claim to be three thousand years old, give or take five hundred years, but I personally believe that is unlikely."

"I'm just here to help a friend."

"The university is extremely secretive about its projects. We could use your help."

"Industrial espionage is way out of my league," I said. "I wouldn't make much of a spy."

"We care nothing for your proclivities, Mr. Greenberg. Shin Bet would like to know who and what is behind Am Ha-b'rit. And we'd especially like to know what project Joseph Solomon is working on at the university."

"I thought Shin Bet knew everything. Joseph Solomon is dead."

"You just do what we ask while you're here on your business trip."

"Anything for Shin Bet."

CHAPTER NINE
GOLGOTHA GENERAL

The limousine pulled up to the edge of the parking lot fronting Hadera University's hospital on the outskirts of its sprawling campus. Built of limestone in the fifties, it was sedate and well kept. Beside me sat Miriam, more serious and spiritual than I'd ever imagined she could be, and not the least bit concerned with me.

The chauffeur opened the reverend's door, and Nation scrambled out quickly, like discovering a cobra in the cabin. Then my door swung open, and I joined him. I turned to Miriam, but she didn't move. Sitting with eyes downcast, deep in thought, as during our ride from the hotel, she took a moment to gather herself. Then she took my hand and emerged from the limo.

Leading from the limo to the hospital's covered entrance was a tree-lined gravel path. On the manicured lawn flanking the path, a throng of men and women held vigil. Groups talking solemnly stood in circles on the green grass and sat clustered under trees. Not a smile or laugh in the crowd, even among the children.

There was no consistency in their appearance. Clean-shaven men in white lab coats; bearded men in prayer shawls and skull caps; some in shirtsleeves or suits and ties; teenagers in jeans, shorts, and logo sweatshirts; women in dresses and slacks; children.

Some in the crowd saw who the passenger was, and a murmur spread; then there was silence as the assembly gathered, lining either side of the walkway. Men cried unashamedly, wiping their eyes with their sleeve or the back of their hand; women dabbed their eyes with handkerchiefs; men *davened* back and forth, quietly chanting Hebrew prayers. No one spoke a word.

I marveled at the closeness, the *gestalt*, of these people, so united in caring for one of their own. Many Orthodox Jews live in my neighborhood back home, and it is inspiring to see their lives so centered on their *shul* and families. The black hats walking to and from *Shabbat* services in all weather—snow, ice, and heat—women in modest dress; some men studying books as they make their journey on foot, their children skipping alongside. I often envy them.

Miriam made her way slowly through the throng down the path with absolute dignity, head erect, shoulders back, eyes straight ahead. The reverend and I followed like two attendants, knowing that her every step was a great effort.

The assemblage, five deep, respectfully watched her pass, craning their necks to see over shoulders, compassion in their faces, tears in their eyes. About two-thirds of the way to the hospital entrance, a rugged-looking man in the front row, in his late-forties, with suntanned face and thick, sandy hair caught her eye. She didn't turn her head, but I knew from the sympathetic look he gave her that the two had a connection that transcended mere friendship. I thought about Miriam married all these years to Solly—workaholic, obsessive, introvert—and guessed she must have sought comfort from her loneliness with this warm and engaging member of the Society.

And why not? Sickly child needing constant attention. Distant husband sleeping in his laboratory. I was happy and relieved for her. And I wondered where that relationship stood.

***

"You'd better go in right away," the handsome young Israeli doctor said to Miriam, placing a gentle hand on her shoulder. As she gathered the dregs of her will, I could see, despite her stoicism, she was only a gentle breeze away from collapse.

The doctor hurried down the long, antiseptic hall, and Miriam turned to me. I offered my arm, and she gripped it for support with both hands. I peered quizzically into her eyes, holding the gaze until she nodded she was ready.

Arms intertwined, she leaned into me, and we entered the room where the boy lay, lit dimly against the night by a cloth-covered lamp. The pitiful waste that was his articulated flesh made barely a ripple in the blanket covering him to his chest. His bone-thin arms and translucent hands rested upon the covers.

His eyes could have been hers, large, brown, and doe-like. They were not filled, as I had expected, with loss and suffering, as were Miriam's, but appeared warm and soothing through some wisdom I could not comprehend, saddened only by Miriam's pain.

I followed Miriam closer to the boy: a mere fourteen, his tender, sweet face never shaved. The strength in Miriam's legs wavered, and after futile attempts to perch on the bed, I lifted her up to place her there. She held my hand tightly with one hand, a lifeline to the sentient world, as she wiped the boy's brow and kissed his forehead.

"Ari, my darling, did you say your *brachot* this morning?" she whispered to the boy, inquiring about his ritual daily prayers. He blinked once, the faintest tender smile struggling its way onto his full lips, answered by her own fleeting smile. Her chin trembled momentarily, her eyes glazing, but she fought courageously to maintain her composure. I slipped my handkerchief into her free hand, startling her that I was even there. "David Greenberg," she said, recovering to introduce me, "this is my son, Ari Ben Joseph." Ari, son of Joseph—Solomon, that is. "David is an old friend of your father's and mine, Ari. From St. Louis."

I nodded, moving closer.

When those astounding eyes of his fell on me, it was as if my entire insides had been jolted, exposed and raw. I was helpless, spiritually stripped naked, yet wholeheartedly open and trusting. I'd never felt more alive.

With an effort that made sweat bead on his forehead and streak down his cheeks, Ari lifted an emaciated arm and, struggling to reach toward me, touched his fingertips to my face. I was startled by their warmth. Seeing my surprise, he smiled, his voice cracking, "I'm not cold yet, Mr. Greenberg."

I studied his hollow face, my gaze fixing upon his powerful eyes, to discover he had already read mine—if I were a religious man, I'd say he "read my soul." He started to speak, but a dry cough stopped him mid-sentence. Miriam held a glass to his lips, and he sipped as best he could. My heart pounded as my eyes remained riveted on the tableau of mother and child. I found myself jealous, having lost my own mother at seven, for whom I'd never sufficiently mourned, let alone cried. My father, harsh and self-centered to the core, found a replacement within months. But his younger wife lacked the empathy, the compassion, necessary for a stepmother, and I descended quickly into purgatory. You get the picture.

Then Ari returned his attention to me.

"Your mother..." He stopped, took a breath, his eyes taking in Miriam and me. "She loved you just as well," he whispered, immediately breaking through every wall of armor I'd devised to protect myself. Having witnessed Miriam and Ari together, and hearing Ari's words, I choked on the lump in my throat, realizing the enormity of all that I had missed in my boyhood, in my failed marriages, which evidenced no children and no pursuit of what could have had real meaning. Instead, I live my days chasing financial security, with side orders of distraction, chess, poker, and women to keep the boredom away.

Here in Israel, Miriam had created a life dedicated to friends, her marriage to Solly, and Ari. I realized, at that moment, that I had been fantasizing about her—that I could never replace that in her life. Miriam was far out of reach. I felt like a jerk for wanting her.

Sensing my distress, Ari said calmly, "You don't have to be alone. You can escape your sanctuary." Then he looked at Miriam before turning his attention back to me.

We talked quietly for only a short time, me with little to say, Ari with little strength to speak. Only a short time, but each word, each syllable, was charged with power. As we talked, the weight of all my regrets washed over me, but, inexplicably, they didn't feel quite so heavy, so dark and foreboding.

Ari's weak arm fell to the bed, and Miriam resettled it for his comfort. I made my way to the corner, flopped into a chair, and there, wiped my eyes with my sleeve. Sighing, I examined this remarkable boy who seemed to see so deeply into those around him, even strangers. I don't believe in magic, in either God or witchcraft, none of that stuff. Maybe I was tired from the long flight, through different time zones, and the stress of being shot at and questioned by the police. But in that dim room, it appeared that sickly child's wasted face possessed some kind of inner glow, a sort of electricity, almost an aura. I rubbed my eyes again but wasn't sure what I was seeing. Had I crossed the line to exhausted hallucination? Being in such emotional turmoil, being so tired, I was in no state to figure it all out.

Miriam stroked Ari's soft hair, his smooth face, murmuring words of love. This mother, speaking perhaps last words to her dying child, whom she had carried in her womb, giving him life, as he gave her life. I looked away, feeling like an intruder into this most intimate of moments.

The boy fell silent, motionless, seemingly fading into unconsciousness. Miriam gasped and searched for the emergency bell, but just then, Ari's eyes blinked awake. His lips moved to speak, and Miriam leaned forward to hear him.

"Bring me the other one, *Ima*," he struggled to say. How he knew Nation was waiting in the hall, I didn't know. "He needs to see me."

Reverend Hubris Nation entered the darkened hospital room looking hesitant and suspicious, like a petty neighborhood thief out for a stroll accidently stumbling into a ransacked house crawling with uniformed police. He paused to give Miriam and me a nervous nod of greeting. Miriam, standing by the door, held out a few sheets of paper folded in half lengthwise.

"Ari wrote this in third grade. He wants you to have it," she said, sliding the pages into Reverend Nation's inside jacket pocket, giving them a pat.

"Ari," Miriam said softly, "this is Reverend Nation. He's come all the way from America to meet you." The reverend shuffled his feet carefully toward Ari's bed as if approaching a sleeping lion. Miriam retreated to the chair across the room from me.

Reverend Nation seemed uncertain of what to do. I studied the pair intently. Ari peered up. His glance seemed to pierce the giant Missourian, who appeared to have gone weak in the knees. The frail boy struggled to raise himself, and Reverend Nation held the boy in his great hands, arranging the pillows to prop him up.

"Do you know what *tikkun olam* means?" Ari asked Nation, coughing out the words.

"Is that some k-kind of... some kind of J-Jewish thing?" the reverend stuttered, taken aback.

"Yes, it's Hebrew for 'repairing the world' or 'healing the world.' It means it is our responsibility to transform the world." Ari sunk back into the pillow to recover after the strain of the demanding exchange.

I listened closely. Most Jews, even semi-ignorant ones like me, know of *Tikkun Olam*, a concept begun in the early rabbinic period and given new meaning in the *Kabbalah* of the medieval era, and today connotes even more profound meanings.

"Oh. Oh, I see, I see," mumbled the reverend.

"You have heard, 'to whom much is given'?" Ari asked.

Nation seemed confused, falling into silence to think over the question. "Yes," the befuddled reverend finally managed to sputter. "To whom much is given, much is required or expected, something like that."

Ari stared into the reverend's eyes for so long, Nation began to fidget, unable to turn away. "Your father," Ari said with gravity, then paused to gather his wind. Recovering, his eyes alight, he repeated the admonition, "Your father!" Then he grew silent, waiting.

I thought about what I knew of Nation's father, the Cape Girardeau judge who sent his son, Hubris, to private school—the son who was kicked out of school. The son who the father assumed was slated to enter a well-established legal firm, perhaps become a judge himself one day, but who never fulfilled his father's ambitions. The son who was entangled in years of drinking and God knows what else? And I imagined the years of conflict that likely had torn their relationship, perhaps permanently.

"D-do you mean," the reverend stammered in shock and horror, "do you mean my f-father-father? Or, or my, m-my H-heavenly Father?"

Miriam rose from her chair, signaling me to follow her. "We'll leave you two to talk," she calmly told Nation. "We'll be in the hall."

Nation's face grew bright crimson, as if his heart had been laid bare, with all his secrets revealed.

CHAPTER TEN
REVELATION IN BLUE

One of Solly's lab techs drove a distraught, exhausted Miriam and me to her home in the Hadera residential complex. Similar to her parents' modest ranch, its wooden structure was one of many broken out of the desert in this comfortable neighborhood: nestled within thick rows of flowers, shrubbery, and other cultivated foliage and cacti. Simple and lovely.

Miriam asked me if I would like to step inside, but she understood when I begged off for the evening. She opened the door, no key necessary, and I caught a clear view of her entrance and living room. Oil paintings decorated every wall, her own works no doubt. They were vivid, breathtaking. I was especially taken with one grouping that featured strong, sweeping black and dark blue foundations providing structure for lively two- or three-color subjects, some abstract, some representational. Works scattered around, both finished and unfinished, were set up on easels. Astounded by her obvious talent, I insisted on a full private showing when we were both rested. She consented in a voice shaky with fatigue and despair.

We embraced at her doorstep, then, with a quick kiss on her cheek, I left for a solitary walk, to ruminate over my life, my current circumstances, and the tangle of mysteries and issues before me. Security had a room set aside for me nearby in special university housing, for which I had been provided a security card, but I wasn't ready for four walls just yet. Other than the walk to the police station, I hadn't gotten any real exercise since receiving Miriam's first call.

The evening was pleasantly cool, the half-moon enchanting, the stars sparkling bright in the clear sky as only seen through the dry desert air. Placing one foot before the other, my thoughts carried me a good distance without noticing how far I'd traveled. I trod along the pebbled walkways, bordered by landscaping stones and plant life lovingly tended by students, faculty, and their families over the decades. Popular theory assumes that owning property in common only leads to neglect, but I saw no neglect within Am Ha-b'rit's domain. Agree or disagree with their philosophies, believers can care.

Within an hour, I found myself on Hadera University campus proper. Multi-story stone buildings were arranged around several quadrangles. For such a prestigious university, Hadera looked modest. I couldn't fathom how they could get millions to fund a school that size *and* millions more to support Am Ha-b'rit's quest to acquire the infamous nail. But maybe the external resources Miriam mentioned, like their foreign investments, weren't reflected in the aging structures I was seeing.

Looking around, I passed the administration area, coming upon the main building. The night was already getting dark, but I could see dim light inside and used my security card to enter. It worked. I was in. As an honored guest, my card supplied privileges, I guessed.

Inside, I made my way along the darkened hallway until I approached the personnel department, where my card again did the trick. Like a young Einstein at the Swiss patent office, a young man who I assumed was a student, surrounded by a half-dozen open physics texts and a desktop computer, sat flooded in an island of lamplight. I greeted a *ma nishma* as I walked past him, as if I knew my business. He nodded back absently.

At the final barrier, I ran my key card through the reader. Still lost in his studies, the young man absently flipped on a bank of lights over a computer station for me. I thanked him, but doubt if he heard me.

At the computer, I entered the system using the password Miriam had given me. My first query was Joseph Solomon, Solly. My old friend had done away with himself, and I wanted some clue, any clue, as to why. I browsed through his files, finding only what I already knew: Solly was from a Jewish family in St. Louis and had been recruited because of his off-the-charts ratings in the sciences. Am Ha-b'rit's talent scouts had done their job well. His job title was listed as "Scientific Maven" for the T'chiat Ha-meitim program. The word *maven* means the expert, the authority that knows more than anyone else does, the know-it-all who really does *know it all*. If any questions, obstacles, or conflicts arise, everyone seeks guidance from the *maven,* and no one ever doubts his or her wisdom. This job title fit what Miriam had told me about Solly's place in his project.

Next, I did a search to find out what the T'chiat Ha-meitim program entailed. No luck; shut out of those files. Then I searched my own memory vaults and pulled out of the dustbin the fact that historically, in Hebrew, T'chiat Ha-meitim literally translates as "enlivening the dead," which in ancient Judaism had always meant the promised "resurrection" of the dead at the End Time. *Resurrection? Isn't that what Miriam and I were discussing with such intensity?*

I went deeper into stream-of-consciousness mode to tap into my very limited, admittedly secular, ancestral background. I connected the word *t'chiat* to the similar-sounding *t'kiah*, the ritual blowing of the *shofar*, or ram's horn, a loud blast that is blown one hundred times on each of the two days of *Rosh Hashanah*, the Jewish New Year and highest Jewish holiday. In fact, some of the *shofar* blasts address Jewish hopes for a messianic era. Indeed, some Jews believe a *t'kiah* blast will herald the second coming of Great King Yeshua, the Messiah, who will be accompanied by the resurrected dead. Of course, this is an entirely different concept than the Christian idea of a "savior," at least to my understanding.

I rapidly surfed the personnel system, clicking into Miriam's file. On impulse, I linked into the pay records. Why not? Miriam was listed as "mother," and her compensation was the equivalent of one hundred thousand dollars a year. This astounded me; it seemed quite a lot for a domestic function. Unless, of course, her husband—or child—was someone extremely important. Extremely.

While in the payroll database, I searched for Solly's payroll records, hoping to get an approximate date of his death. Made sense; his salary would lapse at that point. Then I could quiz Miriam about the date and check her veracity. I was not surprised to find Solly was also being paid a hundred-thousand-dollar annual stipend. Not much for the Scientific Maven of a cutting-edge, multi-million-dollar research project. But knowing Solly, the amount would have meant nothing to him. He was so tied up in his work, he probably never spent a shekel, and likely didn't know how much money he had in the bank, or wherever Hadera University members kept their money. After seeing how modestly Miriam lived, I estimated she and Solly probably had quite a decent nest egg after twenty years. But even added together, these figures were nothing significant enough to arouse suspicion.

But then the real shocker hit me: Solly's stipends were still being paid into his account. Was this part of an insurance or survivor pension plan? Or could it mean Solly was still alive and that Miriam had lied about his suicide?

I had to suppress my anger about the possibility that I was needlessly put through such a heart-wrenching tragedy and wondered what other smoke was being blown up my backside. I exited back into Solly's personnel file. There, I found his office location still listed, building and room number, which I committed to memory. I didn't want to write it down in case I was searched. I was determined to make a visit there, and soon.

Where to next? On a hunch, I went searching for Jarad Weiner, the Jewish radical whom Dov, my Jerusalem detective friend, thought might be involved in murders and assassinations, including, perhaps, poor Levi Asher. Bad move. To my astonishment, the second I pressed "enter" on the query, an alarm sounded, all the room lights came on, and I was shut out of the system. I'd clearly struck a sensitive nerve.

Within seconds, a security guard with a pistol on his hip, breathing hard from running, stood beside me.

***

Reverend Hubris Nation finished shooing out of his hotel suite the myriad hangers-on of his "Hallelujah Hour" entourage: his writers, directors, producers, camera operators and grips, gofers, dressers, tailors, and barbers. He only had to bellow once before gobbling geese underlings scattered out the door.

His brow furrowed in thought, the reverend absently untied the belt of his pleated green silk robe, "Hallelujah Hour" logo stitched in gold thread on the lapel, and dropped it onto the plush padded chair. The silence was a welcome respite from the daily clamor of true believers that followed him wherever he went. He needed to think. Heaving a deep sigh, he paused to pour himself a sherry from the bar, before drifting to the bedroom, tiny crystal glass dwarfed by his meaty hand. There he took a deep breath— alone at last.

Squinting, his eyes searched the brightly lit room. He turned the dial to dim the overhead light, then crossed the carpet and set the sherry on his nightstand. Kicking off his slippers, he snapped on the brass bedside lamp. Satisfied that his surroundings were conducive to rest and reflection, he fluffed his pillows and, muscles suddenly revealing their aches of the day, slid under the covers, which had been neatly turned down by the hotel staff.

Arching his neck, he located his reading glasses on the nightstand, adjusted them on his nose, and then took a sip of the sherry before settling his substantial bulk. His mind was spinning out of control. Taking a deep breath, he opened the paper that the Jewish woman, Miriam, had handed him, and tried to focus. Merely two pages, a child's class assignment, would determine his destiny. It was written so simply, yet it seemed to reveal what no analysis or art could illuminate:

A Fable by Ari Solomon
English assignment, Third Grade
There lived in a distant land a benevolent cantor who was widely known for his beautiful singing voice, which many considered the finest in all the land. His songs, recitations, and readings so delighted the ear that his reputation and his following grew over the years. As he reached his middle age, he was always in great demand, especially on the High Holidays, when he sang for services at the kingdom's Great Temple. In time, the people came to respect his wisdom as much as his singing. As a result, he prospered, accumulating great wealth and prestige.

His life secure, the cantor with the exquisite voice came to dwell in a fine house that had the most magnificent orchard anyone had ever beheld. This orchard became his greatest pride. Surrounded by a high wall, the cantor's orchard bore every type of fruit known in his country, as well as some varieties from so far away that people had no name for them. Pomegranates, crisp apples of limitless colors and shapes, persimmons, sweet dates, olives, there was no end to the bounty from his private orchard. This so pleased him, he began to leave home less and less often, being satisfied to recline among his shaded fruit trees all the day and live off their endless cornucopia of juicy treasures.

Finally, there came a time when he refused to ever leave home. Each morning, he donned fine robes made of red velvet with intricate patterns of gold thread. Instead of going out into the world, he spent all his waking hours in his orchard singing for his own pleasure, to the skies, the birds, the trees, the clouds. He sang and he sang and he sang, delighting in the beauty of his own voice. When a caller came to his doors, he would not even open them a crack to see who it was, but would invariably send the visitor away.

As things would happen, that spring, a drought plagued the land. Very troubled, the king came to the cantor's door to receive the songster's wisdom and to be soothed by his melodies. But the cantor, still refusing to see anyone, sent the king away sight unseen.

Next, the High Priest came to the cantor's door. The annual services of repentance were being prepared, and the cantor's lovely, resonant voice had always graced the Great Temple at that time of year, floating through the air and enchanting listeners to the farthest ends of the Temple courtyards. The High Priest hoped to entice the cantor to the services, believing the man's song could cure the land of its barrenness. But the cantor turned the High Priest away as well, sight unseen.

Then a hungry beggar came to the cantor's door asking for food, but the cantor refused the beggar entry, and the poor man departed, his wasted stomach still empty.

One day, the cantor was singing alone in his garden, as was his wont, and an odd thing happened. His singing was so grand, the note he hit so high, that the fruit on every tree turned to gold and, weighing so heavily on the branches, fell to the ground.

He tried to eat the fruit lying on the earth throughout his orchard, but his teeth could not penetrate the gold. At the end of the day, he went to bed very hungry, hoping to figure out what to do in the morning when he was better rested.

The reverend's fists pulled the pages to his chest, wrinkling them, as his mind raced backward through the years. He remembered his first storefront church in Sikeston, Missouri, with its twenty mismatched chairs, its improvised podium, its hand-painted sign. He thought, too, of his present residence, a mansion off Highway 44, just outside of Fenton, with its state-of-the-art production studio, its massive columns, and spiral staircases. He remembered, too, the years of hard drinking, of unsound relationships with honky-tonk Tessies.

Then his conversation with the sickly boy in the hospital bed leapt to mind, squeezing it in an iron vice, just as the child's dark, penetrating eyes had harpooned his soul. His thoughts were dragged, like an errant schoolboy by the ear, to the last time he'd seen his father, the respected judge. That day had been overcast, the judge's book-lined study draped in shadow. He remembered the terrible row, throwing the glass of scotch at the gray-haired man, knocking over the globe and the dictionary podium, the swearing and shouting, the slamming of the door, the running down the long, manicured lawn, cursing and hysterical…

Without warning, a tear threatened to escape from the corner of the reverend's eye, but he captured it with his fist, then wiped it on the sheet and resumed reading.

The next morning the cantor awoke and found that it was very dark, so dark he could not see his own hand. He felt around until he was able to light his candle, but the candle's flame shed no light into the room. It was then he began to worry.

What the cantor did not know was that, overnight, his eyes had turned to gold, just as had his fruit the day before. And so, he had become blind. Rising, hungrier than the previous night, he made his way through the great house to his orchard. There, he found only golden fruit at his feet. He spent the morning contemplating his problem, growing more and more hungry by the hour, knowing his singing could not cure him of his affliction.

Later, after feeling and stumbling about his great house, the cantor found his walking stick and, still wearing his wrinkled nightclothes, made his way to the palace to seek help from his friend the king. When the king heard that a hungry blind man was at the gates, the cantor was turned away.

The cantor then made his way to the Great Temple to see the High Priest. But when the High Priest was told that a hungry blind man was at the Temple doors, the cantor was again turned away.

Finally, lost, the cantor made his way through the town's warren of streets until he came upon a hovel. He knocked on the door, and the beggar answered. Desperate for something to eat, the cantor begged for a crust of bread. The beggar greeted the blind man warmly and led him into the hovel, bidding him rest on the beggar's own pallet. When the cantor had recovered enough from his ordeal, the beggar led him to the table, upon which sat one piece of stale bread. This, the beggar tore into two pieces. One of these, he handed to the cantor, who ate it hungrily; the other half, he ate himself.

Suddenly, the cantor realized he could see again; his eyes had returned to flesh...

Hubris Nation could not continue reading; his eyes were clouded over, opaque. He crumpled up the paper and tossed it on the floor. Then he sank into a fetal position and began to cry, not in the way he, the envy of all Christendom, often bawled on television, but with ferocious, gut-wrenching sobs. Like ten-year-old Hubris cried the day his mother died. Like the grown

Hubris cried the day his drunken fingers fumbled the phone to his ear long enough to learn that his father had died of a heart attack. Like he cried when the kindly, off-duty truck driver dragged him home from the bar, cut and bleeding. Wept hard, like a little girl. He did, indeed, have sins to wash away, forgiveness to seek, redemption to pursue. As the boy in the hospital bed had said wordlessly, speaking with his eyes alone.

***

I was taken to my guest suite, a cross between a dorm room and a bed-and-breakfast. A guard was posted outside my door. I could go anywhere I wanted on campus that night, including the housing area where Miriam lived, but with a chaperone.

My curiosity, a fatal weakness, was highly aroused by what I'd discovered in the personnel files, especially the Joseph Solomon payroll file. I was determined to follow up. Noticing the computer in the room, I sat immediately. I used my security card to access the network but found the card had been frozen out of all internal Hadera links. Exhausted, I hit the sack.

I rose the next morning, weary like I hadn't slept. I was half-undressed, the shower running, when the phone rang. The caller was a very distressed Bear Brukowski.

"What did you do to Reverend Nation?" he shouted.

"What do you mean, Bear?" I was just as confused.

"He's talking and acting crazy! You've got to get over here now."

***

I never imagined I'd see Bear as anxious as a sinner on Judgment Day. But when I arrived at the reverend's hotel suite in Netanya, Bear was a wreck. When he was playing pro football, during the fourth quarter of the Super Bowl no less, with his Rams down two touchdowns, a sideline camera caught his red-flushed face. With the crowd going wild and his season in jeopardy, Bear's demeanor was calm as he determinedly attempted to whip his team into coming back, which they did to win the championship. Now? *Oy vey!*

He led me across the carpet through the maze of cameras, wires, klieg lights, backdrops, and production people to the suite's spacious outdoor patio. The morning was cool, the final hint of the previous days' storms sneaking off to trouble distant lands. Remnants of the ministry's sumptuous breakfast lay scattered on tables across the patio.

"Bear, what's the matter?"

"Reverend Nation's gone crazy," he whispered, submerged in real pain.

"How do you mean?"

"He's in a total funk. He refuses to wear his wig for the broadcast, gave his watch and rings to the waiters who brought us breakfast, and he won't touch his suits. He wants to wear ancient robes, for goodness sakes!"

"Have you ever heard of what the shrinks call 'Jerusalem Syndrome'?" I asked. Jerusalem Syndrome—Israel's got a whole asylum full of people suffering from it. Tourists and pilgrims step off the plane in the ancient land and suddenly think they're Jesus Christ. You'd think they'd have some real donnybrooks over who's real, but they don't. Delusional or not, I have to admire their consistent approach to a benevolent deity, unlike the violent collision of the world's Great Religions outside the nuthouse walls. Fact is, I often wonder who should be inside the Looney Bin: well-meaning, virtuous tourists who receive the "call" or blood-spilling zealots claiming to be the direct representatives of the Holiest Holy.

"No, that's not it," Bear said. "He's been to Jerusalem many times. Something has changed him, changed his heart…or busted his mind."

I was in a quandary. If I told Bear what I believed had transformed Nation, I'd have to tell him the whole story.

On the plane, the reverend had overheard Miriam talking about the revived Jesus being at Am Ha-b'rit and may had deduced what I had begun to suspect. And now that Nation had met the dying Ari!? Well, the literal-Word-of-the-Bible fundamentalist is likely in utter turmoil, torn with distrust and confusion. Even with my skepticism, my meeting Ari was so deeply profound, perhaps spiritual, that I couldn't get my mind around what I had experienced either. And if I was having problems, Reverend Nation had to be completely *farblondzhet*, lost in a chaotic universe he never imagined existed.

I removed the pistol from my pocket and offered it to Bear. "We're in greater danger than you know, Bear," I said. "You'd better keep this."

"I cannot bear arms," he said, refusing the pistol. "It's against my Christian beliefs."

I slipped the gun back into my jacket.

I had promised Miriam I would keep her secrets, but Bear had saved my life, and he was distraught and suffering. What could I tell him about the source of Nation's sudden madness, and what could I omit? If I stuck to the facts of which I was certain, which were few, nothing would make sense. Yet, something held me back.

CHAPTER ELEVEN
CASTING BREAD UPON THE WATERS

The good Reverend Nation persisted in his ranting, animated and face flushed, waving his arms about. "I, Hubris Nation, will bring God's Kingdom in Heaven to the entire Earth!" he bellowed at Bear and me, as if crying a declaration to God and to the whole planet. "I bear the Sword of the Lord! I am the Rock of Israel! I am the reconciler of the Jews, the Servant of the Faithful."

I shrugged, eying Bear. He nodded in agreement, raising an eyebrow.

"Bring me my automobile," Nation demanded, making a great fist. "I, and I alone, must now face the heathen. I, and I alone, must convert the unbeliever. The End of Days is surely upon us."

Every second spent listening to the reverend raised my blood pressure and delayed my mission. From the moment I woke up, I'd been anxious to get to Hadera's Life Sciences building to see if Solly was, indeed, dead, or if my friends had lured me to Israel using one of the dirtiest tricks imaginable.

"I'm overdue for an appointment," I told Bear, checking my watch for the third time. "But I'll buzz you when I'm ready to leave campus."

"What'll I do with the reverend?" he asked, exasperated.

"Your guess is as good as mine." I looked at him with a due amount of pity.

"I don't have a clue. Any thoughts, any at all?"

"Well, at least he came out of his funk."

***

Security at the Life Sciences building was tighter than a bank on cash delivery day. I was stopped at the entrance by an armed guard and, after removing my keys and watch, was run through a weapons detector. And that was merely to get through locked, bulletproof glass doors to approach the appointment desk.

"I'm here to see Professor Joseph Solomon. I'm an old friend," I said, laying my security pass on the counter. The student working the desk looked up from the computer to study my face. Two armed guards appeared behind me, one at either shoulder.

"Professor Solomon is deceased, sir," the student said grim-faced.

"Well, call up to the third floor anyway. Tell them David Greenberg is here to see Professor Solomon or whoever has taken his place."

The student at the desk simply stared at me as if I'd asked for a chariot ride to Mars.

***

I waited on the third floor near a row of classrooms, like a student killing time between periods. But this time I was chaperoned by a lanky, bearded young man in jeans and shirtsleeves sporting a pistol. He spoke politely in Hebrew-accented English. The school building itself was at least thirty years old, with plastered-over cracks in the walls. Through the closest door's glass panes, I could see a group of seven students, male and female, sitting at old-fashioned desks, encircling a salt and pepper-bearded professor in his late-fifties wearing a brown tweed jacket with elbow patches. The whole scene appeared to be a typical graduate class.

Anxious, I pulled out the cell phone Bear had given me and called detective Dov Landau in Jerusalem.

"Dov?"

"Yes, Greenberg," he grumbled impatiently. "What do you want?"

"Any news from the states on Levi Asher?"

"None," Dove replied irritably. "But I'm in regular contact with the police there."

"Have you checked the airport security tapes?" I asked.

"No luck, David. Neither Weiner nor Shadid were on the plane. No beauty mark matching our nail on any of the passengers' fair cheeks."

There went that theory up in smoke. I had one more straw to grasp, one hope that Levi was somehow still alive.

"Have either of them left for the states yet? Weiner or Shadid?" I speculated that only Levi's abductor, or his killer, would know he didn't make it back to Israel. If we could identify Levi's abductor to the St. Louis police, perhaps we could still save the young man.

"We're trying to keep tabs on them, but they're slippery. But both have been spotted in Israel in the last twenty-four hours."

The disappointment was a blow to my stomach. At least, I rationalized, not convincingly, if both of our main suspects were innocent—if innocent is a word that would apply to them—Levi's captor may still be in the U.S. And if so, perhaps Levi was still alive. Unlikely, but one hopes.

There was a long pause on the line, with Dov undoubtedly trying to decide how much he wanted to reveal.

Finally, he let me have it. "You probably don't know it, but Weiner is affiliated with Hadera University. He's right on the campus where you are."

A ruthless murderer? Not good news! I worked to focus on other theories. "How about the passport forger that took the flight in Levi Asher's place?" I asked. "Is there any way to get a picture of our mystery impersonator?"

"As a matter of fact, Shin Bet is in the process of eliminating all the legitimate passengers. They're a bit busy, what with wars of *jihad*, revolts, civil wars, what have you, going on at our every border. I don't know how long it will take them to find the right man or woman's photo. It could be weeks, a month, perhaps more. Where are you off to?" His curiosity peaked.

"I'm going to visit an old friend from home who lives near the Dead Sea. An artist."

"Be very careful," Dov cautioned me. "Will you take Mr. Brukowski with you?"

"Always," I said. "At least until Reverend Nation pulls him. Thanks, Dov. I'll be in touch."

"You'd better be," he demanded and hung up.

Inside the classroom, the professor stood and gathered up his materials, and the students followed suit, closing laptops, sliding notebooks and materials into their backpacks and briefcases. As they turned toward the door to exit, I could see how animated they were: faces smiling, their eyes alive. Must have been an inspiring lecture.

All eight filed out the door, teacher and students chattering all at once, but when they spotted me, the whole group clammed up. That made me suspicious. I asked my chaperone if I could wait in the classroom—that I had a bad foot and standing for a long time was painful. He nodded permission, and we went in.

I had noticed a handout belonging to one of the students slip to the floor unseen. I chose the rickety desk beside it and seated myself. Then I waited for my guard to be distracted by his cell phone. While he rattled on with his girlfriend, I picked the sheet off the floor and began to read. It was a printout of an Associated Press report from *The New York Times,* the November 20, 2008 online edition. The headline brought me to attention immediately, and I read the article itself.

Scientists Say Copernicus' Remains Found
by The Associated Press

Warsaw, Poland AP – Researchers believe they have identified the remains of Nicolaus Copernicus by comparing DNA from a skeleton they have found with that of hair retrieved from one of the 16th-Century astronomer's books.

Jerzy Gassowski, an academic at an archaeology school in Poland, also says facial reconstruction of the skull his team found buried in a cathedral in Poland closely resembles existing portraits of Copernicus, whose theories identified the Sun, not the Earth, as the center of the universe.

Gassowski and Marie Allen, a Swedish DNA expert, told reporters about their findings in Warsaw on Thursday. Allen said DNA from the bones and teeth matches that of hair found in a book the Polish Astronomer owned. It is in a library at Sweden's Uppsala University.

Pure shock! I stuffed the sheet into my jacket pocket, where the pistol used to reside, and waited, my mind racing, searching for answers, connections, false or otherwise. But one idea kept dominating my thoughts: if my newest hunch was correct, I was farther from being together with Miriam than ever.

Nonetheless, I had held onto the fantasy of Miriam for twenty years already, still hoping to hit on a long shot. The gods may have been teasing me, playing perverse pranks on a foolish man. But if you're destined to go down, may as well be a *mensch* and dare Fate grandly, bravely. Apparently, my friend Solly had made that same decision, in spades, long before.

***

My chaperone showed me into Solly's massive lab and retreated to wait outside, closing the door behind himself. Immediately, the stench of stale cigarette smoke and rubbed-out butts hit me like a sucker punch.

Scanning the room, I saw cigarettes burning in two of the room's many overflowing ashtrays and open packs of Gauloises Brunes scattered about. All around me, every surface of the lab was jammed. The room's counters and desks were filled with all manner of lab equipment, computers, and advanced electronics, with glass beakers and test tubes interlocking in complex Rube Goldberg-like configurations to the ceiling. The floor held a maze of stacked annotated books and scribbled notebooks.

And most oddly, an army cot sat in the far corner, covered with wrinkled sheets and blankets, as if the sleeper had just awakened. An open door in the rear wall led to a private bathroom, complete with shower and rubdown table.

And there was Solly, sitting behind the main desk near the far wall among a galaxy of smoke rings and interstellar nicotine particles. He set his cigarette down and rose, circling the room to face me. It had been twenty years since I'd seen him. He was thin as a rail, his face drawn, with piercing sky blue eyes, and matted, kinky red hair. His freckled skin was sallow, pasty, as if he hadn't seen sunlight in some time, which I guessed he probably hadn't. I was shocked by his appearance, but under the circumstances, not surprised.

He came at me in a herky-jerky manner, as if overdosed on coffee or speed, his arms outstretched, clearly relieved to see me. He gave me a warm hug, but I couldn't return it; I just stood by coldly. Yes, there was a great deal I resented about my old friend.

"David, David Greenberg, do you want coffee?" he asked, ignoring my frigid demeanor.

"Just water, thanks," I replied icily.

Solly crossed to a cabinet and withdrew a fresh glass, then placed it below a long tube at the end of some filtering process. Turning the spigot, he said proudly, "I only drink water that I distill myself. Make my coffee with it, too."

Distilled water? I wondered if he was still prone to paranoia like in the old days. "I'm glad to see you're living so healthily," I said sarcastically. "The key word is *living*."

He shrugged and handed me the glass, then returned to collapse into his swivel desk chair. He rubbed his troubled face, now lined with worry, dark bags under his eyes. He reached for one of his lit cigarettes, then gestured for me to sit opposite him.

95

"This is all your fault, David," he said wearily, half-sarcastically, half-accusatorily.

"What did I do, Solly?"

"What did you do?" he growled bitterly. "You brought love into my life! You introduced me to Miriam. Now I'm losing my son." He paused to recover, in obvious pain. "David, my life is confined to a hospital room or this lab, period. Love, friend, goddamn love was the cruelest trick you ever played on me. You should have known I wouldn't be strong enough to take it."

"Nobody's strong enough for love, Solly," I replied, my expression harsh. "Nobody."

"Ari..." he said, then fell silent, unable to finish his sentence.

A tear trickled down Solly's face as he was overcome with emotion, something I'd never seen before. No doubt he'd been living in denial for these many years. But the truth was unavoidable, there before his eyes every time he stood beside his son's hospital bed. Miriam told me that for the last couple of years he'd been working every waking moment not spent at the hospital in a futile attempt to distract himself from the reality of Ari's progressing illness. But who could possibly put that sweet, pain-ridden face from his mind? I could see the toll the boy's illness had taken on Solly, how much sleep he'd lost over the months and years, and how much Ari's fate had torn up his insides.

Yes, I understood his distress, but I wasn't going to be his shoulder to cry on. Not knowing how much time I'd have with him, I reached into my pocket and tossed the *Times* Copernicus article on his desk. "One of your students dropped this," I said, not smiling.

He studied me carefully, weighing his options. He needed me to get his precious nail. We had been as close as friends could get. Youthful friendships never completely leave you, not really. No matter how much both of you change, how far you drift apart, how different you've become, emotionally, a part of you goes back to the special bond you once shared. For that matter, we had both loved the same woman. And he had, through some trickery, won her from me, and so stole a piece of the prime of my life. You could say, we had a history.

From the depths of his grief, he made the decision to fill me in, no holds barred. He had been living in a secretive cocoon for twenty years. Perhaps it was a relief to unload himself to an old soulmate, to someone outside his constricted circle of colleagues. Perhaps with his son near death, opening up to me gave him a temporary release from the hell he was trapped in. Perhaps he saw my appearance as a chance to brag about things he hadn't been free to discuss.

Regardless, he let me have it, both barrels. He sighed, took a drag, then spoke, cigarette smoke punctuating each syllable. "Ah, you've run into a member of one of my Bisl teams. In Yiddish, *bisl* means 'a little bit'."

"I know what it means, Solly. What 'little bit' are they interested in, these teams? The kids seemed pretty excited."

"Ah, David, the whole idea is the culmination of my DNA research."

"Part of your T'chiat Ha-meitim program?"

"Right. See, Bisl is divided into teams of six students each. Each team's objective is to gather DNA from, ah, from selected individuals around the world."

"By any methods possible," I interjected.

"Well, yes, of course," Solly replied defensively. "In fact, Miriam tells me we can afford to expand Bisl. Why not? My results will benefit mankind in ways nobody can imagine—for now and forever."

Was Solly's declaration megalomania? Insanity? Had my friend lost it? "And who are these 'selected individuals' whose DNA you're after, Solly?"

"Who? Only the greatest minds in history. The greatest minds in history, David!"

I was taken aback, shocked. This sort of thing had always been Solly's obsession—the subject of endless philosophical arguments we'd had. But so many years later, here in Israel no less, none of it made sense. "And what's the purpose of this program? What are you really doing here, Solly?"

"Purpose? Why I'm going to clone them, of course," he said, as if surprised that I would even ask. "What do you think?"

Was Hadera more a madhouse than university? My head was spinning. He saw the look on my face and couldn't help but laugh.

"Solly, come on," I said, perplexed by his cryptic sense of humor. "What's the real deal?"

"No, seriously David." He paused, and I could see he was trying to make a decision whether or not to cross a final Rubicon with me. Finally, he stubbed out his cigarette and took a bottle of whiskey and two shot glasses from his drawer. He set them on the desk and poured. Then, without asking, he slid one across to me.

"I've cloned Jesus Christ," he said matter-of-factly. Then he sighed deeply, shrinking into himself with profound sadness like a punctured balloon. Eyes downcast, he stared at his hands in his lap. Then he raised his gaze into mine. "*L'chiam!*" He tipped his whiskey toward me in salute, then downed the whole shot with one swallow and slammed down the empty glass. His eyes watered, but not from the shot. Unable to say a word, I downed mine, too.

"Yes, it's true, David," he said morosely. "I did clone Jesus Christ. Years ago."

From the sorrowful look on his face, the way he slumped in his chair, I knew he needed to unburden himself.

"Fourteen years ago, right, Solly? Ari?"

He nodded.

"Unfortunately, I had to start with an imperfect specimen," he groaned despondently. "But you play the hand dealt to you, right?"

I simply indicated he should continue.

"Yes, fourteen years ago. I did everything I could, David, everything," he pleaded, pausing to rub his careworn face and collect himself. "Can you imagine what I had to work with? The relatively primitive equipment, the computers that are many generations obsolete now, and the only specimen I had was less than a dust mote, a speck of nothing, almost…nothing." He blew into his palm as if dismissing an eyelash. Then his tears began to flow. With averted eyes, I poured us each another shot, suspecting we wouldn't drink them, not glancing up so as not to embarrass him. Then I waited for him to compose himself, to break the silence.

Finally, he spoke.

Once he got rolling, the words tumbled from his mouth like sludge from an unblocked drain. I became the Royal Society before which he would never present his findings, the Nobel committee that would never know of his accomplishments, and the adoring crowds packing the lecture halls of the great universities of Europe, the United States, and Asia.

"You see, there was an impurity in the specimen I inherited when I arrived, David. The sample from that nail, miniscule as it was, was contaminated by some ancient Hebrew with a genetic disorder. I can't imagine how or why. Maybe the Romans reused execution nails; I don't know. The computers we have now can sort that manner of contamination out, but with the prehistoric programs I had back then…" He snuffled a few times, hands to his nose, his chest rattling.

I decided to change the subject, at least temporarily, to give him time to recover. With the state he was in, I was afraid he would shut down, and I'd still be in the dark about the breadth of what I had encountered.

"So these Bisl students, what's in it for them?"

"What's in it? A Bisl internship is the perfect endeavor for eager young scientists!" His face was glowing, animated. "Part clandestine big adventure; part scientific revolution; part very-well-paid graduate internship; part international travel. We have our choice of the best talent Hadera has to offer. Matriculate to Hadera University, see the world, and fulfill a quixotic quest for the good of all mankind. What student wouldn't want in?"

"But, Solly, these kids, you're putting them at great risk!"

"Look, David, my projects are my business," he said as if representing himself in a court of law. "My biotech discoveries more than pay for themselves—and pay for a ton of religious studies scholarships—so I have *carte blanche* to do whatever I want. Don't judge me, pal." Then he fell silent, lost somewhere in his sad and lonely existence.

After composing himself, he offered, "Are you sure you don't want coffee? That contraption over there contains java made from the finest beans on the African continent. I drink gallons, and look, I'm still alive."

"Yes," I said between clinched teeth, ignoring his offer. "You *are* alive, aren't you?" My fury was building. I don't care to be manipulated, nor was I happy that Miriam had been so manipulated twenty years before—if she wasn't, even now, being stage-managed to pull my strings. I didn't like that from anyone, especially from an old friend.

"So you used your cloning project to lure Miriam to Israel with you, to act as surrogate mother to Ari, your son?" His intense stare answered loudly in the affirmative. "And you used your fake suicide and Miriam to lure me into this chase to get this nail for you. Solly, you were my brother," I half-pleaded.

"And you, mine," he said, attempting to reconcile with me.

"Sure, but Cain killed Abel, didn't he?" I spat, feeling as desolate as I've ever been.

"Enough histrionics, David. You and I don't go back *that* far! See, Am Ha-b'rit security faked my suicide two years ago because bad actors got wind of what we were doing here. One of my colleagues went missing, and the next thing I knew, I was subjected to kidnapping and assassination attempts. I had to disappear."

"Okay, understandable."

"Had a funeral for me and everything. Too bad I couldn't have attended, like Tom Sawyer," he sneered bitterly. "I would have enjoyed hearing all the phony praise heaped upon me. Beyond a few kind words, Buddy, when you're gone, there's only dust and bits of DNA left."

"But Solly, why did it have to be Miriam? You could have gone to Israel without her."

"I wanted her in my life, David, every day. Pure and simple. I wasn't jealous of you. Look, we were friends and competitors. We played tennis, chess, right? Sometimes I won; sometimes you did. Well, I simply won this game, right?" He walked over to a contraption to refill his huge coffee mug, then returned.

"Solly, you knew I was in love with her," I stated, with a slight trickle of venom.

"Ah, a chemical reaction," he said scornfully, "more addictive and destructive than any drug on the black market. Look, David, you always had plenty of girlfriends, far more than I ever did, anyway. I understand you married after Miriam and I left St. Louis. Any kids?"

"Twice. Both ended. No kids."

"And do you regret those marriages?"

"No," I admitted. "I only regret that, in the end, I made them unhappy, or they made me unhappy." I pointed to Solly's cigarettes, and he threw me one of his packs of Gauloises and a lighter. I lit one.

All of a sudden, I am smoking again!

We smoked together, like in the old days, staring at each other's long-lost faces.

"You see, David," he said, calming himself, "I'd hoped Miriam would learn to love me, but she never really did, not enough. I spend all my time in my lab and at the hospital these days. I'm not much of a husband." Remorse flooded his face. "She deserves better," he gulped.

"All right, Solly," I said. "I'll try some of your coffee. Any milk or cream?"

"We should have something to eat sent up," he said. "My assistants keep a chart to see that I eat at least twice a day, but they're all busy with their BisI projects today."

"Sure, call downstairs," I said, realizing I was starving. "Okay, now explain it all to me."

CHAPTER TWELVE
JOSEPH IN BETHLEHEM REDUX

"Cloning Jesus Christ is only the beginning," Solly said, staring at me, becoming visibly uncomfortable. As we talked, he nervously clipped his fingernails into the wastebasket; they were stained yellow from smoking and had grown quite long. It had to have been some time since he'd performed this task, or even gotten a haircut. He clipped all but the thumb of his left hand, which he kept extended—opposing digit long and neatly squared off. Back in St. Louis, he'd sculpted the thumbnail the same way so that he'd always have a screwdriver handy without having to search for a tool. He'd learned this trick from reading an article on aviator Howard Hughes, who'd invented the practice.

"All right, I mean, how did this come about? Why would a group of Jews want to clone Jesus?"

"Miriam must have told you how science has overtaken a lot of the old ways of thinking in Am Ha-b'rit now, our Society being religious-based or no."

"Miriam mentioned it, yes," I said, urging him on.

"It's the 21st Century, right? Even our religious scholars have come around to the idea that God may have methods in mind beyond miracles, burning bushes, and the like. Maybe evolution is part of God's plan. Maybe science is part of it. Ideas evolve, you know."

"I get it," I said simply, not wanting to slow him down.

"Okay. The program, which was begun long before Miriam and I came to Israel, must have been a uniting factor within the Society. In fact, I was recruited specifically for this project. The T'chiat Ha-meitim program was a huge investment for Am Ha-b'rit, but the Jesus clone project was an expenditure the majority could agree on. In Am Ha-b'rit, many of our ultra-Orthodox brothers and sisters are hoping for their 'Messiah,' and they've come around to being willing to use God's Earthly devices—science, what else?—to give it a shot. I did attend one scholarly argument on the subject but didn't stay long. Too boring. Of course, there always were, and still are, factions that are vehemently dead set against the Jesus part of the program, for obvious reasons."

"I can well imagine," I said, thinking again of kindly old Moise Shankman and young Levi Asher, and of the possibility that both had been betrayed from within Am Ha-b'rit.

"On the other hand, my scientific kin want to push the limits of experiment with genetics, ancient DNA, cloning—sky's the limit. Some of the trials this organization had been conducting for decades, just to get to this point, and are nothing short of astounding."

"No side issues, Solly," I said impatiently, although I half-suspected some of the early experiments could significantly affect my quest. Boy, was I right.

"Look," he said, "you know very well I don't believe in God, much less a son of God. Right?"

"Of course."

"But if someone with Jesus' intelligence and charisma were alive today, if he were brought up under the right circumstances, nurtured and encouraged, maybe he could advance the world like he did before, actually fulfill Christianity's Peace on Earth. I mean, with the world as it is today, we could use a Messiah or two, no?"

I was beginning to see. Then Solly's ultimate goal dawned on me. "And if it worked?"

"If it worked, we could revive all of history's super geniuses: Newton, Gandi, Madam Currie, Einstein."

"And Copernicus," I added, fingering the student photocopy I'd picked off the floor, taken aback by the scope of Solly's scheme. I was torn between ethical disgust and possible benefits beyond imagination.

"*If* we can acquire DNA fragments from them," Solly cautioned.

Of course, how could I not have seen it coming? Especially after reading the Times *article on cloning mammoths. Imagine, mankind could leap thousands of years and would keep growing.*

Then another light went on, an even more disturbing one. With stem cell technology and advanced computers, you could keep a person's genetic material alive forever. You could reproduce Jesus multiple times...and Isaac Newton, Copernicus, and the others! Perhaps not all the copies would be geniuses, but those that were...

Then I caught myself. What I was hearing was crazy, and I was going mad listening to it. It's never been proven that genius is inheritable. And the not-so-new notion of "super people" hadn't played out very well down in the mud below where humankind lives, especially not for Jews; although I knew there was no intentional correlation between what Solly was saying and the ignorant, hate-filled interpretation of the concept that claimed six million innocents.

"But Solly, cloning people isn't legal anywhere, is it? And cloning such a culturally sensitive figure as Jesus..."

"Never mind the legalities, David. For that matter, do you expect me to understand the politics of a complex organism like Am Ha-b'rit? My only interest is the science."

Something still bothered me. Was Solly flat-out lying to me? Why did he choose Jesus really? Scientifically, a sample that ancient was not the optimum choice. Why spend all this money, all this effort, even all these lives, to get the nail? It didn't add up. My first reaction was to blame his ego.

"You know what I think, Solly," I said with more than a little accusation in my voice, "I think you see this as the greatest experiment of all time. And you want to attach it to the biggest name in history, to Jesus. Right?"

"Bullshit, Greenberg," he said, throwing down the clippers. "If my name ever gets attached to this project, it'll be because I'm on my way to prison. I'll be infamous, not famous. Don't denigrate my motives. If that's what you think, screw you. I know I'm doing the right thing, and you can help me or just get out."

So there it was. Miriam and Solly had their agenda, and I could help them find the nail or go home. Take it or leave it. At that moment, I decided I was going to spend the next day making my purchases for the shop through my usual sources, which would give me time to think things through. Yes, a drive through the Israeli countryside was just what I needed.

Or so I thought.

Just then, the food arrived, carried in by a pretty, young student, Tzivia. I bantered with her as she directed Solly to eat. She and I both cut subtle humorous remarks about the cigarette odor as she circled the room, cracking open all the windows.

Tzivia was energetic, a bit rushed because she was due in class shortly. She had short, dark hair and warm brown eyes, a gold *chai* hanging from a chain on her ample bosom, and strong legs like a school soccer player. She told me she was majoring in languages and already knew six fairly well, including English and Japanese. She was earning her room and board working the kitchen and carrying trays.

Solly lit a fresh Gauloises and cleared papers from the desk where we were sitting as I dusted my space on the desktop perfunctorily with my sleeve. With a smile, Tzivia set the bowls of vegetable soup, pita bread, and melon before us, then left the room.

As we ate hungrily, Solly enlightened me in his analytic voice. "It was like Am Ha-b'rit's Manhattan Project, you see? I mean, even though Am Ha-b'rit members may not believe Jesus was the Messiah, they think he was a pretty smart rabbi who changed the civilized world, so the whole deal is okay with them. Miriam probably told you we have documents quoting his teachings that aren't in the Christian Bible, right? Interesting stuff, you should read it."

"Yes, she told me. And after you've succeeded, you get the financial support for cloning the others." I took a bite of pita and waited a beat. "All right, the nail, Solly," I said impatiently. "Get to the nail. Do you think the nail will somehow help cure Ari?"

"No," he said glumly. "That can never happen, David." Setting down his spoon, he fell silent. I waited, but he was lost in his own dark thoughts about his dying son.

Finally, tired of waiting, I urged him, "Go on, Solly. The nail."

"Okay," he said, slowly focusing. "Am Ha-b'rit has been caretaker for all three nails for generations, since the crucifixion. We had to split them up some time ago, naturally, to preserve at least one of them. For the T'chiat Ha-meitim experiments, my predecessors had the two nails from his hands, which is where they rescued Jesus' genetic material."

"And the one you're after, the one for the feet?"

"During the Holocaust, the one for the feet was lost. We've been searching for it ever since. Then we discovered it in private hands..."

"Moise Shankman's hands most recently," I interjected.

"Right, and that led to Levi Asher and his trip to St. Louis. That's where we stand."

"Okay," I said, willing to suspend my disbelief for the moment to keep the conversation moving. After all, if, as Solly claimed, they were able to successfully clone anyone, they would have to have some method. "I assume you still have the nails from the hands. So why is it so important to acquire the one for the feet, and at such cost? Why, Solly?"

"That's where what we call 'The Betrayal' comes in, David. I don't know if Miriam mentioned that to you."

"She alluded to it, but I know nothing about it."

"Judas wasn't the half of it, my friend."

"Are you referring to the religious factions against the program?"

"Yes, years ago a member of Am Ha-b'rit, an eighty-five-year-old rabbi named Yourman, hated the very idea of the T'chiat Ha-meitim program, and his hatred only grew more vehement as he got older. Before he immigrated to Palestine, Yourman was originally from a village near Kishinev in Eastern Europe's Pale of Settlement that was wiped out in a pogrom when he was a child. Saw his whole family slaughtered and thrown into a ditch—brothers and sisters, parents, grandparents, cousins, aunts, and uncles. You can only imagine. Yourman was a tough old crow who knew he was dying of brain cancer, with advancing symptoms of dementia, undoubtedly related to the cancer. He destroyed everything: the two remaining nails we had, almost all the Jesus DNA specimens, and as importantly, the computers storing the DNA patterns. Smashed the equipment and set fire to the lab. Wiped out nearly everything except a microscopic fleck of DNA from one of the nails, which had been protected from the flames by its insulated metal refrigerant container.

"Even worse, through his fading perception, Yourman timed his spree meticulously. He cornered the program's top scientists together at their monthly meeting and gunned them all down with an Uzi. All their knowledge was lost. When he was certain they were all dead, he shot himself through the mouth."

Now the tight security surrounding the Life Sciences building made sense. In fact, the whole time I was with Miriam, I suspected we were being watched, even walking near her home at night. At the time, I ascribed the feeling to stress over visiting Ari. Now I knew better.

"So you don't know if there are any other potential assassins from Yourman's faction?"

"No, I was recruited after that tragedy. Naturally, they insulated me from the whole investigation—didn't want to scare me off. I had to build the program back up almost from scratch, with only that tiny sample and a scattering of graduate student notes and experimental records on the program, which I picked through a page at a time."

"And so, the only nail left is the one for the feet, I take it."

"Yes. If it still exists."

"If you already have a Jesus clone, why not start with his DNA?" I asked, avoiding mentioning the name Ari, of course.

"You think I didn't try?" he growled. "We can't, David. Sometimes there just isn't any way. Science isn't magic. Within my technical limitations back then, I had to consume the fleck I used to produce... " He was unable to complete his sentence. "David, I did the best I could. Our Ari has been sickly from birth—destined to die young. We did everything medical science could do. I just wasn't prepared for..."

Commiserating, I walked over and put an arm around his shoulders. He nodded, wiping his eyes with the back of his hand. We finished our lunch without speaking. It was a long time before we picked up our conversation.

"So," I prompted, wiping my mouth with the cloth napkin, "the one for the feet. When someone dies on a cross, the blood flows down. Is that the idea?"

"Of course, I'd have a far better sampling of genetic material from this nail. Plus, as I said, we can now screen out any impurities that might have gotten mixed in with his DNA."

What he didn't say was that he and Miriam would have a healthy Ari to raise to manhood. He didn't have to. His fierce dedication to the program was his tribute to his soon-to-be-lost, oh-so-gifted son, a son that was his one emotional tie to Miriam, and her connection to him.

I could see that Solly had drained his last reserves of social interaction, so our discussion had ended. Where did this leave the three of us? Love triangles are inherently tragic on many levels, with all three aspirants invariably the victims of a despotic fate. And this one? Far, far more than the three of us were at issue.

Obviously, Miriam had known Solly was alive when she called me at the gallery—when we had lunch at Blueberry Hill. She wanted to entice me to help Am Ha-b'rit produce another Jesus, a healthy, complete Ari. Emotionally, in some sense, she was probably a mother instinctively healing her sick child. Perhaps that was her sole aim, nothing more.

Perhaps she didn't love me, never had. The realization that maybe I'd been hustled by my old friends was humbling and humiliating.

But I was in complete denial about any coldhearted subterfuge on their part. If Solly's suicide was faked by Am Ha-b'rit security to protect him and his family, then keeping that secret, even from me, made sense. If I was ever kidnapped like Levi Asher, a real possibility, I wouldn't be able to jeopardize the safety of Miriam and Ari, nor Solly's efforts on the T'chiat Ha-meitim program. Desperately clinging to my illusions, I decided I would never ask either of my friends whether they lied to me for security reasons or to manipulate me…if they'd even tell me the truth. You would think I'd want to know, but I didn't.

And Miriam? Did our kiss lie? Our hands touching? Her tearful embrace? Listen, none of us could make it through a single day without heaping doses of self-deception, and if you claim to believe otherwise, you're lying to yourself. I had to at least pretend that what I felt between us wasn't false just to keep going. The game didn't matter to me anymore.

But within minutes, the game would matter. Bullets and explosions and worse were about to follow, and so were troubling new revelations.

CHAPTER THIRTEEN
THE SNAKE IN THE GARDEN

Overwhelmed with claustrophobia, I needed to get away from that high-tech ashtray. I only had one question. Reaching into my jacket, I slid the police photo that Dov gave me of our local university terrorist to Solly. "One last thing…Do you know this man?"

"Of course, I do," he replied, taking a deep breath. "That's Jarad Weiner. He reports directly to me. Why do you ask?"

A quandary: How much did I want Solly to know about what Dov had told me? I decided to keep my mouth shut. Solly obviously trusted Weiner, and I didn't want to chance that he might alert him to our suspicions. But now, innocent-seeming Solly himself had taken on a sinister patina. Was my old friend the big spider at the center of the web? I wouldn't put it past him. However improbable, hadn't he already somehow enticed Miriam away from me when he had nothing going for him, zilch? At that moment, other events precluded our discussion.

Outside the window, I heard the sudden, rapid pop-popping of automatic weapons fire coming from across the quadrangle. Deafening sirens began to shriek from alarms throughout the building, echoing outdoors. Within moments, I could tell the firing was coming from a variety of weapons. Our young, bearded escort ran into the room, pistol drawn, yelling, "On the floor! On the floor!" Crossing to an immobilized Solly, he pulled him to the hard tile floor and shoved him under the desk. On the way down, Solly grabbed a pack of cigarettes, knocking a filled ashtray onto the floor, spilling its *schmutz* about. I ducked behind the opposite side of the desk, only peeking over its edge as curiosity and fatalism overtook me.

As Solly lit up, resigned to waiting out the emergency curled up in his improvised den, my escort ran to a window and hunkered down. Rising just enough to peer into the courtyard, he could see what was transpiring outside. Just then, a burst of bullets blew through the window, scattering glass, and I flattened on the floor. Quick as a cat, my escort slid to a window with a better angle and began taking aim, firing downward into the quadrangle. Not knowing what was happening, and frightened by the possibilities, I closed my eyes to wait.

Suddenly, the rate of gunfire began to swell, like a crescendo in a symphony when all the instruments join in. Then I heard a single, distinctive shot from a higher-caliber weapon, which sounded like it came from a window on our floor, followed by a loud explosion.

Instinctively, I covered my head as the gunfight below returned to its regular frantic pace. I could smell Solly's cigarette smoke blowing under the desk. The random sound of gunfire continued at its frantic pace. Then the higher-caliber weapon a few rooms down fired another single, loud blast. Shortly thereafter, all shooting stopped. My chaperone rose, slipped his pistol into his pocket, and let us know it was safe to resume our activities. I thanked him, my heart pounding, and went to the window to see what had happened, brushing my clothes. The building's sirens stopped abruptly, replaced by an ambulance wail coming toward us from across the campus.

Below I could see the scorched spot where the suicide vest had exploded, probably hit by that single, high-caliber shot, with a mangled body and the man's detached head sprawled on the ground, a terrible thing to see. I could barely make out the body, too many security men around it, but I saw enough. What a bloody mess.

"Two *jihadis*," the young escort informed me. "One charged the building, but didn't make it. Jarad hit him directly in the belt. The other took a bullet in the head over near those benches." We examined the scene below together, while Solly picked up his ashtray. Kicking window shards away, Solly lumbered over to check an experiment on one of his tables.

"Oh, the bastards shot a student!" my escort cried.

Then I saw her. Tzivia lay curled on the grass, writhing in pain, her eyes filled with terror, blood soaking her sweater. Students and armed men ran to her side. One man held her hand, while another saw to her wound. But not for long. Soon there was a small circle standing above her lifeless body.

I felt disgusted and horrified. Just a short time before, she'd been so

109

full of life, joking, a kind Sister of Mercy aiding two hungry pilgrims. I remember thinking that some poor devil is going to have to break the news to her heartbroken parents, a job I didn't envy. The waves of Tzivia's tragedy would spread throughout Israel, befouling the land like an oil slick hitting a pristine Tel Aviv beach. *Damn fanatics!* My escort headed for the outer office to wait for me, cell to his ear. I faced my friend.

"Where is the nail, David, St. Louis or Israel?" Solly asked coldly, seething with anger.

"I'm not certain." I didn't want to reveal the trap I'd worked out with Dov. I was still guessing that only the person who kidnapped Levi would suspect that the nail had never made it to Israel. If the nail was still in St. Louis—a big if—either Weiner or Shadid, the fanatic or the *jihadi*, would be the first to fly to the U.S., giving himself away, if either of them was the guilty party.

"And Miriam tells me you have a clue? From Levi's text message?" Solly asked abruptly.

"Yes, probably. I think Levi was telling us the location of the nail, whether St. Louis or Israel."

"Yes? Go on," he demanded.

"I don't want my clue getting out. Sorry, Solly," I said defensively.

"Who would I tell?" Solly shot back. Then he took some moments to think. His eyes narrowed, and he glared at me. "Please go," Solly said. "I've got work to do. Get us the nail, Greenberg. I want you to place it directly into Jarad Weiner's hands for safekeeping. You can trust him."

Trust Weiner? I was stunned by this claim and had to take time to recover my composure. "One thing, Solly, can you pretend that you already have the nail? To everyone, even to Weiner. Can you do that?" The request was merely a shot.

Solly tossed Weiner's photo back to my side of the desk. "I can deal with these people," he said ominously, the old, paranoid side of my friend dominating his eyes. "Get your amateur ass after my nail. Remember, Miriam's clock starts one year after I have the nail in my hands."

Could this be the same sweet man I'd known? Was he suggesting that he was resigned to a trade: his wife for the nail? If so, that was damn callous.

I grabbed the photo and headed for the door. Let him find out about Tzivia from someone else, I decided, if he would even care. I had never seen Solly so distant, so calculating, so heartless. But he *had* been dreadfully traumatized by Ari's fatal illness and Levi's disappearance, by the violence outside his office. I wasn't going to judge him in this state. Frankly, I was not in the best state of mind myself.

There was also the likelihood that while Solly directed considerable resources to Weiner's security operations and Bisl, he trusted Weiner enough to give him full autonomy in his actions. Details of Weiner's activities would only interfere with my scientist friend's work.

As I left the building, my escort left me to my own devices. I was relieved to be standing in the sun again, trying to relax enough to absorb its warmth. Around me, people scurried about, bringing order back to the scarred quadrangle. The ambulance arrived with a stretcher for Tzivia, far too late to do her any good.

I thought about what had just transpired. I'd witnessed an aloof, manipulative, unscrupulous Solly unlike I'd ever seen before, a man possessed by a paranoia not unlike his drug-induced college episodes. It made me wonder. If he had manipulated Miriam and fooled the outside world with his fake suicide, what else is he capable of doing? In his jealousy at Miriam's current involvement with me, with his impending loss of Ari, in his current state of agitation and sleeplessness, could he be behind Moise Shankman's murder and the Levi Asher abduction? With the magnitude of Am Ha-b'rit's investment in Solly's program, or projects, who knew what forces and resources he could command? Indeed, by his own admission, or rather braggadocio, he was directing graduate students in his Bisl groups to rob tombs and graves all over the planet. Another question was, would he sabotage his own project to simply gain a suitcase full of euros? I dismissed the whole notion as merely me being shaken by the trail of gunfire I seemed to be drawing.

I took a few deep breaths and called Miriam. I hadn't yet decided if I was going to tell her about the attack. She picked up.

"Where have you been?" she asked, sounding distraught.

"I'm at the Life Sciences building," I said, pausing to not sound accusatory. "Did you know Solly is alive?"

"I did, yes, of course," she answered. "It was purely for his safety—for all our safety. He was in danger." She paused. "I saw Solly at the hospital yesterday in Ari's room. He was disheveled. He's living in his laboratory." Keeping true to my resolution, I didn't ask why she'd lied to me. "When are you coming here?" she half-pleaded.

"I've got a few stops to make between here and the Dead Sea. It'll be late when I'm back in Netanya."

"I don't care how late it is," she said, desperation in her voice. "Come to my house."

"Is there anything more I need to know?" I asked, a little ticked.

"No," she replied. "Nothing. I'm here by myself, David. I need to see you."

I agreed, hung up, and then called Detective Landau in Jerusalem to fill him in on the attack at the university.

"You're a magnet for these assassins," Dov remonstrated. "Where are you going next to be gunned down?"

"I'm driving to Ein Bokek, near the Dead Sea, on business, but I'll return late tonight."

"Wash yourself in the Dead Sea's healing waters," he said. "Clean off whatever substance on your skin that is attracting rabid wolves. Are you taking Mr. Brukowski with you?"

"Wouldn't leave home without him," I quipped, thinking about our strategy. "Have either of our foxes been flushed from the brambles yet, Dov?"

"Shadid is leading protests near Hebron as we speak. I haven't received a report back on Weiner from the university, but we sighted him yesterday."

Is one of them playing the waiting game well, or are our suspicions aimed in the wrong direction? "What about our mystery airline passenger using Levi Asher's passport?"

"This is absolutely confidential," he said hesitantly. "If you repeat it to anyone, you're on the next flight to St. Louis. Permanently. Unless, we're not both locked in prison for a goodly number of years."

"All right, I'm forever mute on the subject. You know you can trust me, Dov."

"Our friends with Shin Bet have identified our mystery traveler, who is now in custody."

So quickly! I guessed that the speed at which Israeli security came up with the mystery man or woman from a crammed international commercial airliner was the reason I had to keep my mouth shut. Shin Bet must be concealing a publically unknown method—probably some advanced biometric modeling. I was astounded that such a capability existed anywhere but in science fiction. But didn't Israel have Iron Dome, a seemingly sci-fi fantasy designed to intercept even small missiles fired from a relatively short distance? Clearly, exposing such a major security asset could set Israel back for a decade or more in their struggle to survive against a myriad-headed hydra of terrorists...and maybe cost many lives.

"So? Who was on that flight?"

"Just some St. Louis lowlife scrounging for a dishonest dollar. He was paid three grand USD to fly to Jerusalem using the ticket, then taxi to Tel Aviv and take the return flight back. We nabbed him at Ben Gurion before he could board the plane home to St. Louis."

"But who paid him? Who altered Levi's passport and gave him Levi's ticket?"

"He claims he doesn't know who was behind it. It was set up by some scum ball he runs into at the racetrack."

Oy, Finkel! So this scheme was just a ruse to throw off anyone searching for Levi. "Did he meet the man behind the local guy, the real bastard with the money and the passport? Perhaps an Israeli or a Palestinian?"

"His only contact was his racetrack friend. He was pretty wasted the whole time the thing was being arranged, which, I take it, is his normal state when he has cash in his pocket."

"Don't tell me. The St. Louis friend's name was Lawrence Finkel?"

"The lowlife is confused on the name—he gets confused on his own apparently—but that sounds like it. A friend of yours, this Finkel?"

I didn't have to confirm it.

"Your claims of innocence are getting more and more difficult to maintain, Greenberg."

Dammit, Finkel! Should I cover for him? Finkel was someone whose overwhelming gambling addiction made me sympathetic toward him; I was even in the tiny minority who liked him, despite his obnoxious personality. Indeed, after his grandmother died, Finkel had proven a generous donor to David Greenberg Antiquities. Hadn't I preyed upon the empire he'd inherited from her, taking full advantage of his continuously escalating, desperate need for cash? If it hadn't been me, someone else would have skinned him, perhaps literally—or so I tell myself. Hadn't I shielded Finkel from his creditors umpteen times? In this case, I knew he hadn't realized he was involved with murderers. But the thought of Moise Shankman, young Tzivia, and perhaps Levi Asher hardened my heart against him.

"Have the St. Louis police questioned Finkel yet? They can find him at his shop on Osage Street. The shop's hours are hit and miss, depending on when the horses are running. But I'm sure if you call his cell and tell him you want to make a big purchase, he'll show up."

"Thanks. Probably won't matter, though. You've already confirmed that one of the two with the spike on his cheek was in St. Louis. And the guy's face and voice were likely well-disguised when he met this Finkel."

There it was, another dead end.

"Any word from St. Louis on Levi Asher?" I queried.

"Haven't received anything. I'll stir their pot later today. The time difference, you know."

"I'll call tomorrow from the university."

I disconnected, discouraged. I needed time to collect myself, to restore my equilibrium and recover from the day's traumas. I figured a drive along the coast and toward the Dead Sea, away from the university and all its heartache, might help. Unfortunately, the nastiness had only begun.

***

Within minutes, I was approached by a squat man with a wide, black East European-style mustache and a bad shave, wearing a rumpled, double-breasted cheap suit. He identified himself as Chaim Turgenev, head of security for the university. We commiserated briefly over the death of Tzivia, before he asked me how he could help.

I explained that I was here to make purchases for my gallery and planned to make a few stops around Israel to see other traders. I was careful not to mention my ultimate destination. He was friendly enough, and, using his cell, he ordered up a car. I then called Bear to settle when and where I'd pick him up and chatted with Turgenev while we waited for my transportation. I learned from him, the attack on the Life Sciences building was the first at the university since Solly "died."

Another welcoming party for me? And thrown by whom? The finger definitely pointed toward Shadid.

His phone buzzed, and after receiving a brief update, he ordered the university's security be stepped up. He told me both attackers had been identified as radical *jihadis*. Remembering Dov's caution, I didn't show any curiosity or surprise that the identification had been accomplished so quickly using only cell phone shots of the dead attackers' faces. Next, without explaining why I thought so, I mentioned that I suspected Edan Shadid to be the man behind the attack. He said he'd pass the idea along to investigators. Homicide was not his area of responsibility.

Within two minutes, I was startled to see the solid figure of the dreaded Jarad Weiner, clad in black leather jacket and jeans, stroll from the Life Sciences building to join us—a high-powered rifle with an advanced scope slung over his shoulder. No black hat, no side curls. His rugged expression was smug, relaxed, satisfied. I presumed his two shots had resulted in two kills. Weiner was quite a marksman.

Naturally, I assumed he had no link to the assault on Life Sciences. To believe otherwise would be cynical beyond reason. As the three of us stood in the sunshine, Turgenev introduced Weiner to me. I forced a smile and offered my hand. When Weiner took my right hand, my left swung a friendly slap to his upper arm, striking his leather jacket in the exact spot where I thought I winged my motorcycle attacker outside the Jerusalem police station. I couldn't be sure if I felt padding or bandaging through the thick sleeve, but his face may have grimaced slightly. He pulled back firmly, without haste. Tough guy if he'd been shot in that spot recently.

He had the beard and the spike birthmark, as in his photo, but it was his black eyes that shocked me. They were a shark's eyes, if a man's can be so described—ruthless, hungry. I had little doubt they were the eyes of a coldblooded killer. Was he also some kind of mole, dead set—and I do mean *dead* set—against Solly's program, or simply ruthless and greedy?

Nevertheless, I realized it was irrational to make such a judgment based on a man's appearance. Especially, when he so resembled another who belonged to a reportedly violent organization.

"What do you do here, Jarad?" I asked Weiner, feigning sincere warmth. He just narrowed those shark-like eyes and glared at me.

"Mr. Weiner is head of security for..." Turgenev nodded his head toward Solly's window.

Oy. Possibly a murderous villain, and he is Solly's, and the program's, keeper! If I wasn't anxious before, I felt weak now. If the cloning project had tentacles throughout the world, and perhaps killers to implement their plans, I was faced by potentially overwhelming threats to my life, as were Miriam and Solly.

Is Weiner a pawn of Solly's? Seeing the discomfort that must have unconsciously crept onto my face, Weiner's lips cracked slightly downward on one side of his face, a subdued cross between a sneer and an evil smile. He knew I was scared.

Or perhaps I was simply being paranoid again. After all, wouldn't Am Ha-b'rit and the university know Weiner better than anyone? Looks can be deceiving, and Weiner's remarkable resemblance to Shadid wasn't his fault. *Why did that resemblance trouble me so much? Wasn't Shadid, the jihadi, the likely culprit in the attack on the Life Sciences building? And didn't the assassin on the motorbike in Jerusalem cover his face with an Arab* keffiyeh—*even though anyone can wear a* keffiyeh *in Jerusalem and not be noticed?*

Police cars with lights flashing and sirens blaring pulled up in the nearby car park, and Turgenev hurried off to meet them, leaving me with Weiner. His cold eyes stared, without blinking, into mine.

"When will you return home, Mr. Greenberg?" he asked.

"Not for some time," I replied. I had to force him into the first move, especially if it was to travel to St. Louis.

He thought for a moment. "Where are you off to next?"

"Just to buy some merchandise for my gallery," I replied. "I also plan to discreetly drop some hints that I am seeking a valuable artifact." I had to sate the hungry beast, but he did not flinch as I mentioned a search in Israel.

"Will you be accompanied by that Nazi, Brukowski?"

"Bear is not a Nazi now," I spit angrily.

"You clearly don't know," Weiner said flatly. "In his youth, he was an ardent White Supremacist, a virulent anti-Semite. He often wrote and spoke about exterminating the Jews."

"Even if that were true, which I doubt, he is a changed man," I answered, furious and confused.

"Jew-haters don't change their stripes," he said venomously.

As I lost an undeclared staring contest with Weiner, a gray Israeli Susita, which means "little horse" in Hebrew, pulled up to the nearby car park. A young, clean-shaven man in gray slacks and denim jacket crossed the quadrangle to join us, surveying the scene of recent violence. He tossed me the keys, then nodded to Weiner. I searched their faces for some sort of tell, but detected nothing. It was only a young man dropping off a car.

"And where did you say you're off to?" Weiner asked me again.

"Just business," I replied, putting on my poker face, albeit a bit too late.

"You ask Professor Solomon. I am the only person you can trust," Weiner said grimly, nodding toward the bodies littering the quadrangle. "As you can see, there are evil elements that have interests antithetical to our own."

"I see that," I agreed.

"You get that material the professor wants into my hands," he asserted, his tone like a spear directly into my heart. "And you get it quickly. Understand?"

"I'll do my best," I replied, putting on my most committed face. But I no longer felt quite so committed to Solly's side of the equation.

I thanked the young man and nodded to Weiner, who nodded back. Then, resisting the urge to look back over my shoulder, I was off, a shopkeeper venturing forth to do some trading in ancient history. I would just keep my mouth shut, play it straight, and see what surfaced. Returning to Miriam that night was all I cared about.

But my agenda had changed. I planned to use Hadera's own internal computer network to find out the truth about Jarad Weiner. To my chagrin, the truth I would discover was more than I was prepared to digest.

CHAPTER FOURTEEN
MESSAGE FROM THE DEAD SEA

I was relieved to see Bear's friendly face, especially when he volunteered to drive. I was shaken up, a mass of electrically charged nerves, and I needed to rest. His gentle smile and soft-spoken words seemed to belie everything Jarad Weiner had said about him. Yet a doubt at the back of my mind troubled me. Added to the new possible revelation of Bear's anti-Semitism, I still hadn't gotten past the ready knowledge the Wentzville sheriff had about Levi Asher's disappearance.

Bear was delighted that the Susita had the latest GPS system, a modern convenience I had never used, stubbornly preferring the challenge of folded paper maps. I told him where we were headed, with two stops before the final pair of stops in and around Ein Bokek, and he entered the data for the four destinations into the system. There are three routes from Netanya to the Dead Sea area, and I most assuredly planned to take the one through Israel proper, not either of the two that passed through long stretches of the West Bank, where the police presence would be heavy after the shootout at the university. Israel is a small country with good highways, and any of the three routes would take only about two-and-a-half hours without stops.

We were off, headed south down the sunny Mediterranean coast, the windows halfway open in the chilly morning air. I needed the fresh breeze blowing off the sea. I told Bear about the attack on the university campus, and his sympathy calmed me. He asked what I had been doing on the university grounds, but I only told him I was out for a stroll. I didn't want to chance blowing Solly's cover. His questions seemed probing, as if looking for some slip that would reveal Solly's ambulatory state. But again, perhaps I was being overly sensitive. As we drove, seeing my distress, Bear attempted to refresh me spiritually, which helped, too. But when he brought Jesus into the conversation, I reminded him that I was Jewish, and we let it go at that. I didn't bother to bring atheism or agnosticism into the discussion, which would only have clouded the already badly disturbed waters. Plus, I wanted to skirt the subject of Jesus, period. I'd began to suspect Bear knew about Solly's cloning program, being an intimate of Reverend Nation's—if Nation had figured it out—another big if. I hadn't decided yet, but I was thinking seriously about bringing my big, kindly friend to meet Ari. Maybe Reverend Nation had not filled him in already. For now, though, I held back.

There were a few extra stops throughout our journey because of heightened security, but nothing of consequence. I popped on the radio to an English-language news station. The *jihadi* attack that took Tzivia's life dominated the headlines, and we listened closely. Israeli security was taking steps to locate the fanatics behind the assault, but the Life Sciences building itself wasn't mentioned in the press reports. Celebrations were fomenting in sections of Gaza. An Israeli cabinet meeting was in session, and the prime minister was scheduled to speak. The PM's job: to toe a miniscule line between projecting strength and resolve, while at the same time reducing tensions within the Arab and Palestinian communities. Elsewhere, a Jewish radical was already demanding revenge, and a peace activist had already been beaten up.

Then the news closed with the announcer reporting wryly that Armenian Apostolic and Greek Orthodox monks at the Church of the Nativity in Bethlehem had, again, come to blows in a dispute over the boundaries of their respective jurisdictions at the shrine. In a reprise of a similar incident on Greek Orthodox Christmas in 2011—a riotous outpouring of anger and pent-up hostility—one hundred dignified, robe-clad priests of the two major Christian religions, including ancient scholars with long white beards, viciously slammed the brooms of their trade against each other's heads and torsos in a melee more of sound and fury than actual injury. As on that fateful Christmas past, the overheated clash had to be broken up by a phalanx of helmeted, shield- and club-wielding Israeli riot police. I'd seen the original mini-war on television and was, thus, able to replay the overheated conflict in my mind. Thankfully, oh kindly gods, this broke my tension. I lapsed into a maniacal spasm of gut-splitting laughter, joined by Bear's belly-deep, rich guffaws.

"Even the broom and the knuckle-sandwich are justified in the defense of the Lord God Almighty," Bear quipped when he had recovered his speech. "Or, at least, in defense of our corner of Jesus Christ's Holy Church of the Nativity."

"Broomsticks, perhaps," I added piously. "But it's a good thing Pope Innocent II outlawed the crossbow, *under anathema*, in 1139, or no telling where mankind's warlike tendencies might lead us. WMDs, like the crossbow, would upset the social and religious order to no end."

"Richard the Lionhearted was wounded by a crossbow bolt, you know," Bear added. "Can you imagine, a king being shot by a peasant?"

"That is certainly not the way God intended," I concluded with a smirk. "You see, the Pope outlawed the crossbow's use against Christians, particularly on church property or on Holy Days. He didn't write a word against shooting arrows into non-Christians."

The ride was certainly a pleasant relief, passing cities, towns, and desert landscapes I had come to love and where I felt so at home. We stopped off to visit three dealers I trusted and often traded with, two Jews and an Arab. There, I made purchases and had them shipped back to my shop in St. Louis. While Bear was busy parking, I quietly informed the three that I was representing a legitimate private collector who was willing to pay handsomely for a special, unique item, but didn't reveal that the sought-after artifact was the celebrated nail. Their faces told me that feelers about the nail had reached them long before. But still, I hoped they might agree to transacting business with me, a friend and honest trader, if they found what I was searching for. That was my only chance.

Bear enjoyed the day and was a big help identifying antiquities and other treasures that the summer swarm of Baptists to St. Louis might pay dearly to own. My Arab friend and supplier, Aban Abdul-Latif, whose name means Servant of the Kind One, had us to his house for dinner, offering a typical display of generosity with a sumptuous traditional meal that we greeted with appreciative approval to his wife. Having been raised in the Bekaa Valley, Aban's wife covered the table with simple, rustic Lebanese cuisine, delicious to the palate and memorable. We feasted on *or kkshik*, a porridge made with bulgur fermented in yogurt and dried on the rooftop for seven days; her own twist on *m'jadanrah*, a lentil stew; and cabbage salad. You learn to love your friends, the people you cherish and trust, and that day, I'd spent time with three of them, and I hoped Bear made it four. But even that balm could not, and never would, wash away the horror of seeing young Tzivia gunned down. If medical science truly wishes to be merciful, let them find a means of exorcizing such torturous memories.

***

It was getting late when I concluded my purchases at Ein Bokek, and Bear and I traveled on into the nearby countryside toward the Dead Sea. In short order, Bear pulled off the highway to drive up a gravel road, now dark except for our headlights, the star-studded sky, and the glowing yellow moon. The landscape through which we passed was rocky, with sparse, hearty, flowered scrub that had somehow taken root and thrived. Life was resilient in this place, a force with real power, and had been for eons. Here, Chick Markowitz, once a lost soul, had also planted roots into the barren stone life and was creating his art again. I was happy that he'd found love with an older man, a fine sculptor, a mixed Yemenite Jew/Gaza-born Palestinian.

The home of the sculptor came into view at the dead end of the road. I was excited about the chance to see Chick again, to relay the good wishes of his brother, Joey, and his mother, and to congratulate him on escaping a lifetime incarceration in the mental institution. The sculptor's spacious house, designed in simple glass and stone with contemporary lines, now posed a troubling sight. Police and ambulance lights flashed, while plainclothes and uniformed officers went about their duties or gathered about talking in low tones over steaming cups of coffee. Bear shut the ignition, and we made our way toward the commotion.

The desert night had descended, and we had to zip up our coats. A tall, thin, well-tanned, older man wearing white linen slacks and matching jacket over a yellow print shirt was crying into his handkerchief, fitfully answering questions from police. This was the sculptor, I assumed. I went up to him and introduced myself, explaining I was an old friend of the Markowitz family, here to say hello to Chick after concluding my business in Ein Bokek.

"Chick is dead," he sobbed, wrapping his arms around me. "This is what I returned home to find!" He cried on my shoulder for some time in a tight hug, his legs so weak from distress I had to hold him up. "There he was! He was..." he wept uncontrollably, near collapse.

A pair of medics surrounded us and gently took over his care. Supporting him and holding his hand, they half carried him to the ambulance before transporting him with lights flashing to the hospital.

"Boyfriend, decapitated," the nearest detective spoke in broken English, pulling his finger across his throat, shaking his head in disgust. "You understand? Head cut off."

"Chick Markowitz?" I forced myself to ask.

The detective grimly nodded confirmation.

Someone had left a gruesome message for me, and I was reading it very clearly.

I was flooded with memories of Chick, Daddy's younger brother, from two decades before when he was still in college. Even then, he tended toward the heavy side, with a round face, pale skin soft as dough, and always slightly flushed cheeks. Chick was such a sweet, shy guy who would never harm anyone, never even utter a bad word against his meanest tormentor, and he had been tormented plenty as a youth for being gay. A guy with artistic potential that he never fully recognized in himself, but others did; he just wanted to be accepted.

Bear and I identified ourselves, and we were led into the house, slipping on shoe covers. There, all the lights were switched on to aid the detectives, forensics people, and security team examining the scene, shooting photos, jotting notes, placing small fragments into plastic bags. There was a lot of blood on the floor and splashed about the room, a lot of blood. Throughout the living room, beneath the sweeping angles of the broad ceiling beams and tinted glass ceiling plates, paintings were knife-slashed and sculptures smashed, creating anarchy upon the polished wooden floorboards.

Is this vandalism a veiled threat to Miriam's art? To Miriam?

A headless torso lay sprawled beside a crimson-spattered white sofa and glass table, its shape outlined beneath a tarp, undoubtedly Chick. His severed head nearby was covered by a blanket. Red Arabic writing was swiped across the large bank of windows that overlooked the dark, peaceful desert night. But even to my untutored eye, from years spent in Israel, the angry crimson lettering looked somehow wrong. Arabic writing has a regular, graceful beauty that this lacked.

"Well, Mr. Greenberg, more chaos in your wake." The ruggedly handsome Ephraim Ben-Hershel of Shin Bet sternly confronted me. "In retrospect, I can't imagine why I was surprised when you arrived."

"Mr. Ben-Hershel, Ephraim," I nodded solemnly, relieved to see him. I politely reintroduced him to Bear. "You know my friend, Mr. Brukowski." The two blankly acknowledged each other. In short order, Bear was led outdoors to the patio to be interviewed by one of Ben-Hershel's underlings, while Ben-Hershel himself led me into the den.

"So," the Shin Bet point man began in his clipped, crisp accent, "you appear in Jerusalem and become the target of an assassination attempt, perpetrator unknown. You show up at Hadera University, and *jihadis* attack, killing a young student—an abomination sending ripples throughout the region. Now you arrive at this lost outpost near the Dead Sea, and a harmless artist is decapitated in an apparently senseless tragedy. I think we are well beyond the point where you can claim your presence at these calamities are no more than bad luck, wouldn't you say?"

I could only shrug hopelessly. For my own sanity, I had clung to the miniscule possibility that my being present when young Tzivia was gunned down was pure coincidence. But the horrendous murder of Chick Markowitz forever placed both lives squarely on my conscience. God's Left Tackle had told me during the drive that God never gives us greater burdens than we can bear, a tired but often quoted cliché. But he was wrong. My responsibility for these two deaths was far more than I could endure.

"I could have you deported immediately and barred permanently from Israel as an undesirable, Mr. Greenberg," Ben-Hershel threatened. "You were carrying an unregistered pistol, for starters. And I am seriously tempted to do so, if only to stave off more troubles for our country. At this rate," he added sarcastically, "if I let you stay another week, Israel will find itself engaged in a multi-front war."

Deported! Am I a pinned chess piece? Had someone butchered Chick Markowitz, taken his life, simply to force me back to St. Louis, either to keep me from recovering the nail in Israel or to hurry me back home to retrieve it? Or, conceivably, to draw me closer to Bear Brukowski? What kind of deviant am I dealing with?

"Who did this, Mr. Ben-Hershel? Who did this terrible thing to my friend? Was it some *jihadi*?" I gestured in a wide arc to indicate the message on the picture windows facing east toward the sea.

"No, Mr. Greenberg, this is not the work of a *jihadi*," he said coldly, as if lecturing a child. "And we must make that clear to the public immediately or there will be chaos. I've been doing this work for some time, and I know when a non-Arab, hopefully not a Jew, has faked a terror attack. The Arabic writing you see is flawed, plus there are a number of other giveaways…but I'm not going to reveal any of my trade secrets.

Besides, the inconsistencies and irregularities may help me to put you away, which would allow me to get some sleep, if nothing else."

"Could *jihadis* have made Chick's murder look like a Jewish subterfuge to obscure their own culpability? For reasons we don't know?" I asked.

"Unlikely," he replied, "but possible."

So that was that. *Jihadis* shot gentle Tzivia, and someone brutally murdered poor Chick Markowitz. Not only murdered Chick, but slashed to shreds his artistic legacy. I was lost in a black torture chamber wishing only for disbelief or madness to free me.

"But why would anyone do this?" I pleaded, grasping for a final straw of my innocence, physically distraught.

"That I will discover, Mr. Greenberg," Ben-Hershel growled angrily, "as surely as God has blessed this land." Then his repressed fury flashed at me. "Are you trying to set off another *intifada,* sir? You are playing with volatile explosives, my friend, and you seem to be tossing matches about heedlessly. Who knew you were coming here?"

I needed a drink or a Xanax, something. My hands were shaking uncontrollably, so my Shin Bet interrogator poured two fingers of bourbon for me from the bar. I was seated in a white leather lounge, Ephraim in a comfortable matching chair. Sweat poured down my forehead, and I swiped it with my handkerchief.

"I only told Detective Landau in Jerusalem," I answered, "and I only told him I was driving to Ein Bokek on business. I never mentioned a word about stopping here, never spoke Chick Markowitz's name." I omitted to mention that I had told Miriam I was coming to Ein Bokek. She had enough problems without getting involved with Shin Bet and a murder so far south.

"You're sure you told no one else?" he asked.

"I am. Not a soul. I told Bear where we were going when I picked him up, but he hasn't been out of my sight the whole trip, except for a few minutes to park the car or go to the men's room, that type of thing."

"So the final stop to visit the late Mr. Markowitz was planned from the beginning of your trip, am I correct?"

I nodded confirmation and took a deep drink, coughing through my burned throat.

"Then Mr. Brukowski had adequate time to call his associates; is that right? And someone working with him would have had plenty of time to do this before you arrived?"

"I guess so. But would Bear be the type to be involved in such a thing? I don't think so," I surmised. What Weiner had said about my new friend's anti-Semitic past and my doubts about Reverend Nation intermingled in my head. Then I dismissed the notion. I finished my bourbon and rose unsteadily to refill the glass, then returned to rest on the chaise, my hand trembling less severely.

"I'll decide who is involved," Ben-Hershel stated.

"But Bear saved my life in Jerusalem," I rationalized, like a boy whose brother was suspected by the principal.

"Anyone can wear a *keffiyeh*," he said. "This is said in complete confidence, Greenberg. Understand? Interpol has had its eye on Mr. Brukowski for some time."

"What would...?"

"You know what: Blood Diamonds. He has friends in the Israeli and Amsterdam diamond districts. That's an odd extension of his ministry."

I was confused and didn't know how to react.

"You told Detective Landau that you may have winged the shooter?"

"Yes," I acknowledged. "In the left bicep."

"This Brukowski, he works for Reverend Nation?"

"They seem to have a close relationship. He works *with* Nation at the very least, and I presume Bear is taking direct orders from him. Otherwise, why would Bear be playacting at being my bodyguard?"

Ephraim nodded, then in deep concentration, fell silent. Apparently, Reverend Nation, too, had been on his radar for some time, but Shin Bet had kept its distance because of political considerations and Nation's profitable Holy Land tourist concessions.

"What are you driving?" Ben-Hershel queried at last.

"We're in a gray Susita, a recent model. It's on loan from Hadera University, from the security people." Then an idea hit me, probably alcohol-fueled. I am not a drinker and was already a bit dizzy. "Perhaps a tracking device is attached to the car. We can inspect it," I suggested.

"That wouldn't explain how your arrival here was anticipated," Ben-Hershel noted. He paused for thought. "Where were you an hour ago, when the murder was taking place?"

"Bear and I were in Ein Bokek proper, doing business. I'll give you contact information for every stop we made. They'll verify everything I say."

"Don't waste my time," he said, dismissing the offer with a wave of his hand. "You received the auto from security at the university, you say? It has a GPS device."

"Yes, it does," I replied, catching on to Ben-Hershel's thinking. "Bear entered our stops, including this one, when I picked him up at his hotel."

"Then it is very possible your GPS is programmed to transmit your destinations to Hadera security," Ben-Hershel stated. "That's a common practice."

Transmitted to the very man, or men, who supplied the car? I pulled the picture of Jarad Weiner from my jacket and slid it across the table. "This man, Jarad Weiner, is in security at the university, in *authority*. Dov Landau believes he may be responsible for murders, kidnappings, and assassinations."

Without glancing at the photo, the Shin Bet man pulled out his cell and barked orders. "Find out where Jarad Weiner has been the last twelve hours, also the other one we discussed at breakfast." He disconnected.

"Can't you arrest him now? At least hold him?" I pleaded, excited. "Interrogate him? Search his house?"

"Israel is a land of laws, just like the United States, Mr. Greenberg. Although it's not as likely, your GPS could have just as easily been rigged to direct your travel plans to an outside recipient, or hacked from a distance by someone with sophisticated technological skills, for that matter. There are many in Israel for whom that would be child's play.

"Regardless, Brukowski, Weiner, or some other entity, Chick Markowitz's murderer knew you were coming here the moment you left Netanya hours ago."

This is way out of my league.

"Now Am Ha-b'rit, I asked you about it yesterday." Ben-Hershel checked his watch disgustedly. "*Yesterday*, when four people were still alive."

"After only a half-day at the university," I emphasized, "Am Ha-b'rit appears to be a religious-based covenant among a select fragment of the Jewish community. But how would I know for sure, Ephraim? I do promise to keep my eyes open for you." I had to get off Shin Bet's bad dog list—a daunting task.

"And Professor Joseph Solomon?" He gave me a hard stare. I felt certain he knew Solly's suicide was a fabrication. If I kept up the charade, I was certain to be on a flight to St. Louis, and quickly. Giving him a crumb was my only chance.

"He's in pretty bad shape," I said solemnly.

"So you've seen him?"

"We had lunch together." *A lunch burned into my memory forever.*

"What do you mean, 'in bad shape'? How?"

"His son has been sickly since birth, Ephraim, and now the boy is close to death. Who wouldn't be in bad shape? He's chain smoking, and I don't think he's eating or sleeping very much."

"What is he working on?" Ben-Hershel asked with deadly seriousness. "Two old friends meeting after twenty years, you had to discuss his current endeavors."

"Give me a break, Ephraim. The man had two Ph.D.'s by the time he was twenty-three. I wouldn't even attempt to understand his research."

"So what is he doing at Hadera?"

"He made *Aliyah* twenty years ago." Solly and Miriam had moved to Israel under Israel's Law of Return, which permits any Jew to settle in Israel. First conceived during the Babylonian Exile, pre-Zionist *Aliyah* signaled a small-scale return of Diaspora Jews to Palestine. The Zionists promoted the concept during the Russian pogroms of 1881-1882 to shelter Jews suffering Czarist persecution. Later, the State of Israel, founded in 1948 after the Holocaust, institutionalized *Aliyah* into law.

"Enough!" Ephraim snorted. "His project?"

"For one, he's in charge of some student fellowship program; I forget the name."

"Greenberg, you're wasting my time." He began nervously tapping his forefinger on the table.

"His work? I don't know. From what I could make out, it's genetics, DNA, all sorts of medical-oriented things. Nothing of military value."

"Why did Am Ha-b'rit fake Professor Solomon's suicide? What are they trying to conceal, or protect?" He stared at me hard.

"I'll try to find out," I said, unable to stand up to the pressure.

"And his wife? She must know he's alive. I thought you were just 'The Beard.'"

"They're separated," I replied. "Look, Ephraim, Miriam's son is dying. Let me go be with her. I've finished my buying jaunts for this trip; I assure you."

"I'll bet you have," he said sarcastically.

"Let me go and stay at the university with Miriam; then I'll go home. Please."

I held my breath as Shin Bet's Ephraim Ben-Hershel thought long and hard, critically studying my face. Finally, he reached into his pocket and handed me an Israeli-made cell phone. "This is not to help you change a flat. But if a real event or emergency occurs, or if you learn something significant, you press that button. You call me first, Greenberg, even before you call Detective Landau. You understand?"

"Yes, I promise. Thank you, Ephraim. Thank you." I was so relieved, I practically hugged him.

"By the way, where did you get the cell you're carrying?"

"Bear gave it to me to summon him."

Ephraim half-laughed at me. "Mr. Bear gave it to you? Don't you think you had better call Dov on the cell I gave you? Using Mr. Brukowski's cell does not seem the best idea." I had never considered that the cell might have a tracking device, nor that Bear could monitor my calls.

"Are there secrets between friends?" I asked self-mockingly, realizing what a fool I'd been. The bourbon, which I had no tolerance for, and the extreme trauma had had a strong effect upon me.

Without further word, Ephraim Ben-Hershel rose abruptly and, stepping briskly, left me to nurse my second drink. And my third. I tried to rise to my feet, but I was too *stickered*, on the edge of puking, and I fell back into the chair, my head a great weight.

When Bear came to get me, I slipped what remained of the bottle into my jacket, a fair exchange for the one I'd donated to Daddy Markowitz on the night my old friend had confronted me at gunpoint.

CHAPTER FIFTEEN
REVELATION

Bear and I were back on the highway, driving fast in solemn silence through the dark desert night. It was cold, the air dry; the Susita's heat was on with the windows only cracked. Bear had to drive, as I was drunk, one bourbon, much less three or more, being a major binge for me. I watched the highway ahead pass, merely a hypnotic ribbon of concrete in the headlights, the desert scrub and a scattering of buildings on either side the only break in the monotony. I nursed a cold cup of coffee given to me by the police support unit at the Dead Sea crime scene, attempting to clear my head, fighting to stay awake.

"Don't worry," Bear said in his calm voice. "I'll be beside you to protect you."

"I know you will," I replied, keeping all sarcasm from my voice. Out here, Bear could have done me in and made up a story about my disappearance, but the alcohol had made me foolishly trusting. "Don't get me wrong, Bear," I ventured. "But there's something personal I'd like to ask you."

"Shoot, David," he said in his soft voice, his hands on the wheel, eyes on the road.

"Someone told me..." I said hesitatingly, "told me you were once part of a White Power movement. Could that possibly be true?"

His face grew grim. I'd hit a nerve. Having said this, I was now embarrassed for him and scared for myself.

"If I tell you this, David," he said, "you've got to keep it to yourself. Word gets out, it would ruin my life. It would destroy my ministry."

I steeled myself for his answer. I had a growing affection for the man. We related to each other like best buddies, nearly brothers. And who wouldn't want Bear for a friend, even if he hadn't been a famous athlete? Strong, kindly, intelligent. We'd had fun together the last few days. Great conversations about NFL locker rooms, even Blues hockey and Cardinals baseball, of which we were both big fans. Plus, his fast actions outside the Jerusalem police station had endeared him to me—unless they'd been staged, that is.

"Bear, you saved my life. I would never do anything to hurt you. I promise, never a word to anyone. I just want to know."

He paused, his jaw clinching, and I could see his mind working. The car slowed by five kilometers, his concentration elsewhere. He gathered his thoughts. "I've told you I had a troubled youth until the reverend rescued me, right?"

"Sure, yeah."

"You know how things can get when you're young? I was angry at the world, filled with hate."

"It happens," I said. "We all go through some craziness when we're growing up."

"See, David, my mother died when I was in third grade," he said biting his lip, still clearly affected by the tragedy. "Dad remarried, but my stepmother was nuts. I figure she was a low-grade paranoid and not too bright either. But she was a slut, just my dad's type. Her relatives were all crooks, a bunch of money-grubbing slime balls always just a step ahead of the law."

"She was a paranoid schizophrenic, clinical?" I asked.

"Probably. Sometimes she imagined wild things, like I was out to get her. She even called the cops on me a few times. Crazy stuff. In thirty years, I never saw her laugh, not once."

"So why did your dad...?"

"She was the kind of woman he wanted; he wasn't good at relationships."

"He isn't the only man like that," I said.

"Anyway, in high school I began running with a pretty rough crowd of bikers; some were skinheads. We were into drugs, motorcycles, all kinds of things. Macho stuff. I dropped out of high school for a while. Our club was into the White Power movement. We beat up some Jews, some blacks, damaged a synagogue. I spent time in jail."

"And this was because...?"

"David, my mother committed suicide. She was so lonely, so unhappy with my dad. He was seldom there for her. She drank a lot, every day. Naturally, I blamed her problems on my father. He was harsh, distant, a real asshole. He was that way with me, too. Anyway, I turned my anger inward and became suspicious about everyone, especially minorities. See?"

"I'm sorry, Bear," I said.

He grew quiet, as did I, leaving him to his thoughts.

"So why hasn't the press picked up on any of this?" I asked. "You know they would expose their own mother's dirty undies for ratings. Or some fan could have Googled you, and that stuff would have surely turned up."

"After I was born again, I changed my name, changed schools, took up football, and hit the books. Brukowski is my mother's maiden name, David. The hate-filled fanatic I had been disappeared for good."

I had pried enough. We drove in silence for an hour. When we stopped for gas, I sensed resuming the conversation was okay, some convivial small talk to relieve the tension we both had felt since Bear filled me in on his sordid past.

A couple of large coffees in the cup holders and a full tank later, we were back on the road, chatting easily, though not about football or racist rants. On newscasts back home, I'd seen Bear hugging many black football players through his ministry, and from our short time together, I felt comfortable that he no longer harbored anti-Semitic, racist attitudes. Heck, if God can forgive, surely a trader in old artifacts can do the same.

"Hey, Bear," I said seriously, "this road trip has given me a lot of time to think—way too much time. I want to get back home as soon as possible. To St. Louis. I've got to be in Israel for Miriam right now, with her son so ill. But whether I attend his funeral or he recovers..."

"Whatever you want to do, David," he replied reassuringly. "I'm just the bodyguard," he added mockingly, putting on a self-depreciating, goofy expression. We both laughed at his characterization of his role in our ill-cast partnership.

"The reverend could have found me a junk consultant who was a few pounds lighter," I bantered, laughing. "Keeping you fed is a major expense."

"Yeah, well, my charge didn't have to be such a *schmuck* either," he shot back.

"How much notice would you need to get the plane ready to take us back?" I asked.

"We'll have to fly commercial, on the reverend's ticket, of course. He's already taken the ministry plane back to St. Louis."

This statement slapped me awake. I was exhausted, mentally and emotionally burned out, and still semi-drunk, which made me suspicious of everyone and everything. Now the original one of my three so-called "suspects" in Moise Shankman's murder was the first to have been flushed from Israel. Reverend Nation had preceded both Weiner and Shadid back to where I strongly believed the nail still remained hidden, in St. Louis. Did this eliminate the person who incited the campus attack, Shadid? And the person who might have slaughtered poor Chick Weiner? It all seemed to be pushing me.

I sat quietly, slumped in my seat, watching Bear guide us through the blackness, seeing Reverend Nation in a whole new light. Were the stories of his Blood Diamond smuggling true? And, if true, what did that say about the good reverend? Why did he return to St. Louis so soon? At my first opportunity, I planned to go online to see what revivals or other appearances Nation was scheduled to make in the states.

My suspicions were growing by the minute, and we still had an hour or more to drive. I now viewed my friend Bear, the "former" White Power advocate, differently, too. Bear was the reverend's man—devoted, obedient, one hundred percent loyal. The fact was, he was acting as my bodyguard on Nation's instructions, which placed him in perfect position to spy on me. Suddenly our friendship seemed a bit less cozy, not so benign; in fact, it felt suffocating. Plus, Bear had the strength to kill me with his bare hands, and we were out in the middle of the desert, no less. I began to wonder if his conversion to Christian dogma was genuine or just a ruse to get ahead in life. Or was he simply a pawn in Hubris Nation's game? On the trip over, I had sensed Bear had Nation's complete confidence. Why not? Bear boosted the TV ratings. Now I wondered how much autonomy the reverend had entrusted to him. How deeply were their interests linked, or how disparately did their interests diverge?

If Bear was hustling me, he had succeeded in spades, making me trust him. If he had a dossier on me, he could have made up a background for himself that paralleled mine. And what hustler worth his stripes wouldn't have taken advantage of that? He and the reverend could have gotten the information about my background easily and cheaply from either Finkel or from Daddy Markowitz. In fact, I remembered that Daddy had, indeed, been questioned—semi-tortured—seeking information about me, leading to my discussion with Daddy over his unregistered pistol. I had never seen Bear preach, but I'd seen his mentor and cohort, Nation, on television, "healing" the sick and performing the equivalent of reading the minds of sinners in the audience. Chicanery? Of course. In the troubled, paranoid state I found myself, I wouldn't have put anything past anyone, much less a former White Power advocate working for the man who'd kidnapped me.

I began to parse Bear's "confession." Why did he so willingly divulge the seamy side of his life to a relative stranger—revelations that could destroy his life and ministry? Unless, of course, his narrative was entirely a fiction and could be easily disproved. After glancing at the front page and international news each morning, I always read the sports page thoroughly, so I'd read everything written about Bear since he turned pro. He had, indeed, only taken up football as a senior in high school. *That fit.* Then he'd been on USC's bench for two years developing, and was elected all-conference offensive tackle in his senior year. Drafted by the Rams in the fifth or sixth round, I couldn't remember which, he had won the starter job in his rookie year, aided by an injury-depleted line, and he went on from there. And, yes, he had been a spokesman for the Association of Faithful Athletes. *So far, it fit the facts.*

Then I examined his tale about his upbringing, especially as it paralleled my own. This, above all, had weaseled its way into my psyche, completely gaining my empathy. My parents had been divorced, and I, too, had been raised by an unstable stepmother. *Check.* And hadn't I lost my mother when I was in the third grade? But she didn't commit suicide; she'd died of cancer. *Check.* Like Bear's dad, my father was distant and high-strung, with a volatile temper. *Check again.* Add to that, in my youth I'd been in revolt against my father, a strong patriarchal figure. *Check a fourth time.* I already had plans to Google two items when I returned to Miriam's, and I now added Bear's formative years to that list. Further, since I'd be using Miriam's passwords—perhaps even Solly's—I hoped to expand my investigations more deeply into Am Ha-b'rit's electronic archives. No telling what I might find.

I pulled the bourbon from my pocket and gulped swigs directly from the bottle. The warm brown liquid burned my throat and unsettled my stomach when it landed in a fiery ball, but I gained tolerance. The wheels of the Susita humming under me, I just kept drinking until grasping the bottle proved difficult. Then I tossed the rest out the window, littering the Holy Land.

I was so distraught by the fatal events of the long day, I was losing it. In my twisted state, a Muslim, Shadid; a Jew, Weiner and maybe Solly; and two Christians, Nation and Bear, were out to get me. Talk about the world being against you! I needed to find some remote desert island to recover my lost peace of mind.

"An imam, a rabbi, and a preacher walk into a bar after a long trek through the desert," I began to babble. Amazed that I had blurted such a thing to Bear, my speech slurred as my soliloquy progressed. "The imam ordered a glass of orange juice, the rabbi a glass of Mogen David, and the preacher a bottle of Lone Star beer. The three were famished, so the imam ordered Lebanese-shank Greenberg; the rabbi, Greenberg brisket; and the preacher, thick slices of barbequed Greenberg ham. How they'd managed to divide my carcass without starting a religious war, I don't know."

The whole notion struck me as ironic, then foolish, then silly. I started giggling like a madman and couldn't stop. Then tears came to my eyes, as much as I fought to repress them. Laughter and tears, two sides of the same counterfeit coin. I was truly in a bad way.

"We'll get you home to bed, David," Bear said reassuringly, giving my sanity the benefit of the doubt—a doubt that was substantial.

Hypnotized by the road, the headlights approaching and whirling past through the darkness, and the car's movement, wild conjectures and fears ran through my distorted and failing consciousness. Then the god Hypnos was merciful. At some point before we reached Tel Aviv, I must have dozed, slipping into a disturbed slumber, the seat belt holding me slumped in place.

***

I was jostled awake by the sound of my seatbelt unclicking, then being slung over Bear's shoulder, and carried from the Susita. Through the fog of sleep and the residue of drunkenness, I panicked, sure that I was being taken to my death. I didn't know where I was—only aware of Bear's heavy tread on gravel under my weight.

Bear paused, knocked on a door, waited, then knocked again. My mind raced to the notion of escaping his grasp, to suddenly leaping from him and running. I also knew I wasn't strong enough to break loose from his iron grip—knew I could never outrun the All-Pro lineman. I had visions of him running me down within a few yards, of his enormous bulk leaping onto me, of crashing down hard on me like he'd smash a defensive back returning an interception.

Then I heard Miriam's sleepy voice. Bear identified himself and told Miriam he had me. I didn't know if I was dreaming the conversation or not. She opened the door, and Bear asked where he could put me.

"In the bedroom," Miriam said. "This way."

CHAPTER SIXTEEN
THIS SIDE OF JORDAN

Bear laid me on Miriam's queen-sized bed, then removed my shoes as the two of them spoke to each other in whispers. I went limp. Bear lifted me onto one side of the bed and slipped a pillow under my head, then covered me with a sheet and blanket as skilled as any trained nurse. The two of them spoke briefly; then Bear's heavy footsteps left the room.

I felt the bed sag as Miriam sat beside me, speaking soothing words, brushing my brow gently. She asked if I needed anything, and I emitted a negative grunt. Then, removing her robe, exposing a silky gown, she walked around the bed and climbed under the covers beside me, pressing close with her body, sliding her arm over me. I could smell her musk and shampoo, her warm breath. She kissed me deeply on the lips.

I was finally, after twenty years, in bed with Miriam. On our earlier call, I'd told her of the attack at the university, and I'm sure Bear filled her in on poor Chick's grizzly murder—on how badly I'd taken it and all the bourbon I'd consumed. The sympathetic manner in which she laid her soft cheek on my shoulder, the way she tenderly stroked my face, suggested to me that perhaps she was open to more than a sympathetic cuddle—that I could have everything I wanted, everything I needed. But I was stinking loaded, stewed, immobile. The gods were undoubtedly rolling in mirth, pointing fingers at my helplessly prone human form, tears of hilarity running down their cheeks and soaking their tunics.

In college, I'd played the clownish inebriated porter in Shakespeare's "Macbeth" who answers the door after King Duncan's murder. I took the part to be near the superbly constructed, raven-haired Selena Simons who played Lady Macbeth. A big mistake! Boy, did she plunge daggers into my heart.

Without knowing why, all warm and comfortable upon Miriam's mattress, I began to slur and mumble my lines from the play:

"*Lechery, sir, drinking provokes, and unprovokes,*" I rambled, "*it provokes the desire, but it takes away the performance. Therefore, much drink may be said to be an equivocator with lechery: it makes him, and it mars him...*"

We poor players enact the role handed to us by The Author. I felt Miriam's soft fingertips sweep across my lips, and in obedience to them, I fell silent. Soon thereafter, I conjecture, I fell to ignominious snoring and wheezing. *Curse you perverse immortals! Curse all of you! Especially, curse Bacchus...*

***

I stumbled through the desolate desert, unable to decide which way to go, unable to recall where I had come from, unsure of where I was headed. I was terrified. I did not recognize anything around me; not the unnatural alien scrub and cacti; not the painted hills and rocks; not the distant cloud-shrouded mountains. All I wanted to do was go home...to go home.

I looked up at the sky to discover it had suddenly grown quite dark, far darker than this early stage of dusk would warrant. Something was terribly wrong. A black foreboding shadow fell over the whole world, and I was desperate to find shelter, any shelter. It was a sky unlike I'd ever seen. But it wasn't just the pitch that frightened me. The whole atmosphere was unevenly dark as if the sky had been hung with a threadbare sheet, with muted patches of pink and red and orange visible through uneven swatches. I saw that the effect was caused by a massive cloud of moth wings, billions and billions of them, its surface uneven as each hovered on its own course. I hurried on, stepping up my pace. I must get home quickly. Since I had never seen such a thing, I had no idea what had caused it, nor what it meant. But I was sure it portended a great upheaval upon the Earth.

I looked down at my painful feet, which were now sandal-clad, bruised, and cut. Stumbling forward, I saw that I was trudging on a rough carpet of broken brick. The ground was painted in a familiar regular pattern, with a white stripe every yard I trekked, a long, extended line every fifth yard. When I raised my eyes, I realized I was on an extended football field covered with litter, more than a hundred yards long, with a goal post visible on the distant horizon. Out of the corner of my eye, I detected a football about to fly past me. Having been a defensive back in pickup touch football, I instinctively leaped for the ball, intercepted it at its zenith, pulled it in, and fell with it cradled to my chest. I rolled, snapping to my feet with my prize, and, like any good defensive back, headed toward the goal post, toward the dark swarm of moths, heedless of their threat.

Running, running, I looked toward the end zone to set my bearings. There, floating a foot above the turf, stood a peaceful Jesus, his tanned face beatific, benevolent, with dark full beard, shining black eyes, and a strong, prominent nose. He had something cupped in His hands like an offering. I focused to see what the object was, but it was obscured by a glow. Then I could make the image out: a nail, resting in his cupped hands on a bed of light.

I tucked the ball under my arm and raced for the end zone, heading for daylight, feeling the thrill of a boy returning an interception, having turned the field to chaos by smashing the order of a planned play. But walls of opponents were closing in on me. Men in robes, turbans, yarmulkes, cowboy hats, wide-brimmed black hats, all manner of dress and headgear were charging toward me, cutting me off. I stutter-stepped and zigged left toward the sideline, but they pivoted toward my path, narrowing the gap. A man wielding a scimitar ran to slice me in half. All at once, the man went flying as Bear crashed into his midsection, opening a gap in the pursuit. I jog-stepped and zagged right, accelerating through the hole.

Then I was slogging through deep, soft sand, my feet churning as if my ankles were weighted, making no progress as men in costumes closed in on me. I ran, ran, ran, but I wasn't moving forward. Bear crashed through once more, driving two cowpokes with blue stars on their Western shirts into the sand with his shoulder, saving me from being hit on a high-low by the pair. But nothing could stop the onslaught. I was swarmed, suffocating, being crushed by a wall of bodies.

"Bear...!" I cried aloud, turning and tossing, flailing my arms about, unable to break free from the tangle of blankets and sheets.

***

I awoke bathed in sweat, my head weighing a ton. From half-closed eyes, I watched Miriam slip off her nightgown and hurriedly begin to dress, a sense of urgency in her every movement. At some point, I mumbled to make her aware I was conscious.

"You were having a bad dream," she said, fastening her bra. Then she stepped into the skirt of a dark suit laid out on the chair. When my eyes cleared, I saw in her face that she was despairing. I rose, sat on the bedside, and stretched.

"The shower's in there," she indicated, and strode business-like from the room.

I dragged myself to the bathroom. Perhaps running hot water onto my neck would take away the pain I felt, from the liquor, from the tortured sleep, from the long drive…from the horrors I'd witnessed.

After my shower, I made my way into her cramped kitchen, wearing one of Solly's old robes. The smell of brewed coffee reminded me of how long it had been since I'd eaten. My stomach cried out from a deep well, demanding attention. Standing at the sink, Miriam downed the last of a cup of coffee, then put on the suit jacket matching her skirt, making to leave.

"I've got to get to the hospital," she told me, stressing each word. "Help yourself to whatever's in the fridge. My friend brought me food."

"What happened, Miriam? What's the matter?"

"The hospital called again," she replied, suddenly sobbing. "When you were in the shower. Ari's taken a turn for the worse. I've got to be at his bedside—to be with him when he...I've got to get there before he..."

So the boy was destined to die that morning. "I'm so sorry, Miriam."

"I've got to go," she said, stopping at the kitchen door.

"Do you want me along?" I followed her into the living room.

I held my breath as she thought this over for a moment, composing herself. "Perhaps you'd better not," she said uncertainly.

I settled wearily into the nearest chair. It was certainly the worst possible time for me to be a complication for her. I wasn't a member of the Society; plus, it was likely Solly would be there.

"I'm being picked up shortly," she said, anxiously checking her watch.

"Listen, Miriam, I need to use Solly's computer to get online while you're gone. I think it might help me find out who killed Chick. It might even save our lives." It was hard to say, but I had to make progress to retain my sanity.

"The computer's in there," she said offhandedly, pointing toward a door to a side room, probably his home office. "I'll write the passwords down. Burn them when you're done." She scribbled them out and handed them to me. Then there was a knock at the door. She kissed me lightly on the cheek and went to greet her escort.

As she pulled open the door, the very man with the suntanned face and long, brown curly hair whom I'd seen Miriam trade knowing glances with when we'd arrived at the hospital to see Ari entered. The same guy. I knew my reaction to seeing him was guarded, emotional, but it momentarily struck me that I wasn't even the Number One "Beard" anymore—to a married woman no less. I was merely one of Fates' damn pawns—not even a rook or a knight or a bishop—just a too-far-advanced pawn waiting to be sacrificed *en passant*.

After they left, I cleared my head. I needed to absorb the loss of Tzivia and Chick, and the adjustment of my worldview by the nature of their terrible demise…and I needed to call Detective Landau in Jerusalem for an update. I was anxious to use Solly's computer. I needed it to check Reverend Nation's appearance schedule back in the states and to Google Bear's links to the White Power movement. More importantly, posing as Professor Solomon with Solly's passwords, I hoped to penetrate the clone program's inner sanctum. Since Weiner was a lifelong member of Am Ha-b'rit, I also could search his entire history. Wanting to know the man's nature was eating at me like a starving parasite. No telling what I might find.

I did feel some relief knowing Bear had driven the Susita to his hotel the previous night. If Weiner was still tracking me by GPS, he would believe I was still in Netanya. I'd be safe, truly under wraps, in hiding. For the moment, I had a chance to investigate numerous, important avenues, unimpeded by fear or paranoia. Only Bear and Miriam knew where I was, and both knew I didn't have the nail.

I heard the front door close and, sipping coffee and nibbling *bageleh*, my mind drifted to poor Ari. I had met him only briefly, but in those potent moments, I had sensed something special in him, which had had a profound effect upon me. I couldn't imagine what those who had known him and loved him his whole life were feeling.

I also could see why the few who knew Ari's precursor so mourned his death that, from a tiny corner of a small ancient nation, the echoes of that tragedy and its implications still reverberate across the globe. I almost envied those who could believe something transformative like that, a God breathing life into his only begotten son. But who was I to judge?

Now alone, I went into the bedroom and located the phone that Shin Bet had given me, making sure I didn't accidently call Detective Landau from Bear's cell. Who knew if Bear or the good reverend could monitor my calls? Then I went outside to the far corner of the back yard to make the call to Jerusalem. Dov picked up right away, and we exchanged perfunctory greetings.

"I have some terrible news, David, but not unexpected, I assume," Dov said. "Levi Asher is dead." The detective had been as kind as possible—ripped the Band-Aid off quickly.

My hands started shaking so badly, I had to set my coffee down on the table and fall into a chair. "I guess I knew it all along, but I was in denial. Poor Levi. How did...? How did he...?"

"They found him in St. Louis. He'd been tortured."

Did whoever was after the nail already have it? If so, all the subsequent deaths were in vain. "Oh, no. So...?" I said before I could stop myself from prompting him.

"His body was found curled up on a concrete floor in an abandoned warehouse just outside of St. Louis, his face bloody, contorted in pain. The crime scene photos are a terrible thing to see."

I was shaken-up, not thinking clearly at all, but I had to know if the nail was already lost, so I wouldn't be chasing a phantom. "Dov, what...what was the death blow?" I had to ask.

"No specific death blow," Dov replied. "Under torture, they can die prematurely. The police are sending the body to the coroner's office to determine cause of death."

So maybe Miriam was right about Levi's fortitude. Maybe his heart gave out before he revealed the nail's location. Levi's killer, or killers, probably didn't know about his heart condition. The cause of death would tell me whether Levi's murderer had the nail, or if I still held the key to its location—in St. Louis.

"One question, Dov. Levi carried a lucky chess piece, a knight's head, black, missing one ear. Was that in his pocket?"

"Nothing like that on the list they sent me. I'll check into it."

"Any word on the attack at the university? On Edan Shadid?"

"Shin Bet has good reason to believe the attackers were from Shadid's faction. I can't tell you how they know."

"I don't want to know; that's Shin Bet's business."

"There is word out to arrest Shadid. But with so much turmoil because of these latest killings, north and south, with the threat of revenge and counter-revenge seething across Israel, our resources are stretched to the limit. Besides, Shadid has the ability to make himself quite scarce in the

West Bank. I wouldn't count on apprehending him anytime soon."

"Did anyone see Weiner on the road to Ein Bokek yesterday? Bear and I were stopped at checkpoints going both ways because of the university attack. Surely, he had to have shown himself at some point."

"I will check to see if any sightings were reported. But with units moving around, reserves being called up, any sighting would be difficult, if not impossible, to confirm."

"What about the logs for security vehicles at the university? We could find the car, find who signed for it, check the mileage."

"I'll consider having someone check the logs when I can free up an agent. But a man like Weiner would have planned for that in advance. I don't think it's a promising avenue of inquiry."

There you had it. Two potential killers of innocent young people, two men I'd shoot in cold blood myself if I was sure they were responsible, and we couldn't touch either one. It made you wonder about justice in the world.

"One last thing, Dov," I said. "The owner of an antiquities shop in St. Louis, a friend of mine, was murdered a few days before the Levi Asher disappearance."

"I've known about that since shortly after our first conversation here," he said arrogantly. "I called St. Louis and learned of that murder and assumed it was related *to you*. Not that a murdered antiquities dealer matters much to me," Dov huffed sarcastically. "Look, foolish man, whatever you're into, shouldn't you drop out before you wind up like Asher or Markowitz, or your friend Shankman? Do you need the money that badly?"

"I've never been that interested in money, *per se*, Dov. This isn't about that. I could probably make as much trading stocks as I do dealing in antiquities. Anyway, I'd like to know what the police in St. Louis have on the Shankman case."

"Nothing. St. Louis knows nothing. Listen, Greenberg, I've got a special slab reserved for you in the morgue here while you're staying in Israel."

"Do you have the Shankman police file?" I asked.

"Check your phone."

The file appeared on my cell. As I perused the documents, my eyes froze on the photo of the crime scene with Moise lying in a pool of blood.

"There's some sort of electronic equipment on the shelf behind him," I observed. "I don't suppose they had those in ancient Ur."

"The police checked that out already. Some sort of genetic comparison gizmo, like they use to check for paternity cases."

"It looks pretty advanced for a simple paternity test," I said, trying to make out the details as best I could.

"That's true. At eighty, Mr. Shankman probably didn't have many concerns personally with paternity. An odd mix of past and present, ancient and modern, I'd say."

Just like the entire *situation in which I find myself.*

"One last thing," Landau said gravely, lowering his voice. "A man's body was found this morning not too far south of Netanya. His throat was slashed. The individual had recently been treated for a bullet wound in the bicep; it was a fresh wound. Unfortunately, we don't have a slug to match against your pistol—your *illegal* pistol."

"Who was he?"

"A small-time thug named Sarnoff," Landau stated matter-of-factly. "Nevertheless, he does serve a number of large-scale smugglers here in Jerusalem who deal in everything from illegal drugs to the black market, to antiquities and raw diamonds."

"Do you think this man, this Sarnoff, may have murdered Chick Markowitz?"

"Sarnoff had blood on his clothing that may not have been a result of his own wounds, especially on his shoes. It is likely the blood on his shoes wouldn't have been his because of the angle at which he fell. Also, the police believe some of the bloodstains dried earlier in the day. The lab's going to try to match the samples against Mr. Markowitz's. If I was a betting man, I'd wager that they match."

"So it could be," I conjectured, "whoever hired this man Sarnoff to shoot me—or to shoot at me but not hit me, as the case might be—and to murder my friend, also killed Sarnoff to cover his tracks. Is that what you're suggesting?"

"What do *you* think? The police are looking into who might have had recent contacts with the late Mr. Sarnoff. If Mr. Brukowski is among them, we will bring him in for questioning."

There was a pregnant pause while he let that sink in.

I wished Dov well and ended the call, anxious to get to Solly's computer while I still had the chance. I took a deep breath of clear morning air, bracing myself for my next steps. There was much I had to know, just had to, about Reverend Hubris Nation, Bear Brukowski, the clone program, and Jarad Weiner. With Solly's passwords in hand, I wanted to know, and I wanted to know *now*.

CHAPTER SEVENTEEN
CAIN AND ABEL

The first thing I Googled was Reverend Nation. He had been the first to break from Israel to return to St. Louis. Regardless of my gut feelings—that the guy couldn't be behind the Moise Shankman or Levi Asher murders—his own actions had made him the Number One suspect. One strike against him: he could have shot his TV sermons in Israel; his backdrop sets were canned. His writers and producers had followed us to Israel on commercial aircraft, so he had everything he needed when he arrived in Jerusalem. To paraphrase what he himself had pronounced, "the Beast will achieve power by convincing the world he is the 'good guy.'" And nobody's much more of a good guy than the reverend, except for his having kidnapped me, blackmailed me, and stuck me with a bodyguard to track my every move.

Bear? Another seemingly "good guy." Oy.

The good reverend was suddenly trending big on the net and subsequently on the news. A photo of him shot from a distance, *sans* hairpiece, was appearing on web sites throughout known civilization. His people had denied that the fuzzy, distant photo was the reverend, but they later retracted their denial. Having seen him up close in his baldpate state, I could certainly confirm that the images on the screen were, indeed, Reverend Nation. I felt a bit bad for old Hubris. Here he'd dedicated his sober life to bringing Jesus into the hearts of the masses and preparing America for the End of Days, and all anyone wanted to do was sneer at his hair loss.

Ain't America a great country?

Taking advantage of the reverend's current notoriety, an industrious journalist had recently blogged about an investigation into his purported

Blood Diamond connections—guns for diamonds—to the Lord's Resistance Army in Central Africa, a terrorist organization responsible for crimes against humanity. In response, or cashing in, the blogosphere was going wild with speculation and commentary on this purported offense. I speed-read the original story and found myself more than half-convinced, but there were some highly tenuous major points that definitely required more proof. Besides, allowing for some latitude, would Reverend Nation be party to all the details of his far-reaching empire? Even if the stories are true, unbeknownst to the reverend, a subordinate could be behind the illicit trade.

Dismissing the bloggers' guesswork, I searched further until I found the link for the reverend's latest telecast. But within seconds, it was obvious the episode had been in the can before his meeting with Ari. Not only was his wig in place, but he was wearing the Rolex and Super Bowl-like ruby ring that he'd used to tip the hotel's servers. The sermon was based on the Amos quote from the Bible, "The Lord roars from Zion," and the Lord was certainly roaring these days, with political turmoil, revenge plots, demonstrations, Knesset speeches, PM Cabinet shuffles, any number of denunciations of Israel from Iran, and the spectrum of *jihadi* terrorists, even from the normally restrained monarchs of so-called moderate U.S. allies. Once the reverend began his sermon, it was hard to stop watching it, but I felt pressed for time and had immediate issues to investigate. No doubt, though, Reverend Hubris Nation is inspired.

Could anyone be devious enough to combine religious fervor and outright murder? Silly question. Fanatics have been killing in the name of their True Beliefs for forever. Yet, I had great difficulty attributing such duplicity to the reverend I knew. My gut rebelled at the thought. He was just so damn likeable once you got to know him.

I finally cut my way through the wig controversy and the Blood Diamond screeds and found Reverend Nation's speaking schedule. He didn't have any appearances planned for another three weeks. This I couldn't ignore. What was his rush to return to St. Louis?

While scrolling through the reverend's site, I did a hasty bit of surfing. Naturally, I was curious about his African operations. *Interesting. Who besides the reverend was the public face of his overseas ministry?* Naturally, the heroic face with the windblown blonde hair most recognizable around the world: God's Left Tackle. There was nothing about the Hallelujah Hour Ministry management structure on the site, but Bear was prominently featured on every page. He had taken several trips to Central Africa. Photos and video were plentiful of Bear visiting orphanages, saving souls, posing with villagers.

But I was getting sidetracked.

Next, I went after Bear's claims about his wayward White Power youth, but I was stymied from the start. Any juvenile offenses would be untouchable under rules of the court. Then I remembered, Bear claimed he had committed his anti-Semitic acts under another last name—that he had changed his name to Brukowski after he'd reformed—and I didn't know that prior name. I even found an article on his high school gridiron feats—which mentioned that he had been a transfer student—but nothing on where he'd come from.

Then I went after White Power articles from the period and location Bear's tale had inferred. Articles with grainy newspaper pictures or no pictures at all. Without knowing Bear's father's name, nothing but dead ends. For that matter, with Bear being such a valuable asset on the preacher circuit, the reverend would have cleansed any reference that would mar his popularity. My only chance to learn more was to query my original source, Jarad Weiner, and I had no stomach for that. Fortunately, Shin Bet had confiscated my pistol or, having seen Chick lying under two tarps five feet apart, no telling what trouble I would have gotten myself into. I considered asking for help, but the Jerusalem police and Shin Bet were busy at the moment. And in any case, I was hoping to remain beneath their radar.

In my search concerning Bear on the computer, I located minor side stories that gave me pause. In the last few years, he had gone through bankruptcy several times: bad investments, real estate collapses, restaurant chain failures, taxes unpaid, as well as IRS agreement deadlines passed. The list went on. The man seemed in constant need of money. Maybe he listened to bad advisors or was fooled by shady business partners. It happens with celebrities, including sports heroes. An American Ulysses, constantly surrounded by lovely sounding siren songs, must pass through rugged shoals, and brave many storms. I felt bad for him. Having slipped on the muddy turf of high finance numerous times, bad knee and all, could he be trying to get away with holding penalties now and then? How many among us, accustomed to plentiful money, wouldn't resort to cheating when faced with imminent poverty? But would that trickery entail cutting off harmless African villagers at the knees? Arranging to have an artist murdered? Now that I thought of it, could it include having someone dressed as a *jihadi* take pot shots near us so that Bear could become my trusted savior? I mean, how did the man on the motorcycle using an automatic weapon miss us both?

I sighed deeply.

Enough procrastination. Time for Solly's T'chiat Ha-meitim cloning program, and more.

Solly's password took me through every gateway in the biochemistry files. I had to cut through mountains of scientific data, through files written in Hebrew—much of the material of no use to me. Under the "T'chiat Ha-meitim" file, I clicked into a folder with the now-familiar label "Bisl," which displayed a list of sub-folders by individual names: "Einstein, A."; "Newton, I."; "Currie, M."; a long list. I plunged right into the "Copernicus" file and opened the document. A list of names appeared, probably the Bisl students I'd seen while I was waiting to meet with Solly. According to the site's notes, one member of the Copernicus team had gained a staff job in Poland, Copernicus' home, and many had their own cryptic project titles. I clicked on other famous names to discover that members of those teams had gained security jobs connected to their favored targets and other professional posts positioning them to acquire samples of the great subjects' remains. I guessed they were waiting for a signal so they could all move at once, rather than striking piecemeal, which might set off alarms at the other targets.

Is this any of my business?

Bisl was, indeed, an international criminal enterprise, far greater than an internship program, but far less than political terrorism or a theft ring. Knowing Bisl's ultimate purpose, I was inclined to be sympathetic toward the students' efforts and wished I had had such an exciting project to spice up my grad school days. If any students were apprehended, I felt certain Am Ha-b'rit would flex its financial muscle to obtain good legal consul for them. If unable to get them off entirely, suspended sentences and deportation back to Israel wouldn't be a tragic outcome.

Then I uncovered it. Jarad Weiner was in charge of the Bisl areas of the T'chiat Ha-meitim program…and who knew what else. His place in the big picture was my next target. What I would find would transform my view of Am Ha-b'rit's ultimate aims, of the T'chiat Ha-meitim program, of everything.

I had been slumped over the computer for some time and rose to stretch my back and refill my coffee cup. Plus, I needed to clear my head and orient myself. The implications of Solly's program were enormous, and I hadn't come to grips with that. If genius was inheritable, and if the

T'chiat Ha-meitim program was a success—both *huge* ifs—Am Ha-b'rit would have, by geometric leaps, the greatest concentration of raw intelligence ever assembled in one place.

Sure, I'm proud to be a Jew, albeit not a particularly observant one, but elites? In his grad school days, Solly wrote copious articles that read like sci-fi on tinkering with human evolution and genius being inherited, crazy notions we vehemently debated late into smoke- and alcohol-fueled nights. Now I wondered if he'd really been serious? Was his mind still stuck in that mode? Indeed, was my friend nuts? I'd have to find out.

I have always been troubled by the notion of superiority of any sort. My thoughts drifted to Solly's fascination with Doctors Harpending, Hardy, and Cochran's 2005 evolution-based theory about Jewish intelligence, which had gained some notoriety, a theory I take with a grain of salt, and which Solly concluded was bad genetics and bad epidemiology. It went something like this: Historically, Jews weren't allowed to own land in Europe and had to find pursuits other than farming. As a result, to adapt, Jews developed an elevated average number of individuals in the higher intelligence categories than the European norm. In aristocratic Central and Eastern Europe, the Ashkenazi Jews, restricted to entrepreneurial and managerial roles, became tax farmers and estate managers for the local nobility, and made ends meet working in the professions and trades.

As Europe developed a mercantile economy and cities began to flourish, the permitted Jewish occupations mutated into banking, finance, outright moneylending—a profession prohibited to medieval Christians—the law, medicine, and all livelihoods requiring advanced mathematical, scientific, and intellectual skills.

Part of the evidence given for this notion was the fact that Jews comprise only one-quarter of one percent of the world's population. Regardless, Jews have won a quarter of the world's Nobel Prizes. I can attest though, having lived around Jews all my life, like any arbitrary classification of people, most are average, with a fair share of dumb-as-a-post blockheads.

Yes, like Uncle Jake, who couldn't operate a cell phone if you sent him to M.I.T.

An alternative explanation is that exceptional Jewish achievement is due to cultural influences. Yes, as a people, Jews typically prize education and learning. But other groups develop that imperative as their economic

147

conditions improve, too. What holds some pockets of people back is basically as Lincoln described his childhood: "The short and simple annals of the poor." Point of fact, I have known people of all faiths and races whom I would consider geniuses, whatever their financial success, whose intelligence and insights I bow to.

Breeding, environment—nature-nurture—I just refuse to buy it. The whole exclusionary ideal has done the "Chosen People" immeasurable harm through no fault of their own. Naturally, the noble's tax collector and estate manager—definably different Jews, who probably lived comparatively well—would be resented, even hated by the local peasants and serfs, a volatile situation. As a result: violence, pogroms, eventually extermination. No wonder the Jews always want peace.

I went back to Solly's computer and scanned the other files, trying to learn about Jarad Weiner. One file was titled "Resurrection," the English word for T'chiat Ha-meitim, so I clicked in. There was Weiner's name. I clicked it, and a request for a password popped up. I entered Solly's password again, but the attempt failed. I tried again, assuming I fat-fingered the keyboard, but another failure. I had one last attempt before I was locked out.

My thoughts went back to Solly's college days. What password would he use when he first came over? I decided his password would be linked to DNA, Solly's favorite subject. And who discovered DNA? As with my Bobby Fischer obsession, Solly had pictures of Watson and Crick, the men who had identified the double helix, on his wall, like one might hang a favorite pitcher or star quarterback. I entered "watsoncrick" and I was in!

I soon discovered the "Resurrection" project had originated before Solly was even recruited, as evidenced by the date of the entries. I remember Solly telling me that his predecessor was British, one of the scientists gunned down by the demented old Rabbi Yourman, along with the other early pioneers of the program. Resurrection had been this Englishman's project, a predecessor of the current T'chiat Ha-meitim program. I clicked in, and there was a folder labeled "Weiner, J." and beside his name, "Shadid, E." My heart started racing.

There had, indeed, been early projects leading to Solly's son Ari. I skipped over reams of data on myriad animal clone experiments. Then I uncovered it: the first viable human clones were identical twins: Jarad Weiner and Edan Shadid. As a further test, approved by Am Ha-b'rit's leaders I assumed, a double-blind experiment had been instituted. Since the infants were identical, one had been placed with an Orthodox Jewish professor's family, the other with a West Bank Muslim professor's family. The idea was possibly to see how religious upbringing would differentiate the resultant "identical" men. Was it better for a child to grow up as a Jew than a Muslim? But no anecdotal double-blind test can ever be perfect. Haven't we seen twins, identical and fraternal, where one is a lazy thief and the other an industrious pillar of the community? Images of the paperwork tying these two to their adopted parents were in the file, too. Shin Bet had missed this connection, having taken place so long ago.

Whose DNA did the English researcher use to create this pair? I guessed that the original donor would surely have been someone living, vastly reducing the test's degree of difficulty. I further surmised that they would have used someone virtuous and extraordinary for so significant a test. The man would probably have been selected for intelligence and bravery, as an honor. Could the offspring of such a virtuous person become ruthless killers, torturers, and schemers? Had there been a problem with this early experiment because of the relatively primitive technology they used, as with Ari, whose limitations were merely physical? Could Weiner and/or Shadid have been created with some moral lack, some flaw? Or is there a potential flaw in each of us that only needs outside stressors to make us into evil creatures? As far as genes go, we're still babes in the woods.

I felt compelled to find out.

CHAPTER EIGHTEEN
SURROUNDED

My investigations were halted abruptly. The front door banged loudly, footsteps stomped to where I sat, and within moments, an angry-eyed Jarad Weiner, all in a huff, stood beside me. He knew where Solly kept his laptop. I frantically tried to close my tabs, but most were still open as he stood at my shoulder. I could see he had a pistol holster at his waist.

"What are you doing on Professor Solomon's computer?" Weiner growled.

"N-nothing," I replied, startled into near incoherence. "Surfing the net."

"You were not merely surfing the net."

"What do you mean breaking in here, Mr. Weiner?" I demanded, attempting to switch tracks.

"I am responsible for the Solomons' safety," he replied adamantly. "I come and go as necessary. Stick to the point. You have broken into sites where you don't belong."

So he knew. T'chiat Ha-meitim's security tracked which computers entered its databases, and Weiner knew Solly was living in his lab. I should have guessed.

"I'm sorry, Jarad. I didn't realize..."

"Sorry doesn't cut it, Mr. Greenberg. There is more at stake here than your curiosity."

"Listen, Jarad, you claimed that Bear Brukowski has an anti-Semitic background. How do you know that?" Hoping to change direction, but also following up on a possible suspect.

"Come with me. I'll show you his dossier."

"How did you get this dossier? Shin Bet?"

"That, too, is none of your business. Come, I'll show you." But I didn't want to leave with Weiner. Once I was in his hands, my fate was far from certain.

"I promised Mrs. Solomon I'd wait for her. I can't go."

"Listen, sir, I must get you away from here. To my great misfortune, I am responsible for your safety, as well, and you are drawing too much of the wrong kind of attention. Consider the incident in the university quadrangle yesterday. By now our Islamist friends must know Professor Solomon is alive, which we've spent the past two years trying to conceal."

"Conceal in what way?"

"We made elaborate preparations. Obituaries, press releases. We even staged a funeral for Professor Solomon. Now, because of you, it's all by the wayside, and both Solomons are at risk."

"How is that *my* fault?" I asked, exasperated.

"Grab your jacket."

"I can't leave until I speak with Miriam. Would you like coffee while we wait for her?" I shut down Solly's computer and spun my chair around to face him, presenting him with an immoveable object.

There was a long pause while he thought the situation over. "Sure, black."

I rose and headed to the kitchen, while he entered the sparely furnished living room and deposited his weight into a worn, cloth-covered armchair. I joined him shortly thereafter, carrying two mugs, and seated myself on the sofa facing him. His pinched expression was none- too-pleased, and he proceeded to nervously tug at his ear lobe, sipping. We stared at each other. His cold, hard, reptilian eyes barely blinked in their fury.

"Brukowski," I said firmly. "What can he do here in Israel? Does he have operations working for him off-the-books?"

"Of course. There is a missing suitcase full of euros to serve as resource," he said pointedly. "Besides, Reverend Nation has a large organization, worldwide. Mr. Brukowski has unquestionable discretion within that organization."

"How would you know that?" I sipped the now-growing-old coffee.

"Come with me, Mr. Greenberg. I'll show you the dossier," he replied, putting down the mug and placing his hand on his holster. Weiner's will was impenetrable. Standing up to his pressure was going to be a leaky boat to manage against gale-force winds.

"All right, but there is something that bothers me, Jarad. The attack at the campus yesterday, it didn't make sense. Why would that take place now? What intelligence could the *jihadis* possibly have, about my arrival or otherwise, to cause them to sacrifice two of their own for so hopeless an assault?"

Weiner thought his answer over carefully. "Almost three years ago, one of Professor Solomon's top assistants, a man named Mayer, was kidnapped by a radical *jihadi* movement indigenous to our area calling itself the Martyrs of the Holy."

"And this Martyrs of the Holy group is headed by a man named Shadid?"

Weiner's face turned to stone. His jaws locked, his eyes grew fierce, his voice grim. "Yes. Mayer was weak. Weak. He would sneak off to meet with his lover in an Arab village, a man, and the Martyrs grabbed him. They performed a ritual slaying of his Arab lover, slicing the man's throat like a sacrificial goat, and hauled Mayer off. I have little doubt that Mayer revealed the perimeters of the entire T'chiat Ha-meitim program to them. As I said, he was weak."

"So do the Martyrs know about the nail?"

"Very likely."

"And their interest in the matter?"

"Are you joking? The man they consider the Christian prophet being reborn? Jews effecting the Resurrection? If they can destroy the nail, the Martyrs can usurp their two enemies at one fell swoop. They will stop at nothing to get it. Nothing. Now, come with me; I'll show you the dossier on the Martyrs as well."

"Where do you plan to take me?"

"I have a safe house set up for you. You can stay there until you return to the states."

"Is Mayer still alive?"

"Shin Bet thinks he is, but no one can be sure. Come, we're wasting time. You mustn't be here when people return from the hospital. They will gather here, friends and families. Such a crowd will create too promising a target for the Martyrs to resist. It is my responsibility..."

"I know, but I'm sure you have taken adequate precautions. These Martyrs, what is their ideology?"

"Hatred, pure and simple. Hatred is running thick on the Arab street in many places, and all manner of false prophets and self-declared caliphs are taking full advantage of it. You know as well as I, people like these, they can't build a World Trade Center, they can't build a jet airplane, their shortcomings are legion, but 9/11 illustrated what their hatred can be directed to achieve."

"A fool with a gun—even a box cutter—can kill any number of wise men." An axiom that troubles me greatly. "Who is backing these Martyrs of the Holy, Jarad?"

"My opinion is they have backing tied to the Saudi security services, perhaps rogue elements in it, but not that far from the mainstream nonetheless. Saudi Arabia is crawling with fundamentalist Wahhabi factions, a quarter of their population, who believe even saying hello to a Christian or a Jew is a deadly sin, and the kingdom must tread lightly not to cross them. Project all the benevolence into the Saudis their oil can buy, neither of us, nor your friend Bear, would receive a warm welcome on a Riyadh street."

"So Shadid's people are Wahhabis?"

"Ha! Wahhabis, caliphates, medievalists, Sharia law! Hatred is his ideology, period. Shadid will promote anything that will add to his own power; his alliances are legion. Fortunately, his resources in men, money, and weapons are limited to what he can squeeze across Israel's borders and the human debris he can recruit locally. Otherwise, we'd be overrun with Uzbeks, Algerians, and who knows what else."

I had to get past my aversion to Weiner to obtain as much information as I could in order to convince him to open up to my questions. Perhaps he had murdered Levi Asher and Chick Markowitz himself, maybe he had someone kill them, or maybe he was just what he claimed to be, a tough, dedicated security agent, loyal to Solly and Am Ha-b'rit. Was I merely being paranoid? I had gone through his file. He had a pair of master's degrees, which meant he was bright. Certainly, he had proved cunning. I also had scanned his early life, which, being part of the Resurrection experiment, was closely documented. Trouble throughout his youth. In one instance, he had been caught torturing and killing farm animals on a nearby *kibbutz*. Am Ha-b'rit was forced to pay compensation. Boys like that can develop into abusive, even violent adults. But people can change, too, once they find their life's purpose. What had Weiner's purpose become?

I studied him, as he glared at me. *Can I possibly trust him enough to leave with him, destination unknown?*

"Wait! Wouldn't planning the campus attack have taken weeks, or several days at a minimum? My coming to the university yesterday was unannounced. The assault on the Life Sciences building couldn't possibly have anything to do with me."

If the attack at the quadrangle had been meant as a demonstration for me—a cold, calculated one, costing three lives—wouldn't it have required coordination between this Martyrs group and elements within Hadera University security? Was it possible Weiner and Shadid were coordinating their activities? Or was this a case of holding your friends close and holding your enemies closer? The Jerusalem police had been wrong about the pair's origins, believing they were from separate parents. Perhaps Detective Landau was wrong about their supposed enmity, too. My predicament was growing more frightening by the moment.

Then again, regardless of their origin story, could the supposed twins somehow be the same man?

"I assume you asked me about Shadid for a reason, having been in the Resurrection file?" he asked, glowering, embarrassed that I knew of his unnatural origins. "Yes, Shadid has gone bad, evil. How do you expect me to feel about the filthy *jihadi?*" His body jutted forward; his hands tightened into shaking fists, his teeth clenched in rage. "I wish I could get my bare hands on him."

Plenty of venom there, but is it genuine? Was blood thicker than nurture, thicker than religious ritual and dogma, thicker than parochial loyalties?

"Your father," I said, hoping to calm him, "your *biological* father must have been a great man to be so honored by Am Ha-b'rit."

"Yes," he replied, sinking back into his chair, becoming reverential. "He was a wonderful man. Warrior, poet, leader, he bravely saved the lives of many, many Jews. A bullet in the back made him a paraplegic for life, but I carry on his legacy. "This is taking time," he said, rising abruptly from his chair, his voice cold again. "Come, we must go now. Gather your things. I'll take care of the cups." To wash away evidence?

"I'm staying." I was determined not to go with him. Let him take me by force or gun me down now; even being shot dead would be better than being his prisoner.

It was a moment of indecision for him. He rested his hand on his pistol. Then he said, "All right, Mr. Greenberg, but it is imperative that you give me your clue to the location of the nail, just in case something unfortunate befalls you."

"Solly has the nail," I answered as confidently as I could.

"Don't feed me that," he said angrily.

So Solly hadn't played along with my lie, at least with Weiner. But was Solly in charge of Weiner, in league with him, or simply his dupe?

"Give me the clue," he ordered, unsnapping his holster.

"I said I gave it to Professor Solomon."

"That is a lie. Professor Solomon told me to get it from you. Listen, Mr. Greenberg, Am Ha-b'rit cannot wager the entire T'chiat Ha-meitim program on your survival. You are not leaving this house without giving me your clue, such as it is. We have sacrificed too much and have too much to lose."

That's what I was afraid of: either being stuck in a situation that couldn't end well for me, or giving away the store, after which I would be superfluous. At that moment, we heard the sound of the front door opening. Weiner re-snapped his holster shut, jerking around to see what the commotion was.

Coming from the hospital, a distraught Miriam was helped into the house by three women wearing long, black dresses. Two of the women were at Miriam's elbows, but she seemed to be walking steadily, independently, her face pale, exhausted, her eyes red-rimmed. I was hurriedly introduced to them. Then one of the women accompanied her to her bedroom, while a pair made directly for the kitchen and began clanging and banging kettles and pans, speaking to each other in hushed, rapid-fire Hebrew. Preparing for a *shiva* no doubt.

Jarad Weiner's implacable eyes pierced my skull like a bullet. "You won't reveal the clue even for Professor Solomon, foolish man?"

I shrugged my shoulders. "Let me think about it."

"Thinking hasn't done you or your friends much good," he spat bitterly. He handed me a cell phone. "When you are ready to leave this house, press this button to call me. You know the condition." Then he turned and left, letting the front door slam shut.

I sunk into the chair, my hands shaking, and tried to breathe deeply. I'd spent a rough couple of days in Israel, and all I wanted to do was go home, especially if that's where the nail was. But I was a prisoner, under an informal house arrest, stuck. Still trying to calm my jagged nerves, I listened to the women. The sound of activity indicated the two in the kitchen would be occupied for some time. And Miriam, I took it, was in bed, resting from her ordeal, being comforted by her third friend. I stared dispassionately at the cell Weiner had given me, like it was some curious alien object fallen from space. Now I had three: one from Bear, my erstwhile personal spy; one from Shin Bet, with all that was transpiring in

Israel, an organization currently as distant as God Himself; and now one from my present captor and potential executioner.

I used Weiner's cell to dial Solly at his lab. A young man's dispassionate voice answered. "Yes, speak."

"May I speak with Professor Solomon?" I whispered into the cell.

"I am sorry, Professor Solomon passed away two years ago."

"This is David Greenberg, his friend. I was just with him yesterday. It's urgent."

"Hold, please." I waited anxiously, tapping my finger on the chair's arm, my stomach nerves grinding, acids burning.

After what seemed like forever, the voice came back on the line. "Professor Solomon will not be taking any calls this week."

"But I must speak with him; it's urgent."

"I'm sorry, but that's impossible."

"But I'm here at his house, with his wife. Can't you get him on the line for a minute?"

"Professor Solomon was quite clear. He can't speak to anyone this week. As you know, his son just died." Just what I feared: Solly was withdrawing further.

"Will he be at the funeral?" I prodded.

"Professor Solomon is not able to attend."

"Is he all right? I'm sure the shock..."

"He is not the best. Please understand, he doesn't want to speak to anyone, not even Mrs. Solomon. Kindly leave him alone."

The line went dead.

How was I to know Solly was still alive? Or perhaps Weiner had made him a prisoner, just as I was. I had to speak to him, to clarify the situation. If Weiner was telling the truth, if he was trustworthy, perhaps I would give Solly the clue and be off.

I stuck my head in the kitchen and told the women, stirring pots and mixing bowls, that I was going out and would return as soon as possible. Then I headed for the entrance hall closet. Fortunately, Miriam had hung my jacket there the previous night. I put it on and checked the pockets. I remembered I'd left the Shin Bet cell in the living room; Bear's was still where I smothered it under a pile of pillows in the bedroom closet. I placed the cell Weiner had just handed me on the shelf above the coat rack, scooped up the Shin Bet cell, then stepped out to the front steps, relieved to be in the open air.

But my relief was short-lived.

I began to head down the walkway, my eyes scanning the placid street. Then I stopped. Two bearded young men in jeans and leather jackets, Uzis slung over their shoulders, headed straight toward me from the corners at the opposite ends of the street, strongly chiseled figures destined to converge on me at a ninety-degree angle. Weiner had left nothing to chance.

I spun about and walked back to the porch, then turned. Both of the young men had stopped equidistant from me and were glancing at each other, a silent communication. Giving up, I went back into the house and peered through the blinds. The street was empty, save the pair of sentinels having returned to their stakeout positions.

What to do? I thought about calling Bear but didn't want to risk a shootout in front of the house where Miriam was inside mourning for her son. I also considered calling Shin Bet. But what would I tell them? I needed a ride to the airport? They were quite occupied at the moment. I also didn't want to expose Solly's program any more than was practicable.

Just at that moment, the woman who had been sitting with Miriam in the bedroom appeared. "Mrs. Solomon would like to speak with you," she said quietly. I thanked her and went back into the house and entered Miriam's the bedroom, closing the door behind me as Miriam's friend left to join the others in the kitchen. I crossed the room to Miriam who was laying on top of the covers, still in her black dress, a damp cloth on her forehead. Our eyes locked as I sat on the bed and took her hand. I could see how devastated she was.

"How are you holding up?"

She squeezed my hand. "I don't know. I thought I was prepared, but..." Tears overflowed her eyes and poured down her cheeks, and she wiped them away.

"Miriam, I am so sorry."

"Don't say anything. I know. How are you? What is your situation?"

"Not the best, Miriam. Are you strong enough to receive more bad news?"

"I think so."

"Miriam, Levi Asher is dead. They found him in St. Louis. He was...was tortured."

Miriam's body seemed to quake. When she had stilled herself, she struggled to talk. "So..." She swallowed. "So what does this mean?"

"I think it means the nail is still in St. Louis, where Levi might have hidden it. I think his heart gave out before whoever tortured him could get its location. The autopsy will confirm that, but I'm pretty sure."

In frustration, she angrily flung the damp cloth from her forehead across the room where it landed on the floor. Then she covered her eyes with her elbow. There were several quiet moments before she could speak. "Poor Levi. So what are you going to do?"

"I'm in a tough spot. Miriam, did you tell Solly I thought I had a clue to the nail's location?"

"Yes, I mentioned it at the hospital. They sneaked him in to see Ari."

"Did you tell him that I suspect the clue is related to a chess game?"

"I don't remember. I've been preoccupied."

"I know you have," I said sympathetically and waited for her to get her thoughts around my question.

Finally, she was able to continue. "Probably not, it wouldn't come to mind, what with Ari..."

"But you can't be sure?"

She shook her head. "No. Why? Why would it matter?"

"Jarad Weiner may be working at cross purposes against Solly. He's been badgering me about the clue."

"Jarad? I've known him for years..."

"How well do you know him? Did you know that the police suspect him of horrendous crimes? He might be the one behind Levi's death, behind Chick's murder. Miriam, do you know about his origins?"

"Yes, I know, the cloning. But I didn't know about..."

"Was he here in Israel when Levi disappeared?"

"No, no, he was in the states checking on a few things."

"Bisl students?"

"Yes. I don't know exactly where he was when the Shankman exchange was supposed to have taken place, but when I spoke to him the night before, he was in Chicago."

"A forty-five-minute plane ride from St. Louis."

"I don't know when he got back to Israel. You don't mean, you think...?"

"I don't know. I do know he's pressuring me for the clue, and he won't let me leave this house until I give it to him. Frankly, I don't think my life is worth two cents while I'm here. He's got a couple of men watching your door. I've got to find some way back home or else I'm a dead man."

CHAPTER NINETEEN
WILL WE ALWAYS HAVE PARIS?

The *shiva* was crowded, as you'd expect, making Miriam's home a beehive of mourners. Men were dressed as conservatively as their religious factions determined, wearing dark suits and ties, blue sport jackets, or Hassidic garb. A whole collage of bearded and clean-shaven members of Am Ha-b'rit talked quietly in pairs and broader circles or huddled in prayer. Women, too, dressed the gamut, engaged in spirited conversations, prepared and organized foods of varied types; trays and platters filled every surface. Children throughout the house ate, supervised by their mothers to shouted admonitions, and played games outdoors. All were in mourning over a special lost son.

I was ready to make my escape in camouflage: pillow tied to my rear, another secured to fashion me enormous breasts, a huge sack-like garment over everything, a headscarf. I wasn't anyone's perfect J-date, that's for certain. Carrying an empty pan covered in foil, I resembled a typical female mourner—from the distance of, say, the Grand Canyon. I opened the window to climb out to the side yard and braced myself. Then I turned to say goodbye to Miriam. But she grasped my arm tightly, urgently, holding me back. Startled, I examined her face, now a swirling mass of sorrow, confusion, and indecision.

"What?" I asked impatiently.

I watched her struggle with herself for some moments. "I'm going with you," she replied, her face conflicted, yet determined.

"Are you sure?" I couldn't believe she would be willing to leave at a time like this.

"I couldn't be more sure of anything," she said resolutely.

"Miriam, think this through..."

"Think this through! I've thought about this for years, David. Who has more invested in this than me? Tell me, who? Now, let's go."

I knew better than to question her resolve. I would have thought she was too grief-stricken to travel, but there was steel in her face. What could I say? It was at that moment that I realized there had to be more to the story than she had revealed. Far more.

I shrugged. She would join me. Maybe I would finally have that conversation with her that I had been holding back.

"Which of these cell phones should I take?" I asked. "I'll take Shin Bet's for sure. But Bear Brukowski, he might be able to track me with the one he gave me. Shin Bet thinks it's possible he, or even the reverend, was behind Chick's murder. And both were in St. Louis when Levi Asher went missing. They also think Jarad Weiner could be a suspect. Miriam, I know you trust Jarad, but he scares me. I just don't want to make it easy for him to track me."

"Then don't bring it," she said offhandedly, seemingly distracted. "By the way," she warned, "we've been told *jihadis* might be watching the roads to Tel Aviv because they've heard about the T'chiat Ha-meitim program."

That was all I needed.

It was settled. As for the university's Susita, I figured Weiner and his associates knew it was parked at Bear's hotel. Just to be sure they found it, we could text the location after we arrived at our first stop outside Israel. They could do without it for a couple of days.

I went out the window, careful to keep my butt and breasts attached, then straightened myself before helping Miriam follow. We carried our empty pans flat, as if they contained leftovers, like mimes in an absurdist comedy, just two women leaving a *shiva* among a thinning crowd coming and going. Beneath my pan's foil, I concealed my laptop and the Fischer chess book, with the notes I had made folded within its cover. We'd have to worry about a change of clothes and other necessities wherever we landed.

Stealthily reaching the front of the house, we joined a pair of women headed home in the same direction we were tending. Miriam and the two women chatted quietly, while I remained silent, aware of their suspicious glances. I can't imagine what they thought of me, but they were too polite to say anything to the grieving Miriam, who merely told them she and her friend were taking a breather from the crowd and would return.

The neighborhood looked so peaceful at night. Like any suburban neighborhood back home, but within a different ecosystem, each of the houses sat on a small plot of yard landscaped to fit its owner's taste. We passed the street's intersection. Without turning my head, I glanced aside to see one of Weiner's security men in dark suit and tie, as if dressed for the *shiva*, a cell to his ear, whispering as he scanned the neighborhood.

Two blocks later, the women we'd joined broke off, and Miriam led me to a small house with moss-green awnings and a matching green door. Without knocking, Miriam opened the door, and we went inside. There, a thin, wizened woman about sixty-five, with gray-streaked black hair, greeted Miriam with a warm hug. I was introduced to the woman, still dressed in black from the *shiva*, whose name was Chaya, meaning "living" or "alive." Chaya's sure, quick movements and assertive manner marked her as the type who everyone in the neighborhood could trust or depend on, a combination town mayor and best-friend-in-need.

Her welcoming personality put me immediately at ease, and I ditched my pillows, dress, and scarf on the couch. With a single knowing glance, a lifetime of love passed between the women as Chaya prepared Miriam for the ad hoc trip abroad, gifting her a castoff suitcase full of incidental toiletries. Then Miriam told our hostess that she wanted me to meet her son before we left. Chaya called his name, and the boy appeared from the back rooms.

I expected a boy in his early teens, nothing more. But as consumed as I'd been with escaping Weiner's net, I found the child monopolizing my attention. He was physically nondescript, at least four inches taller than Ari, slight, with gangly, healthy limbs. His skin was tanned, his hair curly black with dark eyes to match, and a strong Semitic nose; a Jew in his every feature. Yet there was something about him I couldn't ignore.

I don't know what I expected to see—perhaps a boy just having lost his best friend—but his eyes seemed to see far in the distance. In the years he had been close to Ari, he had been touched in some way, and was in some sense a budding visionary himself, as nearly as I could make out. There was a mature wisdom in his gaze, and I felt drawn to this boy who had taken Miriam's late-son to heart and had been his companion.

"David," Miriam said sweetly, "this is Noam, Ari's best friend. They grew up together. They were bar mitzvahed on the same day. Isn't that wonderful?

"Noam, this is my friend David Greenberg from St. Louis."

Normally, I would offer my hand to a boy Noam's age, but I did not. Rather, I simply stood staring at his face, his eyes, as he examined mine.

Then he spoke, "Your heart will change," he said to me in perfect English. "Not right away, but over time. Be patient. You must make important decisions, but you are a good man." Then he nodded and left the room, as if preoccupied.

Ari had clearly changed him. I studied Chaya. Could this woman have been Noam's mother, born to her late in her life? Or had the woman adopted him? How lucky the boy was to have such a mother to raise him— to have such a friend as Ari to grow up with. How else would he be strong enough to accept his friend's loss so calmly?

I hadn't much experience with children, but I knew Ari and Noam were special. Again, the same feeling I had upon meeting the dying Ari came over me, and the old Nat King Cole song "Nature Boy" came into my head, lingered there.

Miriam embraced Chaya, staring into her eyes. "Make your arrangements," Miriam said solemnly.

Chaya nodded, then looked at Miriam questioningly.

"I can't predict what will happen," Miriam explained, "but I want you both in place in case I need you."

"You know we'll be there," Chaya assured her, although I could sense her reluctance and fear. I didn't know what was transpiring, but I had bigger fish to fry at the moment, and so let it pass.

We said our goodbyes, as Chaya dangled a key before Miriam, and soon we were off to the airport in an old Ford sedan, my computer and Fischer book in a borrowed briefcase. We planned to text Chaya the car's location from the airport, knowing her older son would pick it up in the morning.

I drove east down a dark road to the coast, looking to reach the main highway to Netanya, Miriam in the passenger seat beside me. I felt torn by what I was leaving. In the short time I was at the university, I had sensed a closeness among the Am Ha-b'rit members, a trust, a feeling of implicit destiny. If it was hard for me to leave, how much more difficult would it be for Miriam, who had been central to the community's aspirations, at the core of their activities, and they hers?

The night was clear and cool, the stars displayed on a vast black canvas. Along the side of the road, the hills and rocks, the sand and scrub passed in the headlights, stark and serene, bidding me farewell. I loved being in Israel, a place whose familiar streets are safer than most in America, whose vibrant people are direct, yet welcoming, whose ancient culture beckons to be explored like an imploring lonely ghost.

Remembering Miriam's warning about the road being watched by Shadid's people, I analyzed the threats we might encounter, much as would a fugitive. The *jihadis* had displayed their willingness to gamble with whatever assets they had available to stop me. Weiner would try to stop us. But it seemed in his interest not to kill me—that is, unless he was a member of Rabbi Yourman's faction, in which case my death would serve as his checkmate, ending the Jesus-cloning portion of the T'chiat Ha-meitim program. Even if Weiner had gone rogue and was merely out for himself, the nail likely would be his big payday.

As for God's Left Tackle, I couldn't be sure. If money were his aim, he'd want me to live. If he or the reverend had another agenda, was I better alive to them or not?

As the blackness passed around us on the unfamiliar roadway, I noticed in my rearview mirror a pair of headlights following a quarter mile behind. I slowed, and my escort slowed, keeping his distance. I sped up, and he did, too. Not wanting to appear suspicious, I kept my speed steady, and the car didn't accelerate. He was pacing me. About a half mile before we reached Kvish 2, the main highway from Netanya to Tel Aviv, the road narrowed where they'd had to carve through sloping hills to make the surface wide enough for traffic. As we rolled eastward, the shoulder disappeared from either side, leaving no room to maneuver. I checked the rearview, but the car trailing me hadn't closed.

"We're being followed," I said, "but they're not trying to stop us."

"Keep going," Miriam replied.

Suddenly, I had to slam on the breaks to avoid running into a pile of scrub blocking the road. Instantly, an RPG shell struck just ahead, spewing rock and sand. Glancing at the rise above the road's western side, I could see a single figure with an AK-47 automatic rifle rise from his stomach, aiming at us. Then fire rained down, and two bullets struck the back door, one hitting the trunk. I floored the old Ford, crashing and scraping through the pile of debris, which turned out to be just that, hastily thrown together, more visual than virtual obstacle, and was off in a cloud of dust. In the rearview, I saw my escort brake where I had been when the RPG round stuck. Miriam turned to see what was happening behind us.

"What's going on back there?" I asked her, my eyes fixed ahead.

"The car following us has stopped. Three, now four, men are climbing out. They have guns. They're spreading out, firing at the hill, maybe with Uzis."

We were shaken. Being mere feet from a deadly explosion was more trauma than we had bargained for even after the blood-soaked previous day. But I wasn't about to slow down. My guess was that Shadid had had a couple men watching the road to university housing. My trailing escort was probably university or Am Ha-b'rit security, out to tail anyone leaving the area, and now they were taking it upon themselves to clear the road of *jihadis*. At that moment, my assailants were undoubtedly scrambling for dear life to a hidden motorbike on the far side of the ridge. If this was all Shadid could throw at me, he was in a weaker position than I was led to believe. This pair did not seem skilled with the high-powered weapons they'd been given. If Shadid was going to pursue me back to St. Louis, he was going to do it solo. Of course, Detective Landau had warned me that Shadid could be formidable.

Formidable also would be the Saudi money Shadid commanded. Plus, someone had a suitcase full of euros. Not to mention, if Reverend Nation wasn't as innocent as he appeared, his wealth could marshal copious evil. For that matter, Bear alone, lacking access to the reverend's money, might have tapped into Blood Diamond cash and the manpower necessary to operate that trade. There was plenty lined up against Miriam and me.

After being rescued by university security, I felt bad about deceiving Jarad Weiner. Perhaps he was what he claimed to be, just doing his job. But what was I to do? Coming so close to being blown up, I realized I was being selfish to keep to myself what I believed was the sole clue to the nail's location. If I died, perhaps the whole T'chiat Ha-meitim program would be doomed to failure. It was likely someone at the university had already deduced that part of the clue, the Fischer reference, which would be obvious to anyone who knew Levi Asher. But I knew St. Louis, where I believe the nail resided, and I could still be useful. Regardless, I decided to tell Miriam what I'd guessed and let her decide what to do with the hunch. It was her call.

Kvish 2 posed no major problem as we made for Ben Gurion International in Tel Aviv. I didn't even get stopped for speeding and wouldn't have cared if I had. But I couldn't get my mind off our recent close call. Something about it troubled me. Finally, I realized what that troubling thought was. Considering they had an RPG—that they were so close, that we'd stopped, thinking we were trapped—even assuming lack of practice, how did the *jihadis* miss us by so much? In retrospect, the margin of error seemed highly improbable. The rest of the drive, the question would nag at me. Could that roadside attack have been staged for my benefit, possibly like the attack at the police station, and most likely as Chick's murder had been?

Upon our arrival at the airport, Miriam texted Chaya where to find the car and that we would pay damages—three bullet holes.

"Where are we going?" Miriam asked as we made directly to the terminal, moving between the cars.

"The first flight out to Europe…wherever it's going."

In the airport, we examined the boards and made for the counter with the next flight: a red-eye to Paris had an open pair of seats. As we went through meticulous security using my American and Miriam's Israeli passports, a man in gray slacks snapped a picture of us with his cell, then dialed his phone. Someone knew we were Paris-bound.

***

Exhausted and traumatized, we slept on the plane only briefly, fitfully; the wine we were served proved little help. After landing at Charles De Gaulle, we caught a taxi for the Marais neighborhood, where I had good friends. About an hour from the airport, the one-way, cobblestone streets of the Marais form a narrow, twisting warren fronted by 17th-, 18th-, and 19th-Century buildings, excellent for walking or biking, but wide enough for only one car. Nearly every block has a *boulangerie* or two, sidewalk cafes, *bistros*, and *brasseries*, high-end clothing boutiques, and art galleries. The oldest part of Paris and once the city's Jewish quarter, there were long lines to popular falafel stands, kosher bakeries and old synagogues built long before the French authorities, at the behest of the Nazis, shipped most of its Jews to the death camps aboard French trains— a transgression memorialized in the Marais and near Notre Dame.

The Marais had once been home to the magnificent mansions of the Paris aristocracy, but had been deserted in the exodus to marvelous Versailles, allowing their owners to be close to Europe's prime Divine Right power, King Louis, and the limitless wealth that flowed from his good offices. After the French Revolution, the mansions were left vacant, the aristocrats having fled Versailles to England—those who escaped beheading that is. The once-glorious buildings of the Marais fell into disrepair and later were subdivided and occupied by poor working-class families. Now, side by side with vestiges of Orthodox Jews, the area was far into gentrification, broken into upgraded apartments, its streets busy with upwardly mobile shoppers and a robust gay community.

From the taxi, I called my friend, Jean Claude, a restaurateur, and he agreed to put us up for the night. Just to be sure we weren't followed, I had the taxi drop us at the Place des Vosges, where we cut across its sculptured park and made our way on foot the two blocks to his apartment on the rue de la Bastille, turning left twice. We saw no one suspicious as we nonchalantly passed cafes filled wall-to-door with late revelers enjoying their French and Italian foods and wines to the sounds of Edith Piaf and local jazz musicians.

Jean Claude, a man in his mid-fifties, met us at the door, rumpled from being awakened, his gray-streaked hair tangled; his unshaven face shadowed in salt-and-pepper whiskers. I tried to explain our situation without going into too much detail, but he didn't care. He had a friend he could call in the morning whose apartment was vacant for a few days while he vacationed in Marseille. He offered us food, but we were barely able to stand, too wrung out to eat, neither of us having napped in the taxi. He then directed Miriam to his spare bedroom, such as it was, while I volunteered for Jean Claude's broken-down couch.

"Not the couch," Miriam whispered to me sympathetically. "You'll be crippled in the morning."

Too tired to argue, I wearily followed her into the room, closing the door. In moments, I was down to my underwear and under the covers. I turned to watch her finish undressing. She climbed under the covers beside me, resting her head on the pillow, her black hair fanning out.

"I know you'll want to talk in the morning," she said.

"Yes." We studied each other's faces; then I leaned over and kissed her lightly on the lips. In no time, we were in a deep slumber.

***

We slept past ten, waking sore and groggy from our ordeal, with Jean Claude already gone to his restaurant. He'd spoken to his friend staying in Marseille and left the street address for us. Miriam and I dressed quickly. In the clear morning, the sun shone brightly on the alabaster buildings running through the Marais.

Miriam watched out the window as I went downstairs to the *supermarché* across the narrow rue. On my way, I didn't notice anyone out of place, merely a few students and young couples strolling past a row of bicycles in front of an adjacent apartment complex. In the *supermarché*, I bought all the groceries I could carry, planning to leave behind as much as possible as a thank you to Jean Claude: the best cheeses, wines, meats, fruits, and vegetables the store carried. And coffee, of course. Fortunately, I was able to pay with a credit card, as I didn't want to squander our euros. I also picked up a few other basics.

When I returned, Miriam relinquished her vigil at the window to tell me she hadn't noticed anyone watching the apartment. Relieved that we were safe for the moment, we unloaded my haul in the small kitchen, filling Jean Claude's fridge and shelves.

After bathing in the apartment's claw-foot tub, Miriam began preparing breakfast, while I set the table. I joined her and sliced fresh oranges, while she brewed a pot of French roast and prepared omelets with tomatoes and cheddar cheese. I had bought a baguette, being afraid to go to the corner *boulangerie* for that morning's hot croissants, which she sliced. After what we'd been through, I opened one of the red wines to serve at table. Then we sat down for a leisurely breakfast, relishing each bite as if it were our last.

"I guess we'd best buy you some clothes at one of the neighborhood shops," I said. "No telling how long before...before you can go...go home."

The last sentence was loaded, and we both knew it. How many times had I been single and alone in Paris, yearning to share the City of Lights with someone special? Now we were here, but under terrible circumstances.

She merely shrugged, of course. We finished eating, then washed and dried the dishes together, making small talk. Retiring to the living room, the bottle of wine and glasses in hand, Miriam sat on a chair, I on the couch that had been proffered, but rejected, for my sleep the night before.

"I want to tell you my interpretation of the clue's meaning," I said, "so in case something happens to one of us, the T'chiat Ha-meitim program won't be lost. You can do anything you like with it, even pass it along to Jarad Weiner or to Solly. I'm sure someone in Am Ha-b'rit has already figured it out anyway, so Weiner probably knows that much. My main value is being able—hopefully—to apply it to some location in St. Louis. So far, I haven't had the time or peace of mind to think that part through."

"I'll pass what we know so far to Chaya," she said, explaining that Chaya's husband was one of Solly's assistants, a biochemist. "They can be trusted to keep it secret. If something does happen to us, then she can give it to Solly, I guess."

"It's your choice," I agreed, then explained what I'd deduced and handed her the Shin Bet phone to call Chaya. If Shin Bet was monitoring the call, would our cautions to Chaya preclude Shin Bet from passing the clue along to Weiner, a private security operator? I was sure they often traded information, especially intelligence about Shadid and his Martyrs organization. But what other option did we have?

When Miriam finished the call, she joined me on the couch, her legs folded beneath her, wine in hand. I took a sip of mine and put my arm around her shoulders. It seemed so natural, relaxed.

"So, tell me about Ari," I prompted, hoping to clear the air.

"My son's soul was everything promised. His love was as wide as the world, his mind deeper than the sea, his perception as far-reaching as time, beyond time. His beautiful eyes saw everything in the human heart, more than people saw in themselves. I carried him for nine months, and, as his mother, I peered into those beautiful eyes nearly every day." She grew quiet, setting her wine down on the table and reclined against my shoulder, her eyes fixed on her hands. Slowly, a gentle smile emerged.

"His wit was so dry, so droll for someone so young. If he wanted to stick a pin in your ego, there was no stopping him. Just a few words, and you would be laughing so hard at yourself, at human nature, but laughing *with* him. That's what his humor did for people, even at his tender age. Joy, Ari was pure joy. And that smile…" She lowered her eyes.

"I only met him briefly," I said, "but he struck me directly in the heart like, like, I don't know what. It was the most extraordinary thing I've ever experienced."

"No matter what has been made of him—soul, spirit, whatever—he was a boy. My boy. I was blessed to be his mother for nearly every day of his fourteen years…as a baby…as a child. He was so proud at his bar mitzvah. He understood the depth of his Torah portion better than the rabbi. But he needed so much help to get through it. He was so sick by then." She took a deep breath. "I was his mother, David, his real mother. Solly used my egg, you know."

"And will again?"

"Yes, that was the…the plan." She paused, fighting back tears—remembering—uncertainty appearing on her face. "David, I miss Ari so terribly, so terribly. I want him back."

Funny thing, the world has been dwelling on that very notion for over two thousand years. I kind of understand why.

CHAPTER TWENTY
THE MONEYCHANGERS

There are days you always remember.

It was already bright and sunny in the Marais, perfect for drifting through the shops along the rues and boulevards to buy clothes for Miriam. Or, a fantasy of course, taking a picnic lunch with a good Bordeaux to Luxembourg Gardens. Fairly certain we weren't yet being spied upon by hostile elements, we could at least fulfill the former, even if we couldn't risk the latter. I also planned to visit a trustworthy dealer friend whom I would ask to quietly put out word across the EU that I had a client seeking a genuine Jesus Christ artifact, "price no object;" the exact artifact unnamed. I wasn't going to call ahead to alert any unpleasant reception committee.

I called Dov Landau in Jerusalem to see if the coroner's report on Levi Asher had come back from St. Louis, but he was out. I didn't leave a message.

After setting my watch to eleven Paris time, I found the BBC news channel on television. There were still disturbances throughout the Middle East stemming from the attack at the university and the murder near the Dead Sea, Chick Markowitz's. The region seethed with demonstrations from Cairo to Ramallah to Tel Aviv, some fatal, igniting acts of brutal violence, retaliatory acts of revenge. To keep a lid on the anger of its own citizens, the Israeli government made it clear that the police believed Chick's murder was likely perpetrated by a non-Muslim attempting to blame *jihadis*, but they still had no suspect or motive for the killing. Martyrs of the Holy had not claimed responsibility, as they often did. Talk of reasonable restraint, as the Israeli government might, wasn't making much headway in the face of such a despicable and unprecedented bloodletting.

I shut down the TV and corked the wine as Miriam brought fresh coffee to the table. She filled our cups and sat beside me on the couch, deliciously fragrant from Jean Claude's girlfriend's bath oils.

"So you think the nail is in St. Louis?" she asked.

"I'm pretty sure." I explained to her about the imposter using Levi's plane ticket to fly to Israel and about my interpretation of the message left for me at Chick Markowitz's murder scene. But the nail wasn't all I was curious about.

"You and Solly running off to Israel together; that was a real shocker," I stated flatly, pausing for her to absorb that I was changing the subject.

"I'm sorry about that, David," she said sympathetically, her eyes growing tender, "but we had to do it that way." She sipped her coffee. "Solly was their target, naturally. He's made so many discoveries for Am Ha-b'rit since our arrival—breakthroughs that are being adapted by Hadera scientists to genetic-based medicine. So much."

"Then there's the Bisl project," I said, revealing that I knew of the student teams spread over Europe and the U.S.

"You know about Bisl?" she asked, taken aback.

"I do."

"Think of it, David. The chance to bring back the greatest minds of history," she said defensively. "When Solly gets to publish his findings, somehow, someday...you can imagine."

"I can't argue with that. But what about you? You went with him."

"Me, I still paint. I also teach an art class or two at Hadera."

"I saw your work. You have real talent, Miriam. I mean, just to stack them in the living room..." I could see she wanted to evade the subject, but then changed her mind.

"Oh, I do more than stack them. I've had shows at galleries in Tel Aviv, Florence, and London," she stated proudly. "Under the name of Maria Rey— r-e-y, as in Dreyfus? Some of my paintings hang in some pretty fine places here in Europe, and back in the states, too."

"Aha," I exclaimed. "I thought I recognized the style. Maria Rey. I assumed the artist was Spanish. You may not believe this, but I attended one of those shows, Miriam, in Florence. I was dragged to it by a woman friend, a sculptor." I failed to mention that I'd been married at the time.

"You encouraged me to paint, David," she said wistfully, remembering our primeval days. Staring directly into my eyes, she gently brushed my cheek as if no decades had intervened between the last time she'd performed the same act in that college apartment. "You convinced me I could be an artist."

"I didn't encourage you to run off to Israel," I said softly, lowering my voice. Just that simple gesture, brushing my cheek, still melted my ever-tight nerves. "So what happened, Miriam?"

"David, I'd stopped seeing my friends for you. But you were away from the apartment so much—chess tournaments that went on all weekend, all-night card games—you don't remember how often we were apart, or how lonely I was."

"Cards were my scholarship supplement; that's how I won my car. We had so much fun being together, driving everywhere in my used Sirocco."

"Come on, David, 'scholarship supplement?' The Sirocco? I liked it just as well, better in fact, when we walked or rode our bikes around town. Don't you remember? No, you needed the thrill of the games more than you needed the money. Sure, we set up my easel in the living room, so I could paint. Too much time. Where were you? I was young. You didn't need me the way I needed you."

I remembered back to the early days of our relationship, the long walks along Wydown Boulevard, the strolls through the Demun neighborhood with its restaurants and bars, and the bike rides to Forest Park, to the art museum, the zoo. It didn't matter that we had little money. Now I realized how often I'd left her alone, rattling around the apartment waiting for me, while I played fast and loose with the boys.

"I gave up cards way back; it was never really much fun. Chess for the most part, too, except for the odd pick-up game. So, you and me…and Solly?"

"David, it's where you come from. Your family was so cold, so distant, to each other and to you. You lost your instinct to be a part of anything meaningful. You became so alienated.

"My father was a simple salesman, David, and I had that religious upbringing that you didn't. I was part of a community. I needed that; I still do. You were a lone wolf, probably still are."

"So, Solly?" I pressed her.

"It was my decision, and I knew what I wanted, something meaningful in life. I had choices, David, as you well know. At first I was bored, nobody to talk to, nothing to do but paint, but eventually, I found my new self and grew with it.

"Am Ha-b'rit came after Solly, hard. They'd lost all their biotech scientists, the Englishman in charge, the rest. Am Ha-b'rit's biotech people had been tracking his publications, even those crazy speculative articles he wrote that read more like sci-fi. The chance they were offering him, to design and run his own experiments, with big budgets…I mean, David, cloning and genetics; it was his dream come true."

"I can't argue with that," I said.

"Ah, but he had to give up the drugs, and quickly. I helped him. We helped each other, really, and we grew close.

"Solly told me about Am Ha-b'rit, who they were, what they were doing. He told me he could get me into Hadera University to finish my degree. And he understood my feelings about Israel—how I needed something solid in my life. It's not like Solly and I had this big romance; things just developed."

"Evolved." I smirked.

"Anyway, Am Ha-b'rit offered us community, a way of life I could feel comfortable in. And the plans Solly had for his science, the wild ideas—well, not so wild, as it turned out. He finally had his great purpose. We began to feed on each other's dreams, which morphed into a life together." She paused, remembering.

"I'm sorry, Miriam," I said contritely. "I never meant to let you down."

"I don't hold you responsible, David. This was for the best, for me. Don't you see? When Solly revealed the Jesus clone project to me and that he wanted me to be the mother, I had a larger purpose in life, too, a great destiny. I would have a child of my own, a special boy, and a community to be a part of. How could I turn my back on all that?

"I never regretted being Ari's mother for a minute, not a minute. My painting became just a sideline, an amusement. That it was successful surprised me more than anyone."

"Solly's a good guy," I said. "You could have done a lot worse."

"Yes, he is a good guy and a kind father to Ari. He's been a little nuts the last two years, living in his lab and all, but that's the way he's dealt with Ari's illness. He's obsessed with fathering a healthy Ari; that's all he cares about anymore. Can you blame him? I am, too."

She noticed how dejected he looked. "You were a good guy, too, David. And you're a good man now, an even better one."

Do any of us know how we will seek consolation to soothe the ultimate tragedies in our lives? Outside, the air danced with the youthful laughter of cyclists on the rue, the flutter of wings to and fro on the windowsill. She leaned toward me. I put my arm around her shoulders, and we kissed, without thinking, as if the act was foreordained. Our lips touched lightly at first, then urgently, as we embraced, our every sense charged, electric. Wrapped in each other's arms, we descended onto the couch, compelled by instincts that have driven couples through eons—from forest and jungle, through city and countryside—the passion greater for being so long deferred. We were at once a cloud-borne flight of angels and a grappling of lions on fallen prey, primeval and divine. Living for the moment, and seemingly for eternity.

Solly's wait-a-year rule was violated, definitively and repeatedly. I thought about that, but it was, again, her decision, not mine.

We would not be shopping that day.

***

Watched by the three powerful men, the liveried butler set the silver service on the lacquered wood coffee table, carved from a slice of giant redwood. The man placed a sizable mug of coffee before Brady Wilcox, a tall Texas billionaire, wearing his conservative, pinstripe suit and shiny black alligator cowboy boots. Brady lit a Marlboro with his gold lighter, took a sip of coffee, then returned the mug to the table.

The butler then placed a glass of bourbon before Brody Wilcox, Brady's paunchy, shorter, younger brother by two years. Brody wore a white cowboy hat, tan deerskin jacket, string tie, black jeans, and elaborate, brown cowboy boots adorned with colorful Texas flags and longhorns. He lit an unfiltered Camel, took a swig of the rich bourbon, then, cradling the half-filled glass in his gnarled hands, settled back on the couch, crossing his boots on the table.

The butler then placed a large glass of freshly squeezed orange juice before their visitor, Reverend Nation. Nation wore the same wide-brimmed, Australian Akubra bush hat he'd been photographed sporting while posing as an outdoorsman. The Wilcox brothers stared with puzzled curiosity at the reverend's hat, then made eye contact, shrugged their shoulders, and went on as if nothing was amiss. The Wilcox Family Trust was open for business.

The butler laid clean ashtrays beside the two brothers, then circled the room, opening the shades to let in a flood of bright morning sun. Satisfied, he departed, leaving the silver tray holding a two-thirds full decanter of bourbon, a heated coffee pot, and a pitcher of juice. While the door stood ajar, a balding, frail assistant in a neat suit and tie, Coke-bottle glasses perched on his nose, scampered inside. "You wanted to see me, Mr. Wilcox?"

"Yes," Brody growled in his Texas drawl, took a sip of his bourbon and sat watching the ice cubes swirl around his glass. "Cody, have Joe Bob get my plane ready. I've got to meet some folks in Austin for dinner. Gonna whip a deal on 'em."

"Yes, sir, Mr. Wilcox. It'll be ready after lunch, sir."

"And Cody," older brother Brady interjected in his stilted drawl, "call the Gulf. I want a report on that damned rig *this morning*."

"Close the door on your way out, Code," brother Brody added.

"Yes, sir, Mr. Wilcox, Mr. Wilcox," the man said, departing.

The two brothers stared expectantly at Reverend Nation. Brady sucked on his Marlboro twice, then stuffed it out, his face registering his well-known stern, righteous expression. To his right, Brody sipped his bourbon, then his face switched on the benevolent grin of a man truly "of-the people-who-hang-out-at-the-diner." Nothing was said for many long seconds before, businesslike, Brady broke the silence.

"You saw him, Reverend?" Brady asked with profound seriousness. "You met the boy?"

Hubris Nation thought long and hard, putting on his best gravitas. "I did, indeed, Brady. They gave me a long, private talk with him."

"And?" Leaning forward, the older Brady's legendary eagle stare pierced the reverend, who never wavered, never blinked.

"He's the real deal, Brady," Nation said nervously, picking at his tie.

Brother Brody refilled his glass from the bourbon decanter. "Now, Reverend, we're counting on you as our spiritual advisor. There's a whole passel of money riding on this. A shitload. Hell, we've just learned we're up against the damn Saudis. How could you tell? Did he have a halo, a glow, or something like that?"

"No. Now Brody," the reverend cautioned, "that halo stuff, that's medieval crap, and folks just picked it up 'cause it looked good. See? No, *Our* Lord wouldn't have that."

"So how could you tell?"

"I just could, Brody. You heard that song," and the reverend sang in his lovely, deep voice, *"Jesus met a woman at the well-ell-ell?"*

"...and he told her everything she ever done," Brody joined in, the next line of the tune. "Sure, everybody does."

"Well, the boy had these eyes, you see. I'll never forget those big, dark eyes as long as I live. He saw right into my soul, right into my *soul*. Knew everything without being told. Everything."

Brady drank his coffee, his eagle stare never leaving the reverend's face.

Brody thoughtfully sipped his bourbon and dragged deeply on his Camel. "Now, you' sure?"

"Sure as I'm sitting here in front of you," Reverend Nation said definitively. "The child is our Lord, Jesus Christ reborn."

"You sure he wasn't hooking you?" Brody blurted, dropping his sweet-face pose.

"That boy is without guile; his heart is as pure as snow. Gentlemen, he knew I was coming to see him six years ago, when he was a child, a mere child. Wrote something for me way back then to be given to me the very day he met me. What are the chances of that?"

Brody whistled. He and Brady looked toward each other, their faces confirming a decision between them.

As Brady set down his mug, his younger brother and the reverend held their breath, waiting for the eagle's thoughts. "Is there anything that troubles you about this conclusion, Reverend?" he asked. "Not the boy, you understand, but anything else? The Jews, the university?"

The reverend collected himself under Brady's unrelenting gaze. "Well, the St. Louis Jew, the one they got hunting the nail, now he's a big believer in *evil*-ution. That troubles me."

Younger Brody practically spit out a good swallow of bourbon and hooted loudly. "*Evolution*, haw! You remember, Brady, when we tole' Paw evolution was an efficient kind of insertion device for electric motors. Got him to invest money with us in a start-up."

Brady joined in Brody's mirth, his rigid face breaking into laughter. "What'd we say the name of that company was? Evolution Intercourse Insertors?"

"Haw!" Brody laughed. "Paw told the other deacons at church he was putting his money into evolution. That he was all hot for intercourse insertors! Can you imagine!"

"I never seen him so mad," Brady guffawed.

Now Reverend Nation joined the laughter, and the three laughed so hard they had to set down their beverages not to spill them.

"Grabbed his shotgun!" Brody shouted hysterically. "We had to hide in the woods till Maw cooled him down!"

Their hilarity died slowly, coming and going in sputtered fits and starts. As they settled, they wiped the tears from their eyes.

Recovering, Hubris Nation said in a low voice, "Your momma was a saint, boys."

"Momma was a saint," Brody said wistfully, taking a deep draw of bourbon.

Brady straightened the neat Windsor knot on his tie. "Did they let you see the lab?"

"Fellow named Weiner showed me through the place," the reverend replied. "You should have seen it. Tubes and wires and computers and I don't know what all, floor to ceiling, room after room. They was men in lab coats working it, too...it weren't for no show."

Brody and Brady made eye contact again. Brady nodded to Brody to proceed.

"Now, about that Jew," Brody said, smoothing his hat brim, "the dealer from Saint Louie. Can we trust him?"

"He's a good one," the reverend replied analytically. "Wouldn't steal your chickens if he was starving. I got Bear keeping an eye on him, riding along everywhere he goes, all over the Holy Land, too."

"Bear's a good boy," Brady pronounced from his eagle eerie. Brody and Nation nodded agreement.

"Helluva offensive tackle," Brody said fondly.

"With the help of Bear's hard work," Nation stated proudly, "Hallelujah Hour Ministries has converted more Central Africans to Christ than there are colored people in Harlem, New York. That's right. Saved millions of their immortal souls from damnation and Hell. All made possible, of course, by your kind support of the ministry airplane dedicated solely for that purpose. You can go count them people for yourself."

Brady held up his hand to politely refuse the offer of accountability for the brothers' investment in Christianity's march into the darker reaches of the planet.

Brother Brody got a puzzled look on his face, took another sip of his rich brown liquid, and lit a fresh Camel. "More than Harlem, *Jew* York City. Ain't that something, Brady? Tell me," he asked Nation thoughtfully, "do the ni— excuse me, Reverend, I mean the Afro-mericans, the negroes, whatever you s'posed to call 'em—do the coloreds have souls like we do?" Beside him, Brady harrumpfed in remonstration, giving his brother a grave frown.

"Course they do, Brody," the reverend replied. "Why, one of my preachers, black as oil right out the ground, he wrote six books. And not just rah-rah-church stuff, but real thoughtful like. If you want, my Board of Christian Publications sells copies." It was Brody's turn to raise his hand in polite refusal.

"It's just them liberals got them folks all confused on what's right," upright Brady explained to his younger brother as if to a slow-witted child. "They've got souls just like regular folks."

"Well, I was just asking," Brody mumbled as contritely as a dog whipped for peeing on the carpet.

While Brody ruminated over this revelation, his face doubtful, Brady moved the conversation along to tie up loose ends. "All right, Reverend Nation," he said, "is there anything in Scripture against Jesus showing up in—in unusual ways? I mean, he doesn't have to come back riding on a golden chariot or anything, does he?"

"No, nothing in Scripture," the reverend replied.

"Anything in Scripture against a Jew being his John the Baptist in the Second Coming?"

Reverend Nation thought this over with staged studiousness. "No, nothing in Scripture. John the Baptist was a Jew, sort of, originally anyway. Course, they'll all want to be Christian come End of Days."

"All right," Brady said, rising to his feet.

Stubbing out his cigarette and pushing off the couch, Brody removed his cowboy hat and set down his drink.

Seeing the brothers were through with him, a relieved Reverend Nation followed suit. He removed his Australian bush hat, and the startled Wilcox brothers stared at his baldpate—the rumors they'd been hearing confirmed. There was a moment of stunned silence.

Finally, as if from the mouths of babes, Brody spoke. "Hey, Reverend, what happened to your hair? You look like a skinned possum."

"And what happened to the watch and ring you wear on TV?" Brady added, indicating their absence.

"I gave them to the poor," Reverend Nation replied modestly. "You meet Him, it changes you."

Without hesitation, Brady unsnapped his Rolex watchband and stuck it into Nation's coat pocket. Then he gave Brody the eye. On cue, Brody somewhat reluctantly took off his diamond-encrusted ruby ring and plopped it into Nation's other pocket. "That ring's a gift from the King of Saudi Arabia," he said.

"You've got to wear hair and jewelry, Reverend. It wouldn't look right on TV," Brady advised. Brody nodded in agreement.

"I will, Brady. Promise."

That resolved, the three stood together around the table, heads bowed. "Our Father," the reverend intoned, "we thank You for the mercy and kindness You've shown Your unworthy servants. Please continue to bless the endeavors of these brothers and their kin, not only in their daily lives, but in the great works the fruits of their considerable labors have so nobly advanced to bring about the End of Days and Your Glorious Kingdom of Heaven, as was written in Your Holy Bible two thousand years ago. Please, Father, reserve for these deserving souls a special place of honor beside You at Your table. In the name of Jesus Christ, our Lord and Savior, we thank You for our many blessings. Amen."

"Amen," the brothers recited in unison, then raised their heads, a gentle smile spreading across their faces, as Brady removed an envelope from inside his jacket and handed it to Reverend Nation.

"Now this here is for the ministry," Brady said. "We've got to get going on that other project we talked about, the new translation. We need the right Bible in Arab."

"Them rag-heads have got' all crazy," Brody added, replacing his hat on his head. "By the way, that check goes to the tax-deductible side. It's a biggun." He winked.

Reverend Nation nodded thanks benevolently. "As did Christian martyrs in bygone eras, we shall humbly work the Lord's will, even as the heathen wield bloody swords against us."

"Amen," the brothers responded in unison.

Brother Brady nodded to Brody, who reached behind the bar and wheeled out a large leather suitcase. Together, the two brothers lifted it onto the redwood table. Brody popped its locks and opened it. Inside, bundles of American dollars made a pretty picture.

"And this is for you, Reverend," Brady said. "For taking time out of your busy schedule to evaluate the child."

"This is off the books," Brody noted, closing the suitcase and standing it on the floor, as the mood became lighter.

Reverend Nation placed a firm hand on their shoulders. "Thank you, boys. And God bless you both."

"I'll get you some help with that suitcase, Reverend," Brody said. "Where'd you park your plane, out to the Flatbrush strip?

SECTION III. END GAME

"Never Give a Sucker an Even Break."

W. C. Fields Title of 1941 Universal Pictures film
Written under the pseudonym Otis Criblecoblis

I pray you sir, is it your will,
To make a stale of me amongst these mates?

William Shakespeare, *The Taming of the Shrew*

CHAPTER TWENTY-ONE
ARE WE A PAIR?

Well, in for a dime, in for a dollar—or even millions of them.

I shaved using the safety razor I'd bought at the *supermarché*, which, being an electric guy, was a bloody adventure. While Miriam rested in Jean Claude's living room, I turned on the shower and undressed. Neither of us had a change of clothes, so we were going to have to make do with what we had.

As I was about to step into the shower, I overheard Miriam's voice through the door, speaking in a soft whisper. I was shocked. Had someone entered the apartment? I checked my pants, but the Shin Bet cell was still in the pocket. I turned down the shower flow and put my ear to the door, listening to her end of a conversation.

"Yes, I'm safe, we're in Paris. We had that trouble on the way out...

"The Marais, but we're moving shortly. To Montmartre, near Place du Tertre. A friend of his friend...

"I don't know, maybe St. Louis. I'll have to let you know. Did the funds arrive?

"Good. Listen, I can't talk. Purchase Swiss francs with half, shekels with a quarter, put the other quarter in euros. Understand?" She paused to listen. "Yes, I have the clue. Make that exchange," she ordered.

Then she became quiet, fiddled with her purse, rose from the couch and walked into the kitchen.

Turning up the water, I entered the tub and finished my shower.

When I returned to the living room, towel around my waist, drying my hair with another, she was sitting on the couch, lightly sipping wine. She looked me over sweetly.

"There you are, all clean," she said. Sliding down the sofa, close, she slipped her arms around me, her fingertips sliding underneath my towel, onto my buttocks. She pressed her cheek to my stomach for a hug. "I like you a little dirty, but this will do."

"Miriam," I said, reluctantly pulling away, the feelings of being drawn to her still gripping me like a vice after our bout of lovemaking. "I heard you talking."

"Yes, so?" she said offhandedly.

"Where did you get the cell?"

She studied my face, the moment grown cold. "I always carry a cell phone," she said quizzically, shocked at the question.

"But where did you get it?"

"I've had it for years. Security insists I carry it with me."

Oy, *she'd gotten it from Jarad Weiner.* Suddenly, I didn't feel quite so insulated from the world outside the apartment walls. She had obviously intended to conceal the call from me. "But who did you call? Solly? Who?"

"I called Jarad to tell him I'm okay. He was worried sick."

Jarad! *Oy vey.* She didn't try to obfuscate whom she'd talked to, but now it felt like the pair of them must have some deeper-level symbiosis than I'd thought. At that moment, Miriam's demeanor had darkened in my sense of her, but I didn't want to reveal my suspicions. Two could play dumb. "Miriam, I told you I distrust him. I even left the cell phone he gave me back at your house so he couldn't track us. Did you tell him where you are?" I plopped down at the end of the couch, discarding my head towel, stroking my damp hair into place with my fingers.

"Of course, I did, David. Look, I trust Jarad completely. I've known him for many years. He's never done anything but protect Solly and me, and serve *us.* He's a dedicated guy."

I studied Miriam closely. She appeared guileless, but I felt a strong sense of unease. "What were you two talking about?"

"Nothing. Just that," she said calmly, her eyes fixed on me.

"It sounded like someone transferred money to you. Was I imagining that?"

"No, of course not. Jarad's been a big help to me."

I was flabbergasted. "Miriam, you weren't instructing him to pay a bill at the local market. You had him converting the money into many currencies. What's going on?"

"I've sold paintings in several countries," she stated flatly.

"This was no sale of a few canvases," I said, sitting at the far end of the couch. "Swiss francs, shekels, euros..."

Miriam studied my face, which had hardened into skepticism. In the afterglow of so much tenderness, I was still compelled to love her, to trust her. Venus was playing me big time. But what man wouldn't offer the Goddess of Love respite from her half shell, a glass of wine, a warm bed? Miriam and Weiner, that was a different story. That was scary. Yet to believe she could be tied to Levi's torture and Chick's gruesome beheading was more cynicism than I could possibly muster.

"Can I trust you, David?" she asked earnestly. "Completely?"

"Of course," I replied in my most sincere tone.

"All right..." She hesitated at first, eyes fixed on mine. She reached into her purse to grab a cigarette pack and lighter—gold—removed a cigarette, and lit it. She offered me one, but I refused, so she tossed the pack and lighter on the table. "I've been raising money for Joseph's projects for years. You don't think he could sell free soup to a starving man? Look at the expenses we're confronted with. His lab, a wing in the Life Sciences building filled with the latest equipment, his assistants' salaries..."

"Not to mention the multimillion dollar nail. Bisl teams all over the planet."

"Yes, those, too. Recent developments, but exponentially more expensive."

So, Miriam *was* behind the funding for Solly's megalomania. I couldn't have been more shocked if a cattle prod had been driven up my posterior, excuse the scatological reference. In retrospect, the numbers had never added up for me. Religious organizations, never very good at managing their limited assets, seldom are frivolous with their endowments. Solly's projects had always seemed so improbable, so out of proportion. Now my eyes were slowly opening from their slumber. "Miriam, does Am Ha-b'rit even know about the...the Jesus cloning project? About Solly's T'chiat Ha-meitim program in all its dimensions?"

"I don't know, David," she said modestly, blowing smoke. "Joseph deals with those people. I'm not privy to those discussions."

I wasn't going to let her evade my questions; too much was at stake. "I assume Am Ha-b'rit knows about Jarad Weiner and Edan Shadid, that old Resurrection experiment."

"Of course," she replied.

"So where do you get the kind of money you're talking about?"

"Any number of sources. I've been quite busy." She saw my face drop, then stubbed out her cigarette. "Now, David, it's nothing sinister. My donors are all generous people who mean well. It's not important who they are, nor what their motives are, is it? Everyone has his or her own motive. Does a salesperson care about the motives of the buyer, except to make the sale? In the end, our result will serve all of humanity, won't it?"

Well, P. T. Barnum understated his good fortune. There must, in fact, be thousands of suckers born every minute for a showman to thrive. And at her level, Miriam must be quite some show-woman.

"David, I'm not the girl you knew. That I should develop myself wasn't the only thing I learned from you."

Now we were both laughing, the tension released. She slid down the couch and snuggled up against me. I put my arm around her, and she laid her hand on my bare chest, delicately brushing my curly chest hair like she once had.

She trilled from Sondheim's "Send in the Clowns," her lovely lips aglow with mirth, the irony not lost on me. We pecked a kiss, chuckling over what we were, what we had become.

Yes, weren't we quite a pair, indeed? The man immune to being hustled. The woman who could shake down the most recalcitrant wealthy patron. We were the immovable object snuggling with the irresistible force, together again after two decades.

What could I say? She had me. I wanted to remove the bad feelings left by my stern, suspicious tone, to build rapport with her again. We still had over an hour before nightfall, when I planned to chance the Paris subway under cover of darkness to our next hideout—a risk I was not thrilled to take. *Yikes! Now I'm thinking in terms of hideouts, the cover of night. What have I gotten myself into? What has Miriam gotten me into?*

"We've still got some time," I said. "If it's not too painful, you could show me some photos of Ari—if you have them with you."

She reached into her large purse and drew out her wallet. While it was open, I noted her cell phone, lying like a time bomb at the bottom, but felt there was no point in discussing it. As she unsnapped the wallet, amid the row of pockets, I glimpsed a gold Credit Suisse card, her name on the bottom, and others: American Express Platinum, Visa, those of HSBC and other European banks. Handy cash equivalents for wherever she found herself.

She removed the plastic picture holders, returning the wallet to her purse. Then she began going through the photos slowly, pausing one by one. Miriam and baby Ari sitting on a towel at the beach; Miriam pushing toddler Ari on the swing; Miriam spooning in soup as he sits on a colorful highchair. None of Solly. Pictures when Ari was older, of his bar mitzvah, so many, all with Ari seated. *Who took them, Solly?*

Then the grade school headshot. I grabbed the tip of the photo to stop her from turning to the next and studied it closely. I wanted to see the spirit in the boy, perhaps the soul, his youthful personality.

It was then I realized his face looked vaguely familiar. I pulled the picture closer, searching his features intently. Did he resemble the bearded friend Miriam had made eye contact with at the hospital, the man who had escorted her to Ari's funeral? It's sometimes hard to tell with a child, but Ari appeared to share with Miriam's friend the same jaw line, the same forehead. But like Miriam's friend, wasn't Jesus also a Jew, of whom we have no contemporaneous images? Then I stared closely into Ari's eyes, like I'd seen them before.

Ari's eyes were hers, Miriam's! Or so it seemed. Dark pools, deeply black, round, profound. His black curly hair resembled hers, too; his cheekbones were high like hers.

"Miriam, your art shows in Europe, did you ever take Ari with you?"

"Yes, of course, as often as I could. We had wonderful days together…" Her eyes grew sad, but I couldn't stop myself from probing further.

"And today, we made love, Miriam. Doesn't that kind of…kind of violate your plan, Solly's plan?" I couldn't believe she would engage in such an impulsive act by accident.

She took a sip of wine, her brow wrinkled. "I've been thinking about that since the funeral, David," she said slowly. "A lot. I know now that I can never replace Ari. Any child I had now—the same way—I'd look into his face and see Ari. Would that be fair to the child? To Joseph? I've had a feeling that maybe I'm being selfish. Maybe we should find a loving couple...

"Maybe, too, it's time for me to have another child, the old-fashioned way. There's still time. I'm sorry, I shouldn't have said that."

There it was; she was free. Free to be mine, to be anyone's. But had Ari's "divine cloning" been a ruse, merely one of Miriam's gambits? If so, if Ari had been the biological son she'd conceived with her bearded Am Ha-b'rit friend, what about Ari? On their trips to Europe—and probably the U.S.— had Miriam trotted out Ari like a trained monkey? In America, there'd been child preachers, shepherded by their manipulative parents, who'd grown famous, made millions, converted tens of thousands; the tales are legion. Was Ari like that, a circus prop, a Chautauqua tent prodigy?

Was Solly Miriam's puppet, too? Had he confirmed Ari's ancient pedigree at Miriam's behest, being dependent on the money she raked in to keep his research afloat? Indeed, had she planned to exploit his crazy ideas of genetic enhancement all along, since those youthful days back at the apartment? Could she have seen that far ahead? Had Solly, in fact, ever even made love to Miriam?

Or was the reverse the case? Was Miriam Solly's automaton, playing the role he'd programmed her to play, leaving him free to do his work without budgetary limits? Or more the horror, perhaps they were working together, to manipulate me, as well as to sting their wealthy marks.

Or, maybe, just maybe, Ari was just as he'd seemed to be, as Miriam and Solly told me he was. Religious people are fond of saying that God lives within each of us; Christians that Jesus Christ lives in every Christian heart. If that is truly the case, the boy I had met had that spiritual richness in a dazzling abundance.

"That paper you gave Reverend Nation, Miriam. What was it really?"

"Just a school paper Ari had written."

"Homework? With help from his mom?"

"What good mother doesn't?" she asked rhetorically.

She began to laugh heartily, and I joined in with her. Reverend Nation believed he was manipulating us, having kidnapped me in order to extort me into introducing him to Ari, even using his leverage over my bondage to plant a spy with me, my bodyguard, Bear. So what's good for the goose, eh? Still chuckling, Miriam cuddled into my chest and turned her head up toward mine. Our eyes met, really seeing each other fully. She raised her lips. Supporting her chin with my finger, I came closer until my lips met hers, firmly, driven by affection and my wildly accelerating senses. As we remained locked in a long kiss, her hand slid under my towel sensuously, slowly.

At her touch, I laid back on the couch, a frozen dreamer, fallen under the spell of a magical succubus, a lovely warm spirit who had floated as smoke under the doorway to suck away my soul.

Was I now Miriam's partner, or her goat? At that moment, I didn't care.

***

Sulaiman al Kahn, an officer from Mabahith, the dreaded Saudi security agency, wearing a crisp European-cut suit, set a large briefcase on the floor. Satisfied, he settled himself unsteadily on the large silk pillow, reclining against the cracked plaster wall. Persian carpets covered the cramped room's concrete floors, reducing the musty odor that was typical in this part of the West Bank. A flattering gold-framed portrait of the Saudi King dominated the wall across from his seat. The picture fit neatly into a substantially broader clean space on the wall, as if recently hung in place of a larger one.

A woman in a modest, floor-length black dress, her head covered, her face concealed by a scarf, set a tray on the brass table. She placed a small plate and cup and saucer before the Mabahith man, the same before Edan Shadid sitting across from him, and doled out a few *kaak bi ajwas* date ring cookies from a large bowl. She delicately poured the tea, then padded softly from the room, gently closing the door behind her. The leader of the Martyrs of the Holy was open for business.

"May God be with you," Edan Shadid greeted his guest.

"And with you," al Kahn responded, noting the spike-shaped birthmark on his cheek.

The two sipped their tea and tasted their cookies with satisfaction.

"I am honored to see you again," Shadid said. "Your journey to the West Bank was not too unpleasant, I trust?"

"No, not at all," al Kahn replied.

"I sacrificed two of my bravest martyrs to distract the Israelis; God be with our beloved brothers," Shadid said.

"God be with them," al Kahn responded perfunctorily. "You have seen to it that the Israelis will be quite preoccupied during my visit." The visitor smiled, still fascinated by his host's spike-shaped birthmark.

There was a tap at the door. Shadid issued an order, and a man wearing combat fatigues, an AK-47 strapped to his back, led in a raggedly dressed, unshaven prisoner in handcuffs, dragging heavy ankle shackles. The emaciated prisoner's pale face was gaunt, his hollow eyes rimmed in terror.

"This, my brother, is Mayer, the Israeli scientist we captured. Have you anything you want to ask him?"

"Yes," al Kahn replied. "This quest has been a great passion of mine. You told my friend here that only one nail remains. What happened to the other two?"

"They were destroyed in a fire set in 1980 by a crazed old rabbi," the prisoner replied in broken Arabic. "He was against the project from the beginning."

"The nail for the feet is all that remains," the host, Shadid, explained.

"And that nail is in the United States; is that right?" the Saudi security man asked.

"Yes," Mayer replied. "In Missouri, the Midwest."

Shadid made knowing eye contact with his guest. "Any other questions, your Excellency?"

"I am told Western scientists can recreate Jesus using the nail, using modern techniques, cloning and such. Is this true?"

"Yes," Mayer replied.

"They have done it already, successfully," Shadid interjected, an angry scowl on his face. "The Jews have cloned one of their greatest warriors."

"And others have the money to buy this nail?" al Kahn asked.

"Yes," Mayer answered. "Jews, Christians, lots of willing buyers."

"The Jews, the Christians, all seek it," Shadid emphasized. "All have great resources. I understand the billionaire Wilcox brothers are determined to resurrect their Messiah and so defeat Islam in the Final Days."

"We must have it! The King must have it in his hands," al Kahn said, then fell into a deeply troubled contemplation.

"Two enemies combined may be superior in numbers," Shadid said sagely. "But with divided rivals, as are the Christians and Jews, then a wise commander can win the world with one powerful stroke of his mighty sword against first the weaker, then the stronger. Consider Ludendorff's strategy against the Russians in World War I."

Al Kahn thought a moment. Then he waved his hand, dismissing the subordinate pair. Shadid nodded, and the guard took the captive away, closing the door once again.

"What are you going to do with this dog?" al Kahn asked disdainfully.

"Hold him until he is no longer useful. The United States," Shadid stressed, "this makes the acquisition somewhat more difficult. I will have to go myself. Clumsy *jihadis* would only hinder my efforts. I will be risking my own life."

"How will you get past security to America?" a puzzled al Kahn asked. "Interpol, Mossad, the American security services—you are no doubt on all their watch lists."

"I have my methods. It will take time. And money. But with your help, I will acquire the nail. I do not fear my mission, your Excellency. I have dedicated myself these many years to achieving martyrdom for our faith.

"But remember what is at stake, my friend," Shadid prompted his noteworthy guest. "As present events augur, the apocalyptic war between Islam and the infidel is fast approaching. If the Jews or the Christians succeed in obtaining the nail, it will mean the eventual death of Islam. If we succeed in acquiring the nail, Western apostasy will wither on the vine. All men throughout the West, throughout the world, will become our brothers, not we theirs."

The man from Mabahith subtly slid the briefcase toward his host, allowing his skeptical side to weigh Shadid's broad claims. Seeing this doubt on his guest's face, his host pressed home.

"Our enemies have the advantage, a head start in the race," Edan Shadid cautioned. "Mossad, the CIA, the FBI, they are all worthy opponents. There will be bidding, of course. Frankly, your Excellency, at this time, I cannot compete with the resources marshaled by both the Jews and the Christians together. They are fabulously wealthy, and they know what this will portend: by God, the Resurrection of their Prophet! But we must stop them. Fortunately, as I mentioned, the two are pitted against one another. What do you suggest?"

"I must strike!" al Kahn exclaimed, slamming his fist into his palm. "While our enemies squabble, I must strike instantly with my sword. I will have the King's funds wired to your account in Zurich by morning."

"An inspiring strategy, your Excellency. And the bribe money I'll need in U.S. dollars?"

"In this briefcase," al Kahn indicated. "Bring me the nail, my brother. Bring it to me. We will present it to the King together. But whatever you do, don't let it fall into other hands. Understand?"

"If I fear capture, I will destroy the nail rather than give it up. Even if it costs me my life." Shadid reached beside his pillow and picked up a plaque, which he proffered to his guest. "This is a gift in praise to the King, from the people who love him here on the ground. From the people whose children he helps educate, whose children he helps feed and house. All praise to our beloved benefactor. Would you like to visit some of the infrastructure the King's funds have built here in the West Bank?"

"Thank you, but I must return to Amman to conclude some business before I return home to my country." The guest checked his watch. "Ah, which I see must be presently."

"Please see that the King receives our gift. And relay to him the thanks of his humble servants."

"This involves a great deal of money," al Kahn said, rising to his feet and brushing off his suit. "An enormous sum, more than the ransom of many kings. You know what the consequences will be for a failure of this magnitude. God be with you."

"And with you, my friend."

CHAPTER TWENTY-TWO
SEND IN THE CLOWNS

It was time to head to Montmartre, to the apartment a few steep, hilly blocks from Sacré-Cœur Basilica. When it was dark, we left Jean Claude's and made our way through the warren of the Marais, skirting the open Place des Vosges, heading toward the Bastille. A block shy of the monument, we ducked into Brasserie Bofinger for a traditional Alsatian meal, our stomachs, not our souls, starving, having missed lunch. It is always inspiring to dine under Bofinger's glorious stained glass domed dining area ceiling. While we waited for our table, Miriam and I held hands, saying little.

After a while, I left Miriam and stepped outside onto the curb. There I examined the night-shadowed area outside the restaurant, but no pedestrian seemed threatening. I tried calling Detective Landau again, but with the news from Israel what it was, I expected him to be off investigating some disturbance with no time for my petty concerns. This time, I was in luck. He had gotten confirmation from St. Louis that Levi Asher had, indeed, died of a heart attack. I thanked him and told him I would see him on my next buying trip.

"I hope you survive that long," he said in a tone that reflected a grim caution.

That settled it for me. We weren't going to visit my friend in Paris to put out word on the nail. I had fears that *jihadis* directed from the Middle East or Weiner's allies might be watching the city's dealers. Perhaps we wouldn't even stop at Montmartre.

Inside the restaurant, we got a table, and when the tuxedo-clad waiter with an indifferent air finally arrived, we were more than ready to order. For starters,

Miriam chose the foie gras of duck with black cherry chutney and Espelette pepper, I, the crabmeat and avocado in lime with apricot jelly in Gewurztraminer. For the main course, we both selected the grilled chateaubriand. I planned to save room for the profiteroles with warm Grand Vintage Valrhona chocolate, while Miriam commented on the lemon meringue tart with lime sorbet. The dinner was not cheap, but if I was going to have a last meal before my execution, I could have done worse. Fortunately, despite our wrinkled clothing, the waiter probably suspected I might tip like an American, meaning anything at all, so the service was not rude.

As we waited for the starters, I whispered to Miriam, "The nail is still where Levi hid it in St. Louis."

"In St. Louis? How do you know?" she asked.

"Levi died of a heart attack. My detective friend just confirmed it. So, I suspect he hadn't revealed the nail's location yet."

"So what should we do?"

"I want to avoid the airport. I'd like to catch the train to London. We could buy some clothes there, then fly to the states from Heathrow."

For the moment, I felt relaxed, being well fed, no longer a holdout in Jean Claude's apartment. I began to wonder if what we were doing was worth the potential consequences. "Miriam," I asked with all seriousness, "since you may not wish to have another child like, like Ari, how critical is the nail to you really?"

"David, I've made promises to our donors, and I keep my word. Besides, the nail is important to Joseph. He tells me it is important to Am Ha-b'rit. If Joseph's work is to go on, it matters."

"And his experiments matter that much to you that you would risk your life, our lives?"

"Yes. David," she said with urgency. "I've dedicated the last twenty years to enabling Solly's work. Do you think I would quit now because there are difficulties, because there is danger? His work is the most important thing science is doing today; he must go on. You have to see that."

There was nothing for me to say. Or do. I was back to being the Beard.

"David," Miriam confided in me. "Are you sure you're in this? Are you sure I can trust you all the way?"

"Why? What's on your mind?"

"There is more to this than you can even imagine, David—if you can figure out how to help me pull it off."

"Pull what off, Miriam? What are you talking about?" Finally, she seemed ready to reveal the motives I'd long suspected she was keeping hidden, motives so powerful she felt compelled to leave Ari's *shiva*. But this restaurant was not the place to discuss matters of such consequence. I would have to wait.

After dinner, we caught a cab to Gare du Nord station and bought train tickets for the three-hour ride through the Chunnel to London's St Pancras station. The trip was uneventful, and we got a couple hours' rest, but no sleep. From there, we took a taxi to the Sumner, a small B&B I knew near Marble Arch. Fortunately, the young German woman who manages the Indian-owned Sumner had a small room available.

The next morning, after serving ourselves a modest breakfast downstairs, we walked over to Selfridges on Oxford Street and browsed through. I was determined not to cab all the way to Harrod's, with its stock of thirty-thousand-British-pound shoes and thirty-five-thousand-pound handbags, one-and-a-half U.S. dollars to the British pound. Not our style. We weren't off to Buckingham Palace. At Selfridges, we bought enough to fill the old suitcase Chaya had given to Miriam. Miriam's wallet was loaded with credit cards, but I paid.

From Heathrow, we flew to New York's Kennedy International, and after a surprisingly brief wait, from there to St. Louis Lambert Field. I noted a few suspicious characters along the way, but none especially threatening. The train to London ruse had likely shaken a bad actor, or some of them, from our tail.

A half-hour after landing in St. Louis, slightly sleep-deprived, I had the cabbie circle my block in the city's mild spring weather before parking to let us out. Seeing no one on the street, we entered my house. Relief! For the moment...

***

"Finkel can help us catch Levi Asher's killer. I need him."

"He's being held on federal crimes, Greenberg. These are serious felonies," Detective Shay said. "It's not going to be that easy to spring him."

"Look, Detective, the dope was a dupe for this guy. Do you want to put this idiot *schmuck* in the big house, where they'll eat him alive, or catch the monster who tortured that poor kid? I mean, come on, Detective Shay. How many times have I helped you out? Look, I'm cashing in all my chips; we're square."

Shay thought it over, a sour expression covering his face. He pressed the button and spoke into his intercom. "I've got a man here to see Finkel,

Lawrence G. Have someone escort him, will you?" He turned back to me. "Okay, I'll call the Feds for you. But you better be right, Greenberg, because I'm not taking this up the wahzoo for you. Something goes wrong, it's your ass big time, not mine."

***

"You're screwing me, Greenberg!" Finkel groused, pacing around the jail's closet-sized visitors' room wearing his baggy orange jumpsuit. "You told me ten points on the net."

"Finkel, I'm springing you from a long prison sentence. Maybe twenty years! Half your points will be going to Daddy, which is where your cut will end up regardless."

"Screw you, Greenberg. I kick his ass all the time. All the time!"

"Finkel, we need Daddy. Without his help, it's zero return, nada. You can get half of something or get squat and stay behind bars."

"Can't you give him five out of your cut?"

See what I have to deal with? I am springing him from a long, guaranteed prison sentence, offering him a cut of perhaps major proportions, and he's pissed at me. No good deed goes unpunished with gamblers. "Listen, Finkel, I don't have all day. Do you want the deal or not?"

Finkel paced, deep in thought, scowling. "Goddammit, Greenberg, I knew I couldn't trust you. Prick."

"Finkel, do you want the deal? As far as I give a damn, you can rot in prison."

He hesitated, and I could see his face twisting into convolutions of consideration. Finally, he charged the table and slammed down his fist. "Okay, asshole. Get me out of this vomitorium."

"Thank you, Father Finkel," I said reverently. "Now go home and put on your preacher collar."

***

"We need an office in a bank, Daddy. Any ideas?"

Daddy Markowitz dunked his half-pound burger into a huge, red turd of catsup and took an enormous bite. He chewed thoughtfully, his cheeks puffed out, then dipped a French fry and stuffed it into the open side of his mouth. As he worked to chew and swallow the load, he sipped from his Coke straw to dissolve the thick mass. Finally, he swallowed the last of the bite.

"I know a bank guy who owes Tumor a bunch of money. A bunch. Howell's his name, a real loser. We could buy the note. You sure we just need the office for a few minutes?"

"That's it, Daddy. A few minutes. Tell Howell you'll pay off his chit."
I pulled out my checkbook. "How much does he owe?"

"Let me call Tumor."

"Okay."

"And we're talking a quarter-million? My cut?"

"That's possible, Daddy. Same for Finkel."

He dialed his cell. "Tumor. Got a deal for you."

***

I relaxed on my drive home through familiar streets, convertible top down, at the wheel of my beloved azure blue Beemer 4-Series coupe. The sun was bright, the trees sprouting leaves, the grass turning green. It must have rained while I was away. I took the precaution of circling my block, admiring the houses, the maples with their fine broad leaves lining the sidewalk. Nobody stirring. But when I pulled to the curb in front of my house, a black Escalade had my spot. Oy, *the Hallelujah Hour has me in their sights again.*

I entered the front door to find Bear sitting in my chair, the same one Daddy had occupied with his street-bought pistol. I assumed Miriam had let him in. We greeted each other warmly.

"Hey, Bear," I said. "Good to see you. Want something to eat or drink?"

"No, thanks," he said as I sat across from him. He had a suspicious gleam in his eye, and as he leaned aggressively forward, his six-six bulk intimidated me. Clearly, he wanted information. At the same time, I wanted to probe him. It would be a battle of wills and deception, and Bear was very tough-minded—the proverbial "slim customer."

I keep a standard green and white onyx chess set on my coffee table. I slid it between us, white pieces on his side, hoping that enticing him to play might distract him enough to make a mistake, a slip of the tongue. I offered him white because it would be harder for him to turn down the advantage of first move. Also, being white, he'd have to devote more concentration to formulating an attack strategy than I would to defending against him. I'd read that Bear had been the undisputed chess champion among Rams players, and during our drive to Ein Bokek, I'd challenged him to a friendly match. I believed the stories about his prowess on the sixty-four squares, and with average foot speed and agility, Bear's longevity in the NFL was a tribute more to his intelligence than his physical gifts.

At first, his ego made him refuse to play. He didn't want to risk his Rams "championship belt" on an ad hoc pickup game. But I convinced him we would merely be scrimmaging, feeling each other out for some future contest. Either of us could quit any game, at any time, for a draw, and we'd reset the pieces. I playfully questioned his courage in so many words, and he couldn't resist the call to compete. He slammed down a white pawn and we were off, chatting and pushing the onyx.

"What happened to you, guy?" he asked. "Where've you been?"

"Just running errands. How'd you get in?"

"Miriam. She's upstairs sleeping now."

She probably wasn't asleep, but it was as good an excuse as any to avoid being quizzed by our unsettling guest. I had escaped from the university, in part, to avoid Bear and was embarrassed about deserting him. Now he was here to call me on the ruse.

"No, I mean, what happened to you in Israel?" he asked. "I was waiting for you at the hotel in Netanya. I had the university's car."

"That's right," I said. "What happened to it?"

"I returned it. A fellow named Weiner gave me a lift to the airport."

Weiner! I wish I'd been a fly on the back seat during that ride. The possibility of those two conspiring together produced a menace too ominous to contemplate, so my mind rejected the whole concept. Although I did wonder which of them made a fool of the other, and which inadvertently revealed what sensitive information.

We played in silence for a time, struggling through a Ruy Lopez opening toward mid-game. The Ruy Lopez was perfect for my purposes because it's a nice balanced strategy that would be hard to penetrate, one that I could defend without too much analysis. Bear's moves were sharp, direct, but I maneuvered the conflict into ever more complex positions, constructing deep puzzles for him that required him to make increasingly complicated calculations. Always the attacker, he sacrificed a pawn to keep the initiative. I was making him work hard to maintain his attack—establishing a tight pawn structure and a layered, mobile defense along interior lines.

"What did Weiner have to say?" I asked casually.

"Nothing," he replied, keeping his cards close to the vest.

"What did you two discuss?"

"Oh, nothing," he mused. "Mostly Israeli politics, that sort of thing."

"Yes? What did you think of him?" I chanced.

"He's a dedicated guy, being in security and all, but he said some pretty right wing, nationalistic stuff. Man, I got the impression he really hates the...uh, the other side."

"That's my impression, too," I agreed. "Anything else?"

"Not really, short drive," Bear said, closing off the discussion.

"Who contacted who?" I asked. He ignored the question, seemingly focused on his next move. End of topic. "You must have returned the car the next day," I ventured. "You made it back to St. Louis pretty quickly." He didn't exactly let any brush grow under his feet in Israel, that's for sure.

"The reverend needed me for a videotaping session. You were missing. What was I supposed to do?"

Bear was needed for a TV shoot? I made a mental note. If I spoke with Reverend Nation, this was something I could verify or debunk.

I rose and headed to the kitchen for a Diet Coke to calm my nerves and to consider alternative approaches. "You sure you won't have anything, Bear? I've got some frozen orange juice I could whip up. I just brought in fresh apples and pears. What do you want?"

"I'll have the fruit," he replied as I disappeared around the corner. I washed off a few pieces, dropped them in a bowl, opened a Coke, filled a pitcher with ice water, and returned with a tray.

"So what's the story?" I asked. "You seem a little pissed at me."

"David, I was responsible for you." His soft voice did not conceal his displeasure. "That was a nasty trick, disappearing like that."

"I was being watched. I had to slip away."

"And where were you for two days?"

So he was tracking my movements. His barely repressed anger was making me uncomfortable. "Paris one night, London another. Just ditching my tail, if there was one."

He bit into an apple, thinking it over, then took another bite. "So why are you back here?" Bear asked.

"Things were a little hot for me in Israel, wouldn't you say?"

As Bear's competitive heart kicked in, I could see his frustration growing. He wasn't plowing over a squirrely defensive back on this chessboard. Matching his game strategy, his conversation became more aggressive, less guarded as well.

Let it out, big guy!

He finished the apple in a couple bites and picked up another. "The reverend made me responsible for getting some special nail back to the university. Said you'd understand. Any progress on that?"

Aha! Bear knew of the nail, inferring the reverend did, too, but what

195

did the reverend truly know and understand? And how much did Bear know? For one, he knew more than I wished he did. "I just got back," I told him. "I haven't even started looking yet."

"So you think the nail's in St. Louis? Is that why you're here?"

"That nail better be here because I'm not going back to Israel for it."

"Uh-huh. You going to start looking soon? Apparently, Reverend Nation thinks it's pretty important."

"As soon as my body clock catches up." I smiled. "It's been pretty rough, what with all the travel and the trauma. Terrorist attacks, murders, it's a bit much for a shopkeeper. Frankly, Bear, Miriam and I are scared shitless."

"I've been warned," he cautioned, his eyes glaring, "there are some mean players in this game. As you know, *jihadis* and everything. You'd better be counting on me to protect you. You know, once I get the nail, David, I take it back to your friends in Israel, per the reverend's instructions, and you're off the hook."

"That would be a relief," I said with a sigh.

"Do you still have the cell I gave you?" he asked pointedly.

"I don't think so, Bear. I lost it in the scramble."

He pulled another cell from his pocket and handed it to me. "Here's one, same as the other. All you have to do it press the same button, I'll be here as soon as I can, or someone I appoint will."

"Thanks," I said, examining it. Then I noticed a scratch on the case, caused by a ring or rough handling, identical to the scratch on the first phone. *This cell is the one I'd left on a closet shelf at Miriam's house.* Apparently, he'd come to her house looking for me and, seeing I wasn't there, broke in. Probably rather easily. It also meant there was a transponder or tracking device in the phone to enable him to find it. If I carried it around, he'd know where I was every minute.

"Maybe I should stay here with you," he offered, and not merely as a kindly suggestion.

"No, no, we're okay for now. That would be too much for Miriam, I think."

"You're making a mistake, David. A big mistake. You sure?"

"I'm sure, Bear."

"Listen," he said pointedly, "don't fool around with these people. You see what they're capable of. That Levi Asher stuff was no walk in the park."

Levi Asher? What details, if any, of Levi's gruesome torture had the police released to the public? Had Bear revealed knowledge of events that would implicate him in Levi's murder? Since that fateful night outside Ein Bokek, I had considered Bear the primary suspect in Chick Markowitz's murder. From the moment we left Netanya that morning, Bear knew I was headed to Chick's and had plenty of time to call ahead.

"What do you mean 'no walk in the park,' Bear?" I asked, careful not to display any knowledge of Levi's torture.

Bear was a bit ruffled. "I mean, he was kidnapped and killed. What do you think?"

Did Bear make a slip of the tongue? It was a matter of my interpretation, and I wasn't sure. I made a mental note to inform Detective Shay of Bear's comment. They may not be able to arrest him on my suspicions alone, but they could bring him in for questioning.

"Get that nail, get it to me, and be done with it. You hear?" Bear said, jaw tight.

"I will, Bear."

"I don't want you winding up like your friend back in Ein Bokek. Remember?"

Now Bear was throwing Chick Markowitz's beheading in my face, too. Like I would ever be able to forget that travesty. He wanted to win. But win for what purpose? For whom?

***

"One of our suspects has flushed," Detective Landau of the Jerusalem police told me over Shin Bet's cell. "Shadid, the *jihadi*, hasn't been seen in Israel in a couple days. I'll call Detective Shay and warn him that he might be coming your way."

So Shadid was headed here, or here already. Lovely.

I'll call Detective Shay, too," I said. "I think I can help the police catch him. Incidentally, Dov, I have grave suspicions about Bear Brukowski for the Levi Asher murder. I'll follow up with Shay on that, too. Just be aware."

"Good luck," Landau said.

Luck? Lady Luck's fleecing me royally.

CHAPTER TWENTY-THREE
PROLIFERATING THREATS

The flashlight beam shining on his face woke the professor. His stringy hair a strawberry tangle, he forced his bloodshot eyes open, mentally crawling through slumber as the large hand gently shook him.

"Professor Solomon. Please be quiet," Weiner's lips whispered below the familiar thick, black mustache. The professor reluctantly nodded affirmation. Amid the towers of glass, the tubes, and technical equipment structured throughout the busy lab, Weiner paused for some time to study the scientist's thin face as if to penetrate a deep mystery, seemingly unable to continue. Then he quietly set the pistol on the nightstand, pulled down the covers, and helped the slender professor to his feet. With a shhhhh and a finger to his lips, Weiner expertly helped the professor slide on the shirt and pants lying crumbled on the floor beside the cot. When the professor was clothed, Weiner emptied a carton of Gauloises onto the bed and shoved a half-dozen packs into his jacket pockets. That accomplished, he slipped the open pack and the lighter laying on the nightstand into the professor's shirt pocket. Then he took the professor's hand with his left, picked up the pistol with his right, and, tiptoeing, led him through the shadowy labyrinth of benches and lab experiments scattered throughout the elongated room.

In the hall, they passed the body of a young man in his late-thirties sprawled on the floor, lying in a pool of blood. *Too bad; so dedicated. I trained you myself*, Weiner recalled.

The professor's feet hesitated, but the man pulled him along with a forceful jerk. They reached the front door of the building, where a young grad student in a lab coat sat propped up in a chair, his shoulders slumped over the desk at an unnatural angle, blood clotting on a wound from a blow to his head. A can of soda lay on its side, its dark contents having spilled onto the floor. *Sleep well, young man. I hope there are no side effects.*

Weiner let go of the professor's hand, switched the pistol to his left, and tapped numbers into the control panel. The thick glass door slid open. Weiner directed the professor through the entrance, then pressed another panel, and the sliding door closed behind them.

They proceeded across the quadrangle, down a grass embankment under street lamps dim from age and by design. Nearby, twisted under a hedgerow of bushes lay another body of a man in his early twenties. *That's what you get for standing in my way, you arrogant asshole.*

The pair skirted two buildings, then after another hundred meters, cut through the back yard of a darkened house in the middle of a block of sleeping homes. Carefully, they weaved their way through the community, cutting across lawns, through gates and bushes, and over rocky ground. Finally, they reached a car sitting on a dark road. Weiner opened the passenger door, directed the professor into the seat, and, when he was situated, fastened his passenger's seatbelt. Then Weiner paused to study Professor Solomon's face. The scientist's furious eyes glared at him. Weiner removed a cigarette from the pack in the professor's shirt pocket, placed it in his captive's mouth, and held the lighter while the professor puffed it into usefulness. Professor Solomon did not say "thank you."

"I see you have made a decision to dispense with your soul," the professor said sarcastically.

Not to dispense with my soul, Professor. To use it as a trade chip.

***

It was an hour before the onset of dusk, typically the warmest part of the day in St. Louis, with temperatures in the low seventies. I tenderly cradled Miriam against me as we sat on a bench in my enclosed back yard. My patch of grass was still yellow; its manicured borders a tangle of bare vines and dormant bushes. Yet with spring's arrival, the familiar surroundings were returning to life, becoming lush, green, and fragrant. We had an evening to ourselves before we had to begin searching for the nail, a momentary respite from being pursued. Plus, I needed a breather from our latest time zone roulette wheel spin.

Unfortunately, this was not the time for lovemaking, nor even casual affection. Miriam seemed to be taking our plight well, even though I was not. I had to expiate my fears, my suspicions, my doubts, soon or my head would explode.

"Have you told Solly yet about Levi Asher or Chick Markowitz?" I asked, casting out the demons plaguing the darkest regions of my mind. This query brought Solly into the equation, the third point of Miriam's love triangle, or, considering her Am Ha-b'rit friend, perhaps the fourth point of her quadrangle. If the four of us were the extent of it!

"No," she replied matter-of-factly, sighing. "I suppose I should."

"I guess," I mused. "Listen, when we were in Paris, and I overheard you tell Jarad Weiner to exchange currencies. Was that done through a Swiss bank account?"

"Yes," she admitted. "Mine and Joseph's, although Joseph doesn't pay much attention to these things. He may not even remember we have it."

But Weiner has his fingers in it. "Can Weiner transfer funds *out of* that account?"

"No, Jarad's authority is limited. Only Joseph and I can transfer into or out of the account."

I wasn't going to ask her how much money had been deposited into the account, nor who was on the other end of the deal; that was her business. But I figured the sum must have been substantial, just based on the currency transactions that Miriam directed.

Miriam's eyes searched the grounds. "Why did we have to come out here to talk?"

"For privacy," I replied. "Bear spent a lot of time alone in my house, with you upstairs. He may have planted listening devices. Maybe I'm getting paranoid, but..."

"You don't trust Bear, do you?" she asked, knowing the answer.

"I have my suspicions about him, Miriam, in ways I can't explain. He readily found the cell he'd given me, which I'd hidden in your spare bedroom closet back in Israel, so he couldn't track us."

She shrugged and rose, turning toward the house. "I'll use my cell to call Joseph. I should see how he's doing anyway."

"No," I cautioned, taking her arm to halt her. "I put the cell you got from Weiner in my basement. Same reason. Here, use this." I took the Shin Bet cell from my pocket and handed it to her.

She called Solly's lab while I stretched, the back slats on the bench not designed for comfort. She waited a couple of rings, then spoke. "Hello, may I speak to Joseph please? This is Miriam."

She paused, listening. Then a look of horror spread across her face. "Are you sure? Where's Jarad? What does he say?" She froze. "He's what? *What?!*"

Deeply shaken, she collapsed onto the bench beside me, the cell to her ear.

After she'd listened for a minute, she said, "Please call me at this number the minute anyone hears anything. Anything! Be sure to give this number to security, right now." She disconnected.

"What?" I asked anxiously.

"Joseph's been kidnapped," she managed to say shakily, her eyes beginning to tear. "By...by Jarad. He killed Meir and Nachman, two of his own men, and poisoned a grad student."

"By Weiner? How do they know it was him?"

"He used his card to get into the building, to get into Joseph's lab. He didn't even try to disguise himself. They have him on security camera with a pistol, leading Joseph from the building. Now they're both missing."

"Why didn't security call you right away?"

"He'd deleted my phone number from their database."

So Jarad Weiner had cut the cord. He was an outlaw in the worst sense. And he had Solly. If Weiner had been responsible for the deaths of Levi Asher or Chick Markowitz, or both, how much was Solly's life worth now? Both Miriam and I were wrecks. One of us had to come up with a plan of action, or we'd both go crazy.

I rose from the bench. "Wait here," I said. "We've got to call Weiner, right now. We'll use the cell he gave you." *That'll get through to our kidnapper directly.*

"Do you think Jarad will kill him?" a terrified Miriam asked, squeezing my hand.

"No, there's no chance of that, Miriam. No chance. Solly is the only card Weiner holds. This is an extortion attempt to get at your money. He knows what's in your account, or at least he knows about this latest deposit, right?"

"He knows about the nail, too," she said, her voice shaking.

"Maybe he wants to trade Solly for the money and, hopefully, he doesn't care about the nail. I don't know."

Miriam paused, taking a deep breath, her face consumed with hurt and betrayal. "I hope that's the case," she said uncertainly.

***

"What do you want, Weiner?" I barked into the cell.

"Well, my friend Greenberg," Jarad Weiner said. "I think you know what I want. I want to make a trade, a simple trade."

"Trade *what* for *what*, Weiner?"

"A live Professor Solomon for certain assets."

"Which assets?"

"The money in Mrs. Solomon's account. And the nail, of course, when you recover it."

"Why the nail, Weiner? Why not just take the money?"

"Fool. Am Ha-b'rit's not the only buyer by a long shot. The money waiting on the sidelines to purchase the nail dwarfs the chickenfeed Mrs. Solomon received the other day."

What choice did I have? I hadn't the right, nor the *chutzpah*, to wager Solly's life. If I refused and he murdered Solly, the experiments were done anyway. I had to give him everything he wanted.

"Come," I said, my heart pounding, "let's make this trade. I'll do my best to find the nail."

"Get it and bring it to me in Israel," Weiner said coldly.

"How do I know this exchange will be for a live Professor Solomon? First, let him go," I said, stiffening.

"I'll shoot him now," he growled, not taking the bait, "then come after you both unencumbered. You know very well nothing will stop me."

"You won't shoot him," I said. "Solly's your only bargaining chip." I gave a reassuring half-smile to Miriam, who was pacing anxiously by my side, but she wasn't buying any optimism.

"This is your last chance to save your friend's life," Weiner said in his most threatening manner.

What could I do? "All right," I said. "Agreed. I'll let you know when we have it."

"Any tricks, Greenberg, your friend's future will be brief, very brief. If I sense you've contacted the police, if I sense danger, boom, one shot in his brain."

"I'll keep my part of the bargain. But if anything happens to Solly..."

"Haven't I always taken good care of him? *And Mrs. Solomon*?" he added ominously.

"It's always been a matter of trust, hasn't it, Mr. Weiner?"

"Listen, Greenberg, I'm not concerned about whether the Solomons live or die. But when this is over, I will take good care of you, guaranteed."

In this, no doubt, he planned to be a man of his word.

***

The drive to Wentzville, Missouri, can be lovely in the spring, but that hadn't been my first choice for the day.

"How much do you trust Bear Brukowski?" I asked Reverend Nation, resplendent in his white suit, sitting behind his neatly arrayed desk in his beautifully organized, book-lined home office.

Nation seemed taken aback, shifting uncomfortably on the red velvet padding of his gold-leaf, French Provincial chair, as if he had never even considered doubting the former NFL tackle. He struggled with the question, his fingers going to his chin, the gesture showing off his glowing new Rolex, his glistening pinky ring, his wig, and gray-streaked, Elvis-like muttonchops.

"Bear has my complete trust," the reverend said, his brow furrowed. "He's one of my most important advisors. What is your problem with him, Mr. Greenberg?"

"I've been reading about the ministry's Blood Diamond trade in Africa..."

"That is sheer nonsense," he sputtered angrily in his own defense. "I bring those people to Christ; I dig wells and build schools for them. Do you think I would ever use ministry operations to enslave young children or make them into soldiers? Do you?"

"No, Reverend," I answered. "I do not believe *you* would. But who's in charge of your African ministry?"

He paused as if stunned. "Well, that would be Bear, certainly. But his works..." I could see doubt clouding his face.

"Okay, well, who is your accountant?" I asked.

"That would be Frank Levinson. Frank's a straight shooter."

"Does Mr. Levinson have oversight over Africa?" I pushed on.

"I'm not sure. If Bear chooses to use him..." Reverend Nation shakily turned to open a drawer, searched for a folder, and drew out a thick financial report with a blue cover. He opened the document, then fingered through the heavy vellum pages until he came upon a stylized logo. "No, he uses some other firm."

He slid the report across the desk for me to examine. I studied it, page after page, finally landing on travel expenses. I ran my finger down the list. Then it hit me. "Bear's made a significant number of jaunts to Amsterdam. You see here?" I turned the folder and pointed to the entries. "Do you have any operations in Amsterdam?"

After searching his memory, he shook his head "no."

"Then why all the trips there?"

The reverend gave me a puzzled look, shrugging his shoulders. "Amsterdam? What does it mean?" he asked.

"Amsterdam is the diamond capital of Europe. Any Blood Diamonds being polished and laundered would likely have to go through the city's black market. The profit margins can sometimes be higher than those fenced through the Israeli diamond industry. With a commodity of that value, Bear would want to handle the transactions himself. Who else could he trust?"

"I just can't believe there isn't some explanation. Bear is so dependable."

"Why don't you have your man Levinson audit the African ministry? What could it hurt?"

"I will do that," Reverend Nation said, his face a study in pain. "The press has been on me about this Blood Diamond nonsense for so long, I simply dismissed it as mudslinging. I never imagined... Well, let's see what develops. Bear is innocent until proven otherwise."

"Yes, he is," I said sympathetically. "By the way, Reverend Nation, did you recall Bear from Israel for a TV shoot?"

"No. He's not on the schedule till next month."

Hmmmm, Bear had lied to me. He was well within his rights to keep his business from me, but why such an unnecessary fabrication? Murder was but one possibility.

"A final item, Reverend. Does Bear know about the nail?"

"Well, yes," he said, startled that the issue would intrude in the conversation. "I've sought his advice all along on the matter. He's been most useful."

"So how did he become my guardian, a man with responsibilities all over the globe?"

"He volunteered. I needed someone I could..." His voice dropped in volume, "someone I could...trust."

"Well, Reverend, let me tell you. Bear has gotten very assertive with me. Very aggressive, and he's scaring me and Miriam to death. I want you to take him off my case. Tell him you have a need for him elsewhere, preferably overseas. I don't want him coming to my house or calling me on the phone. I don't want to see or hear him. Can you do that in a way that would arouse as little suspicion on his part as possible? Then we'll see what his reaction is."

"I'll do my best, Mr. Greenberg, but Bear has a mind of his own."

Soon Bear Brukowski would be aware of my suspicions, and that frightened me. If the reverend was in the whole mess with him, I'd be betrayed immediately. If the reverend was genuine and instituted the African/Blood Diamond trade audit, Bear would soon know from his own accountant and would guess I'd brought that angle to the reverend's attention. At that point, he'd deduce I knew of his personal interest in the nail. And from that, he might further extrapolate that I suspected him of being behind the grizzly deaths of Levi Asher and Chick Markowitz, perhaps even Moise Shankman, something I would have refused to believe a week earlier.

If Bear was truly a sinister force in this game, what was my life worth? Weiner, Shadid, and Brukowski, my executioners were lining up for their satisfaction, and I had few resources with which to blunt their intentions.

***

The stranger wasn't pleased with the looks of rundown Osage Street, its boarded-up storefronts and scattered litter. Old newspapers blew down the pothole-covered streets, glass and broken bottles crunched underfoot, deformed signs hung by a nail. Osage was not a comforting place to be at night, with streetlights either burned out or shattered by tossed bricks and gunshots. The stranger unconsciously touched his pistol, a hungry-looking German Luger holstered on his belt beneath his leather jacket. Reassured, he checked the address, took note of the hinged accordion security gate covering the picture window, and entered the shop, ignoring the damage inflicted by a beer bottle upon the "Father Finkel Antiquities" sign. Then he shut the door behind himself, slamming it loudly.

He examined the shop's dusty shelves, upon which sat a smattering of objects of questionable value. There were display pedestals jammed into a corner, as if gathered from a much larger space, many of them empty. A frayed red robe draped on a stand near the door declared it to have once belonged to John the Baptist, a gray one to Paul the Apostle, and an erstwhile saint's bone was displayed on velvet—all with disclaimers attached to their labels.

Listening carefully for the slightest sound, he crossed to the counter and stood waiting, ears attuned to the silence. Not a rustle of movement, not a voice breaking the stillness. Finally, he heard a pair of footsteps approaching. His hand went to his Luger.

In the constricted back room, so unlike his late-grandmother's once-prosperous antiquities business, Finkel surveyed the piles of junk disdainfully. His grandmother used to call him Lawrence, but now everyone called him Finkel, just Finkel, never Lawrence or even Larry. No respect. He remembered fondly in his junior year of high school, to cover his poker debts, he'd spent a week kiting checks in banks where the old woman had assets. Ran up a twenty-grand deficit before the bankers finally called her. The sweet lady covered, naturally, but took away his car keys for a week! If only the world at large was so forgiving. Prison had been a tough grind for him.

But now was his chance to change all that. He gathered his courage, and then Father Finkel stepped through the back curtain, adjusting his high white collar, the only contrast to his all-black suit. "Are you the man that called me?"

"Are you Father Finkel?" the stranger replied in a thick Middle Eastern accent.

"Yes," Finkel replied, nervously straightening his jacket and tugging at his sleeve.

"And you are a friend of David Greenberg?" The stranger drew out the Luger and held it flat against his chest. The pistol wasn't aimed at Finkel, but it made its point.

"I am. We are good friends," Finkel stammered. The two men studied each other. Finkel noted the nail-shaped birthmark he'd been told to look for, which, confirming the man's identity, made him twice as nervous. "And you are what, Mr....?"

"Just call me Almar." The stranger glided behind the counter and, pausing momentarily to sense what was in the back room, swiped the curtain aside with one quick motion of the pistol and peered inside. Satisfied the store was otherwise deserted, he came back into the room. "I am an Assyrian Christian, whose roots are in Iran, but I live in Jordon. My family had long ties to the Shah, but we had to flee during the revolution."

"And you want?"

"The nail, yes. The nail will be the centerpiece of a museum our charitable foundation plans to create in Amman."

"That should bring in the Western tourists," Finkel remarked. "All right, Almar, Mr. Greenberg told me I might encounter interested parties. What..." Finkel coughed dryly and had to drink some water before he could finish his sentence. It was chilly in the poorly ventilated storefront, but the small hustler was already sweating profusely. "What are you willing to pay for the nail?"

"What has Mr. Greenberg told you he is willing to accept, Father?"

"A singular artifact like this nail?" Finkel said, eyes to the ceiling as if calculating, periodically glancing askance at the pistol. "No less than ten, ten *million* US dollars. I'm sure Mr. Greenberg could get more by open auction, but that is not his way. That it's for a museum in Jordon *does* fit with his vision for the nail, so that's very good. I'm sure he'll give your museum a reasonable price." From the stranger's subtle reaction, Finkel's hustler instincts made him wish he'd asked for thirty million or more, even though the figure for which he was asking was entirely moot. "Maybe fifteen," Finkel added. "I'm not him."

"I will pay twelve. But that assumes the transaction is agreed to tonight and consummated within three days."

Finkel nervously thrust his hand into the pocket of his jacket, but by the time he'd grasped his cell phone, the Luger was aimed at his heart. "Whoa," he said, his eyes wide. "I'm just getting my phone." Hands shaking, he withdrew the cell from his pocket in slow motion. "We're on the same team here, Almar, my friend. My commission on this deal would enable me to move my operation to Chicago, which is where the big money lies in the Midwest." Once the cell was visible, the stranger lowered his pistol. Catching his breath, Finkel shakily thumbed numbers.

"Yes, Greenberg. We have a gentleman here who wants to buy the nail for a museum in Amman. Twelve million he's offering. But we must agree tonight, and the deal must be consummated within three days...Uh-huh, uh-huh...Okay, a half-million. I'll tell him."

Finkel looked up. "Greenberg agrees to the twelve, but he wants a half-million good faith payment." The scrawny faux preacher held his breath. His free hand shook so uncontrollably, he had to thrust it into his pants pocket.

"I will do this," the gunman said definitively. "How will we transfer the funds? It is late in the day."

"I have a friend at a local bank branch. He can let us do our business after hours so we won't be disturbed."

"Good," the man said. "You will accompany me until the exchange is complete. What account will these funds be transferred to?"

"He wants the account number where the funds are going," Finkel said into the cell. Listening, the faux preacher wrote down the numbers with a badly shaking hand; then, with voice wavering, he recited them twice to make sure he had the correct ones. That completed, he hit disconnect. "Let's go. I'll let the bank know we're on our way."

***

The night janitor, who'd been notified by Tumor's bank friend to let Father Finkel and the stranger in, opened the bank's side entrance off the parking lot. Once the pair was inside, he closed and locked the door behind them, then directed them to a lighted office forty feet down a dark hallway. Without further word, he ambled away and disappeared.

Finkel and the stranger approached the open office door. There, Finkel's guest peered cautiously into the room, his hand on his pistol, before he signaled for Finkel to precede him. Finkel complied, shuffling uncertainly into the room, then slid to a corner. Seeing there was no trap inside, his guest followed.

A rotund man wearing a three-piece suit sat behind the desk with the nameplate reading Richard E. Howell-Vice President. He rubbed his cleanly shaved jowl and glanced at the faux preacher standing scrunched in a corner as if a smaller volume of human might make him invisible. The faux banker produced a smile. "Yesh," he said with his slight lisp. "Happy to accommodate our Jordanian friends."

The large faux banker with the military flattop rose, crossed to a table, and removed a cloth cover, revealing a mechanical device with a wire leading to a 10-key keyboard and another to a miniature screen. He pulled back the chair at the table. "Please have a seat, sir," he said with a diplomatic flourish.

The stranger noted the faux preacher's location and, switching the pistol to his left hand, sat at the table. He looked behind himself a second time, then turned his attention to the simple-looking device. "This machine can transfer money to Switzerland?" he asked skeptically.

"Japanese manufacture," the banker said. "Very user-friendly."

"And this can transfer nine figures? I will need it again in a couple days."

"Nine figures," the friendly faux banker replied. "Anything under a billion, it'll do the job."

The stranger gave a nasty look, then shrugged, signaling with a wave to proceed.

"Now," the faux banker said pleasantly, "just enter your account number and press submit; then wait for the prompt. When the prompt shows here, in green," he pointed to the screen, "you enter your password. Go ahead."

The stranger entered his account number. On the screen, the green button lit up, and he pressed it. The system reset.

"Now you enter your password," the faux banker said.

"I want privacy," the stranger demanded.

"Yes, of course, sir. We will step into the hall until you are finished," the faux banker said pleasantly. "Once you are done with that, enter the transfer amount and press the same green button. You will then get a final prompt. Enter the destination account number, submit a final time, and it's done. That's all there is to it. You can always cancel by hitting the red cancel button. Understand?"

"Of course."

"All right, good. The father and I will step out of the room now. We'll be right outside the door. When you are done, just call us. Any questions?"

"Of course not."

"Then we will leave you now to transfer your funds," the fat man said graciously, and the two Americans left the room, closing the door softly behind themselves.

When he heard the door click, the stranger laid his pistol on the table and took out the slip of paper written in the preacher's shaking hand. He began to work the 10-key. After entering his password, his finger hovered over the submit button. He paused, pricking up his ears. Outside the room, he heard a hurried shuffling of feet away from the door…and other feet, too many, tiptoeing toward him.

The stranger hit the red cancel button. Once he was sure the screen cleared his password, he grabbed his pistol. His very substantial Swiss bank account, full of Saudi lucre, was safe.

***

Finkel and Daddy Markowitz counted to thirty as instructed, but a little too quickly, skipping the one-thousand refrain after reaching twelve, then hurried down the hall, away from Howell's office. As they passed four uniformed officers wearing body armor and helmets, waiting with pistols drawn, Daddy Markowitz, eyes large as saucers, made a pistol motion with his bare fingers. Finkel indicated with his thumb the room from which they were rushing. The two did not slow until they were in the bank's main customer operations. There, they briefly scoped out the area before scrambling under a desk anchored behind a marble pillar, where they covered their heads as if fearing an explosion. Then they waited.

A loud crash, with falling glass, came from Howell's office. But the sound wasn't an explosion. Shortly thereafter, a series of shots echoed in the alley behind the office.

"I just heard a crash from the suspect's location," the team lead officer said into his radio. "Shots from the alley outside. Suspect is armed and dangerous. We're going in."

"Be careful," the radio replied. "Don't take any unnecessary chances."

The four officers gathered at the office door, pistols ready, and made final eye contact, releasing the safeties on their pistols. As the four ducked, the lead officer reached up to turn the doorknob. It turned easily, and he let the door creak open slightly. Next, he counted to three on his fingers; after which, upon his signal the four rushed the room simultaneously, pistols at the ready. The desk no longer had a chair. The window was broken out. The suspect was gone.

"He escaped through the window," the team lead said into the radio, while two of his partners crept to the spot where the cool night air poured into the building through the broken pane. Guns raised, they peered over the sill to see the chair lying on its side amid glass littering the alley behind the bank. No man was in sight. "He's outside somewhere, in the alley. Catch the sonuvabitch."

The team poked their heads above the sill a final time. Satisfied they weren't being ambushed, they climbed down into the ally one at a time, covering each other, then spread out with a well-timed, coordinated maneuver. After checking their body armor and helmets, the officers began checking the back doors lining the alley, one by one, until they finally came upon a door with its handle smashed. They called in their find and, shortly thereafter, gathered together. They checked their weapons a final time, then, on hand signal, crashed through the doorway into the back of a dress shop, pistols raised. Once inside, they spread methodically throughout the shop's storage area, checking closets, dressing rooms, cabinets, any place large enough to hold a man.

"We're in the back of the dress shop a few doors north of the bank," an officer said into his radio. "He's got to be up front."

"We've got the shop covered out here. Go in at your own pace. Careful."

The six gathered at the curtain leading to the front. Then, at a signal, they crashed in, pistols aimed ahead. But the shop held nothing but colorful dresses, hats, belts, purses, and jackets.

"Shit. He broke the door, but never entered the shop," the team leader said into the radio. "He must be in the alley somewhere."

"We've got it blocked out here. But there're plenty of ways he can escape, if he hasn't already."

"Call in all cars. Surround the area. This guy is a killer."

From outside, they heard a team member yell, "There's a trashcan knocked over near the fence, and his coat's on the other side. He must have gone this way!"

***

He had used the tactic many times in the West Bank to evade the Israeli police. The covered pipe opening appeared to be too small for a man, but Shadid's keen eye knew better. *Too small for a fat American, but not for me.* Expelling his breath, he adroitly removed the cover and worked his way into the horizontal pipe feet first, scraping his hands, knees, and hips until they bled, forcing himself ever backward. Finally, still gripping the cover, he was in, his face lying on his pistol, one hand extended above his head. He pulled the cover with his fingertips toward himself, holding the rusted metal with all his might, shutting the aperture from the inside.

He could stay prone there indefinitely, until the police departed. A day or two, maybe three at the outside; he was accustomed to deprivation. He wouldn't starve, wouldn't die of thirst. He would survive to fight another day and to get revenge for this betrayal. This setback was all the fault of that...that dog Greenberg. *I will have your head, Greenberg!*

***

"Shit, Greenberg," Daddy Markowitz said, still wiping the sweat from the layers of his beet-red face and neck. "The damn guy slipped a dozen cops! I don't know how he got by them."

"He's been dodging the Israeli police for years," I said, raising a hand to silence the big man. I crossed the room to the mechanical device we'd planted.

"The monitor was flipped. He must have hit cancel before registering his password," Daddy said apologetically. "We waited as long as we could, David, but the guy had a gun. We had to get our butts out of there."

I lifted the cover panel of the device, exposing in its entrails a plain typewriter ribbon with a string of numbers imprinted on it. Then I counted the number of digits. "Low-tech solution," I said smiling. I carefully pulled the ribbon loose, tore it off, and slipped it into my shirt pocket. "We didn't need him to press submit. We only needed him to type his password. Well done, Daddy."

As the police shooed us from the room, I called Miriam. "He did it; he entered his account number and password in full before he got suspicious."

"Clean him out," she said. "One hundred percent."

I disconnected and dropped the cell into my jacket.

While the police quizzed a hysterical Finkel and Daddy, I watched the front of the bank. After an excruciating fifteen minutes, the real Mr. Howell, shirttail out, wrinkled slacks under a hastily thrown-on suit jacket, entered the bank using his own security pass. He spoke with the detectives briefly before I was able to pull him aside.

"I'm ready to make the transfer," I told Howell, pulling the magnetic ribbon from my shirt, kissing it.

"All right, this way," he said, leading me into a locked alcove adjacent to the main room. Once inside, he sat at a computer screen and, pulling a card with his passwords from his wallet, typed in his master authorization. "Okay…Account to be closed out…"

Broke, stranded in a Western country thousands of miles from home, the second of the twins was probably rabid to kill me, too. Greenberg: zero. Executioners: two…and counting.

CHAPTER TWENTY-FOUR
THE PASSED PAWN

"He had a pistol!" Finkel shouted into my face, his nasal voice echoing throughout the cavernous marble bank lobby. "You didn't tell me he was going to have a goddamn gun, Greenberg."

"Fuckin'-A, Tweety," Daddy Markowitz added. "He could have blown my head off! And I ain't paying for that fuckin' window."

It took a while for Finkel and Daddy Markowitz to calm down enough for their chaotic brains to catch up to what I was saying to them. "Look," I told them, "the guy's probably not very happy with you two. Nor with me either for that matter."

"Fuckin'-A," Daddy said sarcastically. "You think?"

Wait until Shadid tries to transfer money from his empty Swiss bank account. That will infuriate him enough to kill us all.

"Right," I said, handing them a note with a name and directions written on it. "I've registered rooms for you guys at a motel across the river, off sixty-four. You're both paid up for a month. Short drive to the stockyards, ten minutes to the track, fifteen to the Eastside strip joints."

"What a pile!" Finkel whined. "So now we've got to hide out in Illinois?"

"For a month! Greenberg, you *putz!*" Daddy declared.

I withdrew two envelopes from my jacket and dangled them before the furious pair. "Now, boys," I said calmly, "Here's five grand for each of you, cash. Don't lose it all in one place because a second envelope ain't coming. Got it?"

The pair angrily swiped the cash from my hand.

"So no pool hall for a month?" Finkel groaned. "My social life is dead."

"This is the worst thing you've ever done to us, prick," Daddy concluded, counting the bills in the envelope.

"I'm sorry, guys," I said contritely. "I figured a dozen cops..."

"A dozen cops," Finkel said. "I told you, Daddy, Greenberg's a moron."

"Fuckin'-A, Tweety," Daddy agreed.

"I'll call you when the coast is clear," I said.

"So what do we do now, Daddy?" Finkel asked.

"Let's go check out Motel Hell," Daddy replied. "We can pick up some Burgers-2-Go on the way. Later, we can hit the stockyards game for cards till the track opens."

"Jeez, what a crock!" Finkel exclaimed.

They turned to leave, but I stopped them a moment. "Don't forget, guys, there could be a big payoff coming. I doubled-down on the come for us."

"And what's 'the come'?" Finkel groused. "That you live?"

"That's about it," I shrugged.

"Prick," Daddy said, turning to leave the bank. "I'm not going to forget this, Greenberg."

"Asshole," Finkel added, escorting his friend out the door.

***

"Okay, you've got plenty of cigarettes, Professor," Jarad Weiner said respectfully as he tidied six packs of Gauloises in a double stack of three each. "Sandwiches, a tankard of coffee, a lighter...you're all set till I get back."

"Always looking out for me, Weiner," Professor Joseph Solomon growled sarcastically, settling himself awkwardly on the toilet lid, his movements restricted by his right wrist being handcuffed to the sink's water pipe. The walls of the bathroom were solid cement block, like the rest of the small, abandoned house sitting at the dead end of a deserted road. However, the room had not been fully blocked in. Instead, the wall housing the plumbing and electricity had been covered over with cheap drywall panels attached with simple screws, through which emerged the pipes connected to the bathroom's fixtures. "Where are you going, by the way?" Solly added as an afterthought.

"To arrange a boat to Alexandria."

"Yes? Where are we going?"

"To your home town, to St. Louis. I'll be back relatively soon."

"Where are we now?" There was no answer. Professor Solomon rattled the handcuffs. "What if there's a fire?"

"This building is a concrete blockhouse. You have nothing to fear, Professor." The powerful man with the thick black mustache adjusted the pistol in his belt, then exited the bathroom, heading for the front door. Professor Solomon listened to his footsteps, heard the door slam and a key turn in the lock.

The professor turned his attention to the handcuffs. He brought forward his left thumbnail, his portable screwdriver, but clearly, the handcuffs were bolted solidly together in manufacture by pneumatic pressure. After testing them, he saw that the links and the wristlocks were solid as well.

This poses an interesting problem. Hmm. Handcuff, well-made. Pipe, probably twenty-five, thirty years old.

With practiced dexterity, he quickly unscrewed the panel on the wall with his thumbnail-screwdriver, removed it completely using minimum force, and tossed it aside. Then he began to examine the underlying plumbing.

Connections. Yes, yes. Assembled in standard form. Joint, mm-hmm. Workman, probably a local man. Maybe the owner. Jerry-rigged at some point. Probably sprung a leak within the last couple years, two to three I would guess. Water traveling through the pipes at moderate temperatures. Hmm, soldering. Rather, some kind of black muck that's dried on here. What is this cheap substance? Interesting. Perhaps that's the only material they had when they fixed it. Definitely not a professional plumber. Ha! Well, it's hardly a fuel line on a Mars mission. Interesting.

Damn that Greenberg. I should have blocked with the knight. I could have beat him! Or at least forced a draw. The knight block, it was right there. That day.

He fondled the pipe and the joints, shaking them with varying degrees of force; then he listened to their reaction, felt their resistance and examined them with casual disinterest, critically, analytically.

You know, if the male pipe was brought to the process at less than, say, minus two hundred degrees Celsius, then inserted. When it warmed and expanded, its circumference could be a fraction of a millimeter larger. Interesting idea. Hmm. Would that temperature be difficult for plumbers to maintain? That would make for a better long-term result in assembly, certainly. Yessss, wouldn't that also apply to...? I could test for that in...yes. Hmm. Clever notion. I hadn't thought of cooling the specimens, then warming them. Would specimens react to the change of... Of course, keeping a pipe that temperature in this climate. Umm. I'll have to make a mental note to think about that sometime. Hmm. Interesting perspective. Perhaps.

Greenberg! With my *wife. Had I blocked with...I should have traded bishops. Coward! Damn, he had me cowed. If I'd blocked with the...if I'd blocked, then I could have countered with the rook. Countered with the rook. With my wife. I wonder where they are? Where?*

His long, delicate fingers touched, rubbed, tested, pulled, pushed—he even touched his tongue briefly, lightly, to the repaired joint.

He counted on me not blocking with the knight. He knew I wouldn't. Should have. Interesting. I wonder what kind of substances they use on these joints nowadays. Certainly, not. Of course not. That would be foolish. Cool to the touch. Cool. Cold water runs through. Cold water. Hot must be that one.

He lit his cigarette and drew deeply twice, exhaling with relief. Then he puffed repeatedly to make the end glow and touched it to the black muck pasting the joints together.

Ah, see the reaction. Must be made from...Not very, no, not at all. If I simply, perhaps...Perhaps. Interesting. Cool the specimens then warm them, but it must be gradual. Blocked with the knight. Should have. The front door, locked.

He admired his left thumbnail, then picked up the lighter and held it to the joint, waiting for the black muck to react to the heat as he had precisely predicted.

This old blockhouse. Doorplate, screws, the thumb will get them if they haven't rusted. Greenberg with Miriam. Should have warned him. No threat strategy. Should have traded bishops. Goddamn Greenberg, that's my wife. I won her. I won. Should have traded bishops.

What temperature should I cool the specimens to? Would have to warm them very slowly. Should have blocked with the knight. Warm them a fraction of a degree per hour. How? Slowly? Cool them slowly, too. Countered with the rook! My wife. Viscous mass, sticky. I have the coffee thermos, metal, well-constructed; adequate to apply force, perfect. Perfect. Only a few more minutes. New lighter, plenty of fluid. Should have blocked with the knight, countered with the rooks. Or traded bishops. Yes, blocked with the knight, then the bishop trade. But what about his pawn structure, his rook on the open file? My wife. Then traded bishops. Damn, Greenberg. If only I'd blocked with the knight! Equal chances in the end game. Could have gained a draw. My wife. Blocked with the knight.

Warm the specimens one-eighth degree per hour. Yes! Warm them, of course...

***

216

One way or another, I had to get the nail to exchange for Solly. Unfortunately, finding the nail meant solving Levi Asher's cryptic puzzle, then acquiring that holy grail while eluding my ever-expanding host of personal assassins.

Miriam insisted on cleaning up the breakfast dishes alone, so I headed upstairs to my study. The day was sunny, already getting warm. I opened the blinds and raised the window, letting the stale room air out. Below, my back yard was springing to life from its winter narcosis: its leaves, flowers, and shrubbery an insulated outdoor contemplation niche, and an occasional bower for lovemaking al fresco. I hated to leave it, but Miriam and I would soon have to find refuge in some obscure place to survive.

Breathing deeply, I turned to examine my study, with its imposing chess table, its oak desk, and bookshelves. How much time had I spent in here alone, caught up in the adrenaline rush of my own imagination? Maybe there was far more than misfortune behind my solitary life. Perhaps isolation was my natural state, not wholly unlike Solly's past two years living in his lab. Perhaps Solly and I had jelled so well because we were so much alike.

Well, I had a job to do. The basis for my extrapolation of Levi's message was set: the chart equaling "59" that spelled "Jesus Christ" was my key—Bobby Fischer's unparalleled chess game against Donald Byrne the solution. Playing white, Byrne's bishop had threatened the thirteen-year-old Fischer's black queen. However, instead of saving his queen, as any other player would, Fischer retreated with his bishop, allowing Byrne to capture his queen! And that set off the pyrotechnics.

Setting up a chart, I entered the game's moves, starting with move 18, the bishop-takes-queen (BxQ = BxB6) move. Using the "Jesus Christ" key, I placed a numerical value below each move.

Move	White - Byrne				Black - Fischer			Total	Running total
18	Bx	B	6		Bx	C	4+		
	2	2	6		2	3	4	19	19
19	K-	G	1		N-	E	2+		
	3	7	1		5	5	2	23	42
20	K-	F	1		Nx	D	4+		
	3	6	1		1	4	4	19	61

Moves 18 to 20 = 61

Immediately, I ran into a problem: by the time I added up the third row, the running total was already 61. This wasn't working. I played with my chart, adding down, adding only the black moves, adding only the white, adding diagonally, but still no 59—61 was the best I could do.

At that point, I simply dropped all the row numbers and stayed with the letters. Then *magic*, the first four moves, 18 to 21, totaled exactly 59! I was ecstatic, perhaps three-quarters of the way to my goal.

Move	Byrne		Fischer		Total	Running Total
18	Bx	B	Bx	C		
	2	2	2	3	**9**	9
19	K-	G	N-	E		
	3	7	5	5	**20**	29
20	K-	F	Nx	D		
	3	6	1	4	**14**	43
21	K-	G	N-	E		
	3	7	1	5	**16**	**59**

Moves 18 – 21 = **59**

I totaled each of the rows across and came up with *four specific numbers*, one for each move (9, 20, 14, 16), to find my Hebrew *gematria* letters. I was on my way. All I needed was to find the right Hebrew *gematria* chart to find the location of the nail.

However, bad news inevitably arrives before you're ready for it. Just at that moment, Miriam rushed into the room and grabbed my arm, her face a mask of terror.

"David!" she whispered. "There's someone outside the house. I saw him move in the alley behind the fence and in back of the garage. David, someone is watching us!"

CHAPTER TWENTY-FIVE
TO CORAL COURTS MOTEL

Weiner could have safely driven the car up to the isolated cement blockhouse's front door. Instead, he concealed it down the sloping hill behind the house—a stickler for detail, never one to hurry or to take chances. He crept along the back fence with extraordinary dexterity for a man of his solid build, pistol in hand, pausing only to crouch behind an abandoned trash dumpster, shielding himself from the back of the blockhouse ahead. He wore a lightweight black leather jacket and dark jeans, matching his mustache. Balancing on one knuckle, he peered around the dumpster, his menacing stare searching the front driveway and the dirt road from which it branched.

Everything clear.

He glided swiftly to the side of the house, then, pistol raised, worked his way around to the front. The daylight was potentially his enemy, revealing him to the world, yet he calculated he faced little risk in this deserted place. Stepping onto the porch, he discovered the plate covering the knob hung unhinged, the door ajar. Bad sign. His pulse quickened. He took a breath, gathering his poise.

In one violent motion, he kicked the door inward, slamming it against the interior wall, and burst inside, pistol aimed ahead.

But the dusty room was empty.

He paused to listen. Only the faint sound of a water trickle coming from the bathroom. Not a good omen. He quickly made steady strides to the bathroom where that door, too, was open. Pushing in, he saw it. The coffee thermos he had left for the professor was dented and lying on the floor, the water pipe leading to the sink disconnected, running, the clear fluid mixing with the brown stimulant in a widening puddle. His captive was gone. *I won't clean up your spilt coffee this time, Professor!* He spit.

He turned and hurried back through the house to the front porch and halted. His eyes searched in every direction; he saw nothing but desert scrub to the horizon, a wasteland in sand, stones, and cacti. No movement.

Then from below the hill back of the blockhouse, he heard his car engine kick in with a throaty growl. In panic, he slapped his pocket and felt his key fob right where it should be. *How could this be?* Of course, he realized despondently, a man like the professor could, in effect, "hot wire" a car in seconds, even the most sophisticated model, using whatever knick-knacks were in his pockets. *I was a fool not to think of that.* Then with a stab of anger, it dawned on him. *The professor must have deduced I wouldn't make a naked approach to the front. He must have concealed himself to take advantage of me hiding the auto in the back.*

In panic, he ran around the house and down the hill, but the car was already speeding off, kicking up dirt and rocks three hundred meters ahead. He raised his pistol, but did not fire. He knew he couldn't catch Professor Solomon, but there was no logical reason to harm him either. Now, transportation must be his top priority. He had a boat to catch.

Unfortunately, his strategic alternatives had become geometrically more difficult to effect. And as an incidental consequence, further killing would be absolutely necessary.

***

They must have spotted him from Greenberg's kitchen. Through a slit in the fence, he could see David Greenberg and Miriam Solomon scramble down the walk to the blue BMW parked at the front curb, wheeling suitcases behind them, a computer bag slung over Greenberg's shoulder. Greenberg popped the trunk and threw in the suitcases, then joined Miriam in the Beemer's cabin. Taking a deep breath, he started the car, threw it into gear, and sped off.

***

He hurried from his hiding place back to where he'd left the flame-painted Trans Am on an adjoining street, only to find a parking ticket lodged under the windshield wipers. Angrily, he grabbed the ticket off the windshield and absently stuffed it in his pocket, then climbed behind the wheel. He turned the key and gunned the motor into action. Frowning angrily, he frantically pressed the GPS control. On the dashboard screen, the yellow light indicated Greenberg's car was heading south, down Euclid Avenue. Teeth clinched, he released the brake, threw the car into gear, and sped off in pursuit.

***

Maybe I'm being paranoid, but it's possible my BMW has a tracking device attached to it. I drove straight to a car dealership on South Kingshighway to rent a plain gray Nissan Altima, hoping to make it difficult to track my movements, while lowering my profile as well.

As an added precaution, I gave the grinning young salesman the Beemer's key fob and slipped the woman behind the desk sixty bucks in twenties to buy them both lunch in the U. City Loop, which was in the opposite direction to where I was headed. If my car was bugged, their lunch excursion would provide a false scent for my tracker. They were thrilled to hit a good lunch spot, showing off a late-model Beemer instead of enduring another brown bag lunch at the dealership.

While the salesman and the clerk made their arrangements to desert their posts, I slung the computer case over my shoulder, and Miriam and I headed to the back of the rental facility. Miriam was still tense, frightened, as was I, so I took her hand as we strode down the hall, then through swinging doors to the repair shop. We cut through the shop, trying to ignore its pungent odors of oil, gasoline, and chemicals, its cacophony of automatic wrenches and high-pressured power tools, its cadre of uniformed technicians tending open hoods or the undersides of elevated new-model cars. Finally, more relaxed, we headed out the employee exit in the back.

There, we waited in the sunshine until my BMW pulled up alongside the Nissan, having circled the complex. The young salesman popped open the Beemer's trunk, and I hurriedly transferred our luggage to the Nissan. That done, I waved a thumbs-up to the salesman and clerk, and the young man laid rubber around the corner and disappeared. When the BMW was out of sight, Miriam and I went back inside the shop and waited a nerve-racking five minutes, giving anyone tracking the BMW time to pursue it in the wrong direction.

Ready to run from our hiding place, we climbed into the Nissan, and I navigated between the lot's patchwork of colorful cars around to the front, where I put the car in park. Letting the motor run, I stepped outside to examine the street, but it was a normal, busy thoroughfare, with no street parking permitted. No cars were parked illegally on either side of the street, and the few sitting on the side street north of the rental lot were older models, unoccupied. With a sigh of relief, I exchanged a confident smile with Miriam, climbed back in the Nissan and drove south.

***

Clumsy and amateurish. Now Greenberg believes he is loose in the city he knows well, driving a car unknown to me. Let him continue to think that.

Pressing a hand to steady his knee, he stood from his hiding niche to his full height. Relived to be upright, he took a second to stretch his back, then made for the Trans Am. He had Greenberg right where he wanted him.

***

In the rapidly fading dusk, the only movement was his intended victim, whom he'd initially spotted from a hundred meters away driving an older-model, Israeli-made Carmel into the open garage. Whistling a tune, his prey crossed the small back yard, entered the house, and conveniently emerged shortly thereafter carrying two large black garbage bags.

He quietly crouched behind the stone wall and screwed the silencer onto his revolver, listening to the man's footsteps, to the clunking of the trash bags. When his prey reached the trash container, he dropped one bag and reached for the lid, his back to the wall.

Quick as a leopard, he leaped over the wall, grabbed his victim's thin neck with his powerful left hand, and in one motion, he pressed the muzzle against the man's temple, pulling the trigger. He felt the man go limp immediately and released his grip, letting the body fall in a heap. Then he went through the man's pockets and pulled out the key.

He paused a moment to examine the lifeless body, the blood pouring into the sand, which had drunk so many crimson seas over the millennia. It never ceased to amaze him how much blood there always was. The man's face was frozen in shock and horror in reaction to the impact of the bullet. It was a common face, nondescript. *Was this man a Jew? A Bedouin? A Palestinian? A Christian?* It was impossible to tell, and the grimacing lips would never self-identify again. *Well, his nationality, his religion, his tribe, don't matter anymore.*

He slipped into the garage quietly, making barely any sound. The auto wasn't even locked, typical in an Israeli neighborhood with little petty crime. He slipped behind the wheel, started the motor, and drove off at moderate speed, his mind planning his next approach. He rapidly considered all the obstacles, what set-up the police and university security würde haben

would have devised to stop him, how to traverse Israel through Netanya, to Tel Aviv, to Egypt, all the way to St. Louis. By necessity, his plan had had to be altered, delayed, but it had hardly changed. Tens of millions of U.S. dollars, perhaps more, were at stake. All methods were at his disposal.

He would not be stopped.

***

"Don't lock the door," I said, popping the trunk of the Nissan rental before climbing out onto the street.

"But this neighborhood," Miriam said nervously, examining the aged city street's two-story bricks houses, some with boarded windows, and the abandoned warehouses at the end of the block. Behind the lone mom-and-pop grocery, ramshackle rusted-out trucks and old cars with mismatched hoods parked on glass-strewn, broken concrete lots.

"There's nothing to steal. I'd rather have someone ransack 'nothing' than break a window."

We went into the office, the sordid lair of a brutish woman of roughly sixty with cotton-candy hair, chain-smoking before a Dr. Phil angstfest on an ancient, twelve-inch TV. With barely a glance to appraise us, she slid a plastic-covered chart of the complex toward me, then returned her attention to the shouting emanating at full blast from the scarred TV. I looked over the chart, trying to sort out the available cabins from the occupied. Certainly, the woman had X-ed with a marker the occupied, but not clearly, and the unoccupied, smudged in a variety of colors, weren't well-erased from years of one-night mattress-bouncers. I selected a corner cabin for Miriam and me, plus the only other cabin with a view of our door.

"Two cabins? Two?" the gruff ninny hawked at me.

"Yes, please."

"Two? All right. But no wild parties, no naked running between cabins, no noise. We got folks trying to sleep around here. Understand?"

"I understand. We just want quiet, too."

She gave me her stock threatening look. Then I signed and paid for three nights in advance for both.

A legendary South St. Louis landmark, the Coral Courts Motel, its pink thirties-style half-acre of planned disorder, was a welcome relief from the adjoining street. Still nicely preserved, the motel's curving pathways were lined in multi-colored, rock- and glass-embedded, two-foot-high walls giving it a "coral" effect, I assumed. It was washed in blue floodlights stuck in the ground every five yards or so. The myriad paths led to a series of small cabins made of the same rock- and glass-embedded concrete as the pathway borders, each sporting a peeling, pink door and two small, barred windows. I considered the window bars a big plus.

We wheeled our luggage up the walk. Our cabin felt cramped, with a sagging queen-sized bed, a beaten-up, cigarette burn-scarred dresser, and a cheap, wobbly nightstand. I raised the windows to air out the stale, pungent residue of dust and the musty, former smoking-permitted days' odors permeating from deeply within the walls and ceiling. I raised an eyebrow to Miriam, and she shrugged back.

Before we were settled, the phone in Miriam's purse rang. She hurriedly retrieved the cell and, noting the number, plopped down on the bed and sat back against the headboard, kicking off her shoes.

"This is Miriam." Her face brightened suddenly, a wide smile spreading over her lips. "Joseph? Joseph! Where are you?…What?" She paused to listen. Finally, I caught her attention. "It's Joseph," she told me. "He's back at the lab! How?" She began to laugh, an absolute delight in every feature. "He escaped from Jarad! He stole Jarad's car!"

All I could do was shake my head. I was laughing, too. Never underestimate a super nerd.

"You what, Joseph?…You had an idea while you were being held?…Yes? You cool the specimens, then warm them up? Which experiment is this, Joseph?…Which experiment?"

She listened and laughed for some time, shaking her head. As Solly's dissertation went on and on, she shrugged to let me know she didn't understand a word, encouraging him periodically with "that's wonderful—that's brilliant." Then he must have been anxious to get back to his work.

"I love you, too, darling," she cooed and slipped the phone into her purse. Oy. *I'm the Beard again!*

I stared at Miriam, wistfully taking in her beauty. Longing for her. Yet believing in my gut she was not, and never would be, mine. Then I noticed she was staring back at me with the same uncertainty.

"Well," I said, "Solly's safe. The nail's still ours…if we can find it."

She merely shrugged and began to unpack, unable to meet my eyes. Speechless, I followed suit.

Now I knew Jarad Weiner was really angry.

***

Night arrived, and the street's sparse traffic dwindled to nearly nothing. Slipping on his soft, deer hide gloves, he walked calmly toward the Nissan rental and tried the back door. It was unlocked.

Didn't that simplify matters?

He marked the empty street in all directions, the nearby upstairs and downstairs windows, the vacant lots. No one in sight. He pulled the car door open wide and, bending over, placed one foot on the back floor for leverage, reached in, and swiftly jiggered the back seat loose. Then he fastened the combination GPS-tracker and microphone transmitter firmly in place. Reaching into his pocket, he pulled out his cell and checked the GPS—it was working. Next, he spoke in a normal voice, a receiver to his ear. Satisfied that his words were coming through clearly, he pocketed the cell and resettled the seat securely.

Fine. Now he could track the car and listen to any conversations taking place.

He took a deep breath, taking stock. His stomach was growling; he'd missed a feeding. Pausing to think, he recalled passing an old diner a few blocks back. Dollar hamburgers, shakes, all kinds of junk. He'd order a half-dozen burgers and a large shake to see if they'd hold him; then he'd get some rest. He strolled back to his car, removing his gloves.

There was nowhere Greenberg and the woman could move to, nothing they could say in transit inside the car's cabin that he wouldn't know instantly. All he had to do was wait, and they'd lead him directly to the nail.

***

"Okay, Reverend, thank you. Please let me know right away if you learn anything."

I disconnected the call. Miriam gave me a concerned, questioning look.

"Reverend Nation has no idea where Bear is. He's thinking of cutting him off from the ministry completely, taking away his airplane privileges, even his credit card. I didn't know what to tell him, but I explained that I didn't want Bear to be aware of our suspicions if at all possible."

"What are you going to do?"

I could see that she was frightened. I, too, was terrified. So much coming at us, so much risk to sticking our necks out in order to get the nail. No, there was no playing it cool here; my attempts to act calm hadn't fooled her. "I'm going to call a detective friend of mine to see if we can get some protection."

"What about the Texas thing?" she asked. "Won't that interfere?"

"Ah, yes, the Texas thing." I lay down onto the bed beside her and began rubbing my temples, which did not relieve my headache one iota. "Are you sure you want to do that?"

"Are you kidding?" she asked, incredulous. She sat up on her knees and starting rubbing my temples, my forehead, my neck. "We're talking over a hundred million dollars," she said soothingly. "That's a lot of lab equipment and scholarship money."

"And DNA bits from long-dead scientists and such," I added.

"We're too close, David; we can't stop."

"Well, maybe the cops can help us with the Texans."

We kissed lightly, and I picked up the phone. I got past the screener to Detective Shay rather quickly—he must have left word to pass me through—and he made it instantly clear that I wasn't his favorite caller.

"What do you want, Greenberg? I'm stretched up to my neck with local problems. Do you read the news?"

"I know, Detective. But we need some protection. That murderous Shadid is loose."

"Tell me about it. Twelve of my best goddamn men, you'd think..."

"I know, Detective, I know. And I hate to tell you, but the twin brother I told you about is on his way here. He just killed two of his own men in Israel and maybe an innocent bystander, some civilian. Help us, please."

"Goddamn, Greenberg! Goddamn. Now we got two of them animals? Look, I'd like to help..."

"*Please*, Detective Shay," I pleaded. Then I waited while the line grew silent.

"Okay, David, okay. I'll scrape up what I can. But understand, all hell's breaking loose around here, and I got layers of big shots over my head, every one of 'em ready to dump damp cow patties on me. Where are you?"

"The Coral Courts."

"Oh, Mr. Class. What cabin?"

"I've rented three hundred and three oh one. One last thing, Detective. You remember Bear Brukowski?"

"Bear? Sure. One helluva tackle."

"Well, I hate to tell you, but he is a prime suspect in both Moise Shankman's and Levi Asher's murders. Prime. And they're looking at his activities in Israel, too."

"What? Are you nuts?"

"Detective, did headquarters reveal to the public that Levi Asher was tortured? Did they? Because Bear seemed to know about it. Can you at least bring him in for questioning?"

"Not on your word alone, David."

"Well, do check, Detective."

"I'll check, but don't hold your breath. I mean, Bear Brukowski? Give me a break."

"I'm willing to make a statement that may implicate him," I said.

"Just keep your head down, David. I'll send you whatever help I can spare."

We agreed on details—I'd have some discretion—but I wasn't expecting much.

And I didn't receive even that.

***

It was sundown when I opened the door to find Doggie and Casey.

Oy. *These were going to be my protectors?*

I had them come in out of the rain.

Doggie was in his late-fifties, a man with a thick, salt-and-pepper mustache whose considerable weight had settled into his substantial stomach and seat padding. He wore his rumpled service blues with two buttons open at the collar to accommodate his multiple chins.

Casey was a woman in her early-fifties. Her blue uniform was pressed and starched, her neat brown hair tied up in a bun. They were more anxious about this unexpected duty than I was about having them.

Doggie explained that for the last thirty years he'd been the guy sitting by the door guarding the private areas at city hall where politicians freshened up for mayoral events. His father's alderman had gotten him the job when he was young and less obese. Casey, on the other hand, had spent her career deskbound at the station. Both wore pistols, but the shiny holsters told me that the hardware had been issued that day solely for this purpose. The whole time we spoke, Doggie constantly tugged at his holster, trying to make it fit comfortably around his expansive middle. The heavy leather belt so irritated him, you could see it on his face. Orderly Casey, no problem.

"That pistol," I said to Doggie, "do you know how to shoot that thing? Are you qualified?"

He did some thinking, massaging the gun on his hip. "When I was a rookie, I passed the test. Now that I think of it, I'm probably expired." He chuckled easily in his pleasant way. "I wished I'd thought of that when the captain wanted to send me here." He smiled broadly.

"How about you, Casey?" I asked.

"I'm intermediate Word- and Excel-qualified," she chuckled, her eyes constantly searching the Coral Courts environs, nervous as a squirrel in a dog pound.

Talk about scraping the barrel. "All right," I said, pointing. "You two take the cabin next door and keep watch on my door. Anyone approaches, you come out with your gun drawn. They could be dangerous guys, very dangerous."

"Our guns?" Casey asked, alarmed.

"Yes, your guns," I replied. The pair did not look pleased. "Now I'm going to order in some dinner. What will you have?"

"Where from?" Doggie's face brightened, as he thrust his thumbs inside his waistband with a pained grunt.

CHAPTER TWENTY-SIX
PERPETUAL CHECK

He swallowed mouthfuls of the thick brown liquid until he felt the familiar, sought-after click in his head. A welcome, warm glow of Southern Comfort washed over him, bathing his mind, stomach, chest, and extremities in a peaceful state of grace. It would be maintenance sips from here on in, until his nap on the return flight to Texas. He lit a fresh Camel and settled back in his padded white leather chair, a half-glass of bourbon lodged in his fist. He was ready, braced, manly.

The pilot, in his crisp, white uniform trimmed in gold braid, exited from the cabin and stopped smartly beside him. "The ground crew's finished running the tests, Mr. Wilcox. We're fueled and ready to go."

Taking a deep drag, Brody Wilcox turned to study the darkness outside the nearest window, which was being pelted by rain. Waves of insane atmospheric tantrums that had whipped across southern Missouri from the previous night's Oklahoma tornados were violently swirling across the St. Louis area into Central Illinois in an attempt to reach north. A series of lightning strikes cracked loudly into a unified, great explosion, flashing brilliance to light up the nearby tarmac and hanger. "What about the storm?"

"Should break relatively soon, I'm told," the pilot added. "We'll get clearance in about ten, fifteen minutes."

Brody made eye contact with his bodyguard, a former FBI agent, sitting across from him. The bodyguard, a powerfully built man with a blonde flattop, strong chiseled face, and neatly pressed, blue pinstripe suit, clinched his jaw and nodded. He, too, was ready.

Brody took a final belt of bourbon. His mind working, he took a last drag on his cigarette, stubbed the butt in the ashtray, and stood decisively.

"Okay, let's go save the world," he said, thrusting his cowboy hat down on his head. "We'll start the motors on my orders."

The pilot saluted and headed back to the cabin. Reentering the cockpit, he slapped his co-captain on the shoulder and gave him the thumbs up. They'd be heading home soon.

***

The lightning flashed repeatedly, its crash and thunder echoing from the distant hills, reverberating back again as the plane's door was lowered. With a clank, the hatch touched the tarmac, its steps now escalating downward into position. Brody examined the threatening sky with extreme trepidation. He'd always been afraid of lightning. When he was a boy, he'd been so terrified during thunderstorms that he'd been unable to sleep, and his parents had had to set up a makeshift bed for him in the root cellar for just such occurrences. But what had to be done had to be done. He and the ex-FBI agent finished slipping into their trench coats and opened their umbrellas. Taking a deep, tremulous breath, Brody nodded grimly to the ex-FBI man, who spoke into a cell. Then the pair made their way down the stairs, holding the railing with their free hands against the wet steps, until they finally set foot on the pavement. The hanger stood ahead like some low-budget torture chamber.

One of the two enormous doors, together wide enough for a private airplane's wingspan, slid open when they were still twenty yards away. When he saw the gaping aperture, Brody's heart began to pound. His mind shouted to pull back, to run to the safety of his jet, but he resisted the impulse. Too much was riding on his courage. He patted his coat, but then remembered he hadn't brought his flask on purpose, and he sure could have used a final swig. His hands were shaking. He shoved his free hand into his coat pocket so no one could see.

After pausing a moment for a final, brief consultation, his bodyguard entered the large structure, and Brody followed. The pair closed and shook out their umbrellas. Inside the vast, dimly lit space, a private jet with a single red stripe rested beside testing equipment and a wild tangle of wires, its proverbial hood lifted as if abandoned in mid-repair. Brody noticed that, for a place made to work on engines, the concrete floor was immaculate.

Appearing like four figurines in a shadowy ancient tableau, they seemed innocent enough standing there, two of them real-life versions of their dossier photos, the Jewess and the St. Louie Jew, who was some kind of Middle East tradesman. Beside them stood an odd-looking, pint-sized preacher, five-four or five-five tops, white collar and all, his arm around a skinny fourteen-year-old Yid with curly dark hair. Brody swallowed hard. He had to remember that the boy had God in him, not like a sinner on Sunday morning, but the real stuff.

God, I need a goddamn drink. If only this wretched storm would shut the fuck up! As if in reply to his wish, overhead thunder boomed and lightning cracked anew. It was a good thing he hadn't brought Reverend Nation along because he knew he was going to really tie one on the moment his plane was airborne again, Jesus Christ or no Jesus Christ.

The Jewess stepped forward, an exotic-looking, pretty, little thing with black hair and fetching eyes. Nice build, too. She held her hand open toward him.

"The Swiss escrow account, please," she said with an earnest smile.

Brody nodded, and the bodyguard handed Miriam an index card with three lines of numbers written across it. The woman glanced at the card, then eyed the Jew shopkeeper, who took it from her hand, then slipped behind his group.

"It's legitimate?" the woman asked Brody, who stood still as a statue, hands in his pockets.

The bodyguard replied, "It is."

While everyone stood around studying each other, the shopkeeper lifted a cell to his ear and began reciting the numbers on the card into it. Then the shopkeeper waited. And waited. And waited. It was unnerving. Finally, he nodded and slid the index card and the cell into his jacket. The transfer must have gone through.

The woman put her arm around the boy and nudged him forward. The boy slipped her, walked right up to Brody, and looked him squarely in the eye.

"Your mother's worried about you. She wants you to stop drinking and smoking," the boy said calmly, a slight smile on his innocent face.

"I been...I been meaning..." Brody stuttered before falling silent. Of course, the boy would know about his drinking. Crestfallen, he removed his cowboy hat and hung his head, fixing his eyes on his boots.

At that moment, a red-faced, barrel-chested man with a crew cut, wearing a three-piece suit, strode toward them, his wingman a seriously pudgy uniformed cop mumbling into a walkie-talkie. Simultaneously, glaring lights snapped on above them, and when his eyes cleared, Brody could see military-style helmets behind the walkway railings above. "Hold your fire," the big sloppy cop yelled more loudly into the walkie-talkie.

"What is the problem here?" the bodyguard asked in alarm.

"Violation of the United Nations Convention against Transnational Organized Crime, specifically the United Nations Protocol to Prevent, Suppress and Punish Trafficking in Persons, Especially Women and Children," the heavy man in the three-piece suit said with a lisp. "This is a clear violation of the Trafficking Protocol. You're all under arrest."

The overweight cop flashed his badge. Brody was immobilized, shaken to his boot heels. All he wanted to do was get back on the plane and in the air to Texas. A drink wouldn't hurt either.

"No such thing is going on," the bodyguard said firmly, resting his hand near his pistol holster.

"Oh, yeah. Well, we'll see," the three-piece suit answered, nodding to the rotund cop.

"Bring them forward," the cop said. Then growling in a gruff voice, he began to round up the Jewess, the shopkeeper, and the preacher.

Meanwhile, as everyone watched, a thin female cop in a crisp uniform escorted a wiry-boned woman in her sixties, headscarf covering her gray and black hair.

"Is this your boy, madam?" the three-piece asked.

"Yes, that is my son," the thin woman answered in heavily accented English.

"Is that your mother, son?" the three-piece queried the child, a gentle hand on his shoulder. When the boy nodded "yes," the three-piece turned to the gathering. "We're going to have to hold all of you until this is straightened out. International child trafficking is a very serious crime."

A suddenly terrified Brody looked quizzically, pleadingly toward his bodyguard. "Arrest?"

"You can't hold us," the bodyguard said grudgingly. "We only came in here to stretch our legs until the storm lets up. We've done nothing wrong. We're going to walk straight back to our plane and head home."

"But the money," Brody sputtered to his sidekick. "That's a shitload. A shitload!"

"Child trafficking is thirty years in the federal slammer, minimum, Mr. Wilcox," the bodyguard whispered to Brody. "We just want out of here." He turned to the authorities. "We've done nothing. You've got nothing."

"Oh, yeah?" the three-piece replied, reaching his hand into the shopkeeper's coat and confiscating the index card. "And what is this?"

"We don't know nothing about that," Brody hurriedly spit out. "We found it on the floor. Figured it belonged to somebody."

"You can't hold us," the bodyguard said. "We're leaving this hanger right now."

The heavyset cop looked questioningly toward the three-piece.

Deadly silence fell over the party as the three-piece rubbed his double chin. "All right," he said at last, making a reluctant, but understanding facial gesture toward the ex-fed, the sympathetic expression of one veteran law enforcement man to another. "But I want both of your contact information before you leave this hanger. Understand?"

"I'll give that to you," the bodyguard said. "This is Brody Wilcox, the chairman of three old drilling firms and a co-chairman of the Texas State Republican Congressional Campaign Fund."

"All right," the three-piece said. "Officer Lynch, take down their info. Then they're free to go. We'll bring in the other three for questioning. They'll look pretty good in orange jumpsuits and cuffs."

The boy serenely approached Brody a final time. "You cannot buy the Kingdom of Heaven," he said in his even, placid voice.

"Don't I know it," Brody replied. "A camel has a better chance threading a needle than what rich folks got for that. That's scripture. Anyhow, you tell my mamma I'm gonna quit drinkin' next week. You tell her for me."

The boy gently patted Brody's cheek; then his pale face warmed to a kindly, glowing smile. Brody smiled back sheepishly, turned, and headed for the open hanger door without looking back, lighting a badly needed Camel and popping open his umbrella. "Just like Pontius Pilate," he said, "I'm gonna wash my hands of the whole dang mess and have myself a drink. 'Cut your losses short' is what I always say." *Only, my God, what is brother Brady going to say about this fiasco!*

Inside the hanger, the bodyguard finished dictating their contact information to the overweight uniform and followed Brody shortly thereafter. Within a half hour, the jet was headed home with Brody half nodding off in his chair, the drink in his fist dribbling bourbon onto his lap.

Screw them Jews. The world is just gonna have to save its own doggone self. I ain't gonna mess no more with God's own plan, and sholy with no plan that locks me in no prison for thirty years. Ain't Jesus done give us free will of our own? Well, ain't He?

***

We were lucky. Lucky that Miriam was farsighted enough to preposition Chaya and Noam in St. Louis, so they'd be here when we needed them.

So there it was: perpetual check. In chess, there are games when one player is compelled, to stave off defeat, to keep the other player's king in continuous check. If the opponent's harried monarch is unable to escape, but his king cannot be cornered either, then the game settles into endless repetition. Since neither player can win, neither loses, the game is declared a draw.

That was similar to what had transpired in the airplane hangar. In this case, the Wilcox money was safely in Miriam's Swiss bank account. Stalemate or not, we were willing to settle.

***

Once the six had piled into the two cars, four into one, Greenberg and Mrs. Solomon into the rental, he lowered his field glasses and rose from the mud. He was drenched, coat over his head notwithstanding, mud-streaked, and shivering.

It was a puzzler. What the Israeli woman and the child were doing in St. Louis with Greenberg and Solomon, he couldn't guess. And the rent-a-cops? Brody Wilcox's man could have taken them both, blindfolded. From what he could see, Brody appeared so dejected, he could barely climb the plane's stairs. If he had to wager, he'd bet the ranch the nail hadn't been exchanged. In fact, there wasn't the slightest indication Greenberg had even snatched the nail yet. He'd bet the ranch on that, too.

He'd change into something dry and make his way to Coral Courts. They'd return there. Then he'd just have to wait in his car for Greenberg to make a move. Greenberg, who still didn't have a clue that he was watching their every movement.

He climbed back over the hill to where he'd hidden the Trans Am, the pouring rain soaking his socks, chilling his feet. A quarter of the way up the hill, his shoes and pants cuffs were covered in muck, and he had to balance on his hands to keep from falling face first into it. Reaching his car, he tore off his soaked shirt, used it to wipe his hands, and climbed in. Throwing the shirt onto the shotgun seat floor, he popped the suitcase lid, grabbed a towel, and began to dry his hair and chest. Next, he donned a clean shirt, wrenched off his shoes and socks, and tossed them on the back floor, leaving a gunked-up floor mat, before peeling out of his pants. He sighed relief when he was in warm, dry clothes.

Flipping on the GPS, he saw they were headed east on 64. Coral Courts Motel, no doubt, or dinner somewhere close to it, and then back to the motel. Smiling, he flipped on the receiver, and their voices came through clearly, with little static. He paused to listen closely.

"That was Doggie," Greenberg said in the Nissan. "They'll easily make the New York red eye. Once Doggie and Casey have Chaya and Noam safely on the plane, they'll meet us back at the motel. In the morning, Chaya and Noam will catch a flight to Tel Aviv."

"It was so good to see them again," Miriam said wistfully. "And wasn't Noam great? 'You cannot buy the Kingdom of Heaven.'"

The pair broke into laughter.

If Brody Wilcox seemed depressed, Greenberg and the woman were the opposite. Only getting skunked for real money could explain it. But for now, however, he had no idea of what had transpired in that aircraft hangar. It would have to remain a mystery.

"Okay, one final objective, David," Miriam said. "Then you're off the hook."

No need to spy on them to know what that meant.

***

Finkel's eyes searched the littered street in both directions, turning his flashlight this way and that. Even in the dimness, under its knocked-out street lamps, among its boarded-up windows, empty shops, and apartments, he detected no movement, nothing sentient. Even a rat couldn't make an honest living on Osage street.

He unlocked the accordion gate and slid it open half way, then unlocked the front door and slipped inside, locking the door behind him. Quiet and darkness. The same old odor of dust, the empty display stands jammed together in the back of the room, the phony artifacts in front. He pulled his cell to check the time and the results of the fifth race, then shoved it back into his pocket.

Fuckin' nag blew it in the stretch again!

He had a half hour before the sucker arrived, plenty of time to set up. Grumbling under his breath, he scurried to the cash register. He inserted and turned the key, then popped the drawer with a fist. Three dollar bills. Three lousy dollars!

Suddenly, he felt a pistol at his temple. "Father Finkel. Good to see you again." Out of the corner of his eye, Finkel glimpsed the nail-shaped birthmark on the man's cheek. A burning lump dropped into his stomach. He had that sinking feeling that he wasn't going to make the poker game tonight.

"Into the back room, please, sir. Where is the nail?"

"The nail? What nail... Oww, that hurt!"

"If you play coy with me, Father, your chances of survival are not good."

"What...? What do you want to know? Ow, that really hurt!"

"Now, the nail."

"A guy named Greenberg. David Greenberg. Ow, that really... I'm bleeding. I'm fuckin' bleeding."

"Are you going to cooperate?"

"Yes, yes. It's Greenberg. He knows where it is. He's the guy. Owwww, stop it, please, stop!"

"You're no priest, are you, Father? You're a Jew."

"No, I'm simply... Oww, please, please!"

"Tell me you spit on the Torah."

"I spit on the Torah. Owww, stop, please..."

"Tell me you piss on Moses' grave."

"I piss on Moses' grave. Owwww."

"Tell me there was no Holocaust."

"The Holocaust is bullshit. Bullshit. Owwww! Please! I think it's broken!"

"Oh, you wet your pants, Father. Not very sociable. Now, where is David Greenberg hiding?"

"I don't know. I... Owww, you're breaking... Stop, stop, please!"

"But you can reach him, can't you? Can't you?"

"Yeah, sure. I can call him. Owww, stop, please stop! You're breaking my..."

"Then don't you think you should call him?"

"Yes, yes, I'll call him. Owww, it's bleeding."

"You don't need both these eyes, do you, Father? Can I have one?"

"Please. I'll call him. I'll call him right now, right now. Owww. Don't, don't..."

"And what will you tell him, Father? How will you get to him?"

"I'll... Let me think... Owww, I'm thinking. Give me a moment to... Owww, don't, please don't... That hurts. That hurts!"

"It certainly focuses the mind, doesn't it, Father?"

***

Only one final step was required to extricate myself from this whole *mishugganah* mishmash. Levi had hidden the nail in the St. Louis metropolitan region, an area with a population of three million spread over eighty-two hundred square miles, and using *gematria*, the ancient Hebrew numerology system, I had to find it.

Oy, *what a headache.*

The primary idea in *gematria* is to turn Hebrew letters into numbers, based on the belief that God's truth is most perfectly revealed with mathematics. Whether the religious theorists who believe this are correct is way beyond me. Not that I'm not a believer in math; I am. The Greeks' Pythagorean Society—remember the Pythagorean theorem?—believed the truth lay in numbers, but even they kept *pi* a secret from outsiders. They believed knowledge of *pi*, an irrational number that never ends, would only confuse the average man and bring their beliefs into question. Since the Greeks, Western science has gone pretty far in proving that the universe is written in the language of numbers, whether inked by the Great Mathematician Himself, God, or conforming to some other, natural explanation. Math led Newton to our understanding of gravity, Copernicus to the secrets of the solar system, and Einstein to the mysteries of space and time, among multitudes of other breakthroughs. But to my knowledge, no math has yet proven or disproven the Torah, Scripture, or the Koran, although some might argue it has given us insight into their wisdom.

I already had my numbers: 59, thanks to Levi Asher's text message, and, from Bobby Fischer's chess game, the numbers 9, 20, 14, and 16. What I needed to do now was the opposite of *gematria's* standard method and, instead of turning Hebrew into numbers, turn my numbers into Hebrew. From those Hebrew words, hopefully, I could extract the nail's location. My problem—the only Hebrew I remember from my childhood are the four letters on the dreidel, a spinning top used by children to gamble for candy or pennies at Chanukah. That wouldn't get me far.

Fortunately, Miriam had been Bat Mitzvahed and has lived for two decades in Israel. We propped up the pillows against the headboard. Then she poured two cups from the motel coffeemaker, while I fired up my laptop and made myself comfortable beside her. She reclined against her pillows, curling her feet under, and took a sip of coffee. When I took a deep breath to calm my nerves, the heavy scent of her fragrant musk drifted into my nostrils, and I sensed the warmth of her body beside mine. But I forced myself to push the feelings these engendered within me into the back of my consciousness.

Work to do.

My stomach tightened as I Googled various *gematria* paradigms. There were so many! My first discovery was that in *Kabbalah*, there are ten basic *gematria*, corresponding to the ten *Sefirot*, or "emanations," through which *Ein Sof* the Infinite reveals himself and continuously creates both the physical realm, like here on Earth, and the chain of higher metaphysical realms which maybe Plato understood, but will forever remain a mystery to me. The sources admit that few understand the relation of the *gematria* method to the corresponding *Sefirot*, and, further, there are many different methods that are subsets of the major types.

Easier to evade pursuing killers.

Simplify, simplify, simplify! After further exploration, I was able to find standard *gematria* reduced to four basic methods.

Now we're getting somewhere. But where?

As a student, the brilliant young Levi had undoubtedly obsessed for hours with these numbers and methods in his *Kabbalah* and *gematria* endeavors. I was certain that he had found, back in Israel, perhaps playing around, the "Jesus Christ = 59" method, and with the number 59 sticking in his head, maybe the Fischer game moves matching that sum had clicked at some point. I know he was in a hurry when he texted his clue, so I didn't expect perfection but rather something slapped together on the dodge that might make sense, just as he'd mistakenly fat-fingered the X in his clue as a Z.

The method that seemed most likely, the Ordinal Value Method of *gematria*, assigned a numerical value to each of the 27 Hebrew letters. Promising. Since twenty was the highest number of my four suspects—9, 20, 14, 16—that meant, working backwards, I could find which Hebrew letter was represented by each number. I showed the online chart to Miriam, and she slid shoulder-to-shoulder with me to examine my screen. Her warm nearness was not good for my concentration.

I had to go entirely by the chart because the example given on the site identified the word *shalom* as having an ordinal value of 52. That said, the site "clarified" by noting that "52 is the number related to the Tetragrammaton associated with *Zeir Anpin* and *Yesod*." Also, way beyond me. And no help.

Nevertheless, if I was lucky, the resultant four Hebrew letters would spell out the nail's location. The chart assigning numbers to the Hebrew letters read from 1 to 27, with one or more Hebrew letters assigned to each number. From these, I opened a new tab in my spreadsheet, then created my own four-character chart with the values revealed in Bobby's chess game: 9-ע-16, נ-14, ר-20, ט. *So far, so good.*

Number	Hebrew Letter
9	ט
20	ך
14	נ
16	ע

Miriam studied the result, groaning and wrinkling her brow. Pointing, she showed me, "Two non-adjacent letters spell 'awake' and two spell 'candle.' Two others mean 'very bad.' They can sound like the English word 'rotten'? Does that mean anything? That's all I can find."

Naturally, no arrangement led to a word or a series of words that made the least bit of sense.

Bad start.

The next method I found was *Mispar Gadol*, which means "Large Number." But I didn't want a big number, so I went to the next related method, the *Mispar Katan*, meaning "Small Number" or "Reduced Value."

Aha! A small number is what I want!

In the *Mispar Katan*, the numerical values that have multiple digits are reduced to a single digit. This seemed promising.

Fortunately, I found the Buzzle site where the Hebrew letters related to single digits. Adding the digits of my four key numbers together (9, 20, 14, 16), I came up with 9, 2, 5, and 7. These produced the Hebrew letters *teth-beth-hei-zayin*.

Number: Name	Meaning	Symbolization
1: Aleph	an ox or bull	strength, primacy, leader
2: Beth	**a tent, house, in, into**	household, family
3: Gimel	a camel	to be lifted up, pride
4: Dalet	a door	opening, entry, pathway
5: Hei	**a window**	behold, the, to reveal, inspiration, what comes from
6: Vav	a nail, hook	to fasten, join together, secure, add
7: Zayin	**a weapon**	cut, cut off
8: Chet	enclosure	inner room, heart, private, separate
9: Teth	**snake, serpent**	surround

On the chart, these letters equaled four words, **snake-house-window-weapon**. But the letters themselves, forward or backward, even scrambling their order, produced no sensible word. However, I thought, perhaps snake-house-window-weapon had some meaning. The famous Snake House at the zoo, its window, some sort of weapon? I wasn't very confident of this hypothesis.

Then I had a breakthrough. I saw that adding the digits together was the *Mispar Katan Mispari,* or "Integral Reduced Value" method. Another obscure version of the *Mispar Katan* required *multiplying* them together. As required by this method, I dropped the zero on the 20, making it a 2 (multiplying times zero always produces zero), and when I multiplied the rest, the new sequence was **9, 2, 4,** and **6**. I created a new chart using those values.

Number: Name	Meaning	Symbolization
1: Aleph	an ox or bull	strength, primacy, leader
2: Beth	**a tent, house, in, into**	household, family
3: Gimel	a camel	to be lifted up, pride
4: Dalet	**a door**	opening, entry, pathway
5: Hei	a window	behold, the, to reveal, inspiration, what comes from
6: Vav	**a nail, hook**	to fasten, join together, secure, add
7: Zayin	a weapon	cut, cut off
8: Chet	enclosure	inner room, heart, private, separate
9: Teth	**snake, serpent**	surround

Suddenly, in order, my four-digit chart shocked me: *Teth*-serpent, *Beth*-tent or house, *Dalet*-door, *Vav*-nail. *Nail!* Jackpot! This startlingly lucky find was, indeed, promising.

"A nail, Miriam, a nail!" I practically shouted. "It has to be 9, 2, 4, 6: serpent-house-door-*nail!*

"Yes," she said excitedly. "In Hebrew, *Vav* is a nail or a hook, like you hammer into the wall to hang a picture."

"Do these four letters spell a word or a group of words?" I asked, my nerves alive like I'd taken a straight shot of caffeine.

"Not really," she replied. "It's nonsense."

"Nothing?" I pleaded.

She studied the four-letter Hebrew word for some time, shaking her head "no, no, no." Then she stated hesitantly, "If you drop the *dalet*, the letters *teth-beth-vav* do read as the word 'taboo' in Hebrew."

Number: Name	Meaning	Symbolization
9: Teth	snake, **serpent**	surround
2: Beth	a tent, **house**, in, into	household, family
4: Dalet	a **door**	opening, entry, pathway
6: Vav	a **nail**, hook	to fasten, join together, secure, add

Taboo! Surely, even in his hurry, bright young Levi would have seen the pattern emerge immediately when he simply ignored one letter, like a priest would see "God" in the letters "GOXD." It's only natural.

"Taboo? Are you sure?" I exclaimed so animatedly it startled her.

"Yes, sure," Miriam replied, a bit bewildered.

"Where was Levi staying in St. Louis, Miriam?" I asked.

"The Central West End," she said sheepishly. "He was staying at my old friend Becky's apartment on McPherson, just up the street from your gallery."

I hurriedly Googled Taboo Tabernacle, a local gathering edifice that welcomed people of all beliefs and lifestyles, very loosey goosey.

"Miriam, they're having a costumed fundraiser tonight," I cried, springing from the bed. "There's a costume rental not far from here. We've got to make a few purchases. Then we're going to retrieve our nail."

CHAPTER TWENTY-SEVEN
THE TREE OF KNOWLEDGE

"All right, Finkel. I'll put some cash in an envelope with *both* of your names on it and slip it into the mail slot at the gallery. You can pick it up tomorrow morning. Don't be wandering around looking for a sucker. You hear me? Double park and run in. Then back to the Eastside, lickety-split. No stops. Finkel, these guys are killers. Got it?"

"Got it. Will do, David. Right back to Motel Hell."

"And Finkel, no more envelopes. This is the last one, period. Your cut is coming, goddammit. Understand?"

"I promise, genius. Thank you. Thank you so much."

Returning the cell to my front pocket, I put my hands on my hips, fervently hoping that Miriam was nearly done with her makeup job. I checked the window, but the weather wasn't going to change. A great Midwestern thunderstorm was trailing the one that passed through the previous night, with fifty-mile-an-hour wind gusts swirling destruction in its wake. The motel window was a solid waterfall, with lightning flashing, crashing and exploding all around.

Well, maybe the rain would supply additional obfuscation to the cover of a moonless night.

"They blew the whole wad already?" Miriam asked laughingly, applying the final touches to her black lipstick.

"Every cent," I said, laughing nervously. "Bad night at the track. I couldn't let them starve, could I? That would force them to return to St. Louis, to their normal sources for cash, where Shadid could get his hands on them."

We were set to attend the Taboo costume fundraiser as Morticia and Gomez of the Addams family. I crossed to the mirror to stand beside her, where we both froze to admire the pretty picture we made as a couple. Surrounded by the shabbiness of the cheap bedroom furniture, Miriam made a...well, I'll say a *fetching* Morticia. She appeared to have recently emerged from the netherworld in her deathly white mortician makeup, long black wig, thick, cat-like black eyeliner, and matching black lipstick and fingernails.

I may be no lady-killer, but in suave Gomez maroon velvet smoking jacket, slicked down hair, and fake mustache, I made quite a sight myself. Add the black cape, and we were ready for the cover of *Rolling Stone* or *Vanity Fair* as the case might be.

"How could I have ever left that?" Miriam asked my reflection.

"Your sexy new look is a definite turn on," I replied.

I called our intrepid law enforcement pair in the adjacent cabin to be sure they were ready. They were. Doggie and Casey knew their separate roles.

That confirmed, Miriam slung her bag over her shoulder and fastened her cape against the maelstrom outside. We'd leave our luggage and the laptop and swing by to retrieve them the next day, assuming we were still sentient. Then we clicked open our umbrellas and headed out. I waved to Casey watching for our departure from her cabin window. She signaled back. One brief stop at my gallery to drop off Finkel's money, and it would be two blocks to the nail. The whole time, I'd been two damn blocks away.

***

I pulled up to my gallery and threw the Nissan into park. After patting Miriam's arm to reassure her, I opened the door and popped the umbrella. Getting soaked the whole way, I ran to the front door, splashing into broad Missouri rivers running along the curb, drenching my pants, shoes, and socks. Lightning flashed while I slipped the envelope through the mail slot. Then I ran back to the car, soaked through my flimsy cape. Even ducks would have been depressed by this weather.

I flopped back into the car and took a moment to examine the area. Visibility was limited, but I saw no one who looked suspicious. Only pouring rain, and more rain.

"Okay," I said. "You ready?"

Miriam nodded.

"All right. Next stop, Taboo Tabernacle and the nail. Minutes away."
Time to buck up my courage.

***

"Is that the Jew Greenberg and the woman?"

"Yes, that's him! That's Greenberg. Oww..."

"You said he had a blue BMW."

"Yes, but he's tricky. He's tricky. Oww... Don't, don't..."

"Are you certain that's him?"

"Yes, yes, that's him, that's him and the woman. Owww. Don't, please, don't... Don't you see their costumes are a frigging disguise? Who would go around in shit like that? Oww..."

At long last! He'd had setbacks, reversals, but now he would behead this apostate, this blasphemer, Greenberg, then singlehandedly defeat the Christians and the Jews, and put an end to their insidious Satanic plotting. He and he alone would decapitate the serpent!

He paused for a bittersweet moment to realize he may never again see his beloved West Bank, and to remember nostalgically Switzerland in the spring. It would not be long now. Then he focused on the task at hand. "All praise to Allah. I am your humble servant."

He checked his Luger automatic and slid it into his belt. Then he slid his golden dagger into its jeweled sheath. "God willing, I will have their throats."

***

He was so fortunate, so lucky. Another half hour and he might have dozed off. Clearly, that was Greenberg—the ridiculous disguise wouldn't have fooled a child—and Mrs. Solomon in the seat beside him. All the waiting, the desperate travel, the hardship, the loss of his former life at the university, all worthwhile. God was unquestionably directing him to recover this nail. He must put an end to this infernal, atheistic, scientific blasphemy! "Thank you, Hashem. I am the instrument of your will. I am your servant."

He checked his automatic pistol, then snapped shut the holster at his hip. Satisfied he could catch the pair, he started the motor and threw the car into gear. Greenberg owed him a debt, and he would extract every drop of revenge. Every drop.

***

The GPS put Greenberg and the woman right at...his gallery? Strange that he should drive there. Was he returning to his home around the corner? Or had he another purpose for breaking cover? He turned up the volume on the receiver. The static from the box increased, but at this volume, he would be more likely to hear any nuances. He heard Greenberg's car door slam shut again, the seat belt click. Then he heard the man's voice coming through the listening device quite distinctly.

"Okay," Greenberg said. *"You ready?"*

There was a moment of silence on the other end.

"All right. Next stop, Taboo Tabernacle and the nail. Minutes away." Through the receiver, he heard the car's gears engage, then heard the motor roar.

He punched the coordinates into the GPS, and the street map was revealed on the screen. Simple, right there. Easy as good ol' American apple pie. He had the defensive back right in his sights.

Pancake time.

Damn, the kid hid it right near the spot he'd kidnapped him. He could have saved himself a lot of trouble by catching the skinny Jew nerd a half hour sooner.

He slipped on his calfskin gloves, wriggled his fingers, reached under his jacket, beneath his left armpit, and checked his pistol in its leather holster. Then he slid the machete lying on the seat beside him into its jerry-rigged sheath under the jacket's other arm. Satisfied that nothing could stop him, he started the motor. Let Greenberg get the nail first; then it was his. As were they, his. He'd teach them to run him around, to sneak out of Israel while he waited for Greenberg's call. He wouldn't even bother to dispose of their bodies. Let them rot.

The downpour began in earnest once again. All he could see through the headlights were sheets of rain blowing sideways. He couldn't even see taillights. He slowed to a crawl.

Careful, no need to rush. Plenty of time.

He had them pinned, big time.

***

When the light changed, I turned left onto Kingshighway from McPherson, made a quick right onto Waterman, and slowed to a crawl. There it stood on our left, looming in the darkness, a monolithic temple to...well, I had little idea to what. Brotherhood, the Earth, peace, that kind of liberal *schmaltz.* Twenty yards from the building stood a tall statue of what appeared to be stylized upper torsos of a man and woman clinching in the heart of a giant phallus. Well, that was my interpretation. Above the building entrance, large black letters read "Taboo."

"What would Levi be doing here?" Miriam asked.

"My guess, he sensed he was being followed and ducked into it. There'd be people, a crowd maybe. He probably found a niche in there to hide the nail, and a place to formulate and send his text."

"So we guessed right."

"He was a smart kid. You'd have to know him well to know about the Bobby Fischer chess and the *Kabbalah gematria*, and you'd also have to know Hebrew to find the nail. Any of those three missing, there'd be no way to unscramble the clue. Talk about encrypted."

We fell into silence. As we drove into the parking lot, I could see a message board similar to those fronting any church. In permanent, illuminated blue letters, the sign read, "Taboo Tabernacle—A Refuge from Convention." Below that, a quote of the day.

We circled the small parking lot slowly, searching through the thick storm for a vacancy, but all the places were taken, even those reserved for the handicapped.

"You sure you don't want to wait at the wheel while I go in?" I asked.

"No, David. You can't leave me out here by myself."

We exited the lot and drove west on Waterman, until I finally found a spot three blocks away. We parked, opened our umbrellas, and hurried toward Taboo, pelted by the drenching downpour. There were singles, couples, and groups on both sides of the street, making their way quickly toward Taboo, umbrellas open, raincoats buttoned. Against my better judgment, I kept glancing back at the people behind us, kept tabs on those across the street, made sure the ones ahead didn't slow to let us pass. With three ruthless killers after me, it was a fright-filled sidewalk.

Upon reaching the entrance, we felt great trepidation, yet exhilaration, that our bloody search might be at an end—if my guesses were right, that is. Our eyes locked a moment, trying to give each other encouragement; then we went in. In the foyer, we could hear John Lennon's "Imagine" wafting from loudspeakers. Very apropos.

The high priestess, I guess you'd call her, stood near the door, greeting the communicants entering the holy place. She was pretty in a country-girl way, with long raven hair flowing down her back, thin pale lips, wearing a simple brown robe adorned by golden chains—and colorful tattoos down both her bare alabaster arms.

Cool.

She flashed the peace sign with a wide smile. "Heal Mother Earth," she said sweetly. *Nice. No dogmatic rabbi, priest, reverend, or imam here.*

"Heal Mother Earth," we responded in unison, flashing the V-sign back.

"You're newcomers," she said.

"Yes," I answered. "We're visiting from Michigan. This is really awesome."

"Welcome," she said warmly. "Umbrellas and shoes over there. Donations at that table."

When the priestess shifted her attention over my shoulder to other groups entering the building, Miriam and I used the diversion to slip by. We removed our sneakers, sheathed our umbrellas, and I wrote a check. SOP. The planets appeared to be in alignment.

We passed a tanned, blonde man with a Hollywood smile, wearing a white buckskin Indian chieftain outfit and magnificent headdress, and his dark-haired wife dressed in a Native American wedding robe. They gave us the "how" sign as we passed, hands raised, and we returned the greeting.

Nearby, another couple stood dressed as mimes, with whiteface and broad red mouths, wearing berets and black tights, an oversize flower in their lapels. A young man, standing alone, perfectly resembled a not-as-handsome Don Draper, fedora hat and all.

We stood in the corner for two or three minutes, our eyes searching the eclectic crowd. Nothing suspicious, no threatening characters. Then we slipped into the main gathering hall, with its high ceiling and post-modern, multi-colored stained glass windows. The place was already filling up, but we managed to find two seats together in the back near the doors. The room held no symbol of worship, no Cross, Star of David, no Crescent, no Buddha, nothing but an American flag hanging loosely from a pole topped by a golden eagle.

I looked over the crowd, happy to be together, to have a common spiritual core, a sense of community, and wondered, *Is this what I've missed in life? Having no family? What was I trying to avoid? Did I see nothing during my trips to Europe, to the Middle East, but lifeless treasures, overlooking the people surrounding me?*

Then I glanced aside at Miriam, slumped in her seat, her eyes fixed on her hands resting in her lap. She had seen the laughing couples, the families, just as I had. Now with her son dead and her husband living in his lab, what did her life mean?

The crowd quieted as the high priestess strode to the podium. She welcomed everyone and thanked them for coming out in such terrible weather, cracking a few clever jokes about the storm. *Funny. She could easily pursue standup if the spiritual game ever went sour.* Then some words about the recent interfaith conference she attended with a few members.

Before she could break into the day's topic, I tapped Miriam's knee, and we slid from our chairs, crept out the back door, and closed them carefully, trapping the good humor and spiritual communion inside. Once in the foyer, we headed through the dimly lit corridor leading toward the back of the building lined with classrooms, its corkboard-adorned walls alive with children's construction paper cutouts and watercolor pictures depicting various themes of brotherhood and pacifism.

We reached the end of the corridor and, seeing nothing but more classrooms to the left, turned right onto a darkened hallway. Miriam found a penlight in her bag and handed it to me. Walking down another long hall, we found only offices and janitor closets. Then we turned again and saw it: the entrance to a new annex.

Directly ahead loomed a black door with a snake wrapped around a tree trunk carved into it, a not-so-subtle allusion to the Tree of Knowledge. A sign beside the door read "Sanctuary," with its stylized S a twisting, coiled snake, its gargantuan head projecting toward the onlooker. The snake's hinged mouth gaped widely, its curved giant fangs exposed and dripping, ready to bite. There we had it—the "serpent-door" of Levi's clue. I swallowed hard.

Miriam and I exchanged wary but relieved smiles. She took my hand, and we pressed forward together toward the door, the creaking floorboards echoing in the cavernous empty chamber. *Just my luck.* When we entered the darkened sanctuary, the sky outside picked that exact moment to begin exploding with renewed thunder and lightning. Obviously, God didn't think we were scared enough.

I shined our little light around. The room was designed for contemplation, with futons, pillows, and mats along the perimeter. In the room's center was a large, glass-enclosed diorama, at least eight feet long by six feet wide, with ferns and flora, giving the chamber a sense of serenity. In the center, a gurgling waterfall tumbled over a windmill replica, attached to a yard-high 19th-Century log millhouse. There, right on the millhouse, a door.

Serpent-house-door, I thought excitedly. *Of course!*

I dropped Miriam's hand and went right to the little millhouse. But nothing is easy. The miniature jungle setting was occupied by a large, scaly black snake lying curled up against the millhouse door, its body resting in the pool below the waterfall. I know nothing about snakes, poisonous or not, as you'd assume this one to be; but the prospect of sticking my hand into his territory was not my first choice. I shined the light on the snake and saw it was awake, and, to me, appeared none too pleased with being disturbed.

While Miriam held the flashlight on the snake, I tentatively reached for the millhouse door, but the snake must have felt threatened and opened its mouth, so I pulled back. Then I had an idea. I had Miriam move the light slowly away from the snake, and its attention followed. Quickly, I grabbed its tail and tossed it to the other side of the atrium. When it landed, Miriam held the flashlight right in its face, freezing it in place.

Sorry to disturb you, pal, but no time for niceties.

I pulled open the millhouse door and reached inside. My fingers felt around its rough cedar floor, but no nail. As I withdrew my hand, it accidently bumped against the door, which came loose on one hinge. Investigating, I felt along the top of the door. It wasn't solid. Taking a gulp of air, I squeezed my fingers into the hollow of the door itself and felt around. There, my fingers lighted upon something solid wrapped in plastic. I worked the object loose and brought it out: inside the plastic wrapping was a large nail. I held the nail up for Miriam to see, dropped it into her bag, took her hand, and we left the poor snake to catch up on its napping.

Jubilant and relieved, all smiles, we half-skipped hand-in-hand back down the hall from which we'd come. Ahead, we spotted him before he saw us. There was just enough light to make out the man in the silver-gray suit, pistol and dagger in hand, a nail-shaped birthmark on his right cheek. Instant death in Armani. We turned and ran the opposite way, our hearts beating madly, down an unfamiliar hallway in the direction of what we hoped was the parking lot. Seeing our flight, the man with the birthmark broke into a run, chasing us. We didn't get far.

From the opposite end of the hall, another man was coming straight for us, finger on the trigger. This one wore jeans and a black leather coat, a nail-shaped birthmark on *his* right cheek, identical to our first pursuer. Terrified, we stopped, searching for a way out. Trapped! They were coming, weapons drawn, from both ends of the hallway, Am Ha-b'rit's slightly flawed first attempts at cloning human beings. Weiner and Shadid, our executioners.

A short hallway teed out from the one we were fleeing, which ended in a brown metal door that housed a maintenance and HVAC facility. I pulled Miriam toward the brown door and tried the handle. It was locked. We were, indeed, cornered. We turned back, arms around each other, our backs to the door. Our eyes kissed briefly, tenderly, and then we faced our doom together.

As Weiner and Shadid, his mirror image, confronted each other for their first time since the womb, each knowing of the other only by reputation, each hating the other like some contemptible phantom, an instinct kicked in. It was like those Samurai warriors who were taught only to attack, who never knew the concept of defense. Taught to keep killing forward, their swords always chopping, chopping, chopping forward, implacably forward for their Lord, never slowing, never retreating, never fleeing. To kill and kill and only to kill, all sense of self-preservation sublimated to the Lord's will. To fall and be replaced by the next ant killing forward, to be replaced by the waves of armed ants behind.

The brothers halted simultaneously, delighted at finally facing The Unequivocal Enemy they had despised so passionately for so long. A great smile crossed both of their lips. I would never have guessed that either one could smile so broadly, so naturally. The whole clash took only seconds really, although it seemed much longer. Pistols locked on automatic fire, both began blasting with sheer glee into each other's bodies from point-blank range, shouting cursed insults in Hebrew and Arabic. Shadid's pistol locked, and he tossed it aside, drawing his curved dagger. Weapon raised, he charged Weiner, dagger slashing, impelled forward by an absolute animosity. He stumbled momentarily, as rapid-fire bullets struck his midsection before his will drove him on. Then Shadid was upon Weiner, his dagger plunging repeatedly into his brother's neck as an animal struggles in a death clinch, taking bullets the whole time. Then they were still except for their final shudders. The pair lay twisted together, motionless, like a perverse mockery of the sculpture couple entwined in erotic rapture outside the Taboo Tabernacle. Blood was everywhere, their common life essence covering them both, as a lake of sentience poured onto the carpet, spreading rapidly. Two men of enormous potential, learning, and courage—everything a father would want in his sons—yet their fanaticism brought them to this end.

Miriam and I were both in shock, having witnessed the spectacle of two brothers so brutally destroyed by their own enmity.

"Jacob and Esau," Miriam said breathlessly when she was finally able to speak. "But with no reconciliation. Such a shame. Poor Jarad," she cried bitterly, turning her eyes from the bloody wreck of her former protector and family friend. Tears poured down her face, streaking her mortician white makeup with solid black from her heavily drawn eyes. She buried her face in my chest. My arms went around her, and I averted my own eyes from the grotesque tableau before us.

Officer Casey came running down the hall, a novice to such traumatic catastrophes. Breathing hard from her gallop toward the shots, she stopped before the crimson pool of blood, five feet from where we stood, aghast at the horror at her feet, her virgin service weapon still in its holster. She, too, began to cry from the shock of the nightmare before her, her handkerchief to her face.

I put my arm around Miriam's shoulder as we passed through slippery blood, which soaked our bare socks. There was no avoiding it. Soon we heard the Taboo security guard running tentatively toward us from the offices near the front of the complex.

"You collared two internationally wanted serial murderers, Casey," I told her. "You need to take credit for this." I'd see if I could get her a commendation for her undaunted courage. Who knows if she heard me? She was shaking, unable to stop crying.

"Casey," I said. "Can you handle this? Can you call it in?"

She nodded into her handkerchief, still sobbing.

"Call me at home when you're back at the station," I said. "I'll file a statement. All right?"

Casey nodded again. "It'll probably be tomorrow," she said, confident with her long experience writing reports. She pulled her radio from her belt and, still wiping her eyes, called the station, reporting a double homicide in a public venue.

With Casey's permission, Miriam and I disappeared out the side door onto the parking lot. The night had reduced its fury to a steady rain. We'd left our umbrellas and sneakers back near the entrance, but we weren't going back for them. The deep puddles and lawn-gully wash would dilute the red sludge on our socks, as we tracked the liquid remnants of the twin brothers down the sidewalk. It was cold, uncomfortable, yet with the nail in Miriam's purse, it felt like a very hard-won victory, and a very real escape from death.

As we approached the rental car, my arm still around Miriam's shoulders to lessen the chill, she began to recite from Genesis the passages about Rebekah's physical discomfort from the already active *in utero* rivalry between twins Jacob and Esau and her conversation with God about them.

"And the children struggled together within her; and she said, If it be so, why am I thus? And she went to enquire of the Lord. And the Lord said unto her, Two nations are in thy womb, and two manner of people shall be separated from thy bowels; and the one people shall be stronger than the other people; and the elder shall serve the younger."

Those two we'd left behind in a macabre death embrace were more than twins. They were genetically identical, the same man, except for what they'd been taught and had come to venerate...and to hate.

I'm not a believer, as I freely admit. But during that chilling stroll, I fervently prayed to whatever good pervades the universe, be it God or love or whatever, that like the biblical Jacob and Esau, there will be a reconciliation between these two long-suffering peoples, between these two nations living side-by-side through a seemingly hopeless, endless mutual fratricide.

And then I discovered that I, too, was crying, crying hard. I wiped my eyes on my drenched Gomez cape in a vain attempt to clear my vision, but the damn tears just wouldn't stop.

CHAPTER TWENTY-EIGHT
LITTLE DAVID, SANS SLINGSHOT

"Hey, Sarge, there's a guy tied up in this car."

The sergeant joined the patrolman, rain drumming on his hat's plastic cover, on his poncho, on his face. He shined his flashlight into the car. Sure enough, there was Finkel scrunched into the back floor, bound and trussed, a rag stuffed into his mouth. The cops worked the door open and began to untie the man. As they worked, the sergeant ripped the tape from the captive's face, freeing him to speak.

"Careful, goddammit, I got broken bones here!" Finkel shouted as the officers cut him loose. "Shit," Finkel screamed at them, "that hurts! Where the fuck have you been, eating goddamn donuts?"

***

Shaken and exhausted, we left the rental at the curb and made our way through the rain to my house—visions of a warm shower and dry clothes shimmering before us. Once inside the foyer, we removed our stained, soaked socks and dropped our capes to the floor. When we looked into each other's faces, our makeup streaking into death masks, we were quite a fright. It was reassuring to hear Doggie's police radio squawking inside, the excited myriad voices and sirens issuing forth through the static, directing police cruisers to the Taboo Tabernacle. After a brief, damp hug and deep sighs, we made our way into the living room. I hit the light switch, and our relief turned into terror.

"Hello, David. Welcome home."

My worst nightmare: Bear sat in my armchair pointing a pistol at us, the same chair in which an armed, drunk Daddy Markowitz had greeted me seemingly ages ago. But Bear was stone cold sober and six-feet-six of muscle. He wore tan calfskin gloves, no doubt to conceal his fingerprints.

Good cop Doggie lay on one couch, unconscious, blood dried on his forehead, his hands locked behind him in his own cuffs. With a tilt of his head, Bear directed Miriam and me to the other couch, immediately across from where he sat. We complied.

"Well, it looks like that police APB hasn't ensnared you yet, Bear," I said, hoping the potential threat might affect his tactics. "They ought to spot your gold Porsche rather easily."

"Wish them luck! I'm driving a loaner from a friend," he replied.

"Did your friend give it up voluntarily?" I chided him. "What do you want, Bear?"

"The money and the nail. Period."

"And then you'll leave us alone?" I asked, my tone of voice indicating I knew his answer.

"Sorry, David. The knight isn't going to get his chess game against death," he said, recalling *The Seventh Seal*. "It's checkmate right here and now, pal. Pressing business."

So much for mercy. "Unsportsmanlike conduct, Bear," I admonished him bitterly, my wrist flipping an imaginary yellow flag.

"So give me a fifteen-yard penalty," he retorted, a sadness upon his rugged brow. "This can't be stopped, buddy."

Miriam squeezed my hand. Our eyes met momentarily. Then I faced the third, most resilient of our executioners.

"There's no limit to what you could have been, Bear," I said wistfully. "No limit. Do you really have to kill us?"

"Things might have been a lot different if I'd had an older brother like you, Greenberg, instead of the so-called 'friends' that latched onto me," he said, feeling sorry for himself. "But it is what it is."

"I'd have been proud to have a younger brother like you, Bear. Too bad it turned out this way. Listen, with all you've done, with the big contracts and the ministry, why do you need this so badly?"

"I just have no head for business, brother David, especially against those real estate development sharks. None. I kept parleying myself into the ground. That high leverage will kill you quickly. Believe me, I had plenty of help doing it."

His jaw locked in anger; this tack wasn't getting me anywhere.

"I had a little problem with gambling that got out of hand, too."

"Can Miriam put on a pot of coffee for us, Bear? We're awfully cold. Look, she's shivering."

"You won't have that problem long, David." He swung the pistol toward Miriam. "You stay right where you are, Mrs. Solomon. I apologize for your discomfort."

Miriam merely gave him a resentful, dirty look.

"How did you get in my house?" I asked.

"Upstairs window. I came up over the eave. A little rough on my bad knee."

"Except for the knee, you could have played another three, four years," I said.

"Well, it was the concussion syndrome that really did me in," Bear said. "I kept getting my brains knocked out. It's no fun to go for a clean block and wake up on a stretcher in the training room when everyone else has dressed and gone home."

"So, you mentioned a police APB? What do they want me for?" His face told me he didn't believe a word I said.

"Everything, pal," I said, "starting with Moise Shankman's murder. Too bad Levi Asher beat you to Moise's shop. Then, of course, there's Levi's death."

Bear reached in his pocket and pulled out a brown wooden horse head with one ear broken off, Levi's lucky knight. He turned the chess piece adroitly in his fingertips, examining it closely, then plunked it on the glass coffee table like he'd moved it in a game. "I didn't mean to kill the kid. His heart gave out."

"You tortured him, Bear."

"If he'd just given me the nail's location, he'd still be alive," Bear said defensively and rubbed his eyes wearily.

"You can lie to yourself, friend, but don't lie to me. Either way, you couldn't have turned Levi loose."

Bear rose and began to pace nervously, never averting the pistol from us for very long. "I needed the money, David. It had all just gone down the drain. I have big-time creditors that aren't going to take 'please-be-patient' for an answer any more. You know the type. Goons."

"Ah, poor Bear, victim," I cooed sarcastically. "You lost your killer virginity with Moise Shankman and so became one of those murderous goons yourself. Did killing come easier after that?" I waited for his answer, but he voiced no words of self-condemnation or regret. "And the motorcycle 'assassin' at the Jerusalem police station? You intended for him to miss us, so you'd save my life and I'd trust you, I'd depend on you. Right?"

"Clumsy, very clumsy. I figured you saw through that ruse." He poured a glass of water at the bar and drank it down.

"Then you ordered your assassin, Sarnoff, to perform Chick Markowitz's decapitation. Later, you gave Sarnoff the Moise Shankman treatment to cover your trail. Murder, murder, murder, pal. Oh, yes, Shin Bet and the Israeli police have plenty of questions for you, too. The U.S. and Israel have an extradition treaty, you know. It's just a matter of time…and justice. Actually, you were quite lucky you got out of Israel before they nabbed you."

"You think?" Bear asked, surprised.

"Sure. You only reached the plane because you were driving the university's car, the Susita. They weren't looking for that. The car and the chaos created by the suicide attack at the university enabled you to evade their net. Nobody's perfect."

"Markowitz? How can you be sure that was me?"

"How? Bear, Bear, Bear," I remonstrated. "The only other person who could have conceivably known I was going to visit Chick in Ein Bokek was Jarad Weiner, and that was a real stretcher, highly unlikely. Weiner was wise in the ways of the various radical factions. He wouldn't have made such a ham-fisted attempt to make Chick's murder look like a *jihadi* had done it. Nobody was fooled—not the police, not Shin Bet, not even me. It was just far too inept, too ridiculous. After my head cleared the next day, I knew you had to have ordered Chick's murder. That's when I called the Israeli police."

"Well, you got that right. I do congratulate myself, though. Killing that gay paint-pusher did have the intended effect. You left Israel the next night. Right?"

"Wrong, my friend. You had Chick murdered so I'd cling to you, my savior. That way, you could keep an eye on me until I had the nail. Instead, I fled Israel, I escaped *from you*."

He thought a moment. "Wait a minute. I think you're BS'ing me, David. If you suspected me from the beginning, why did you ride back to the university with me? Wasn't that a little foolhardy?"

"First, I was drunk. Drunk and despondent. And I still hoped that you were innocent. We'd become friends, brothers. Most importantly, I didn't have the nail yet. There would be no purpose to killing me until I acquired the nail."

"Which isn't a problem anymore."

"We don't have the nail, Bear, but we can get it for you."

"David, David, David," he said, tsking in reply. "Delay of game, five yards. You do so have the nail."

"Why would you think that?"

He pulled a miniature receiver from his jacket and displayed it proudly. "Because I've heard every word you've said in your rental car since Coral Courts. How do you think I showed up here ahead of you at just this moment? Luck? As I said, checkmate, my friend." He flipped the receiver onto the table, where it landed beside the knight's head with the broken ear.

"Okay," I said. "What do you want?"

"Like I said, the money and the nail," he replied bluntly.

"Do you mind if we have a drink first? To take the chill off?" I asked. "Under the circumstances..."

He waved Miriam to the bar with his pistol, saying politely, "Mrs. Solomon. I guess the Lord will overlook this one sinful indulgence." To me he said, "You stay where you are, Greenberg."

Miriam poured two long stiff ones and added ice. "Do you want anything to drink?" she asked Bear. He simply stared daggers at her, and she returned to my side.

"Okay," I said after taking a hard slug of whiskey. "The money is in a Swiss bank. I'm sure you have an account there, too." He nodded in the affirmative. "Miriam can give you the account number and password. I don't have it. Listen, you can keep her as a hostage until the transfer clears. You'd do me a helluva favor if you'd turn her loose after that. Would you do that, Bear, do it for me? She can't hurt you."

"Maybe, David. I'll consider it. No guarantees, though. I'm not so sure I want to leave a witness." He reached in his jacket and withdrew a notebook and pen, which he slid across the table. "Please, Mrs. Solomon, write them down for me."

"You're not going to spare us, are you, Bear?" I asked angrily through clenched teeth.

"It's not likely, David. Sorry."

"You can't shoot us," I said passionately. "Cops are keeping a close eye on my house. Someone will hear the shots."

He reached inside his jacket with his left hand and pulled out a machete, like a starving tribesman eying a goat tied to a stake. "Yeah,

257

well," he said, "I've thought of that. Going to have to soil your décor a bit. Sorry. Incidentally, nice place, David."

Seeing all that grizzly, sharp steel in the hands of a colossus, Miriam glared at the transgressor, giving him no satisfaction.

"Look, Bear," I said. "I don't know the details, but there's got to be around a hundred million dollars in that account. Why do you need the nail, too?"

"A hundred mill," he said whistling his surprise, pleasantly calculating. "I never figured it might be nine figures. Why do I want the nail? Because there's a lot more where that came from, that's why. I could wind up the biggest TV evangelist in the world. Or shacked up poolside on an island paradise right here on Earth. Lots of choices. Now," he said to Miriam dropping the smirk, "we're wasting time. Please, Mrs. Solomon, write down those account numbers."

"That money belongs to the university, to my husband's research," she said, either bluffing or, since she was already condemned to a horrible death, willing to go down sooner rather than later to protect Am Ha-b'rit's money, a latter-day martyr to Israel.

He set the machete down, picked up the knight and the receiver, and stuffed them into his jacket pocket, leaving no physical evidence. Then he took up a pair of ropes lying in neat loops by the couch and threw them over his shoulder. He paused a moment to listen to Doggie's radio, but there was nothing about my street. All the attention was focused on Taboo.

He stopped to admire himself in the room's full-length mirror, still a man in great shape, before he turned my way. He was invincible, and he was fed up with being polite.

He came toward us with fire in his eyes, and it did not take him long. Miriam screamed at the top of her lungs, but my house was too well insulated to disturb the neighbors. Doggie stirred slightly, but fell back, inert. Miriam made to run, but Bear grabbed her neck with one great hand and flung her onto the couch. He pinned her down with his leg, using all his weight, placing the pistol to her head. I knew he wouldn't shoot her; Miriam still had the bank code.

I probably should have run, but my instincts to protect Miriam kicked in, and I grabbed Bear's wrist, reaching for his pistol. Using just his hand, Bear pushed me down with his considerable strength—no contest. Then, while he held Miriam at bay by sheer leg strength, her punches and fingernails landing harmless as an ant's on an elephant's hide, he wrestled me into submission. I fought furiously with my limited strength, trying to bite his hand, but in short order, he had my hands tied behind me and my feet bound together, bundled up on the couch like a hog for slaughter.

He checked to make certain I was immobile, then grabbed Miriam like a ragdoll and tied her hands in front of her so she could write, pulling tight on her wrists as she cried out in pain. Then with the end of her rope, he tied her to the couch leg, where Doggie was lying still. We were helpless.

"Holding, ten yards," I growled, but Bear merely sneered. He paused a moment to listen to Doggie's radio, but still nothing that would disturb him. For a second, I wondered why he'd kept Doggie alive. Then I realized he planned to have Doggie call the police over the radio to divert their attention from his avenue of escape. Before killing Doggie, too, no doubt. He'd thought of everything.

"All right, Mrs. Solomon, I want those account numbers."

"Screw you," Miriam said, pulling at her bindings.

"We'll see how long you hold out when I disassemble your boyfriend a piece at a time, starting with his eye." He withdrew his cell phone from his pocket, pulled up a photo, and held it in front of Miriam's face. "Here's your friend, Levi Asher, or what's left of him. It would have been worse if he hadn't died on me. This will only be the 'before' picture of David when I get done with him."

Miriam turned away. I could see that she wasn't going to give up the money, not even under torture of the vilest sort.

Bear set down his pistol, picked up the machete, and held it inches from my eye. "I want to make this clean and quick, Mrs. Solomon. Otherwise, it's his eyes first, you see? Then his fingers, one at a time. Next, his hands, his feet. It won't be pretty. Now that number, please."

Miriam gritted her teeth, remaining silent.

"After David, it's your turn, Mrs. Solomon. Think about that. What you see is what you'll get, in spades."

"You think I'd turn over the future of the human race to you? Who the hell are you, you selfish beast?" she spit. "I'm sorry, David, but many people have devoted their lives to my husband's experiments; too many have already given their lives."

In no rush, Bear lumbered to the bar and drank a glass of water. Then he washed the glass in hot water and dried it. Setting it neatly with the rows of other glasses, he headed back for me, menacingly wielding the machete. "All right, lovers. I think your right eye first, David. Isn't that what the Lord decreed that an adulterer should forfeit?"

Just at that moment, Doggie, having regained consciousness, rolled off the couch and in one motion, ran two steps and leaped with his full three hundred pounds onto the surprised Bear, mass *in extremis* times velocity not so great equaling force. The two of them crashed onto the coffee table in a heap, Brukowski's head clunking loudly against the hard surface, the machete clattering across the floor. When the officer finally managed to roll off Bear, Brukowski was out cold. He'd suffered another of his notorious concussions. Now he was more helpless than we were.

"Oww, my shoulder," Doggie groaned, having difficulty catching his breath from the sudden physical exertion. "I think I really hurt my shoulder."

The rest was simple and logical. Still able to walk, Doggie, huffing and puffing, worked himself to his feet and trundled over to the police radio. He scooted the device with his feet across the room, right into Miriam's bound hands. Then he instructed her which button to push to transmit to the precinct, and she called the police to free us.

Within minutes, uniformed officers were untying us and unlocking Doggie's handcuffs. A medic was seeing to Doggie's forehead and shoulder, which, fortunately, wasn't dislocated. He'd be sore in the morning, but he'd live another day to grab a beer and guard the corridors of city hall. The still unconscious Bear was well-covered by drawn pistols, and soon thereafter handcuffed. He never felt a thing.

Released, Miriam gave Doggie a grateful hug and thanked him for saving our lives. Once freed, I joined the pair, hugging Doggie, too, and gushing thanks like a schoolboy to a superhero. Then Miriam and I embraced so hard I thought we'd never let go.

At last, our horrendous quest was over.

As Miriam headed upstairs to gather herself, Doggie explained the situation to the officers, who went about their standard protocol. More and more police kept arriving, along with the ambulance and fire department. I lived less than five minutes from Taboo, where they'd all gathered. The street outside became filled with cruisers, their red and blue lights flashing. Medics, it took quite a few, loaded the prone Bear onto a stretcher for cartage, while officers took pictures, picked up evidence, and asked questions. I watched as six men maneuvered Bear's stretcher out, his body a motionless hulk like a great king lying on its back, the loser in a titanic chess game.

As the cruisers and the ambulance pulled away, the neighbors went inside and back to bed.

I offered the disheveled Doggie a cold Michelob, and he nodded a weary "yes." He was content to sit and let the medic finish treating his head and shoulder, while I brought a six-pack from the fridge and sat beside him. We clinked bottles and took a couple of deep swallows, as the EMTs packed up and walked out with one last admonition to Doggie to go directly to the ER when he left for a thorough exam.

"Down the hatch," I said, tilting my bottle toward my newfound friend.

While we drank our beers, Miriam returned from upstairs, wiping off her mortician makeup with washcloth and towel. Seeing her, I imagined I looked pretty outrageous myself. She took one of the beers and joined us.

"By the way, Doggie," I asked, "did you remember to turn on the security system when you came into the house?"

"Sure. Just like you told me, Dave," he replied.

"Then we have the whole thing on tape!" I shouted, laughing. "Every word!"

"Open and shut case," Doggie said. "Three witnesses, a taped assault, and a taped confession." He and I smiled at each other, satisfied. Miriam quietly drank her beer, too wrung out to emote, to even smile.

"Here's to you, Doggie," I toasted, handing him a second Michelob and taking another for myself. "You nailed a major, major celebrity criminal. Bear's an important man in Blood Diamond trafficking and a quadruple-murderer. You're a big-time hero, guy. You and Casey are going to be on TV, the nightly news, CNN, the works."

"Brukowski will never steal gift baskets on my watch," Doggie joked with mock toughness.

"Check and mate, my friend," I noted.

The game was over.

CHAPTER TWENTY-NINE
RESETTING THE PIECES

I hate this stuff. Kaplan, my thieving accountant, sat at my desk in the gallery reviewing my books. He claims I have to submit a quarterly estimated tax, so I do. I reached in my drawer, pulled out the aspirin, popped the lid, and downed two with my coffee. Miriam was off spending a week or so with her mother, so this was my chance to get it done.

Just then, the bell above the door tinkled. In walked Daddy Markowitz, Finkel, and their acquaintance, Felix Johnson, a full six-foot-four of soft baby fat. Johnson's deportment is vacuous, as if his eyes are out of focus, his head empty.

Finkel looked the worse for wear: the whole left side of his face was a mass of purple bruises, his swollen lip zippered with stitches, his left arm in a sling, and his left hand in a cast. Daddy and Finkel furiously slammed a check on my desk simultaneously, self-righteously.

"Why don't you take lunch, Kaplan," I said. "I've got to talk to these gentlemen."

Noticing Finkel's condition, the anger on my guests' faces, and Johnson's size, Kaplan snapped his laptop shut, slid it into his briefcase, and scurried to the door. The second the little bell tinkled again, Daddy and Finkel started shouting.

"Hold it! One at a time," I said. "Calm down. I can't understand a word you're saying."

They stopped shouting and turned to each other, trying to decide who would speak first. That gave me a chance to break in.

"What's Johnson doing here? Is he supposed to represent muscle? You bringing muscle into my shop?"

"Fuckin'-A, Tweety," Daddy said threateningly, his own considerable bulk resplendent in his pinstripe suit. What, had he been watching *The Godfather* again?

"Johnson," I said, "why don't you go in the back and get yourself something to eat? The fridge is on the right. There're frozen Snickers in the freezer, but don't touch the ice cream. That belongs to one of my employees."

"Thanks, Mr. Greenberg," Johnson said, eyes brightening, and he circled the counter, heading for the back of the shop.

"Hey, Johnson," Daddy ordered, his face flushed and sweating, "you stay here. I want him here!"

"Go ahead," I told Johnson. "These gentlemen will be all right. Take whatever you like."

"Thanks, again, Mr. Greenberg," Johnson chirped and disappeared.

"Now," I said, turning to my guests, "what is the problem?"

Daddy grabbed one of the checks and waved it in my face. "A thousand dollars!" he shouted. "A thousand fuckin' dollars!"

"Right," I said. "So?"

"So? You told us a quarter million!" the diminutive Finkel shouted, his horse-like face knotted in fury. "A quarter million!"

"Right. I bought each of you a quarter-million-dollar annuity. They're in your name. You'll each get a thousand forty-two dollars a month for life, minus withholding, much of which you can recover at tax time."

"So now we have to file taxes!" Finkel said, growing angrier by the minute.

"An annuity!" Daddy said, incredulous. "I want cash money. All of it."

"Cash on the barrel head," Finkel added assertively, slamming his good palm on my desk.

"Now fellahs," I said. "If I gave you all that money at once, you'd both be dead in six months. Daddy, you'd be broke in three and an addict to boot. Finkel, in a month, you'd have every shark in two states out to cripple you, and you'd be in debt to the year 2100. This way, you guys will eat regularly for a few days a month the rest of your lives. Think of it: racetrack chili dogs, triple bacon burgers, real food."

The groans were so loud I was afraid the neighbors might call the cops.

"We don't want no fuckin' annuity," Daddy barked. "We want our quarter mill, U.S. big ones."

"Cash dollars," Finkel echoed.

"Too late, fellahs. I already set up irrevocable trusts for both of you.

You know what 'irrevocable' means?"

Daddy looked quizzically at Finkel. Finkel appeared crestfallen.

"It means you can't take it back."

The groans were thunderous.

"What about your cut?" Daddy asked hopefully. "Ninety points should be about four-and-a-half million."

"I already donated my cut to Doctors Without Borders and some to Taboo Tabernacle. It was the least I could do."

More deafening groans. "Fuckin'-A," Daddy exclaimed. "Greenberg, you're a moron."

"Doctors Without Borders is a bunch of crooks," Finkel declared, his resentment forcing his face to wince in pain. "I told you we couldn't trust him. The prick cheated us."

I reached in my desk drawer and pulled out a dossier, opened it, and slid two certificates across the desk. "You need to sign these," I said. "Right next to the X."

"I'm not signing shit," Daddy said.

Finkel nodded agreement.

"Suit yourselves. If you don't sign, the checks stop coming."

The two entrepreneurs eyed the other, their demeanors those of men who'd gotten a tip from a jockey at the stockyards on a 160:2 underdog from a Chicago track dropping in class at Fairmount; wheeled the double to obscure their bets, splitting the wager among the four favorites in the second race; won the first race on the thoroughbred, natch. Then, just when they're deciding which new car to buy, saw their windfall disappear when a nag in the second race slated to finish last, pumped on drugs, miraculously finished first, then collapsed dead of heart failure in the winner's circle... and don't say this hasn't happened to you.

They signed, reluctantly, Finkel scratching out script with his good hand, and slammed the pens down so hard they bounced onto the floor.

"I'll never trust you again, Greenberg," Finkel groused. "You can pull your next scam without me."

I gathered the signed certificates, placed them in the dossier, and returned them to my drawer. Then I handed them each a copy of their contracts, which they shoved under their arms as if the insurance documents were yesterday's newspaper. "I know you won't thank me, gentlemen, but it's for your own good. I'd lose two pretty good friends if you were both dead."

"We're not your friends, asshole," Daddy said.

"Yeah, we're not your friends," Finkel echoed.

"Not at the moment," I said, "while you have cash equivalents in hand."

Finkel winced, bringing his good hand to his jaw, and turned to Daddy. "So what do we do now?"

"Cash these friggin' checks."

"And then?" Finkel queried.

"Let's get up a game at my mother's house till she comes home from work. I can deal for both of us."

"Well, I want to cut before every deal. And no second-dealing or bottom-dealing, fucker."

"Sure, Larry. We'll pick up Hamburger Haven on the way. Then we'll hit the stockyards game till the track opens."

"Wealth awaits you," I cracked, laying a Grant on the desk. "Lunch is on me, boys," I said.

Finkel snatched up the fifty with his good hand faster than Daddy could blink. They turned to leave.

"Wait a minute, wait a minute," I called, halting them in their tracks. I yelled to the back, "Johnson, your ride's leaving."

Johnson shuffled into the front of the shop chomping on two ice cream drumsticks, trailing flakes of sugar cone, nuts, and chocolate on the Persian rug. "Johnson, I told you not the ice cream; it doesn't belong to me," I said.

"Sorry, Mr. Greenberg, I forgot," he said through a full mouth. "There might be one left."

"Aw, shit," Daddy said disgustedly. "We got to drop off Johnson way the fuck out..."

"Isn't this a pile...?" Finkel groaned.

"Fuckin'-A, Tweety," a despondent Daddy concluded. "Fuckin'-A."

Daddy held the door open, but Finkel wasn't ready for life outdoors quite yet. "You know," Finkel said to Daddy thoughtfully, furiously formulating a new angle to shoot, "this annuity is guaranteed, right? Like by a big insurance company?"

"Right," Daddy replied.

"Maybe we can borrow against it from the bank. It's ours, isn't it?"

Daddy considered the proposition. "It's been almost two weeks since we paid Howell's chit," he said, his countenance brightening. "Sure, he's got to owe Tumor more money by now."

I watched as the rear ends of the mighty musketeers dissolved into the sunlight, having strut and fret their hour upon the stage, leaving nothing but calm in their wake. "Yes," I mused, "as evinced by Macbeth, '[Life] is a tale told by an idiot, full of sound and fury, signifying nothing.'"

A tale told, as is mine, now nearly complete, and considerably less portentous than I had originally aspired to convey. A tale, perhaps Shakespeare's "second burthen of a former child," a poor copy of a poor copy.

***

According to the Native American Ute, Pokoh, the Old Man, created the world. He created every tribe out of the soil where they once lived. That is why every man wants to live and die on his native land. He came from that very same soil.

I paused a moment to catch my breath in the crisp, thin air high in the Colorado Rockies. There had been a snowfall the night before, and my shoes made a pleasing crunching sound along the path I had worn to the woodpile, a trail of smeared footprints behind me and ahead. Above, rose the majestic snow-covered mountain peaks. Surrounding me, among the great boulders and running river, rose the spring-renewed red cedar and pine. I turned to gaze absently at the peaceful knotty pine cabin where we'd spent the past three days and nights recovering from our ordeal. On our daily hikes through the hills and picnicking beside the roaring falls, we talked about everything. Everything but the one thing foremost on our minds. One final armload of wood would see us through our last night in this idyllic refuge.

Miriam emerged from the cabin and ran to me, zipping her coat. "There's a moose in the back," she said excitedly, taking my hand. "A big one with his velvet antlers growing. I've never seen one before."

I let her lead me around the side of the cabin. She wanted to cross the gulley and approach him, but I held her back. "We can't friendly up, Miriam," I cautioned. "They're wild creatures." This wasn't Disneyland. Tourists get killed all the time trying to pet moose, tempted by their splendid beauty and seemingly calm demeanor.

We stood together watching the creature, standing erect on his powerful, knotted legs like some natural monolith, our arms wrapped around each other. We felt the mountain chill chapping our faces and the tips of our noses as we watched the great male continue his journey beyond our sight, unhurried and unthreatened. We kissed lightly. With a sigh, Miriam went back to the cabin while I saw to my last load of wood.

The nail had arrived, or should arrive shortly, at the Hadera University Life Sciences building, escorted by a pair of Bisl project students, a young man and woman. The pair had been doing research in the states, hoping to locate the secret burial place of Albert Einstein. They would place the unique artifact, if indeed it was, directly into Solly's hands. I could barely even contemplate the consequences of that handover. Solly would probably thank them and go right back to work.

Perhaps now, finally, he could remove his laboratory cot and return to his own home. To sleep in the comfort of his own marital bed.

After a light dinner, we cleared the dishes and sat before the modest fire. I added a shard of wood and closed the glass door, turning the latch, and slid the vent wider to burn more brightly. I joined Miriam lying in her jeans and sweater on the bearskin rug, her head nestled in her glorious curly black hair. In Ute mythology, when Puma was off hunting with his son, Bear convinced Puma's wife to run away with him. Puma found Bear's trail and tracked him down, then killed him in a fight. Maybe some Ute found Bear's body and this rug was his fur. It didn't quite fit; yet it did.

My arm around her, we watched the fire dim, deep in thought. This would be our last, our only, chance to talk about what to do next. It couldn't be put off any longer.

"Do you feel okay now that Solly's projects and the university have everything they need?" I asked hesitantly, then paused, wondering how to articulate what I'd been feeling since our lunch at Blueberry Hill only weeks before, perhaps since that day she went missing twenty years before. Then, I simply said it. "Can you stay with me?"

I could see the conflicting emotions surge across her alabaster face. Her tender lips pursed, her cleft chin trembled. "You can't ask me that," she replied, a catch in her throat.

"Why?"

"Why? Am Ha-b'rit, the university, are my world, David. They have been for two decades." She hesitated. "My son is buried there," she said, her voice catching. "My husband..."

We both fell silent.

"David, I've decided I need to have a child, to raise and to love." She stared into my eyes. A child? Did she mean a more perfect Ari? Mine? Had our fling in Paris or our sojourn to Colorado already tied us together forever, with our seed the embodiment of our love? Somehow, I knew she wouldn't answer those questions before I made my decision. And I understood that. She was leaving it up to me.

"Come live at the university," she said. "You can lecture as little or as much as you want. You can still follow your own interests." It was true; moving there would pose no hardship for me. I could give Arnie a half-interest to run the gallery by himself. He'd do well; he was a far better salesman than me. So, what was holding me back?

"We couldn't live together at Hadera, could we?"

Her fingers went to her lips. Then she said what I feared she'd say. "I'm married, David. We could see each other, but... Do you love me? Do you love me, David?"

"You know I do. Do you love me?"

"You will never know how much," she whispered. "You *can* never know."

There was my quandary. David Greenberg, again the outsider, the loner. Twice divorced, burned and scarred by his past. David Greenberg, a man unanchored among the centuries, swept helplessly through the scattered relics and fragments of ghost civilizations like an ancient parchment in the whirlwinds of time.

And what awaited me in Israel beyond moments stolen with Miriam? A group whose beliefs I would never fully understand or appreciate, for the most part based on faith in a God, or at least in a tradition, that I was estranged from regardless of its familiarity. No, Miriam and I lived existences separated by far more than the thousands of miles between our two beds: existences torn inexorably apart by a chasm called life.

From the look on my face, Miriam knew my answer without me saying a word. We embraced, holding onto each other like we had no tomorrow.

In the morning, I would see her to her New York flight for the first leg of her journey home. At the gate, a kiss and a final wave, and that would be it. Then I would wait for my flight to St. Louis with a copy of *The New York Times* bought at the gift shop, unable to read the neatly printed pages. I'd probably buy a portable chess set for future visits to Bear. By then, he'd likely be a gang leader in Beaumont penitentiary or a prison ministry spokesperson—or both, knowing him—awaiting his ultimate fate, inevitably keeping a keen eye toward an escape to parts unknown, to some African jungle or European underworld haunt.

And Miriam and me? Maybe, just maybe, I'd change my mind and buy a ticket to join her. Or perhaps she would trade in her ticket for a seat beside me, to dwell within local call range to her mother. But in a race that time had already fixed, neither of those horses were the way to bet. Yes, God—malevolent, capricious—or Fate as the case might be, does cheat at chess. We do, in fact, endure frantic lives imperiled at every turn, unable to escape a remorseless perpetual check—ever listening for a clarion summons to a serene celestial stalemate that never sounds.

Yet what is our choice but to listen for those trumpets, that shofar? Aren't those fantastical stories, those mythologies, the mortar that seals the foundations of our civilization?

***

My story ends with me in my walled garden, alone, staring through the clear night air at the planet Venus, Goddess of Love, seeing Miriam as she was that night in Paris. Her radiant face never fades from my memory; her absence never fails to strike my heart.

I tear a leaf from a nearby shrub, crumble it, and toss it aside. My thoughts dwell on Tantalus, the Greek mythological son of Zeus and the nymph Plouto—yes, offspring of a god and a woman—and wonder, aren't we all part mortal, part divine? Like Tantalus, I have tricked death, and in scorning the gods' will, brought down their punishment upon me.

Yes, as with Tantalus, haven't the gods condemned us all to eternally reaching for spiritual fruit just beyond our grasp, to forever thirsting for love from a pool our parched lips can never touch?

All we can do is keep searching for tales that give us a momentary glimpse of some distant, dimly glowing truth, and yearn, in vain, for the happiness that has inexplicably eluded us.

ADDENDUM
DAVID'S METHOD OF UNRAVELING THE CLUE: 59CBZQ

Chart A

In Bobby Fischer's Game of the Century, Byrne played white (lower case), Fischer played black (bold upper case). Byrne's bishop at c5 threatens Fischer's queen diagonally on square b6.

Fischer (black)

	A	B	C	D	E	F	G	H
8	**R**				**R**		**K**	
7	**P**	**P**				**P**	**B**	**P**
6		**Q**	**P**				**P**	
5			b					
4			b	p			**B**	
3	Q		**N**			n		
2	P					p	p	p
1				r		k		r

Byrne (white)

Chart B

Instead of saving his queen, Fischer retreated with his black bishop at g4 ("o") to e6, threatening Byrne's white bishop at c4, thus allowing Byrne to capture his queen.

Fischer

	A	B	C	D	E	F	G	H
8	R				R		K	
7	P	P				P	B	P
6		Q	P		B		P	
5			b					
4			b	p			"o"	
3	Q		N			n		
2	P					p	p	p
1				r		k		r

Byrne

17. ... B-e6

Chart C

Byrne captured Fischer's queen at b6, naturally, giving the veteran chess master a seemingly insurmountable material advantage. In reply to the loss of his queen, Fischer took the white bishop at c4, checking Byrne's king at f1 [see position below]. Thereafter, Byrne never escaped check from Fischer's minor pieces, in the process losing most of his defending power pieces, until Byrne's king had nowhere to run.

Fischer

8	R				R		K	
7	P	P				P	B	P
6		b	P				P	
5								
4			B	p				
3	Q		N			n		
2	P					p	p	p
1				r		k		r
	A	B	C	D	E	F	G	H

Byrne

18. Bxb6 Bxc4+

Chart D

David found this chart for converting letters to numbers.

A	B	C	D	E	F	G	H	I	J	K	L	M
1	2	3	4	5	6	7	6	5	4	3	2	1

N	O	P	Q	R	S	T	U	V	W	X	Y	Z
1	2	3	4	5	6	7	6	5	4	3	2	1

When he applied the chart to the words "Jesus Christ," it totaled 59.

J	E	S	U	S		C	H	R	I	S	T	Equals
4	5	6	6	6		3	6	5	5	6	7	**59**

Chart E

Seeking the number 59 to locate the nail, David entered the game's moves into a chart, starting with move number 18, the legendary BxQ move. Then, using the "Jesus Christ" key, he placed a numerical value below each move. The row numbers in the chess notation, he kept the same, so move 18, b6, would equal 8: 2 [for the letter "b"] + 6 [row 6]. This first attempt didn't work. By the time he got to the third row, move 20, the running total was already 61.

Move	White - Byrne				Black - Fischer				Total	Running total
18	Bx	B	6		Bx	C	4+			
	2	2	6		2	3	4		**19**	19
19	K-	G	1		N-	E	2+			
	3	7	1		5	5	2		**23**	42
20	K-	F	1		Nx	D	4+			
	3	6	1		1	4	4		**19**	**61**

Moves 18 to 20 = 61

Chart F

Next, David dropped the row numbers and stayed with the letters. He added the resultant numbers in each row, producing four specific numbers as keys: 9, 20, 14, 16—and these totaled 59.

Move	Byrne		Fischer		Total	Running Total
18	Bx	B	Bx	C		
	2	2	2	3	*9*	9
19	K-	G	N-	E		
	3	7	5	5	*20*	29
20	K-	F	Nx	D		
	3	6	1	4	*14*	43
21	K-	G	N-	E		
	3	7	1	5	*16*	*59*

Moves 18 – 21 = **59**

Chart G

David researched *gematria* and produced a chart with these Hebrew letters. But the Hebrew letters meant nothing.

Number	Hebrew Letter
9	ט
20	ר
14	נ
16	ע

Chart H

Next David added the digits of his four key numbers together (9, 2+0, 1+4, 1+6), reducing the numbers to a single digit, and came up with 9, 2, 5, and 7. Using these, he found the Buzzle site and produced this chart. But the result, in proper order, *Teth-beth-hei-zayin*, was also meaningless.

Number: Name	Meaning	Symbolization
1: Aleph	an ox or bull	strength, primacy, leader
2: Beth	**a tent, house, in, into**	household, family
3: Gimel	a camel	to be lifted up, pride
4: Dalet	a door	opening, entry, pathway
5: Hei	**a window**	behold, the, to reveal, inspiration, what comes from
6: Vav	a nail, hook	to fasten, join together, secure, add
7: Zayin	**a weapon**	cut, cut off
8: Chet	enclosure	inner room, heart, private, separate
9: Teth	**snake, serpent**	surround

Chart I

Next, he tried an obscure version of the *Mispar Katan* and multiplied the values together, dropping the zero on the 20. The result (9, 2, 1x4, 1x6) produced a new sequence: 9, 2, 4, and 6.

Number: Name	Meaning	Symbolization
1: Aleph	an ox or bull	strength, primacy, leader
2: Beth	**a tent, house, in, into**	household, family
3: Gimel	a camel	to be lifted up, pride
4: Dalet	**a door**	opening, entry, pathway
5: Hei	a window	behold, the, to reveal, inspiration, what comes from
6: Vav	**a nail, hook**	to fasten, join together, secure, add
7: Zayin	a weapon	cut, cut off
8: Chet	enclosure	inner room, heart, private, separate
9: Teth	**snake, serpent**	surround

Chart J

Put in the correct order (9, 2, 4, 6), David produced the final chart. He then dropped the letter *dalet,* and the remaining letters, *teth-beth-vav,* spelled the word "taboo"—the building where the nail was found. There, the symbolization **serpent-house-door** enabled David and Miriam to find the actual **nail**.

Number: Name	Meaning	Symbolization
9: Teth	snake, **serpent**	surround
2: Beth	a tent, **house**, in, into	household, family
4: Dalet	a **door**	opening, entry, pathway
6: Vav	a **nail**, hook	to fasten, join together, secure, add

ACKNOWLEDGEMENTS

I greatly appreciate the insights and support of the many friends, rabbis, theologians, and others who informed and enhanced my understanding of Judaism, Christianity, Islam, mythology, Hebrew, Yiddish, Kabbalah, gematria, chess, biotechnology, and millennial religious movements. And to my agent Jeanie Loiacono and TouchPoint Press for their enthusiastic embrace of this story

OTHER BOOKS BY ED PROTZEL

DarkHorse Trilogy
The Lies That Bind, Book One
Honor Among Outcasts, Book Two
Something in Madness, Book Three, coming soon!